Also By Elizabeth F. Shearly

Endless Sea Of Stars

Dread Spring

Project Pardus

Syphon Bound

A Bond of Storms and Stitches

A Bond of Armour and Artfulness

Syphon Bound Novella

A Tourney Bond

Second Acts of Weary Warrior Women

The Swordswoman and the Vampire

To Break A Dragon Bond

A Pentagram Of Candles and Spectres

Her Castle, Her Howl, Her Pack

The King's Pixie Seer

A BOND OF STORMS & STITCHES

ELIZABETH F. SHEARLY

Copyright © 2025 by Elizabeth Shearly.

All rights reserved. No part of this book may be reproduced, stored, or distributed without express permission. No part of this book may be used for AI training without express permission.

ISBN (ebook) 9781068934650

ISBN (paperback) 9781068934643

For more information, visit www.elizabethshearly.ca

Editor: Maggie Morris, The Indie Editor

Cover art gold frame via DepositPhotos.com.

This is a work of fiction. The story and characters are strictly products of the author's imagination, and any resemblance to real people, living or dead, is unintentional and entirely coincidental.

Content Notes

Broken bones, mortal peril (falling from heights, wild animal scratch, freezing to death, drowning), ostracism, incarceration (FMC, MMC, animal companion).

Please see the book's web page at www.elizabethshearly.ca for detailed content notes

A Bond of Storms and Stitches is written in Canadian English and contains many references to North American flora and fauna, along with Ice Age flora and fauna, some of which is renamed to blend better with the world.

To see some of the inspiration for the world, check out my Pinterest board.

Prologue

When another *boom* shook the ground, drowning out even the groans of the wounded, the mage looked up from the bloody soldier she was healing to her husband on the crest of the hill. These people had trusted them, followed them across the lake, and now they lay here in anguish, or worse, cold and still. He turned, as though he could sense his mage's gaze on him. She watched him take in the wounded surrounding her, and when their eyes met, she nodded deliberately. His eyebrows drew together, but he nodded back.

She closed her eyes and reached out to the wounded, felt for the places where their bodies were broken, took a deep breath, braced her feet, and syphoned energy from her husband—her source—knitting the sundered flesh back together before they could die of blood loss or sepsis. The syphon wavered. She was drawing too much magic from her husband. Why was he delaying cutting her off? If he was pulled into an ephemer with her— Her whole body jerked, and her magic winked out.

The wounded around her stirred, their broken armour and torn clothes revealing fresh pink scars beneath the unwashed blood. Some sat up, others slipped into tranquil slumber. One tried to stand, and she reached to help, but her hands were wispy and incorporeal; anything she tried to touch now would pass through her as though she weren't there. Good. They'd done it.

But this was only the beginning. Nothing but a few dusky clouds graced the bright sky. She squinted. Where was Escelius? As if in reply, an avian scream rent the air, the clouds glowing from below as her firebird shot into the heavens. *Thank Hiorach.* The bird screamed again and swooped toward the source of the mage-fire, the clash of weapons, and the cries of battle. Embers rained from her wings as she crossed battle lines to the Empire's forces.

The mage drifted to the crest of the hill. She tried to take her source's hand—force of habit. It would be days before her body regained solidity. The forest was burning, but the Empire retreated.

"Their ships will burn if they stay." Her source, her husband, her king, had his gaze glued to their corporeal ephemer.

And what will become of us if we *stay?* But she couldn't speak, not in this form. Their Loyalists would be granted asylum. They were Lake folk after all, and what would unite all the Lake kingdoms if not their common enemy: the Empire?

1

Mellia

And so their twisted mockery of a holy firebird ephemer set the ships ablaze, good free men burning, trapped in their vessels, and the blaspheming false king and queen gained the favour of the heretical kingdom of Carille. Thus have their descendants and supporters been harboured in Carille's province of Nordval for centuries.

Mellia tuned out the Grist brother's historical account. The centuries-old story of King Lorthran and Queen Olena would never be immortalized in stained glass like the window currently fogged by her breath. Grist brothers crowded the lawn behind her, the usual New Bridge brothers, mixed in with pilgrims from other hives. The crowd was no reason to shirk her work. This window needed to be fixed before the Grist queen's funerary service tomorrow.

The window shone blue, green, and gold in the afternoon sun. A farmer, wielding a dull shovel, frozen mid-hack at a verdant riverbank, though no sign of his efforts showed in the green glass. A huge golden hand, taller than the foolish farmer, sprang directly from the ground, as though to block his next blow. That's where the trouble was: The Golden God's thumb had cracked away from the rest of his hand. Perhaps if the farmer had cracked, Brother Prospus wouldn't have insisted the window be repaired before the service. And since the brothers were without their Grist-queen-derived power, it fell to a sister like Mellia to do the repair today.

Mellia reached out to the crack. The pane couldn't be fixed with magic, of course, but with the replacement pane in hand and the sun sparkling over the glass and leading, it would take but a moment to complete the repair. She drew her round knife and pressed it to the leading around the pane. Just a touch of magic would be enough to soften the black metal precisely where she was shaving away—too much magic and the whole window might bow and collapse.

Bright Prince Canis drove his heretical brother from Sudra's shore. Thus did Sudra become a beacon of welcome for the Golden God Doloman and His faithful Grist, in the heretical land of The Lakes. And so, too, did Sudra prosper from is membership in the Eichsburgh Holy Empire under newly appointed Archduke Canis.

If she hadn't heard this text a score of times already, it might be fascinating to learn as the soft metal peeled away from the glass, a half-hour's painstaking work done in a moment with the help of her magic. She dug the corner of the half-moon knife in above Doloman's thumbnail and popped the first piece of the pane from the window, followed by the second. She *had* done a beautiful job painting the details onto the new pane, the lines on Doloman's palm and the way His skin sparkled in the light, perhaps better work than the original glassmaker. Of course, she only had this one pane to perfect, while the glassmaker had created twelve full windows.

Mellia lifted the new pane by the edges and fitted it into place, prying the leading here and there to make space for the slight difference in size.

The Sudrans rejoiced and welcomed Doloman's favour, welcomed the Grist, who bestowed on them the binding ritual, granting Sudran mages power to syphon as they had never seen before.

The pane almost slipped from Mellia's fingers, but she held it steady with both hands. The blessing of the binding ritual. Did anyone who had been through it still believe it a blessing? Was she the only mage who despised it? In fairness, most mages only went through the ordeal once, established their bond, and carried on. Not five times. Five *failed* times.

The window. Mellia coaxed the new pane into the window and pulled a strip of leading from her pocket. The sunlight was enough to melt it into place, with a judicious application of magic, of course. Doloman's golden hand, telling the farmer that only He can form mage bonds. Or choose not to, in Mellia's case. She stirred up a light breeze to help the chill air cool the fresh leading, then clambered down the ladder to the walkway by the hive wall. She craned up at the repair, sunlight glinting in her eyes too brightly to actually see the thing, though it had been starkly visible from inside. And they couldn't have a crack in the Golden God's hand, not with so many visiting New Bridge.

She wiped her palms on her apron as the reading brother closed his leather-bound tome, and the others began to disperse. Hopefully, one of them would help her carry the ladder back to the builders' hall. The thing was damnably heavy, and no amount of magic would make it easier to carry. She caught a red-bearded brother's eye, and he sauntered over, squinting up at the window, and stopped beside her.

"You sisters have many talents," said the brother. He must be a pilgrim, since he wasn't normally around the comb.

"Thank you. If you wouldn't mind helping me with the ladder—"

"That looks much better, Brother Padril." Grist Father Glimar didn't stop to admire it, striding by on his way somewhere important, his piercing gaze taking everything in despite his hurry.

"Thank you, Father," said Brother Padril.

Mellia swallowed her protest. What good would it do to petulantly call after the Grist father, insist that it was *her* work? Besides it feeling exceptionally good to see the look on Padril's face when she called him out. But the look would swiftly be followed by a scowl or a glare. Unbound mages, even sisters, were not supposed to use magic out in the open like this. Mellia needed as much support among the Grist brothers as she could garner today. So she smiled at him.

And he had the good grace to look sheepish. "It does look better. I spent half of Igneo prayer this morning staring at that crack."

"I suppose you're a pilgrim?" And still, Father Glimar knew his name, despite him never having been around the comb before.

"An outrider, actually." Come back for the ascension of the new Grist queen next week. Of course. All the New Bridge Grist brothers would gather to bind the new Grist queen, once she was chosen from among the handmaids. "Shall we deal with this ladder?"

Mellia and Padril wrestled the unwieldy ladder down from its lean against the wall, and Mellia took the rear while the brother hefted the front.

"You're Sister Mellia?"

How did Brother Padril know her when she hadn't recognized him at all? No sense in denying it. Maybe he wanted to make sure she got credit for fixing the window after all. "That's right."

"I have a message for you. I came through Falvair on my way here, and your father charged me with it."

That's why he had come over. And she'd roped him into helping her haul a ladder. Mellia's face heated. Best to get the message over with. "Please, deliver it."

Padril manoeuvred the ladder between the beehives dotted about the cloister lawn, and Mellia watched her footing across the dormant brown grass, toward the builders' hall opposite the hive. Padril cleared his throat and recited. "Dearest daughter, Your most holy age is upon you, and as such, the time has come to bind yourself to the heir that I have selected for Falvair. Your presence is required here for the proceedings, on the occasion of my sixty-sixth and final year as marquess. Etc., Falvair."

Padril downplayed the lack of love and affection at the message's end gruffly, as though embarrassed that he couldn't convey warmer regards. But what regard would her father have for the daughter who had failed him five times already? Should she fail this final time, he would be left with no one to carry on his lineage. To have two children fail him so completely—no. Thinking about her brother never helped anything.

"Thank you for delivering the message." Returning to Falvair would mean undergoing yet another harrowing binding ritual with a pompous or even cruel lord chosen by her father. A pit opened in Mellia's stomach. No, she wouldn't do it. She wouldn't go through the ritual again only to have it fail. She had a chance to become a handmaid, now that Grist Queen Arista was dead, and she would take it, just as soon as the brothers' conclave offered it to her. And they would, since the handmaids openly used magic, and she was the best mage in the comb.

Padril led her by the ladder into the builders' hall, and they tidied it in the storeroom.

"Thanks very much for your help"—Mellia curtsied—"and the message."

Padril blushed. "I— You're welcome, sister. Congratulations on your upcoming binding."

Mellia forced a smile. "Doesn't every mage dream of her binding?" She had to get out of here right now. "Please excuse me, Brother Padril. There's so much to attend to before the Necrophoresis Ritual and only three more days to attend to it."

"Of course, please, don't let me keep you. Give my regards to the handmaids."

Mellia curtsied, and Brother Padril scampered away. She crossed the cloister, back toward the hive and the Grist Queen's Keep. The keep towered over the small hive buildings, only matched by the hive itself, the smooth granite facade broken by the sparkling stained glass. Its beauty never dimmed, no matter that Mellia had been admiring it for the past three years, ever since her father had shipped her off to become a sister. Clearly, he hoped that becoming closer to Doloman would finally make the binding ritual succeed. Instead, it had given Mellia a way out of the binding entirely.

And now was the time to tell her father that. She'd have to get Livine to write her letter out for her and send it right away. The handmaids were busy, but Livine would find a few moments to write out a short missive.

Mellia smiled as she approached the entrance to the Grist Queen's Keep, but the guards frowned at her. *Fallo's green garters*, her bee pin wasn't on her cloak. They wouldn't let her into the keep without it, not with all the pilgrims wandering about underfoot in the cloister this week. Even without its bond to the Grist queen, the Grist Guard's brothers were a formidable group; there was nothing for it but to run up to the dormitory and fetch the silver brooch.

By the time she got back to the gate and the Grist guards let her through, she had mentally composed practically her entire reply to her father.

Dearest Lord Falvair,

I am pleased to impart that an opportunity to ascend to handmaidship has presented itself to me. This is a great opportunity for our family to be blessed with Doloman's favour, and I'm certain you wouldn't want me to decline it. I'd like to respectfully request that you await news of my handmaidship.

Sister Mellia of New Bridge Hive

That should do it. Diplomatic enough to placate him, but firm enough that he wouldn't argue. After all, having a handmaid in the family would be prestigious. Some distant cousin would take over the marquessate and be thankful in a way Mellia could never be if tied to a source who would see her as nothing more than a channel for magic.

Mellia climbed the spiral stairs to the handmaids' chamber. Their six curtained beds stood against the walls, neatly made for the day. The drapes stood open, despite the chill, and the fire crackled in the hearth. Livine sat in the window embrasure, her logbook propped on her lap, pen moving quickly over the paper.

If Mellia waited for her to finish, she'd be here all day. "Livine?"

The handmaid glanced up. Then back down.

"I need a letter written. I can come back if it's not a good time..."

Livine sprinkled sand over her page and snapped her logbook closed. Hopefully, she had used her magic to dry the ink, otherwise her logbook pages would stick together. "It's a fine time, Mellia." She drew a coveted sheet of paper from her writing desk and dipped her pen.

Mellia recited the message, and Livine copied it, her eyebrows rising as the scribbles covered the page.

She paused before signing the letter for Mellia. “You told me you wanted to stay a sister even if you don’t become a handmaid. That you would never submit to the binding ritual again.”

Mellia shrugged. She *had* said that. Back before Grist Queen Arista had passed away, when the prospect of becoming a handmaid had been a distant dream and refusing the next binding ritual just as distant. But now, both were happening. “My father would never allow me to stay a lowly sister. Besides, everyone in the hive knows that I’m the most skilled mage ere.”

“That’s true. It wouldn’t make sense to choose another sister as handmaid.” Livine nodded, case closed, and signed the letter with a flourish. “I’ll make sure this gets sent to Falvair.” She sprinkled it with fine sand and folded it neatly.

“Thank you.” Mellia settled herself in one of the wingback chairs by the fire and pulled a dress for the Necrophoresis Ritual out of the chest between them. It was the blue one, Sathred’s. For a ritual taking place *on* a waterfall, the Grist certainly weren’t worried about expensive fabrics being ruined. The silk slipped between her fingers as she felled the neckline down.

Voices echoed up the spiral stairs along with the patter of slippers on stone. The handmaids seldom left the keep, so they were given only the most delicate of shoes. Morath and Runas swept into the handmaids’ chambers, the former short and stocky, her cropped hair sticking out from the edge of her veil; the latter the most willowy handmaid, her long blond hair pinned neatly away.

“If you hadn’t said anything, then we’d still be down there, wouldn’t we?” Runas peeled off her gloves and tossed them on her pristine bed.

"Would you have had me keep quiet? We don't even get a say over our own new handmaid." Morath crossed to the hearth, gave Mellia and strange look, and busied herself poking at the fire.

"What was the discussion about? It'll be Mellia." Livine had picked her logbook back up and barely paused in her writing to pipe up. "I'm sending the letter to her father today."

Morath froze.

"You're not going to tell her, are you?" Runas said to Morath's bent head. She rolled her eyes and took the seat opposite Mellia.

"Tell me what?" Mellia's hands were frozen mid-stitch, so she laid the silk down in her lap.

Runas took her hand, and Mellia let Runas baby her instead of snatching it away. "The list of handmaid candidates was settled upon this afternoon. We just came from the obedientiary conclave. The trial will be held the day after tomorrow."

"We tried to speak up for you." Morath gave the fire one last vicious poke. "You're not even being considered."

"And that's when they kicked us out." Runas squeezed her hand.

Not being considered. Mellia was not even being *considered* as a handmaid candidate. Not even being given a chance to show off her skills at the trial. Her skills that wildly surpassed all the other sisters, and everyone knew it.

"I know it's a shock, Melly." Runas's sympathy seared her. "We can still work together with you as a sister." Her smile turned out more like a wince.

They could keep working together with her as a sister, that was true. Except that her father would never let her stay here in the comb as a sister. She needed to be chosen by Doloman; she needed to be a handmaid! And she would be.

"Good thing we haven't sent that letter to your father yet," said Livine, flapping the paper her way. "Do you want me to rewrite it? Tell him you're staying here regardless."

"No." Mellia brushed the silks off her lap onto the top of the chest and got to her feet. "Send it."

"Send it? But it says that you're going to be a handmaid, and you weren't chosen—"

Mellia planted her fists on her hips. "Send it. Chosen or not, I'm going to be the new handmaid. If I go now, the conclave might still be in session."

"That's true, Melly, but they've already..." Runas trailed off as Mellia turned her glower on the handmaid.

"You tell 'em." Morath pumped her fist.

"Don't encourage her!" Runas scooted to the edge of her seat. "Mellia, there's nothing you can say that will change their minds now. No one is supposed to interrupt the conclave. They'll kick you out, and it'll ruin your chances—"

"What chances? They've already *declined to consider* me, so what could make it worse?" At least she could find out why they had rejected her as a candidate. Maybe she could clear up some mistake. What could they do to her that would be worse than having to slink home and be bound to an obnoxious lord—or failing to bond...

"I can see that you're dead set on this course." Runas pursed her lips. "We'll be here when you get... back." She'd been about to say *Kicked out of the conclave*, most likely. And so what if Mellia was kicked out of the conclave? Or barred entry to begin with? The alternative was to sit here and cry. Crawl home to Falvair.

Mellia rounded the chairs and held Livine's gaze. "Send the letter."

Livine nodded. "You're the best mage." As though it were a foregone conclusion that the conclave would logically select the best mage as the next handmaid. And they should. Hence the trials. It benefitted the Grist to have the best mages supporting the Grist queen. They would see that. They would choose her. Or at least let her try. She wasn't asking for special treatment, just fair treatment.

She swept down the stairs, all five foot nothing of her standing tall as she stalked across the inner cloister and rapped on the conclave door, the guard outside too shocked to stop her.

The door cracked open. "What's the emergency?" The brother's gaze raked her and softened. Brother Padril. He opened the door wider.

"Brother Padril. I understand that I'm not being considered for the handmaidship, and I'd like a justification from the conclave. I think I can reasonably say that I'm owed that." Her stomach clenched. Was it because Padril knew that her father wanted her to return to Falvair to be bound and married? Had he convinced the other obedientiaries that she wouldn't want to be a handmaid anyway? He hadn't mentioned being the outriders' obedientiary when they'd met...

But he nodded and made way for her. The guard's mouth hung open now, but he closed it and saluted as Brother Padril shut the door behind Mellia. The room was close, the shutters cracked. Unlike the handmaids' chamber, the conclave didn't have glazed windows. It was either stuffy or frigid at this time of year. Smoke hung in the air from the two obedientiaries puffing on pipes.

"I presume you have something prepared?" said a gruff voice before Mellia's eyes adjusted to the dim light filtering through the closed shutters. One of the brothers coughed.

"Fresh air perhaps?" Mellia smiled around at the grey-headed brothers, the leaders of each role in the comb. She gestured, and a thin breeze blew from the doorway, catching the wispy hair of the brother who had spoken.

A collective sigh hushed through the room.

She turned to Brother Prospus, puffing on his pipe, as usual. "I fixed the cracked pane in the first chorea window, Brother." As the builders' obedientiary, he'd given her the task. And where was the healers' obedientiary? Ah, yes. The one with the unbelievably huge white beard. "You know that half the salves in the infirmary were set by me." She turned to the brother with long plaited hair—the fanner obedientiary. "And half the fabrics were woven by me." Brother Padril had taken his place at the table, and she gambled. "The mantle that warms you on your journeys is my work, even some of the hand tools your foragers take to the field," she finished, turning to the other pipe-smoking brother, the forager obedientiary. "I'm sure you all see that I could support a Grist queen like no other sister. Seeing as I do all of this in addition to my regular duties, and I tutor Lord New Bridge's children." *Fallo's green garters*, with it all listed out, it seemed far too much for one person.

"Can you mend this?" A grizzled brother, the Grist guard obedientiary, brandished a riven chunk of boiled leather. Not exactly within the scope of a handmaid's duties, but certainly a tough feat, mending a material that would require so many steps. Did they think that magic was omnipotent?

She took the bracer and ran her finger along the crack. "I can't make something from nothing, brothers." Reversing damage was not something magic could do. Without any supplies, at least.

The grizzled brother nodded and took the piece back. Maybe that had been the test on its own?

A brother with long plaited hair spoke next. "Recite the first of the Choreas."

The Six Mage Edicts? Did they think her a child? Did she not have her tutees repeat this every week? "A greedy mage drains her source dry.

A selfish mage refuses her source's direction. A hard mage cares not for her source. An ambitious mage eclipses her source. An inconstant mage doubts her source. A loose mage bonds indiscriminately. Or would you like them in the original Eichian?"

"That will suffice," the fanner snapped. Perhaps she should have been more demure. But did they really expect her to stumble over the *Choreas*?

"And have you ever undergone the binding ritual before, Sister?" The bored forager didn't even bother to look at her.

"Yes, Brother."

They all looked at her then.

"Your bond was broken?" Brother Padril spoke gently.

She held her head high. "No, Brother. The rituals failed."

"Rituals?" The grizzled brother's attention was riveted to her. Damn her tongue.

"Yes."

"Sister, speak plainly. How many rituals have you undergone?" snapped the fanner.

"Five." Let them hate her, dismiss her, laugh her out of this chamber. She was the best mage they'd seen all day, and they knew it. Having her as handmaid would make all of their lives easier.

"Thank you, Sister. I believe we've seen enough."

Mellia's nails dug into her palm. She didn't argue; she didn't have a hope of hiding the tremor that would wrack her voice. Nothing would make her case any better than she already had, and arguing would just paint her as difficult. She strode out into the glaring evening sun slanting over the roofs of the comb into the cloister. She wandered onto the grass, the stained-glass windows of the hive sparkling in the evening light.

"Mellia!" Sathred waved her down from nearer the hive. The handmaids weren't supposed to be outside the keep, were they?

"Sathred! What are you doing out here?"

"I told Glimar I needed to know more about preserving Arista's body. He didn't want to risk having her decompose before the Necrophoresis Ritual. So I get to see the sun!" Who else would call the Grist father "Glimar" so cavalierly? Sathred tapped a beehive affectionately, and two disoriented bees buzzed out and meandered to the ground.

"Clever." The Queen's Garden was open to the Grist queen and her handmaids whenever they wanted to *see the sun*, but the walls were high, and the sun was not, at the moment.

Sathred wrapped her trailing sleeve around her hand and coaxed one of the bees onto it, then the other. "Were you just in with the conclave? I swear, the best part about being a handmaid is never having to answer to them again." Just the Grist father.

"I was." Mellia planted her fists on her hips.

Sathred nudged the bees to the beehive's opening, and they crawled inside, one after the other. "Everyone knows your magic is the strongest. You've been practicing since you were a kid. You'll get it." She smiled at Mellia, but all the handmaids knew about her past bond attempts. How could any of them expect her to be accepted?

No matter. If they rejected her, she'd go to Father Glimar. Even if the obedientiaries refused to see reason, surely the Grist father would want the best mage for his new Queen's handmaid.

2

ALROTH

"Without any assurance of repayment, I can't lend you the silver you've requested." The moneylender grimaced as a spider the size of Alroth's hand scuttled across the wall and froze. "You know, the Grist can help repair these buildings."

Yeah, for a tithe that would eat up more of the harvest than they could spare.

"For a very reasonable tithe, you could have a few brothers out here to guard the place, and then there would be no need to move inside the town walls at all."

Alroth nodded, as though considering *that* asinine statement. "Thanks very much." *For nothing.*

"Your larder looks well enough stocked." The moneylender sniffed, eyeing the stacks of preserves and scrounged and bartered foodstuffs. He clearly wasn't used to meeting in a stuffy, spider-infested larder. In all fairness, this was a close to a back room as Alroth had.

The spider scuttled behind a barrel and out of sight. The moneylender would not change his mind. They would find another way to scrape together silver. They would have to. But how? They'd made some coin accompanying pious lords into New Bridge for the Grist queen's funeral rites, but not enough. Not before winter really set in.

The moneylender straightened his mantle as he stood. "If you change your mind about indenturing any of your people, you know where to find me."

Alroth rose as well, jostling a hanging dried ham with his head, but even that didn't keep the moneylender from cringing away. "I won't change my mind." Most of the folks who lived here in Mill Hamlet had come to avoid exactly that fate, and Alroth would never condemn any of them, even to save the rest.

The moneylender held his ground. "It's your first winter here in New Bridge. You might change your tune by winter's end." He brushed the seat of his tunic, even though just this morning Alroth had meticulously cleaned the crate the little weasel had been sitting on.

Inviting him here at all had been a mistake.

A knock on the door interrupted before Alroth could do anything he'd regret.

"Captain Alroth, sir?" The kid's voice barely made it through the paper-thin door.

Alroth heaved a sigh and resisted the urge to scrub a hand over his face. What was the trouble now? He opened the door. Tarrin shifted from foot to foot, eyes fixed on the ground.

"Hey, kid, what can I do for you?" Alroth wrapped an arm around his shoulders and drew him away from the back room. No need for the moneylender to hear about Mill Hamlet's difficulties.

"It's the harvest, Captain. Vernis says the ground's going to freeze overnight. We got to get everything in before..."

"And we will." Alroth clasped Tarrin's shoulder. "Let me grab Del and Kai, maybe Falkirk and Etienne if I can rustle them up. We'll be there in two shakes. Get on."

The kid's face split into a grin, and he trotted away. He was recovering well from his near drowning in the fall. Looking stronger. Happier.

They'd all benefit from having the harvest in. If they were going to bring it all in today, though, the next week would be all preserving and storing. Any crops they didn't save meant one more hungry day next spring. Etienne couldn't beg time off from his castle guard duties right now; they were already woefully short on men up there. Was Falkirk even back from their journey to Hiorach-cursed Munificast?

The moneylender emerged from the larder, just a little too close to Alroth.

A young mother with her tiny babe sat by the fire. The two of them had been holding up since the birth; capable old Selena, dozing in the sturdy armchair across from them, had mothered her, just the same as she mothered the rest of them. The mother had even gained some colour back since she'd crawled in here six months past, half starved, fully with child, no doubt turned out by her parents. Alroth hadn't asked, had just sat her by the fire and handed her a bowl of broth and hard bread to sop it up. They'd all been woken more than once in the night by the babe's cries, but it was a reminder that the mother and child were safe and warm here, not slowly dying on the streets.

They could still starve if Alroth didn't get the harvest in, and they could still die if he didn't get them all moved inside the town walls soon. Overwintering out here would be bad enough, but come spring, when the March River was navigable again, they could have worse to contend with. But no use worrying about that until Falkirk returned with news.

"Pretty mage like that shouldn't have any trouble making coin." The moneylender said it just like that, as though he didn't expect Alroth to blacken his eye for it.

But Alroth kept his clenched fists to himself and jerked his head at the door. If she wanted to make coin that way, she would, and no one here would think less of her for it. But she didn't. The moneylender scuttled out the door.

Alroth followed and shut it tight behind them to keep the little family and Selena's old bones cozy against the biting wind, and peered at the sun. Etienne wouldn't be off duty until dusk. They'd have to make do with Tarrin and the boys, plus his handful of strong folk able to wield sickle and hoe.

The moneylender said his farewells, probably still hoping to change Alroth's mind about indenturing his people, and Alroth made sure he was off toward Mill Gate before trudging to the fields where Del and Kai already worked, bickering incessantly, along with anyone else hale enough to help.

After spending the afternoon hauling potatoes and parsnips, the chilly breeze was welcome, cooling the sweat running down Alroth's back under his shirt. Even Del was quiet as he hefted another basket of vegetables and headed for the storehouse. The one they'd rebuilt midsummer after the old one burned down. Alroth sighed and ran a soil-caked hand through his windswept hair. He couldn't prove it had been folk from the town proper and not roving bandits who'd lit the blaze, but no bandits had been seen either before or after. Inside the town walls, nothing of the kind would be permitted to happen. If only he could scrape together the coin to get them a place, tiny though it would be compared to their knot of cottages and cruck house. At least none of those had been the arsonist's target this summer. Alroth shuddered, the sweat suddenly cooling on his skin as the sun dipped below the town wall behind him.

Alroth retreated to the storehouse to ensure their harvest was well stored, away from prying rats, at least. He turned the corner into the back storeroom and came upon Del and Kai, heads together. Quiet, for once.

"Everything well out here?" he said.

"Yes, Wolf," said Kai.

Del stuck his hands in his pockets. "How did your big meeting go?"

"A bust." Alroth waved it away, as though it hadn't been their last hope.

"I'm sorry. It was a good idea." Kai rearranged a basket of vegetables.

"Nah, don't worry about it. We'll sort something else out." He just didn't know what yet. Day labouring would only get them so far, but it would be better than nothing. As long as they could get the work. "You two pulled more than your weight today. Every pound of food we saved is a hungry belly filled. Worth more than coin, that." He punched Kai lightly on the shoulder. He meant it, too. Starving in a hovel inside the town walls would be no better than starving outside them. He would know.

When the three of them got back to their cruck, Etienne sat with his boots up on the table, combing his bushy blond moustache.

Falkirk sat across from him, leaning on their elbows, eyes narrowed. "You did not."

"I did! I swear to you on Sarilla's golden petticoats." Etienne brandished his tankard.

Falkirk rolled their eyes. "As though that means anything to you at all." They caught sight of Alroth and stood. "Captain."

"You have a report for me."

"Yes, sir."

Alroth jerked his head toward his back room, and Falkirk followed him into the larder and closed the door, for all the good it would do. Alroth sank into his rickety chair, and Falkirk sat opposite on the low crate.

"I should be offering you the proper seat after you travelled so far."

They shrugged. "It was mostly sitting today. Got a ride in the back of a farmer's cart."

"Jolting is more like." The road from Munificast isn't bad, but some of those carts...

Falkirk didn't let him delay any more. "You were right. There's talk of war."

"Talk?"

"Whispers, for now."

And if war came? From Carille? New Bridge Castle had been built for that eventuality, the town walls fortified and built higher, but their little settlement would be raided, burned, maybe worse.

"We should be safe until spring, sir."

"That's if they don't have bound mages."

Falkirk didn't answer. They knew it was true. Mages could make the treacherous winter winds of Lake Val passable if they had enough power, and Carille might not have the Empire's backing or the Grist presence that Sudra did, but they had plenty of powerful bound mages. No, Alroth and the folks under his protection couldn't stay here. Inside the town walls was the only safe place for them.

"Anything else, Falkirk?"

They furrowed their brow. "Probably just idle talk, but something might be brewing with the Grist."

"Brewing?"

"Nothing specific. Just some rumours of Grist fathers promising land and title in exchange for loyalty."

"Is that really news?" The Grist were always buzzing around making deals behind closed doors and putting their loyalists in places of power. Why would that concern them out here in New Bridge? No one wanted this worthless spit of land, strategic though it might be. Calornith Province didn't have the mines of the mountains, the fertility of the lowlands, or the wealth in trade of the Western Road.

"It's news because the titles being promised already belong to families with secure lines of succession."

"Let me guess, the families are not particularly pious?"

"That's right."

"They're planning to, what? Take their lands?"

Falkirk shrugged. "They're just rumours. I'm sure the Grist are making promises they can't keep, as always."

Petty squabbles from folks who already had everything they could ever need, still clawing for more. That kind of manoeuvring would never affect them out here. What in the name of the Great Golden God would Alroth do with a title? Not that there was an ephemer's chance of moving a boulder that he would ever have one. Becoming one of those pompous, selfish lords would be a nightmare anyway. No, he didn't need fancy words, just solid silver. If war came, only coin would protect them.

But how to earn it? They couldn't risk what little reputation they had by thieving; they needed coin and lordly approval to move inside the walls. There wasn't time to hire on as guards for any more travelling merchants. Anyone with sense stayed off the roads by this time of year, including bandits, though once the ceremonies were done, all the smallholders and pious folk leaving New Bridge might not know that. But what if the snows flew while they were away and they were cut off from New Bridge for the winter? It was too great a risk. Which just left day labouring in town. But even if they all managed to find work every day, they would come up short. No, only a regular guard post like Etienne's would have a hope of providing the legitimate coin they needed in time.

"How's everything been here, Wolf?" Falkirk stretched out their legs.

"Del and Kai have been up to their usual squabbles. Selena's been a mother hen over that little one."

"As have you, I'm sure."

Alroth glowered, drawing his eyebrows together, and Falkirk laughed.

"Very convincing, Wolf."

Mother hen. How dare they? A smile tugged at the corner of his mouth. The babe was precious, in more ways than one. Every child deserved a warm, loving home with folks to dote on them.

"The little one will be climbing all over you, tugging on your beard in no time."

"Doloman willing."

Falkirk nodded seriously. "How are our coffers looking?"

Alroth jangled the keys to his lockbox. "Lighter than we'd hoped. I'll talk to Etienne about getting a permanent guard post in the castle."

"Coin and prestige." They gave him a shrewd look. "Etienne isn't around much."

"There's nothing for it, Falkirk." It was either earn coin away from his folks or stay poor with them. At least as a castle guard he would be able to come home every night, make sure they were still alive and fed. Protect them from nighttime raids, Doloman forbid.

"I can take care of things."

Alroth's shoulders rose. Falkirk was capable of taking care of things while Alroth was away, but long-term? No one had ever looked out for these people, not until Alroth had stepped in and brought them together, providing guidance, protection, and resources. He'd hunted down the timber they needed, rustled up the folk to build the cottages, bargained them down through friendship and pity. He'd secured the right to farm the flood plain through the summer, found folk willing to teach the skills they all needed to survive, even got some Grist foragers to come help out once or twice, not that they could afford the tithe, but he'd been the one to convince them to lower that, too.

Yes, while Alroth was away, Falkirk would hold everything together, but that's all they would do. Alroth was the one who needed to be here and advocate for his people and draw them in to work as a team.

But he was the only one with a hope of joining the castle guard. Del and Kai were too hotheaded, and Falkirk... the guard captain would take one look and dismiss their willowy frame out of hand. So it had to be Alroth. Getting the position would be hard enough—he would figure out how to do that later—but even if he did, would he end up like Etienne? Drifting away, practically living at the castle, sleeping there most nights, too late or too exhausted to get home after his shift? Not that Etienne had ever been interested in running their hamlet, but even if he had been, the castle guard were expected to be available. There was nothing for it. Alroth would get a post with the guard for long enough to earn the coin they needed, and once his folks were safe inside the walls, he'd come back to them.

He got Falkirk abreast of the harvest situation, and the two of them left his back room for the hall. Del had his drum out, and Kai his horn. The pottage on its hook over the fire bubbled, the scent of stew filling the room, which was getting warmer by the moment as folks clapped and sang along to their tune. Tarrin pulled Selena to her feet and started the line of a dance. The babe looked on from her mother's lap with wide eyes, the mother's knee bouncing, her cheeks round and pink. Etienne joined the dance, pulling the person next to him along until the earthen floor trembled with stomping feet and the air with shouts and catcalls.

Alroth had to keep these folks safe. Even if it meant leaving them for a while. Someone tried to pull him onto the floor, but he smiled and shook his head. His shoulder was tired enough already from the harvest, and he'd have an early start if Etienne could get him a temporary post tomorrow.

As Alroth sopped up the last of the gravy from his bowl of pottage, Etienne flopped onto the bench beside him.

"You could try one dance, Wolf."

Alroth scraped the last drops from his empty wooden bowl. "You're dancing enough for the both of us, Drake."

Etienne laughed. "Not possible, my friend. What's on your mind? You've been staring deep into that bowl like it's your long-lost lover's—"

Selena sauntered by at that moment and lifted a grey eyebrow.

"—eyes," Etienne finished.

"Any chance you could put me down for a guard shift tomorrow?"

Etienne slapped his knee and crowed. "You? A castle guard? But how will you keep from stabbing the kidney of the man next to you? Wolf, no offence meant, but you will never convince the guard captain that you don't want to butcher every one of us up there. For a day, perhaps, when I vouch for you, but for a week? A month?" He shook his head sadly.

"I didn't ask for your opinion on the matter, just your recommendation, puffed-up dandy," Alroth growled, drawing a chortle from Etienne.

He held up his hands in surrender. "Fine, fine. You want to beg the captain for a posting? On your knees? I'll take you to see him in the morning. But there are fifty other men, mostly mercs like us, wanting a permanent position. They heard Lord New Bridge is making a good offer, and they've come, probably to overwinter. Even if I get you one shift, it won't guarantee you more. They'll stage a mock battle most like."

"With the rumours of war."

Etienne nodded, suddenly serious.

"So you've heard them, too?"

"They would never hire so many guards just for the funeral rites. The smallholders are boisterous, but they can be taken down in one stroke, for the most part. Lord New Bridge is tight with his coin. He wouldn't pass it out so freely unless he was trying to lure the likes of us into loyalty."

Selena returned with a tankard for Etienne, who took it with a wink and a "Thanks, love." He took a long pull of the warm ale, foam coating his moustache as he thunked the stone mug on the tabletop.

Alroth could take fifty men, perhaps not all at once, but he could win out in the ring against practically anyone, sometimes even Etienne. "What are you really worried about, Drake?"

Etienne shook his head. "Never worried for you, my friend. But if they find out who you are..."

If anyone with a grudge against the Wolf recognized him, they would most likely fight to kill. Dirty. But why would they? Etienne certainly wouldn't tell them, and Falkirk, Del, and Kai were the only ones here who knew. Though, mercs from Nordval might recognize him, even with the beard. He would deal with that if it came up. What other option was there? Besides, just because someone recognized him didn't mean they'd go crawling to the guard captain with the information. His treason had benefitted them all.

"I'll need to turn in if I'm going to be up when the gates open."

Etienne waved him away, already at the bottom of his tankard and looking longingly at the dance floor once again.

Alroth absently greeted folks as he skirted the dancers to the bedrooms. The noise wouldn't keep him awake; in fact, it would keep the nightmares at bay. It would remind him that he was no longer alone. Even the clash of weapons during the war days had helped. It had reminded him that he was no longer unarmed.

3

Mellia

Mellia woke up in the silent dormitory before dawn. The brothers weren't going to choose her as the new handmaid. It didn't matter that she was one of the best mages among the sisters. She had proven herself unable to bond with five different lords, despite performing the binding ritual exactly as instructed—meticulously so. She got up and dressed quietly in the dark. Other sisters were stirring now, rising to tend the fires for the brothers.

Mellia had to tell Elenta about her father's letter. She of all people would understand, bound to Lord New Bridge as she was. The cloister's silence was broken by Mellia's footfalls and the sound of her breath puffing into the still morning air. A glitter of frost coated the hive roof where the sun touched the spire. She stole through the crowded guest house, picking her way around the sleeping blanketed lumps, across the glittering granite floor, and past a pair of sleepy-looking guards. Not Grist guards but mercenaries hired for the funerary period. Sleepy merchants filtered into Iram Square, the clatter of their stalls being set up seeming to annoy the hulking Doloman statue that towered in front of the huge hive doors. He glared down at the ruckus, arms crossed over his golden chest. Mellia hurried on.

Hive Street was nearly deserted, and she made good time down toward the water. Lower Gate clanked slowly open as she turned onto Water Street. New Bridge Castle, its pennant hanging despondently in the still morning, lay before her. The brothers hadn't selected her to participate in the handmaid trials—not after her performance yesterday—but she could still go over their heads. Father Glimar knew who she was because of her role at the castle, tutoring his niblings. If she asked him, he would at least grant her an audience. And once she had that, she would convince him to let her participate in the trial.

She climbed the stairs to the castle drawbridge, already lowered and admitting a steady stream of practically dressed folks like her. A breeze caught a strand of Mellia's hair as she crossed the southern barbican to the gate. The outer ward was already bustling, the kitchen chimneys releasing a stream of smoke that rose almost straight into the chilly air, and a couple of smallholders sang a bawdy song as they leaned against each other on their way to the great hall to pass out, probably still awake from last night's revelry. Perhaps they were celebrating a marriage and bond alliance negotiated over last night's dinner. Likely, the promised mage wasn't even in New Bridge, still blessedly unaware of her fate. Mellia sighed and hurried past the well and across the inner drawbridge.

The guards nodded at her Grist pin, and she passed into the inner ward. She climbed the steps to Lady Elenta's chambers, since the drapes were open behind her large mullioned windows. Elenta would sympathize about her father's edict, even if she could do nothing to change it. The lady in the antechamber nodded and waved her through into Elenta's chamber.

Another of her ladies was pinning Elenta's hair, both of their backs to the door, and another offered Elenta something from a tray of food.

"Good morning, Elenta," said Mellia.

Elenta's cheeks went pink as Mellia came around in front of her. "Mellia!" She waved the food away and Mellia toward a seat. "I'm sorry about yesterday. I should have told you to keep the children..." She swallowed. Ah, yes. Yesterday morning, after tutoring, Mellia had released the children from their studies, and they'd gone tearing off to bother Lord New Bridge. Elenta had borne the consequences. But somehow, she was the one apologizing.

Mellia tried to smile. "No apology necessary."

The lady was almost done with Elenta's hair. They would be listening at the door even after they left, but speaking freely in front of them wouldn't be appropriate.

"Morgan told me yesterday he wanted to be Grist father after Father Glimar."

"You're a good influence on them, sister." Elenta's hummingbird ephemer buzzed past Mellia's head and darted through the wall, its translucent form passing through the stone with ease.

Best not to mention that Delia also wanted to be Grist father. Elenta would have thought it hilarious in days past, but now... Lord New Bridge would be livid if he found out his daughter had said such a thing. And if Elenta's ladies knew, he would inevitably find out. Elenta would take the brunt of his rage, but he might well dismiss Mellia too, and without her excuse of tutoring the children, there would be no justifiable reason for her to visit Elenta like this anymore.

The lady finished her pinning, curtsied, and left, followed by the lady offering food, when Elenta waved her away. The heavy door shut behind them.

Tears welled in Elenta's eyes.

"Oh, Lenny." Mellia went to her knees next to her friend and wrapped her arms around her.

"I'm fine, Melly," she sobbed out. "I have all these ladies and my beautiful children and we're all safe here."

"I know." Mellia squeezed her friend close. The door to the lord's chambers on the opposite wall was closed, but it didn't lock from this side. He could appear without announcing himself at any moment. They could never forget that. He wasn't a cruel man, as such things went. He just wanted things a certain way and never seemed to explicitly tell Elenta what that way was.

Elenta pulled back and wiped her face with her handkerchief. "I'll do better today." She pasted on a smile. "Now! We have something to discuss."

"We do?" Mellia went back to her seat and smoothed her dark wool skirt. The edge brushed Elenta's fine silk hem. No one could accuse Lord New Bridge of being stingy with his matron.

"Yes. Lord Ainsley arrived yesterday after you left."

Ainsley... why did that sound so familiar? There were so many smallholders and minor lords in Calornith Province here for the funerary rites, why should she care about Ainsley?

"Your parents sent him."

"As their representative?" Since her brother's death, Mellia was the de facto heir to her family lands and title, and her position in the Grist meant that her father often had to make do with vassals as representatives. Strange that she had never heard of this one though. She hadn't been gone that long.

"No! As your betrothed." Elenta grinned.

Mellia's stomach tightened, and she swallowed the bile climbing up her throat. Her father had sent the suitor to her. It made no difference that she'd refused his summons. Once it became clear that she wouldn't become a handmaid, the suitor would pounce... She tried for a smile, but she must have looked as sick as she felt, because Elenta's grin faded.

"You get another try, Mellia. Isn't that wonderful? You'll get to go home and be a lady. No more working all day as a sister. You'll finally be a matron!" She gestured, and the fire leapt in the grate. Elenta's tiny silvery hummingbird reappeared, squeaked, and hovered next to Elenta's head.

I can already do that. But Mellia didn't say that. If her magic was strong now, how much stronger would it be if she were bound? But she'd *tried*. Five times she'd tried, and all of them she'd failed. That another lord was willing to go through the ritual with her now spoke to how much he wanted her family lands and title. She'd never met a Lord Ainsley, so it was not her personality that had captured his attention.

The door behind Mellia creaked open, and Elenta's gaze jumped over her shoulder. "My Lord."

"What could possibly have needed my power, mage? Sitting alone with a sister is hardly strenuous." His quiet tone prickled goosebumps over Mellia's scalp.

"I—I was demonstrating the power of a strong bond to Sister Mellia." She gestured Mellia's way. "This is the sister Lord Ainsley will take as his matron."

Mellia bowed her head. Elenta didn't need to be wrenched into an ephemer again today.

Lord New Bridge's scathing gaze was palpable on her dark sister's garb, the simple veil over her hair, the scuffed toes of her boots. She could practically hear him thinking that she was unfit to be bound to a lord. "I'm sure Sister Mellia is fully aware of the implications of binding. You must learn not to squander my power so frivolously."

Mellia didn't move. What could she do?

"My Lord, please, I have work to do this morning. I can't—"

"Surely not so much work, considering you sit here gossiping with a companion." His eyes flashed.

"No—" Elenta's protest was cut off as she fell to her knees, a wince twisting her face. The colour drained from her, blew away in a non-existent wind as her hummingbird ephemer gained solidity. Elenta's mouth moved, but no sound reached them.

"I hope you appreciate these lessons, matron." New Bridge's hard gaze flicked to Mellia, who quickly focused on her own feet on the floor.

The door closed with a click.

Mellia sank back in her chair.

Elenta's back bowed, the bed beyond her visible through her slumped form.

Mellia shook her head, trying for a smile. "I should be more excited about the prospect of bonding." She swallowed the lump in her throat again. Something, perhaps a slimy frog, was trying to crawl up it. Lord Ainsley was probably perfectly nice. Once they were married and bound, she would be a matron, as Elenta had said. Except if the bond didn't take. Again. "I'm sure the ritual will go smoothly this time. Six is a sacred number, after all.

"Now, go ahead and show me what needs doing."

Elenta squeezed her hands together, her shoulders rose and fell on a deep breath, and she climbed to her feet. She gave Mellia a tense nod, and they began their painstaking process of translating gestures into instructions. All their years of childhood etiquette lessons together helped immensely, when they used to talk silently behind the matron's back, as did Mellia's having trained to run a large household of her own. The two of them managed to ensure that Lord New Bridge's breakfast was prepared to his satisfaction, sent some of Elenta's ladies to ensure the visiting lords were taken care of, and wrangled the children, all without Elenta being seen in her indecent ephemeral form. It wouldn't do for the household to know she'd required the lord's correction, after all. Mellia shuddered.

By the time tutoring was to begin, Elenta was corporeal once more. Mellia, Elenta, and the children crossed the inner ward together.

"Lord Ainsley wanted to meet you. I told him that you'd be here this morning. After your lessons with the children. He'll meet you in Hive Tower."

A pious lord. No doubt assigned by the Grist, in exchange for prestige for her father and Lord Ainsley, once he inherited. He would perform the binding ritual to the letter. Mellia shuddered. At least last time hadn't been painful, not like the first...

"I'll meet him." Mellia hugged Elenta and corralled the children up to their classroom. How would she get through lessons today knowing she would meet her betrothed after them? Her stomach roiled. Hopefully the children wouldn't notice her discomfiture.

The lesson passed in a blur, but she kept Morgan and Delia in their classroom until Elenta came to retrieve them. Elenta squeezed Mellia's hand and whispered, "Good luck," before chivying the rapscallions away.

Perhaps they should have sent a guard to escort her to Hive Tower. Was it too late to escape back to the comb and claim she'd never got the message about meeting Lord Ainsley? No, Elenta would be blamed for not passing the message to her. Mellia took a deep breath. She had done this before, and she would survive it again. Strangely, the thought of failing to bond *again* was no more unpleasant than the thought of the bond actually taking. Why wouldn't she be pleased to have a bond finally take? To finally have the security of a bound mate and live like a lady again? Chills skated up her spine. Was that anticipation or dread?

She wrapped her mantle around her, though it did nothing to dissipate the chills, and descended into the courtyard. Instead of turning toward the gate and inner drawbridge, she turned to Hive Tower. She took the narrow stairs into the lord's hive, the steps clinging to her feet, slowing her progress. She turned the last corner and paused in the hive doorway. Stained-glass windows let in tinted sunlight, bathing the altar at the head of the room, a constantly running fountain, powered by the magic of the Grist.

A lone man knelt there, nothing to cushion his knees on the wooden floor. Pious. Perfectly suited to bond a Grist sister. Mellia's footsteps were muffled by the fountain's trickle, and he didn't move until she was next to him, even then just cocking his head, not looking at her. Her skirts rustled as she surreptitiously folded them for extra padding as she knelt. Playing at piety came naturally to her after three years as a sister.

"I understand you are thirty-six years old." His accent marked him as from the Western Road. Likely a rich merchant wanting a more prestigious title.

"Yes, my lord." Ah, thirty-six, the most auspicious of ages. The last chance for an unbound mage to bond into matronhood. Any mage not bound between twenty-four and thirty-six years of age would never be. According to the Grist and their love of the holy sexternity.

He nodded sagely, still not looking at her. "Your father assured me you would be cooperative."

Mellia clasped her hands as if in prayer to stop her fingers' tingling. She deliberately slowed her breathing. "Of course, my lord." What choice did she have but to be cooperative?

"Good. We'll wait until after the Necrophoresis Ritual, but I see no need to delay further. We'll be bound directly after the ceremony and return to Falvair for the solstice."

He was so sure the bond would take. Did he not know her history? She had to make sure he was aware. It might be the only way to change his mind.

"My lord, I have failed the binding ritual five times."

"Excellent. The sixth will be successful, I assure you." His voice was grim, as though he would personally make sure that the bond took. He couldn't be worse than her third attempt, could he? That one...

Maybe if she assured him of her good intentions, he would be less... thorough. "I will also make every effort to perform the ritual perf—"

"That won't be necessary." He stood. "Perhaps such attempts were the cause of your past failures. Good day, sister." His footsteps receded from the hive.

Mellia stayed on her knees, squeezed her hands together in genuine prayer this time. No. No, no, no. He was just like Lord New Bridge. He would *perform the ritual*, and if the bond didn't take, would he try again? How many times would he attempt it? And what would become of her if it *never* took? She would lose his protection; her father would have no use for her...

And if the bond was successful? Her heart might beat itself out of her chest. She couldn't breathe. To be bound to *that* for the rest of her life? A pompous, pious ass who would see her power as *his* and wrench her on a whim. Wearing silks, being tended, and being called a lady were not worth that... perhaps that would even make it worse. Having ladies chosen by her source watching her day and night, listening at doors, reporting back to him. And she'd never be allowed to visit Elenta again...

But how to prevent it? Resisting him would make him "take her in hand," no doubt. She shuddered.

Father Glimar was her route to becoming a handmaid, and she would go crawling to him if that's what it took. She could not allow the ritual with Lord Ainsley to proceed. With any luck, Father Glimar was either unaware of the betrothal or would take pity on her. If he succeeded in helping her, as a handmaid, she'd be free of Lord Ainsley's suit, committed to Doloman for life. And handmaid duties would put her not insubstantial magic to good use. She could work with the other handmaids, unbound though they were, to make beautiful things. Hard work? Yes, but not the ties of a matron, subject to the whims of her source, dogged by the threat of wrenching for the smallest perceived infraction.

Mellia dusted off her skirts and strode down the narrow steps back out into the inner ward, wrapping her mantle more firmly around her shoulders and straightening the bee-shaped pin on her breast as she emerged from the circular stairs. The guards by the inner drawbridge recognized the Grist's symbol and nodded as she approached.

"How are you today, sister?" The big blond one with the immaculate moustache always chatted to her, as though he couldn't help himself.

The other one was new and assessed her as though she were a threat.

She focussed on the friendly guard. "As well as can be expected while mourning the Grist queen."

"Can anyone be well after such sad news?" He shook his head.

"I'm sure the visiting lords are keeping you busy enough."

The guard threw back his head and laughed. "So they are, sister! Alroth here is benefitting from their skullduggery. More mischief means more guard posts."

Alroth nodded curtly, his gaze still assessing. She drew herself up. Who was he to judge a sister so? A temporary castle guard?

"Good day, sister." His voice rumbled from his chest.

Mellia fiddled with the bee pin on her mantle. "And good day to you." Why was her voice so breathy? She hurried on across the inner drawbridge. That guard—Alroth—was probably still watching her with his piercing gaze. But that didn't matter. It was unsettling, certainly not exciting. Just because a man looked at her that way didn't mean her future lay there. Though her luck with lords had been abysmal. Perhaps a mercenary guard would break her streak of misfortune. As if binding herself to a mercenary would help her position at all. Her father would disown her.

The outer ward bustled, the kitchen chimneys pouring smoke, and whinnies and neighs of horses floating from the stables next door. As the day wore on, the cacophony of the great hall would drown out both, but this time of the day was for work, not amusement. The revelry from last night when all the smallholder lords arrived would have left them slow to wake this morning. Not that the occasion was happy. The Grist queen was dead, after all.

And this might be her only chance to become a handmaid. All she had to do was get that handmaid position, and she wouldn't have to worry about being bound to a lout like Lord New Bridge. She picked up her pace as she passed through the south gate into the south barbican, down the steps, and across the drawbridge.

The streets were even more crowded than the castle, oxcarts passing slowly toward the lift at the east end of the castle, working day and night to move supplies into the purser's tower. Water Street was just as crowded, what with the supplies coming from the Lower Gate, but at least the street was wide enough that Mellia could avoid the endless dung piles that were laid faster than they could be cleaned on a day like this, and the nip in the wind kept the smell at bay.

She turned down Hive Alley, narrow enough to bar cart traffic, at least, and into Iram Square, the golden statue of Doloman glittering in the late-morning sun but still passing judgment, particularly on any who would enter the hive's sanctum. Mellia shuddered and skirted the statue. Thankfully, she didn't have to enter through the hive proper every day. Brothers worshiped six times a day, but sisters only on holy days. Most of the bustling activity would be round the back entrance, next to Upper Gate. While the smallholders resided in the castle, ten times as many pilgrims resided here in the comb behind the hive. Brothers and sisters had come from all over Calornith Province to say their farewells to Grist Queen Arista and see which handmaid would take her place as Grist queen.

Two guards were posted outside the makeshift guest quarters in the echoing entryway. Both had axes at their hips, and right now, they looked about a hairsbreadth from using them on each other.

"Aye, I'll say it again, and to your face. Your glyptodon face breathes too loud. What do you say to that, eh?" The fair one's nose was about a handspan from the darker one.

The loud breather didn't move back. "Your humming drowns it out, not to worry." His eyes were flinty though.

"Humming like a damned stinger? Your mother hums!"

The dark one rolled his eyes, and the light one drew his fist back.

"Gentlemen!" Mellia used her teacher voice. "What seems to be the problem?"

Both men immediately straightened to attention. They glanced over her Grist pin.

"No problem, Sister," said the fair one. "Just horsing around, you know how it is between friends."

Friends? These were mercenary guards hired to supplement the Grist Guard brothers for the funeral period. Maybe that's how mercenaries showed friendship? Either way, it was no way to act on duty.

"Even if I did, you've been hired to do a job, and the Grist expects that you will take your role seriously."

They both looked at their shoes and *yes Sister*ed her. Better.

"See that I don't catch you brawling again."

Chagrined *no Sisters*.

She swept between them into the guest hall. Arista's body would sit out for a total of six days, salted and dried, and then on the seventh, the husk would cascade over March Falls and be left to float out into Lake Val—if it didn't get hung up on a sandbar or Mud Island. The water was low this time of year. Maybe one of the Grist outriders would troll the March River and ensure the Grist queen's body made it to the bay. It seemed undignified for the Grist queen to be eaten by dire wolves, bears, or titanis before she could reach the Vita Maris, where spirits gathered.

Granite glimmered under Mellia's boots, and scores of voices blended together as a few knots of brothers and sisters spoke in hushed tones. Likely catching up with old friends. None of the sisters travelled in their roles in the comb, as a rule, and of the brothers, only outriders would be likely to visit other hives in the course of their duties. Except, of course, the Grist father, who ventured to the heart of Sudra regularly to speak with Sudra's Pater Patrum and the archduke.

At this time in the afternoon, Grist Father Glimar should be in the sacristy, having finished the mid-afternoon Locus prayer.

Mellia crossed straight into the cloister and hurried past the dormant beehives to the guardhouse. Unlike the rowdy mercenaries at the gate, real Grist guards protected the entrance to the inner cloister. Even with their diminished power without a bonded Grist queen, no one would dare accost them. They didn't move as she approached, the butts of their halberds resting on stone.

"Sister Mellia, to prepare the handmaids for the funeral service." She strode by, heart in her throat. Was that the first time she'd lied to a Grist guard? If they wanted her to stop, they would say something. The portcullis was already raised, despite the hundreds of unknown brothers and sisters coming and going today. Then again, with the Grist queen dead, fewer remained to guard.

Waiting would be too excruciating. She'd waylay Father Glimar outside the sacristy. Before she could lose her nerve, she stalked across the cloister lawn toward the sacristy door, nearly colliding with Brother Padril coming around the corner. *Bonds.* She wouldn't be thought fit to be a handmaid tromping through the grass like this. She curtsied and held it. *Please nod and walk on...*

"Sister! Where are you headed in such a hurry?"

Going over your head with the Grist father. Perhaps not. "I'm going to meet with the handmaids."

The hem of his black mantle shifted, showing a glimpse of his black boots. "Best of luck with your betrothal, Sister Mellia." Was that pity in his voice? He knew she wanted to be a handmaid, and yet he wished her *luck* with her betrothal?

"Thank you, brother." She clenched her teeth before anything more could escape.

Brother Padril joined a group of brothers for a reading in the inner cloister. She couldn't loiter here waiting for Father Glimar now that she'd lied to Brother Padril about going to see the handmaids.

Mellia trudged to the Grist Queen's Keep, where Grist Guards were clearing out the barracks and a harried Morath directed the flow of provisions into the cavernous space turned kitchen for the solstice feast, which would follow on the heels of the funerary period. The barracks had no windows; she couldn't watch for Brother Padril's departure, or Father Glimar's, from here. She climbed to the handmaids' chambers and poked her head in.

"Mellia." Runas bustled over with a steaming bowl. "Will you take this up to Dayma, please? I don't think she's eaten at all today, and she's been up there working since before dawn."

"We've all been working," said Sathred. "Keeping a cadaver in a form fit to be seen is difficult enough without the instructions being written in some godforsaken code."

"Livine is doing her best," Runas insisted.

"I'm sure you all are." Mellia smiled thinly. She held the bowl steady as she climbed the narrow stairs to the Grist queen's chambers and took the last turn at a crawl, the close air of the death chamber stifling her breath. The shutters remained firmly fastened. She couldn't keep an eye on the inner cloister from here, either.

Dayma sat hunched in the embroidered chair next to the huge bed. There could be no mistaking Queen Arista for asleep. Her hollow cheeks clung to the bone, her skin darkened, her closed eye sockets sunken into her head. Her dress had collapsed in strange places—her thighs, her pelvis—likely only supported by its own structure. Or perhaps Dayma had added supports inside it to keep it from collapsing completely.

The handmaid in question didn't stir when Mellia entered, seemingly staring through the queen's headboard carved with a stylized beehive, the queen bee sitting in the centre, the walls of the comb all around her. That was how the Grist queens lived. They were too important to risk them out in the world. In their keeps, they were protected from those who wished to harness their power, and thus the power of the Grist. Was Dayma imagining becoming Grist queen? One of the current handmaids would. And if she was, was she perhaps dreading it? Her face was starkly blank.

"Dayma?" whispered Mellia.

Dayma turned to her, expression fixed, and goosebumps prickled Mellia's arms. Could some of the death Dayma had been surrounded by these past few days have invaded her? Were her eyes more sunken than they'd been?

Mellia hovered in the doorway. Death lived in this room. It was not a place for the living to linger. "Would you like something to eat?"

She shook her head slowly. A deep breath racked her body, and she shivered all over and pushed to her feet, leaning on the back of her chair. A fixed smile twisted her face. "Thank you, sister. I haven't had a chance to come down today." She gestured to the corpse before her. "Queen Arista will be ready for the Necrophoresis Ritual as planned."

"You can take breaks to eat, Dayma." Mellia thrust the bowl and spoon into her hand.

Dayma looked politely inquisitive.

"A break, Dayma."

Dayma took the food and placed it carefully on the small night table by the bed. "I'm perfectly all right, Mellia. My sacred duty to prepare Queen Arista for the Necrophoresis Ritual is not to be taken lightly, passed off to another, or shirked."

"I hardly think eating can be counted as shirking your duty."

Dayma looked down her nose at Mellia, as though she was too ignorant to know that handmaids were above such mortal pursuits as *eating*, which they definitely were *not*. "If you'd like to be useful, fetch me Sathred's dress. I haven't finished the embroidery on the sleeves."

Dayma was expected to dress the handmaids as well as the queen's husk. All the handmaids had more work than they could realistically do on their own. That's why they had Mellia. "I'd be pleased to help with the embroidery, Dayma."

Dayma's face shuttered again. "Fetch the dress, Mellia. That's all." She turned to the shuttered window and drew close enough to peer through a crack, her back rigid. As she'd said, these were her tasks, and she would carry them out if it killed her.

Mellia slunk downstairs and gathered Sathred's blue dress.

"Did she eat the stew?" Runas called from the window seat.

Mellia shrugged.

"You could go see for yourself," said Sathred from her chair by the fire. "You're supposed to be up there with her."

"I can desiccate the husk perfectly well from down here." Runas closed her eyes, as if to prove her point.

Sathred started to retort, and Mellia escaped back upstairs to the death chamber. Why did Dayma feel she had to stay up here when even Runas refused? Dayma took the dress and laid it across her lap, set her needle embroidering, using her magic to affix a row of tiny blue beads in a heartbeat, and leaned back in her chair.

Mellia pulled up a chair across the bed from Dayma and sat straight, watching Dayma's needle across the queen's husk. If Dayma insisted on staying up here, she wouldn't be alone.

"You could work downstairs, couldn't you?" Mellia should have brought a dress to work on, even though Dayma might admonish her rather than thanking her for her help.

"And leave Arista alone?" Dayma shook her head.

Grist Queen Arista had been young when she'd ascended to her role. One by one, her original handmaids had moved into retirement as sisters or passed away and new young handmaids had been appointed to care for her. Since the Grist queen was not allowed to leave the keep, the handmaids did everything for her. *Had* done everything for her.

It was wrong to leave Dayma alone with her grief, but Mellia had to see Father Glimar today, before the handmaid trial. She would use some excuse about helping Morath in the kitchen to make her escape. Even if Brother Padril was still in the inner cloister, surely she'd been in the keep long enough not to arouse suspicion.

Father Glimar, on the other hand, would have left the sacristy long since—

"How is your progress on the handmaid trial coming? Do you know what your demonstration will be?" Dayma's eyes were open, and she was navigating a tricky section of beading.

"I'm not sure yet." Trying to get a chance to be included in the trial was taking up all of the time that she should be spending preparing her demonstration.

"Your strength is the same as Sathred's, right? Comfort?"

"Yes, that's right." Embroidery, furniture, keeping a room temperate. "I did a little magic for the brothers already..."

"But for the trial you'll need something special. Don't go too far though. If you use too much power as an unbound mage, you can accidentally syphon from someone nearby."

Mellia smiled. The handmaids were always in lecture mode. Just one more thing that would make her a perfect handmaid. Though of course, she'd be teaching sisters instead of the lord's children as a handmaid. She'd no longer be permitted to roam in town once she took her place here. "I was thinking perhaps a show with the weather. If it's cloudy, draw a ray of sunlight to the brothers, if it's sunny, try for a rain shower."

"Rain shower? It would be snow for certain at this time of year. Be careful not to chill them with a gust of winter wind. That will turn them against you for certain." Dayma closed her eyes and leaned her head back, finally past the tricky beadwork and on to a simpler section again, her needle working of its own accord across the satin.

It was a good point. She would be taking a chance playing with the weather when winter was on the way. Perhaps something smaller, making a flower bloom out of season. That wasn't her speciality, but it would be well within her capacity to grow one spring flower.

"Perhaps I'll grow a handmaid's nightcap. The brothers will surely enjoy seeing a flower during these grey days."

"Perhaps… it's less practical than they might prefer. And possibly more suited to a companion handmaid, but flowers do bring joy to a space." Dayma's small smile seemed more genuine this time.

But Mellia had to focus on getting into the trial first. She said her goodbyes to Dayma, who still hadn't touched her stew, and left the keep.

She didn't look for Brother Padril's red head as she crossed the inner cloister, though the brothers were still attending their reading. She marched past the Grist guards and through the cloister, past the guards at the entrance to the comb—bickering again, if more quietly—and into Iram Square.

Doloman's golden gaze watched her as she crossed the square and strode up the lane to the Grist father's house. A footman eyed her suspiciously as she approached. As a member of the Grist, access to the Grist father was afforded her, provided he was available. She gave her name to the usher, who gave her a critical look.

"The Grist father is quite busy right now, sister. Perhaps after the Necrophoresis Ritual… ?"

"I'll wait." Mellia planted her hands on her hips.

The usher huffed and disappeared inside. Was he planning to leave her standing here until she gave up and went away? If he was, he would be disappointed, because she wasn't going anywhere. She'd stand here all day *and* all night if she—

The usher reappeared and bowed her inside. She wiped her feet and crossed the corridor.

Each wall of Father Glimar's, of course, hexagonal chamber was hung with a tapestry of one of Doloman's tenets. Mellia's boots sank into the thick rug. Good thing she'd had the presence of mind to wipe the road filth from them. Father Glimar sat between the glazed window and the large crackling fire.

"Come in, child." He gestured to the chair across from him. "Warm yourself." He must be wondering why she was here. Unless he'd heard of her barging into the conclave yesterday from one of the brothers. Did he know of her betrothal as well?

Mellia perched on the edge of the seat, holding her chilled fingers out to the fire's warmth. The tips of Father Glimar's black boots gleamed in the firelight, peeking out from beneath the hem of his cassock.

"The brothers refused you."

The fire crackled, and a log fell. Mellia nodded. Even the rug in here was patterned with hexagons.

"They don't believe you can bond."

Mellia nodded again and picked at a golden bee embroidered on the arm of her chair.

"You believe that you can?" He watched her, his fingers steepled, elbows on his chair's arms. He didn't sound doubtful or hopeful, or anything much. Just curious. His gaze was soft, patient. Not skeptical like the obedientiaries.

She couldn't lie to him. "I don't know, Father."

"But you think you should ascend as a handmaid nonetheless?" Again, he seemed simply curious.

Mellia shrugged. "I won't be called on to become Grist queen. I'm older than most of the handmaids, so by the time a new queen is chosen, no one need worry about my ability to bond. I'm the best mage among the sisters, even the brothers will tell you that."

Father Glimar's face remained impassive. "Why are you so desperate to become a handmaid?"

Should she tell him about the betrothal? If she told him now, he might not help her. But if she tried to keep it from him and he already knew, it would make her look dishonest. "I've been betrothed."

He crooked an eyebrow. "Congratulations. May Doloman bless your union."

Was he being facetious? "Thank you, Father." Maybe appealing to his piety? "I would much prefer—that is, if I had a choice in the matter—I'd prefer to devote myself to Doloman as a handmaid."

A smile flitted over the Grist father's face. "You don't want to be bound to anyone, or you don't want Lord Ainsley?"

Mellia let out her breath. He knew. He'd known this whole time, and he'd let her stumble around and reveal it to him. It wasn't the bond that repelled her, more that she didn't want Lord Ainsley, but it wasn't *just* Lord Ainsley. None of her suitors had been at all appealing as a source. Mellia opted for the truth. "I want to be a handmaid, Father."

Father Glimar nodded slowly. "I see." He crossed his legs beneath his cassock. "Then we shall have to prove to the brothers that you are capable of bonding."

Mellia jerked back, as though pulled by a string. He wasn't suggesting the ritual. He couldn't be. No, the Grist queen was bound to the brothers and Grist father, and they didn't perform the binding ritual. Father Glimar must be speaking of something else. His gaze was piercing. He'd seen her reaction.

"The Grist bond is not carnal in nature, child." His face softened. "Our bond to the Grist queen is spiritual." He closed his eyes and tilted his head up, as though savouring the memory of the bond he'd lost with Grist Queen Arista. Glimar got to his feet and reached a hand out to her. "Kneel with me, sister."

The two of them lowered to their knees before the fire, face to face, knees pressed into the plush rug, and Father Glimar took her hands in his. His gold rings pressed into her fingers.

"Don't look away, Mellia," he said, quietly.

Mellia swallowed but held his green gaze.

"I detest court events," Glimar continued in a low voice. "Entertaining in this house. I would much rather live as a brother in the comb."

Was that true? But he'd been called by Doloman to his current position. He performed it so well.

"Now you, Mellia."

Now her... what? Was she supposed to say she hated being a sister, toiling all day, sleeping in the dormitory... perhaps she was. Her knee half covered a golden hexagon on the rug.

"Eyes on me." He squeezed her hands gently. Glimar's soft admonishment made her jump, but his eyes were kind.

Mellia licked her lips, but Glimar's gaze didn't flicker from hers. "I'm not overly pious." Her voice sounded too loud in the empty room. Her own *heartbeat* sounded too loud. "My parents sent me to be a sister after I failed my fifth binding." A tug in Mellia's chest made her gasp.

Father Glimar's mouth crooked. "There it is." He squeezed her hands again. "I feel that I'm too young to be Grist father, with the obedientiaries being older than I am, to a man."

The tug in Mellia's chest was stronger this time, and Father Glimar rocked forward, as though he felt it, too. He nodded to her. Her turn again. She was supposed to admit something to him, but what could she say? She was afraid of being bound to someone like Lord New Bridge—his *brother*—for the rest of her life? She didn't want to go through the binding ritual again? She envied the handmaids their freedom, the support they enjoyed to work magic, even unbound? If he found those things out, he would never let her become a handmaid. Handmaids were devoted to the Grist queen, not their own selfish desires, certainly not using the role to escape a proper bond to a well-respected lord. But she had to say *something*. He was waiting for her.

What did he want her to say? His admission had been about being younger than the obedientiaries who answered to him. She was older than the handmaids. That had never seemed like an obstacle before, but perhaps it could be.

"I'm older than the other handmaids. Perhaps I'm too old?" The last part came out as more of a question.

The thread between them faded, the grip on Mellia's chest loosened, and Father Glimar dropped her hands. His face returned to his unreadable mask, and he returned to his chair.

She'd failed.

He'd given her the chance to prove that she was capable of a Grist bond—something he had no obligation of any kind to do—and she'd squandered it. The hexagons on the rug blurred before her and a tear dripped onto her skirt.

"There now, sister. None of that."

She shook her head. He'd been so kind, and still she'd failed. She *was* incapable of forming a bond, whether her partner was cruel or kind.

"It seems to me that the brothers can be convinced."

What? Was he going to speak on her behalf, even though she'd failed?

"Lord Ainsley wants your family lands and title, no doubt."

It hadn't seemed prudent to tell Father Glimar that, but now that he'd said it aloud... "Yes, Father. My grandfather was created Marquess of Falvair at the end of the war."

"Rise, sister. It seems clear to me what Doloman wants for you. You needn't worry about being denied the handmaidship based on your... bonding history."

He really was helping her. Mellia bowed her head. She'd failed, but still, Father Glimar was caring for her. "Thank you, Father."

"But one simple task will prove Doloman favours you for the position." A task? The trial, of course. Maybe she should tell Father Glimar about the handmaids' nightcap, see what he thought of— "Before the trial tomorrow, bring me information from the castle."

Information. Before the trial. This was a task from Doloman that she had to complete before she could even participate in the trial? The time for such a task was far too short, and none of the other handmaid candidates had to... But it was a chance. Which was more than she had now. "What information?"

"A young lord went missing a few years before the Canal War began. I understand that he was seen at the castle yesterday. Bring me more information. His family has been looking for him for twenty-five years and would like nothing more than his return, Doloman willing."

Yes, of course..." She'd ask Elenta. Surely either she or her ladies would have heard this gossip about a long-lost lord... wait. Twenty-five years ago? But that was... the heretic prince disappeared twenty-five years ago. It was a huge scandal in Nordval. The descendant of the heretical King Lorthran and Queen Olena just up and vanished when he was almost of age. Obviously, Mellia had never met him, since she was a child at the time, and even if she hadn't been, Nordval folks, especially Loyalists, didn't mix with Sudran, even in Falvair, the nearest to Nordval one could get without leaving the mainland.

So why was Father Glimar looking for the heretic prince here? It didn't matter. It would secure her place as a handmaid. No need to question it further. If it kept her from having to bind herself to Lord Ainsley, she would do it.

4

Alroth

Alroth woke up early, enough dawn light filtering through the horn window across the room that he could dress and sneak out without disturbing the rest. They needed the sleep; another long day of harvest and preserving lay ahead of them. With any luck, he'd get a permanent post and wouldn't be back until dusk.

Mill Gate would open at full dawn, and Alroth would be ready when it did. The fire in the hall burned low, and Alroth's breath misted. He stirred the embers and fed them until the flames leaped and crackled. Now the hall would be warmed when the next person rose. He went into his back room and pulled out his war chest.

His jack of plate, once patterned grey and red, smelled of rust. He spread it before him in front of the window, the heavy plates thumping on the sill, the iron dulled with time. No obvious rusty patches stuck out, but what if a plate cracked and he got a festering wound today? What would his people do? But he had no time or money to repair his jack, so he pulled his gambeson over his head and laced it by rote, followed by the faded armour. He slid on his cesti over his knuckles, the leather still supple from regular care, the metal studs glinting in the patch of sunlight under the window. Alroth belted on his twin short swords, tucked his helm under his arm, and swiped an apple from a barrel. As he strode out of the cruck, he stuck the apple in his pocket. His knotted stomach was too tight to eat anything this morning. He would succeed in proving himself, of course, but being discovered could mean he was driven out of town, or worse, and being wounded could mean the end for his folk.

He drew his swords, Volnus and Ictus, and went through a few forms to loosen up his stiff shoulder. His reach would be shit, though in the chaos of a mock battle, it would hardly matter. Someone would always be within reach, and it was easy enough to get inside an opponent's guard. He sheathed his blades and joined the procession climbing the path to Mill Gate. The portcullis had already been raised, and Alroth passed a creaking cart and a plodding pack mule that couldn't be coaxed forward, as hard as its driver whipped it. Alroth held up a hand to the infuriated driver and retrieved his apple breakfast. He held it out to the mule, who eyed him skeptically but still got moving, stretching its neck out to snatch the morsel, munching as it plodded placidly under the stone archway into New Bridge.

Alroth strode under the gate alongside it, the portcullis hanging overhead for that one long moment. This was the sort of protection his people needed, protection that he needed to secure for them. The towering limestone walls, gatehouses with watchful guards, an iron portcullis to stave off bandits and invaders alike. And he would get it for them.

He turned up Castle Street, along the palisade that separated the castle's outbuildings from the rest of the town, the castle's towers peeking over the spiked wooden stakes.

"Eh! Wolf!" An arm wrapped his shoulders from behind, and Alroth's elbow jabbed at its owner's gut reflexively. They groaned. "Your bite hasn't softened with age, I see."

A wiry blond man, mailed from throat to knee, braced his hand on the pommel of his sword. Hasburgen. A woman followed two paces behind him, also mailed but unarmed.

Alroth nodded to him. "Good to see you still breathing." They'd fought side by side, but that didn't make them friends or even allies. And it meant that at least one person here knew who he was.

Hasburgen laughed. "Still the same old Wolf. Come to try your luck in the lists? Weigh down your purse?"

"That's right. You?"

"I don't need luck, my friend." He gestured to his companion.

A shining, translucent hawk fluttered to land, weightless, on the woman's shoulder. Hasburgen had bound a mage? Alroth must have shown his confusion on his face, because Hasburgen laughed again.

"Gertie makes me nearly invincible. Harder blows, faster blocks, sometimes even destroys opponents' weapons." He gave her a pat on the shoulder as if she were a loyal warhorse.

Alroth turned away. The matrons he'd met were good for cooking, laundry, mending... not battle. During the war, some men had insisted on always fighting together, been able to enhance each other's strength, speed... Of course, that would never be permitted in Sudra. That a man would bind a mage and use her for battle? Their bond couldn't be sanctioned, could it? But here they were, about to show themselves plainly in front of the New Bridge Castle guard captain, not known for his forgiving nature.

Hasburgen slung an arm around his shoulders again, undeterred by Alroth's dismissal. "I know what you're thinking, Wolfy, and yes, our bond is sanctioned. She's a proper matron, in accordance with the divine teachings of the Grist." He raised his gaze to the sky. "We didn't bond in Sudra, of course. The Grist brothers in Carille are ever so much more cooperative about such things. They're so glad to be consulted at all, they'll sanction practically any bond. You should think about getting your own mage."

Alroth bit his tongue. Speaking of getting a mage, as if from a market. Any response on his part would start a brawl right here outside the castle, and he couldn't afford that. Likely, the woman, Gertie, hadn't had any choice. Had found herself attached to a mercenary against her will and was terrified of battle, poor thing. Surely the Grist here in Sudra could free her of their bond, if she asked? The Grist in Nordval might be desperate for crumbs of power, but the Grist here in Sudra decidedly were not.

They were waved inside the palisade, the guard nodding to Hasburgen as though recognizing him.

"I guess it's too late for that, this time. Maybe after I pound you into the dust, you'll reconsider." He shook his head. "Still with the short swords? I'll never understand how you manage to stay alive, Wolf." He shoved Alroth's shoulder as they approached the practice field. "Don't die out there today."

"And you." Alroth nodded to Gertie, who trailed Hasburgen like a shadow, the hawk on her shoulder taking flight at the clash of weapons from the field.

Two men were already at it in the lists as Alroth strode up to the wooden rail. The guard captain watched from across the yard, his lip curled. Hasburgen had joined a group of five men nearby, two more mages standing next to them. Thankfully, no one else looked familiar. Not that Hasburgen wouldn't give Alroth away, but he would at least wait until it gave him some kind of advantage to do it.

One of the competitors in the lists threw the other to the ground, and the guard captain waved at them to stop.

"Men on this side, you're castle. Men on the other, you're hive. Form up." It would be a miniature mock battle then, about twenty men—and mages—on either side. If you were borne to the ground, captured, or turned tail, you'd be out of the fight.

The man next to Alroth grumbled through his bushy black beard, fingering his sword hilt. "They got mages over there."

Hasburgen and his party were on the hive side.

Alroth shrugged. "Mages go down, just like men." He followed the pack around the end of the lists and onto the field.

"No shield, red?" Another man elbowed him companionably as they lined up in a loose formation.

Alroth smirked. "Don't worry, I'll cover you without."

The man's eyes narrowed, but he shrugged and knocked on his own shield, painted blue with a yellow snake. "I'd never give up mine."

"Take down twice as many men with two swords than with one." He tapped the other man with his elbow and drew Volnus and Ictus.

The man cracked a smile. "Suit yourself. Looks like you've survived so far."

The guard captain's squire pointed to each side in turn, all the fighters letting out whoops and hollers of "Castle!" and "Hive!" Alroth put on his helmet, the nosepiece in the inner corner of his eye grounding him. *Just disarm, don't kill.* Blue and Yellow banged his spear on his blue-and-yellow shield and bared his teeth.

The squire shouted, and both sides shuffled forward, holding their formation. Hasburgen was farther down the opposite line, his party on either side of him, minus the mages. Good, they were safe behind the line. The man across from Alroth wielded a pike and shield, but his face was pale and beardless. Was this the closest to battle he'd ever seen? He'd break easily.

Alroth bellowed as he got in range of the pike, and the youth dropped his weapon and stumbled backward, away from whatever he saw in Alroth's eyes, breaking the opposing line. Blue and Yellow moved in on his man, giving Alroth the space to advance and disarm the opponent to the right of the fleeing youth.

The opposing line was broken in two, Blue and Yellow quickly stepping into the gap with Alroth and flanking his man. It was risky to break their line as well, but their opponents were melting away. Black Beard bellowed and broke through the line farther down, close to where Hasburgen and his party were. *The mages.* Alroth locked Ictus with another man's axe and twisted it out of his grip, dropping it to the hard-packed dirt. Yes, Black Beard was advancing on Gertie and the other mages, sword raised. Hasburgen and the others hadn't noticed, perhaps didn't care. They wouldn't turn and run back—that would mean forfeiting the melee—but Alroth could get to them. He dodged a thrust from a halberd and jogged toward the three mages, who stood shoulder to shoulder facing Black Beard's longsword.

"They're unarmed!" he called.

Black Beard turned, glaring at Alroth. "They don't belong here, with their unnatural magic."

"Back off, man." Alroth planted his feet, brought his swords up, Ictus at Black Beard's kidney, and Volnus toward his face.

Black Beard shook his head. "Turning on your own side." His gaze flicked to Alroth's faded jack of plate, and his eyes widened, realization dawning. "No more than I'd expect from the Wolf." He whirled back to the mages and brought his sword up as Gertie thrust her palm out, stepping into Black Beard's blow. A blow not intended to disarm—the mages had no weapons. Was he trying to take the mage's head off?

Should have brought a shield. Alroth raised Volnus to deflect the blow, but it was a strange angle and would glance off and hit his arm.

Black Beard choked and sputtered, gasping for air as his sword came down, clanging with Alroth's blade and making his ears ring. Sure enough, it glanced off and slashed Alroth's gambeson, pain searing up his arm, and Volnus thudded to the dirt. Gertie eyed both men coldly as Black Beard stumbled to one knee, dropped his sword, and clutched at his breast. He was out.

Alroth curled his—likely broken—arm into his chest, Ictus solid and reassuring in his other hand. Gertie reached for him, but he batted her hand away with the flat of his blade.

"I don't want to fight unarmed mages."

Gertie smiled coldly. "Mages are never unarmed, Wolf."

The mage to Alroth's injured side stepped forward, reaching toward him, but Alroth sidestepped. Three of them could easily flank him now that he had lost both Volnus and the use of his cestus on that side. Trying to hit or block with a broken arm would mess him up for life. He didn't dare turn to see how the rest of the fight was going. The thud and clash of weapons behind him meant he wasn't the last castle fighter left standing. These mages were on the opposing side. They would need to be beaten, borne to the dirt. One touch had been enough to fell Black Beard. How to take them down without harming them?

Footsteps thudded behind him, and Alroth chanced a peek over his shoulder.

Blue and Yellow charged toward him, axe raised, and settled next to him, shoulder to shoulder. "It's almost a rout," he panted. "What are you waiting for?"

"They took him out," said Alroth, jerking his chin at Black Beard, still collapsed on the ground where they'd left him. "Don't let them touch you."

"Right," said Blue and Yellow and drove his shield into the left-hand mage's belly.

Alroth growled as the mage doubled over and fell to her knees. Out. Brutal for an attack on an unarmed opponent, but as Gertie had said, the mages weren't unarmed. Alroth raised Ictus, and Gertie stepped forward. She swiped out with her mailed hand and grabbed his blade. The hilt hardened under his fingers, almost as though the leather was drying out, cracking, sloughing away, and his blade—*no*—rusted and cracked. *Fuck.* What had she done? He clutched his ruined sword hilt tighter, drew his elbow back, and struck a heavy blow to Gertie's middle. Her breath whooshed out, and she staggered and toppled to the dirt. The last mage took two steps back, turned, and fled.

"It's a rout," said Blue and Yellow.

Alroth barely heard him. *Ictus.*

The guard captain called the melee for the castle side, but how could this be a victory? Ictus was destroyed, rusted and cracked right before Alroth's eyes. The first weapon he'd bought with his own pay, the blade that had saved his life more times than he could count. He sheathed the rusted ruin and bent for Volnus, sheathing it on the other side.

This was what he'd wanted. He would join the castle guards, make a fat purse of coin, and get his folk settled inside the town walls for the winter. So he had lost Ictus. Hopefully, he wouldn't need his short swords again anyway. His days of fighting as a mercenary were over. He'd be outfitted with a shield and spear, like the other castle guards, maybe a halberd one day. He'd won. The void inside his chest twisted.

Hasburgen came up next to him, where he stood over Gertie's slumped form. "Good luck for you. If we'd been on the same team, we would have routed them in half the time." He made no move to help his matron from the dirt. He looked Alroth over, gaze catching on Ictus's ruined hilt. "Ah! I warned you, Wolf! Don't tangle with a mage!" he crowed.

"He tried to save us," Gertie half groaned as she dragged herself to one knee.

"Want her to help with that?" Hasburgen waved at Alroth's arm, still cradled against his body.

Alroth reached out his good hand to help Gertie up. Clearly Hasburgen wasn't going to.

"It's the least I can do," she said as she stumbled to her feet.

Alroth shrugged, shooting pain down his injured arm. "You got him, in the end."

"I would have had my shoulder sliced open, but yeah, I would have got him without you." Her gaze flicked to Ictus. "I'm sorry about your blade." She winced.

"You can't undo it." Could magic fix what magic had ruined?

She shook her head, and the last spark of hope for his blade flickered out. "Your arm."

Alroth nodded and gingerly held his arm out to her.

Gertie touched two fingers to the slice in Alroth's gambeson—not all the way through, thankfully—and the pain slowly eased, the feeling came back to his fingers, and Alroth flexed them.

"Enough," said Hasburgen.

Gertie snatched her hand back.

"Let's get you to Jule." His fingers wrapped her upper arm, and Hasburgen marched her away.

The mage who had run was crouched over a man lying on the ground, a dark pool of blood around his thigh slowly soaking into the dirt. Another man, presumably her source, stood over her with his arms crossed. The bleeding man stirred, sat up, and patted his leg, still covered in blood, and the source strode to the guard captain, who nodded and flipped him a glittering coin.

The mage got shakily to her feet, an ephemeral rat poking its nose out of the neck of her hauberk. *Fuck*. She'd snatched him from the jaws of death. That much blood? If he'd survived to be carted from the battlefield, he would have died of sepsis or, at the very least, lost that leg. But she'd made him good as new in but a moment.

The guard captain caught Alroth's eye and waved him over. Too late, the man next to him turned. Black Beard. Either he was telling him that Alroth was the Wolf, or he was telling him that Alroth had turned on his own side. Their side might have won the melee, but the guard captain could send Alroth away regardless, or worse...

"I've been hearing interesting stories about you, Wolf."

Shit. "Name's Alroth."

The guard captain's face didn't change. "Seems to me you're a man who changes sides on a whim. We don't abide defectors in the guard."

And how could Alroth argue with that? No matter which story Black Beard had told the captain, he *had* fought against his own brothers in arms, both times. But what else could Alroth do? If he didn't get this post, he'd have to turn to, what, thieving? Extortion? Murder? No, none of that was acceptable.

"I was defending unarmed mages—"

"The same unarmed mages that took down armed men?"

"They didn't have weapons." Alroth gestured toward where Hasburgen and the mages stood dejected. "I couldn't just—"

"Wait." Black Beard's eyes narrowed. "Your arm. Blow like that, should be broke, sure enough."

The guard captain's gaze flicked over the slash in Alroth's gambeson. "Fighting for the mages all along, were you? I let them fight, figured what harm could it do, but seems like it did plenty of harm. Get out of here, Wolf. Show your face again, and I won't let you off so easy."

Alroth's spine stiffened, and he squared his shoulders. He wasn't getting the post. And even if he was able to change the captain's mind—unlikely—he'd have to work with the likes of Black Beard, who would no doubt spread stories about him before the other guards even had a chance to make up their own minds. He inclined his head, turned on his heel, and strode out of the lists.

Still, how could he regret what he'd done? Black Beard had been ready to slice a woman open in a mock battle. Had he stood by and watched it happen, he'd never have been able to live with himself, even if he had won the castle guard position. The sun was high enough now to beat down on him, so he swiped off his helmet and tucked it back under his arm. His miraculously healed arm. He'd met mages before, even on the battlefield, but he'd never been healed by one. No wonder the guard captain had paid that source for healing a deathly injured man.

It would be handy to have a healer like that around. Just last month, after Tarrin had nearly drowned in the river, he'd been in bed with a fever for a week. If they'd had a mage, she could have healed him up right quick. But no. No Grist father would ever gift them a mage. Selena, of course, could heal cuts and scrapes, stop the bleeding if someone was badly hurt, but mend bones? Staunch a man's lifeblood pouring into the dirt? Alroth shook his head, squinting into the sunrise.

He passed through Mill Gate. The cluster of huts, the cruck house, the storehouse, and their few little fields stretched before him in the near distance. There were root vegetables to preserve and pickling to be done. No use daydreaming about magic that would be forever out of his reach.

5

Mellia

Mellia arrived at the castle as dawn broke, the grey light enough for her to pick her way through the frozen streets. She'd get Father Glimar's gossip out of Elenta before she tutored the children, and she'd pass it on to Father Glimar at his manor house before Munis prayer. He'd confirm that she would be included in the trial this afternoon, and she would still have a few hours to help Morath in the kitchen before the trial.

A chorus of shouts went up from within the palisade adjoining the castle. There must be some kind of contest taking place in the lists this morning. Mellia crossed the south barbican and hurried through the outer ward. The guards on the drawbridge to the inner ward were familiar, but they never spoke to her like the moustached guard, Alroth's friend. Strange that she knew Alroth's name after meeting him once, but not the friendly guard's after chatting with him all season. Her bee pin let her through to the inner ward, and soon she climbed the wooden steps to Elenta's chambers. This time, she didn't wait for Elenta's ladies to leave before she asked her questions.

"Did you hear the rumour about the heretic prince?" Mellia took a sweet bun from Elenta's breakfast tray and broke it in half.

Elenta's eyes gleamed. "Ooh! No, tell me everything."

Damn. Maybe one of the ladies would chime in.

"Apparently, he was spotted right here at New Bridge Castle!"

Elenta leaned forward. "One of the visiting lords?"

"Maybe, I'm not sure."

Elenta ran through the list of visiting lords, their ages, and the likelihood of them being long-lost royalty as one of her ladies did her hair and speculated on the prince's identity along with her. None of them knew anything more. *Ignis's flaming fingers.* If they didn't know, who would? How did Father Glimar expect her to discover more about his rumour with the crumbs he'd given her? He hadn't even told her it was the heretic prince; she'd had to piece that together herself. No matter how unreasonable Father Glimar's task, she'd complete it. She had to.

Who else could she ask? Who would know which lords were visiting? Maybe have a better idea of who the heretic prince was? Lord New Bridge would surely know, but asking him was laughable. Mellia shuddered.

"Mellia, are you all right?" Elenta touched her arm, and she jumped.

"Yes, I'm just distracted." *Being repulsed by your husband.* "The handmaid trial is today."

Elenta frowned. "Why is that worrying you? You don't have to do the trial anymore, Mellia. Lord Ainsley is going to bind you to him in three short days!"

Exactly. Elenta's face was patient, guileless. She didn't understand. They'd been raised to anticipate their binding rituals above all else. Turning away from that was inconceivable.

"Of course I am, but I know most of the sisters in the trial."

"Oh, Mellia. I should have known, you're anxious for your sisters. I'm sure the trial will go smoothly for all of them."

A platitude; only one sister would become a handmaid.

The ladies chattered about Elenta's preparations for the Necrophoresis Ritual and the upcoming solstice celebration. Many lordlings would probably stay for the festivities here at the castle.

The hive bells pealed, Mellia's signal to see to the children. She was halfway to the door when Elenta called out.

"Oh, Melly! I almost forgot! Lord Ainsley will see you after tutoring."

No. Absolutely not. If she never saw Lord Ainsley again, she'd die happy. Except he was a visiting lord... Surely he'd spent time among the other lords. If he knew anything about the heretic prince, Mellia needed to know it, too. She pasted on a smile. "Thank you, Lenny, that will be lovely."

The tutoring session flew by much too fast, and Elenta arrived to retrieve the children, Lord Ainsley in tow. The children's eyes went wide when they saw him, and they quieted immediately, following their mother out of the classroom in uncharacteristic silence.

He'd come to collect her himself. Did he think that she would stand him up if he summoned her to the king's hive as he had the day before?

Lord Ainsley waited in the doorway, glowering, while she tidied after the children. Could he have heard that she wanted to become a handmaid instead of letting him bind her? Was he here to convince her to change her mind? No, he wouldn't have heard. Father Glimar was the only one who knew about their arrangement, and why would he tell Lord Ainsley? But Father Glimar was Lord New Bridge's brother, and they had perhaps spoken of Lord Ainsley between them.

There was no tidying left. Her betrothed filled the doorway, his shoulders padded out by his fashionable pourpoint, his beard trimmed piously short. He held out her cloak in his pale hand, the bee pin glinting in the late-season light slanting through the north-facing windows. The snows would come soon, and once they did, no one would be travelling anywhere, not even back to Falvair. No wonder Lord Ainsley wanted to be bound and off as soon as possible. He wanted to be comfortably situated on their lands for the winter.

He wrapped her mantle around her shoulders, and Mellia didn't resist as he fastened the clasp.

"There's a chill in the air today." Lord Ainsley's cool fingers brushed Mellia's throat, and it took all her willpower to fight back her shudder. Memories of other fingers, not nearly so light, clutching her throat, stopping the air in her lungs, would surely show on her face.

Mellia looked down and turned from Lord Ainsley. "Yes, my lord. We'll be fortunate if the water is high enough for the Necrophoresis Ritual."

Lord Ainsley waved dismissively as he stepped through the doorway, clearly expecting Mellia to follow. "The handmaids will take care of that. That is, after all, their only use." He didn't head for the king's hive this time, once they reached the inner ward, but straight through the eastern gate to the north barbican. The walled gardens.

The fruit trees and flowering shrubs had all been covered for winter, but the sun hitting the whitewashed walls at their backs spread a welcome warmth over them, and the walls protected them from the wind that, come winter, would screech down the river carrying biting ice crystals with it.

Lord Ainsley settled himself on a bench with the sun on his face, and patted the stone beside him. Mellia planted her hands on her hips and faced him, a cloth-wrapped pear tree prickling at her back. He sighed. "This is how it's to be?"

She was going to be a handmaid. "You wish to bind me to you to secure my lands and titles. How did you expect it would be, my lord?" She took a breath. She was supposed to be asking him about the heretic prince, not shooting barbs.

"I won't endeavour to deny that, Sister. Are you really so pious that you would begrudge me my ambition and deny yourself the life of a lady that you were born into in favour of remaining a Grist sister?"

She wouldn't *be* a sister. She would be a handmaid. But only if she brought something useful to Father Glimar. "Of course, my lord." She perched on the bench beside him, not quite able to bring herself to touch. "Forgive my abrasiveness." What excuse would she give? The handmaid trial excuse had worked on Elenta. "The handmaid trial is this afternoon, and the sisters are all in an uproar."

Ainsley's mouth twisted. "Hardly becoming of Grist sisters."

What an Ignian ass. Grist sisters were people just like lords were. Why shouldn't they be excited and nervous for the trial that would change one of their lives forever? And that Mellia would only join if she got the information she needed. "Have the visiting lords been very disruptive? I've heard so many rumours." *Careful.* Rumours were probably not becoming of a Grist sister. "I've even heard the heretic prince himself is present." She smiled as though it were a joke, but Lord Ainsley's revulsion was plain.

"If he is, he should count his last days. If I ever discovered him, I'd run the traitor through."

Mellia recoiled at his vehemence. Certainly, the Loyalists' leader, the heir to the heretic King Lorthran and Queen Olena, who had attacked the Empire simply for bringing Doloman's teachings to Sudra, was an enemy of the Empire, of the faraway archduke. But it had been fifty years since Sudra had been at war with anyone, more than two centuries since the heretic king and queen had been driven away to Nordval with their supporters.

If Lord Ainsley had heard rumours of the heretic prince's attendance at this castle, he would have hunted him down. Which meant...

Mellia swallowed the lump in her throat. What if she couldn't secure her place in the trial today? Or what if she did and failed?

To be bound to this man for the rest of her life... Except, of course, she wouldn't be bound, because she wasn't able to bond. After five failures, that was clear to her, if not to her father. Let Lord Ainsley try to bind her to him. If he did, he would see that none of it mattered. The binding ritual, as unpleasant as it was, would only be one night, and she would be free of him, her sacred word intact. He would have to give her that, at least, that she had never lied to him and had kept her word.

After she failed again... No, it wasn't the time to wonder whether her father would take her back, keep her as a spinster. No sense in thinking about whether his heir, likely a distant cousin, would keep her fed and sheltered. She would consider her likelihood of being turned out onto the streets later.

Lord Ainsley made small talk until he tired of her listlessness, then he inclined his head and left her there.

She would have to tell Father Glimar that she'd failed. What did she know now that she hadn't before? She could make something up. That might get her into the trial if Father Glimar didn't have a chance to verify her claim. But what would happen when he learned of it? Would he rescind her handmaidship in disgrace—maybe even deem her a drone for her fabrication? No, lying wouldn't get her what she needed.

Mellia hunched in on herself as she trudged out of the garden and across the inner ward.

"Oy! Sister!" The moustached guard was back on duty at the inner drawbridge.

Mellia smiled, in spite of herself. "Good day, sir."

"I've heard more convincing *good days* from men being marched to the gallows. What in Fallo's name could make a person so dour?"

The other guard wasn't Alroth. He stood at attention, ignoring them. Probably still listening to every word though.

"Just discouraged. I... have a task from Doloman, and I'm not looking forward to telling the Grist father that I've failed."

His sympathetic look made the lump rise in Mellia's throat again. "I can see how that would get a sister down. Anything I can help with?"

Mellia smiled wryly. "Not unless you can find the long-lost heretic prince for me before the noon bells."

The guard's face froze behind his moustache, and Mellia's heart joined the lump in her throat. Was it possible that this guard had heard rumours the ladies and Lord Ainsley had not? "Doloman is looking for the prince, is He?" The guard's voice was a fraction more strained than his usual offhand manner.

"There's a rumour that he was seen here at the castle. If you know anything—at all." She cleared her throat—that cursed lump made it hard to speak. "It would mean a lot to me..." She swallowed.

The guard frowned. "Completing Doloman's task really means that much to you?"

Should she tell him about the handmaid trial? About Lord Ainsley? What if Lord Ainsley found out what she'd said? As long as she got the handmaidship—and she would—Orbitus take Lord Ainsley. "It would change my life, sir. Free me from a betrothal to a man... I don't care for."

The guard studied her seriously. "I know something of the heretic prince. Mind you, it's been some years since I've heard his name. When he left home in Nordval, he started a mercenary band, fought in the Canal War. After, well..." He trailed off and shrugged.

Mercenary. Hadn't there been mercenaries hanging around for the funeral period? Their mismatched armour and well-used weapons made them stand out around the hive and here at the castle. It would be enough for Father Glimar. It would have to be. She resisted the urge to fling her arms around the guard, and instead took his hand in both of hers, squeezed it through his leather gauntlet. "My eternal thanks—" She still didn't know his name, this strange friend she'd made.

"Etienne, Sister." He laughed at her vehemence. "Glad to help, what little I could, at any rate."

It might seem small to him, but she wouldn't forget what he'd done for her. Mellia crossed the drawbridge into the outer ward at almost a jog and left the castle, just in time to watch a cart being overturned on Water Street. She'd never get by, so she took Castle Street past the palisades around the castle outbuildings, toward the hive.

The Grist father's manor sat, dwarfed by the hive, right there before her. The staff waved her through this time, as though expecting her return. She crossed the hall to Father Glimar's study, head high. She would do this. She stepped over the threshold.

Father Glimar was not there, so Mellia sat in her place by the fire to wait. He would be here soon, and she could tell him what she'd learned about the heretic prince. And if it wasn't enough, she'd go back out and find a mercenary to question. She shivered. Mercenaries had weapons. She had a little silver but perhaps not enough to buy information from a mercenary. The majority had fought in the Canal War and, by all accounts, made plentiful coin. They were coarse and, well, mercenary. Not bound by honour. But if she had to confront one to gain her place, she would. She would confront a score of them until she found the one who would treat with her if it meant she was free of Lord Ainsley. But she wouldn't know if that would be required until Father Glimar arrived.

The tapestry across from her showed a long waterfall, the Grist depiction of a syphon bond, flowing over a high cliff with the face of a source into a pool, a mage's face looking up from the bottom. The source's bearded visage looked down benevolently into the pool, the mage's fine features reverent as she looked upon the source of her magic. *Magic, like water, always flows downhill, from strong to weak.* Mellia's arms prickled with goosebumps. What did it say about her, then, that she had tried to bond—five times—and had failed? Was she too headstrong? Too determined to hold on to her own self to accept the power that the sources had clearly been trying to give her?

Lord Ainsley had claimed that was the problem, that she'd been trying too hard, that she should leave it up to him to form the bond, simply remain receptive. But hadn't she given herself to the sources? Allowed them free rein to do as they pleased with her? What if Father Glimar agreed with Lord Ainsley? What if he thought she was too headstrong to be a handmaid? The fire crackled and danced higher. The autumn wind rattled the windowpanes. She wasn't supposed to use magic outside the comb. Not until she was a handmaid.

The door latch clacked, the door swung open, and she froze.

"Sister Mellia, good to see you again. My apologies, I haven't much time to speak." Father Glimar latched the door and settled in his seat.

"This won't take long, Father."

"Good, please, tell me."

"Do you think I'm too headstrong to bond?" That wasn't what she'd meant to say.

Father Glimar regarded her thoughtfully. "That's what you've come to ask me?"

Mellia shook her head and straightened the veil over her hair. "No, I..."

He smiled at her in that comforting way of his. "I understand that you wish to know why your binding rituals have failed, Sister Mellia. The truth is I can't tell you that. Only Doloman, our Golden God, can decide whether to gift us with a bond or refuse us. Perhaps He knew that those sources were not right for you. Perhaps He wished for you to become His handmaid." Father Glimar raised his eyebrows expectantly.

If that was true, then Mellia agreed with Doloman—not that it was her place to disagree with the Golden God—but none of those suitors had been at all appealing to her on any level, and none of them had cared about her on any level. Could Doloman be as benevolent as the Grist believed? Could he have recognized Mellia's indifference toward her suitors and withheld a bond in recognition of her feelings? She could ponder this when Father Glimar wasn't watching her, stopping just short of tapping his foot.

"I discovered more information about the heretic prince."

His eyes lit up.

"He's a mercenary, not a visiting lord. Since there are mercenaries in town at the moment, I can only assume that one of them is the heretic prince."

Father Glimar's gaze shifted past her. He was losing interest.

"I can ask around more, find a mercenary to question—"

"Thank you, Sister Mellia, for the information." He fixed her with a benevolent look. "Having completed Doloman's task, I'm sure you have preparations to make for the handmaid trial this afternoon." Father Glimar waved toward the door.

Mellia jumped to her feet. "Of course! Thank you, Father." She'd done it. Somehow, she'd done it! She was going to be a handmaid!

She excused herself and retreated to Iram Square. Was it possible that it was Doloman's will that she hadn't yet been bound to a source? That all this time, Doloman had wanted her to be a handmaid? Either way, next time she saw Etienne, she would have to thank him. She didn't have to perform the ritual. She was going to be a handmaid in three days' time.

6

Alroth

Alroth paced the three steps from his tiny desk to the grubby horn window in his back room. The closed door did nothing to muffle Del and Kai's bickering.

"You're the one who didn't shut your trap when the sister came up to us."

"You didn't warn me she was coming. What, do I have eyes on the back of my head now?"

Best to get their wages from them before they came to blows. Alroth threw open the door. "You two done already? Where's your pay?"

Del swaggered forward and dropped a handful of dull coins onto Alroth's desk. Kai laid his stack beside Del's meagre pile.

They'd been promised more than that. Much more. "You come home by way of the alehouse last night?"

"No, Wolf, Del couldn't stop antagonizing me yesterday long enough to stand guard. They docked our pay."

"I'm not the one who was breathing like a bellows! You should have heard him, Wolf, he—"

"That's enough from both of you. They cut your wages because you're sad excuses for guards. Get out of here."

Del slammed the door as they scurried out, the two of them already tearing into each other. Whose fault it was didn't matter a mite. Without coin from the extra guard posts over the next week, he hadn't a hope of making up the sum he needed. He swept the coin into his lockbox to sit with his earnings from yesterday. Etienne had been able to get him one lucrative shift, but that would be his last after this morning. He could take a shitty position, like the ones Del and Kai had taken yesterday. The pay would hardly be worth the time—but it would be better than nothing.

Alroth dragged Del and Kai down to the docks with him. They could unload some crates for the solstice festival and make a bit more coin. Del and Kai followed in his wake, barely even pausing their bickering to breathe. Alroth chatted with the dock workers until they directed him to the foreman, who was chuckling amiably with a hovering clerk. Alroth's folk had worked as day labourers before, unloading barges in the fall or ships in the spring.

"You're in luck. We're expecting two more barges this afternoon," said the foreman when Alroth explained that he was looking for work for himself and his men. They were a hairsbreadth from shaking hands when another man sidled up. He looked familiar. Maybe he'd helped them out in their fields earlier this year?

He spoke quietly to the foreman, who stuck his thumbs in his belt.

"Now, I don't want to be petty, but I understand you're an unreliable sort, and I can't have any unreliable workers." He glanced over at Del and Kai, who were engaged in a shoving match to topple the other off the edge of the dock.

But the familiar man was watching Alroth. *Ah.* He'd been there this morning, at the mock battle. On the hive side. Alroth had two handspans on him, and he used his size along with a glare to make the man scuttle away.

He toned it down as he turned back to the foreman. "I understand." It wasn't the foreman's fault he had to restrict whom he hired. Keeping the peace among his workers was his priority.

He beckoned Del and Kai and trudged back through Lower Gate and into New Bridge. Where else would they be looking for extra hands for the Necro Ritual preparations? The three of them had worked odd jobs around town for the last half a year, but steady work was hard to come by. Chances were that wherever he went today he'd be recognized and denied. Perhaps after a month or two, the black mark on him would wear off, but they didn't have a month or two. If Del and Kai could behave themselves for even a moment, he could send them off without him to get work, but they would earn mere pennies if he wasn't there to keep them from being turfed out at the first sign of a squabble.

As the sun rose overhead, as high as it got this late in the year,, it was clear that they wouldn't find anything. They'd checked the inn, the livery, the farrier... When the noon bells rang out from the hive, Alroth send his Turbatius-spawn back home to help with the last of the harvest and the packing of root vegetables in barrels of dry sand.

They couldn't move house once the snow flew. They'd had a light snowfall the week before, but it hadn't stayed. They were unlikely to be so lucky again.

Alroth crunched down the lane, emerging in Iram square, the gaudy great statue of the Golden God looming over him. He wandered to the steps of the fountain. Two women chattered as they filled their water buckets, and another dourly scrubbed her laundry, her hands bright red in the cold water.

Alroth couldn't make the money. The castle guard captain knew who he was. Not only was he never going to make enough coin in time, but his folk might be denied a place inside the walls of New Bridge on principle, simply because he was the one asking for it.

What had made him believe that he could hide his identity? He hadn't even bothered to dye his jack a different colour. It wasn't as though cesti were common here, and a man who fought with two short swords was bound to be noticed. It had been foolish to believe that it would go smoothly today.

He sat himself on the fountain steps. They would have to endure the winter outside the town walls and defend themselves from any attacks come spring. Mill Hamlet was sheltered by the low walls intended to protect Mill Gate, the hip-height one in the northwest and the castle's spur at the mouth of the Sinu River. But that still left New Bridge Road from the west up the March River and over the millworks across the Sinu. Not that an attack was likely to come from there—New Bridge Road was an old track that led to crumbling Old Bridge Keep, the tiny village of Bridge, and not much else. Perhaps they would be protected if they stayed where they were. But someone had been allowed to burn down their storehouse at midsummer.

Alroth scrubbed at his face. The only other available option was heading down by the docks and taking on a disreputable job. After all, Alroth's reputation was ruined already. That could give him *better* standing for such a job. Perhaps he could find something not too nefarious: taking from a wealthy traveller on the road or hunting down a known brigand. Surely there would be someone looking for muscle to carry out such a task?

He straightened his houppelande and strode down Hive Street to Water Street. Syreni's Rock sat on the corner of Water Street and Hive Alley. The type of employer who wouldn't look too carefully at his history would be found there, and if they did look, they might even consider it admirable.

The horn windows were further hazed by ash, and the hall was dim and smoky, the firepit's smoke collecting under the rafters. They were lucky to have a proper chimney in their little cruck. Alroth's eyes watered.

"Wolf!" Hasburgen waved him over from a table in the back corner.

Say it louder next time so the whole of New Bridge can hear you. Alroth ignored the other patrons' stares and joined Hasburgen, Gertie, and another bound pair at their table.

"Here to celebrate your win this morning?" Hasburgen clapped him on the back. His shoulder twinged.

Gertie wouldn't meet his gaze. Was she still sorry about destroying Ictus?

"Nothing for me to celebrate. A little bird told the guard captain that I'm the notorious Wolf."

Hasburgen raised his hands in front of him. "I had nothing to do with that."

"I know. I did what I did, and I'll live with it." If only the other option hadn't been years more bloodshed, then maybe he wouldn't have had to turn traitor.

"Ah, don't worry. Nobody liked that bloodthirsty Bellator-spawn." Hasburgen slid his tankard in front of Alroth.

Julius might have been hated, but Alroth's actions had paved the way for peace, and in peacetime, rich lords didn't empty their coffers into mercenaries' pockets. "Are you going to keep looking for work here?"

Hasburgen nodded. "We'll stay a few more days. See if anything turns up. Fingers crossed we don't get snowed in for the winter. Think we can make the twin cities before the snow flies?"

"Only if you leave soon." The journey would be two or three days by foot. Going by ship would risk Dolomast harbour being iced over by the time they arrived.

"And yourself? Still looking for work?" Hasburgen grabbed back his tankard and gulped the warm ale.

"If anyone will have me."

"What about that fancy gentleman? Did he find you?"

Fancy gentleman?

"A lord, seemed like. Looking for the Wolf. We sent him down to Mill Hamlet after you. Must not have crossed paths."

"You what?" Alroth leaned on the table, light-headed, and blinked the spots from his vision. Hasburgen had sent a lord looking for the Wolf to Mill Hamlet, which was full of defenceless folk. Del and Kai had gone back, but had they arrived before the lord? And even if they had, could they hold him at bay, whoever he was? Alroth had to go. Now. He scraped his chair back.

"Something about a job. He sure looked rich. If you turn him down, send him my way, will you? Old Hasburgen is always in the market for coin, no mistake."

Alroth mumbled goodbye and strode out, back into the biting wind. He gripped Volnus's hilt until his knuckles ached. If anything happened to Mill Hamlet, he would gut Hasburgen like a littlefield bird.

The guards at Mill Gate gave him a dirty look, but they didn't stop him. He squinted toward Mill Hamlet. No smoke, thank Salus. But two armoured guards lounged in the square between the cottages. Everyone else was inside. A shout echoed around the corner of the cruck, and Vernis rounded the house, Del rushing after him.

Alroth stepped into his path and brought the old man up short with a gentle hand on his shoulder.

"Alroth! Don't worry, we outnumber them now. They won't take anyone." He pulled his belt knife, and Alroth put his hand over Vernis's bony knuckles.

"That's right, they won't take anyone." He tried to catch Vernis's skittering gaze.

"Damn right, they won't." Del clasped Vernis's other shoulder. "We'll watch them. Won't even blink, we'll watch so carefully. We can take them if they try anything."

Vernis shook his head. "We can't wait for that. We'll take them out *now*. Just to be safe." He nodded sharply.

"Woah, old man." Attacking a gentleman who was perhaps here to offer Alroth work would be disastrous. Alroth raised his eyebrows at Del, who shrugged helplessly. Vernis had come out to Mill Hamlet to escape the constant presence of armed guards. "I'll get them out of here. Where's Kai?"

"Inside, with his lordship," said Del.

A rich gentleman indeed.

Del coaxed Vernis to plant himself in the square while Alroth drew the guards into the cruck and out of sight.

The lord warmed his hands by the fire, Kai close at his back. Selena sat stubbornly in one of the chairs next to him. The other, where the mother and child normally sat, was empty. Maybe they were napping? Unless they didn't want this lord to see them...

"I heard you were looking for me, my lord." Alroth tacked on the honorific just in time to seem natural.

"The Wolf? Are you the one who almost killed your own man this morning?"

Only a fool would admit to being such a hated figure. "Why?"

"I have a proposition for that man. I think he'll find it very compelling—and very lucrative."

Alroth gestured the gentleman toward his back room. What was the worst that could happen? No one else was looking to pay him. But a knot tightened in the pit of his stomach. Why was a lord looking for him? Did he think Alroth had no morals? That he would do anything for coin? Had the lord so misjudged him? He huffed out a breath. He could always walk away from this gentleman once he heard the proposal.

The gentleman followed Alroth into the larder and closed the door behind them. He pulled out a silk handkerchief embroidered with an elaborate A and dusted off his crate before taking a seat across from Alroth's proper chair.

"I have been authorized to promise you a place in the castle guard if you carry out this task, along with conventional payment." He shifted on the hard crate. Used to upholstered furniture, then.

Alroth didn't budge. He didn't want a place in the castle guard, not now. He'd be "accidentally" spitted during drills at this rate. Conventional payment would be excellent, but it wasn't enough. He might as well listen. If the job was simple enough, he would take it and pocket the coin.

The gentleman cleared his throat and eyed the shelves of preserves. "Firstly, the amount of payment." He named off a sum equal to what Alroth would have made in a season as a castle guard.

The knot in the pit of Alroth's stomach clenched. Men like this didn't part with coin easily. What was the catch? "Tell me about the task." He leaned back in his chair.

"Ah, yes. The task." The gentleman glanced around the room. What was making him so furtive? The amount of money at stake? The job itself? "At the Necrophoresis Ritual, the handmaids must be taken care of."

"They no doubt have competent Grist guards." If this gentleman was saying what Alroth suspected he was saying, he would have to voice it aloud. Alroth wouldn't do it for him.

"Well, yes, of course, they do. I mean, they must... not return to New Bridge after the ceremony."

"Where should they be taken?" Alroth raised his eyebrows. If the gentlemen meant that they should be murdered, he would need to say that outright.

"Taken where they shall never return." Not necessarily murdered, then.

Alroth shook his head. "I don't want a place in the castle guard. They wouldn't accept me, as I'm sure you know. What I want is assurance that the money will change hands." No matter what happened to him, this gentleman would need to be responsible for paying up. He would not agree to this deal on the assumption that the gentleman would expect him to die trying to kill the handmaids and save him from paying. The Grist guards might be weakened without their Grist queen, but Alroth and his mercenaries still wouldn't be a match for them.

"Of course." The gentlemen inclined his head. "I will leave the coin with whomever you wish."

"Half now."

"I don't have—"

"Half before the ceremony. Well before."

"As you wish, of course. But I will require proof that the task has been carried out."

"Such as?"

"There are conventions about such things, I believe. A head would do."

So murder. Murder six innocent handmaids for coin. Alroth's stomach churned. Good thing he didn't drink much of Hasburgen's sour ale. He shook his head, crossed his arms, and sat back. Let the lordling try to convince him.

"Before you make your decision, you should know that Lord New Bridge doesn't seem concerned with Mill Hamlet's safety."

What was that supposed to mean? Was it a threat? Kill the handmaids or Alroth's folk would be attacked?

"He might even welcome this little eyesore being dealt with."

The trap closed in around him.

"If you do this one task, I'm sure I can convince him to hold off for a while, at least. I might even be able to clear your name, Wolf."

This one task. Murder. And he would be free. Free of the judgment that had dogged him for years, rich enough to make a life for his folk. Could he really do it? One act of unjustifiable violence and death in exchange for leaving his burden behind? Yoked with guilt and even more nightmares than he currently endured.

No.

No amount of coin, no amount of absolution, could be earned with others' lives. Being revealed as the Wolf was inconvenient, but he would sort it out himself. Perhaps it was time to leave New Bridge after all. Leave Etienne behind; he'd built a life here and would not want to uproot it. But how long until someone like Black Beard or Hasburgen blew into wherever he made his new home and revealed his secrets once again?

The gentleman still waited for his answer. He pulled his handkerchief from his pocket and sniffed from it. The letter *A* twined with flowers and vines in glittering silver thread, even in the dim light that filtered through the window. He tucked it away.

If Alroth refused, would the gentleman attack Mill Hamlet right now? Del and Kai were ready to fight, and the lord had only brought two guards. They could take that many...

"Do remember, Wolf, that this task will be carried out whether or not you refuse."

They would hire someone else if he declined. Someone to kill all of the handmaids at the ritual. It made sense, in a way. The handmaids never left the hive and thus would be uniquely vulnerable on the waterfall during the ceremony. It was likely the only time they could possibly all be captured or killed, certainly the only time they could all be taken at once. It wouldn't even be that hard. How many Grist guards would they have? Six? Eight? With fighters on either side of the river—easily crossable at this time of year—they could set up an ambush. Whoever took the job, naturally, not Alroth.

No, focus on keeping Mill Hamlet safe. He shook his head. Regardless, he could not do this. If he took the coin and balked, came back without the head of a handmaid, this gentleman or his men would burn Mill Hamlet to ashes without hesitation. That gleam in the gentleman's eyes said as much plainly.

He couldn't kill the handmaids, but nor could he refuse the job and let some immoral mercenary like Hasburgen take it. And the best way to protect Mill Hamlet *would* be to play along, at least for now. Two days remained before the Necro Ritual. Time enough to think of a way out.

He sighed. "All right."

"All right?"

"Half the payment before the job—that's standard, by the way—and half to my associates here afterward." He loomed into the smaller man's space. *Now get out.* He bit back his growl.

The lordling seemed to take the hint. He bowed and strode out of the damned larder.

He'd bought them some time, but that was all. He couldn't kill the handmaids, and when the lordling discovered that, Mill Hamlet would have to be cleared. Hopefully, the first half of the payment could get everyone safe inside the walls. Then only Alroth would be at risk when he didn't come through. In the meantime, he had to do something, warn someone, that the handmaids were in danger. What if the lordling hired a second line of mercs as insurance against the very thing Alroth planned?

Someone rapped on the doorframe. "Alroth, we need you out here. Vernis thinks there's going to be a storm..."

Alroth sighed. Right. His own people and his own problems. For now, he'd get Mill Hamlet ready for the winter that would come no matter what insignificant mortals like him did.

7

Mellia

Mellia helped another sister haul a hogshead of pickled trout from the storeroom. Morath's panicked gaze fell on them while she frantically stirred one of two cauldrons over the roaring fire in the huge hearth at one end of the temporary kitchen.

The two sisters bent their backs to the hogshead, huffing and puffing. Morath motioned them to a nearby corner, and they pushed together to tip the hogshead up. Mellia wiped the sweat from her forehead with her nettlecloth scarf before it could run into her eyes, and the other sister did the same. What next? There was always something.

Mellia sat next to another sister at the table, pulled her belt knife, and peeled sunchokes. They weren't allowed to use magic for this. It seemed arbitrary, but sisters weren't officially permitted to use magic at all—a rule that was often overlooked at the convenience of the brothers, as evidenced by all the magic Mellia used to make their tasks easier. This sisters' work, of course, didn't qualify.

The handmaid trials would take place in the afternoon, and the score of candidates who had been selected from the sisters' ranks would all show their suitedness. Mellia would grow a flower. A tiny spring flower, when others might summon a spring breeze, make a whole bolt of cloth, spin a fleece, sew a kirtle or a tunic, embroider cuffs with lovely beads, or clean a soiled garment—

Her knife slipped and sliced her thumb. *Bond and Grist*. She cursed and squeezed her fingers to the cut, but blood oozed between them. Spots clouded her vision, and the sister beside her took her shoulder. Was she calling Morath? No, Morath already had enough to deal with... but yes, there was the handmaid.

Morath gestured to Mellia's bloody hand, and the sticky blood stopped. Mellia gingerly opened her hand and brushed over the cut lightly. Yes, through the blood, nothing but a pink scar. She took a deep breath and mumbled a thank you. Morath squeezed her shoulder.

"It's no problem at all, Mellia. I'm glad to help. Once you've gathered yourself, go to the fountain and wash up. Then rest. You don't want to be exhausted for the trial this afternoon."

"I don't need to..." But Morath had already returned to the hearth. Now that her thumb wasn't actively oozing blood, Mellia didn't need to clutch the table to keep upright. She kept her crimson hands away from her white apron as she got up and climbed the few steps to the Queen's Garden. It had its own fountain where she could wash.

Mellia squinted as she emerged from the dim keep, the noon sun glinting off the stained-glass windows of the hive, these ones set in a honeycomb pattern instead of a rectangle like the window she'd fixed on the side that faced the cloister. The remaining leaves on the tall maple rustled gently, and the fountain's trickle drowned out voices from the bustling comb beyond the wall. On the other side, the corridor leading from the queen's keep to the hive loomed. The Grist queen never left the keep, so she had a special corridor leading directly to her balcony in the hive proper, where she spent services behind a wooden screen. That was as close as she ever came to seeing the outside world.

A handmaid sat on the edge of the fountain, speaking quietly into her cupped hands. Her generous curves and kindly face gave her away: Alinace, the companion handmaid.

She looked up when Mellia approached, taking in Mellia's bloody hands, her mouth curving into a silent O. "Mellia, what happened?"

"I cut myself, but it's all right, Morath already healed it. It looks worse than it is."

Alinace waved toward the fountain and the sheet of water pouring over a flared lip.

Mellia swiped her hands under the chilly stream and rubbed her fingers together, the pink water sluicing away down the grate. "How are you faring, Alinace?" As the companion handmaid, she didn't have many tasks now that the Grist queen was dead.

Alinace glanced down at her hands, now closed around whatever she had been speaking to. A tiny squeak emerged from between her fingers along with a twitching pink nose.

"Who have you got there?"

Alinace blushed. "It's nothing, no one."

Mellia shook droplets off her hands, pink from the cold water now instead of her own blood. "Seems like someone to me."

"Yes, well, he's a... rat."

"A rat?" Didn't they carry diseases? Mellia recoiled.

"He's not dangerous, I promise you! I raised him myself, and I've kept him very clean, and he loves to curl up with me, and I've never gotten sick from him. He's not even fully grown yet—" Another squeak cut her off, and Alinace loosened her grip.

A tiny wiggling nose poked out from between her fingers, followed by surprisingly long whiskers, two black eyes, and round pink ears. Fine. It was a bit cute. Two little paws tucked under the rat's chin.

Mellia sighed. "He's adorable."

A smile lit Alinace's face. "You think so?"

"How could I not? Look at that little nose."

"Do you think the next Grist queen will want him as a companion?"

That was assuming Alinace didn't become the next Grist queen. Livine would be worried that the rat would chew her manuscripts, Dayma would have the same fear about her textiles, and Morath would quite rightly worry about her food supplies. Sathred might tolerate the thing, but would never be as attached as Alinace, and Runas? Runas would shudder, hold it by the tail, and order it out of her sight.

"May I pet him?" Changing the subject was better than disappointing her.

Alinace nodded, and Mellia stuck out her finger and stroked between the rat's ears. He squeaked indignantly and scurried up to Alinace's shoulder and under her veil.

Alinace blushed again. "It's warm in there, that's why he likes it. He'll sleep in my pocket if I give him some corn."

Mellia squeezed her hand. "I'm glad you have a companion right now." Plenty of work waited for her in the keep. She should probably get back there.

"Mellia, I can't talk to any of the other handmaids about this..." Alinace wrung her hands.

Her work could wait. Mellia sat next to Alinace on the edge of the fountain. "What do you want to talk about?" The last of the dead leaves rustled overhead. One strong gale, and the branches would be fully bare.

"You don't think... I mean, I couldn't be the next Grist queen, could I? I don't even know what I would do with that kind of power. I don't think I could..." She sighed heavily.

No, Alinace was unlikely to be the next Grist queen. But that was just a feeling. The Pater Patrum, far away in the capital, would choose the next New Bridge Grist queen on the recommendation of the other Grist fathers across Sudra. They wouldn't care that Alinace had no desire to be queen or that she wasn't suited for that level of responsibility. They would probably look at all the handmaids' family ties and how much power they had. Who was to say that they wouldn't choose Alinace?

"If they do choose you, you'll make a wonderful Grist queen." Mellia had attended masses six times a year at the holidays along with the rest of the Grist, when the hive was divided into sections: brothers, sisters, lords, and peasants, and the Grist father and Grist queen addressed them all from their high seats. Grist Queen Arista's soothing voice had flowed through the rote prayers like honey. Alinace's voice squeaked almost as much as her rat's, and she stumbled over her words more often than not. To be Grist queen wouldn't be easy for her. But she would learn—she would have to, should she be chosen.

Mellia gave Alinace's hand one last squeeze, unable to summon any more words of comfort, and swept back down into the ground floor of the keep. She avoided Morath's eye as she resumed her place at the paring table. Sitting in the garden until the bells rang for the trial... her stomach clenched.

All too soon, the bells pealed, echoing throughout the comb. All the sisters fell silent and slowly put down their tools, looking at one another uneasily. Mellia wiped her knife on her apron, sheathed it, and tossed the apron on the bench beside her. She stepped out from behind the bench and smoothed her skirt. She would impress the brothers, and she would be the next handmaid.

"Sisters, gather your materials. Don't keep the brothers waiting." Morath's voice rang through the hall.

Mellia scooped her pot of soil and seeds from the hearth, the clay pot warm under her fingers. She climbed the few steps to the inner cloister where two brothers waited. They fell silent when she emerged and eyed her pot of dirt. The other sisters filed out after Mellia, some holding pots like hers. Were any of them planning to grow a flower? A handmaid's nightcap like her?

The brother led them to the outer cloister, and they were greeted with hoots from all sides; the whole comb had gathered, under the roofs of the pathways and on the sunny lawn, to watch the trial. The sister next to Mellia shook like a leaf, and Mellia grabbed her hand and patted it, shushing her softly. A brother trailed after the twelve sisters, his arms wrapped around a large stone. An animal whined in a cage in the circle the brothers had cleared inside the ring of Grist beehives.

Father Glimar sat under an awning at the edge of the circle, his rings tapping the arm of his chair as he drummed his fingers. "Welcome, comb. This is not a trial that we perform often, and it is not to be taken lightly. The sisters here have come forward to be judged. Once they have proven themselves to their own satisfaction, we will commune with Doloman and relay his choice of handmaid to you."

A buzz of whispering voices filled the cloister as Father Glimar's words were passed back and around through the comb. Father Glimar flicked his fingers, and the brother next to him called a sister's name. She stepped forward, hitched the harness of a backstrap loom up on her shoulders, and began to weave. She closed her eyes, and the loom filled with a full bolt of fabric. Cheers and hollers filled the cloister. The sister grinned and bowed.

Next was the sister with the stone. She brushed her chisel over the top of it, and a carving emerged—a bee sitting in its comb. Rough, but certainly recognizable.

Then came two sisters in a row carrying plant pots. The first grew a handmaid's nightcap—Mellia winced, sweat prickling her skin. And worse, the other grew strawberries handed proudly to the brothers to taste. Granted, the plant had already been in its flowering stage, but still. Mellia's stomach clenched. Her little flower would be pitiful after this.

She needed a task that would stand out. Something practical that would prove she was the most suited to being a handmaid. But what would impress the brothers? She should do something big, perhaps fix something in the comb. Another of the stained-glass windows desperately needed to be replaced. If she could get the materials, then she could put it in place. That would certainly be impressive, but where would she get the materials now? She could clear some of the dry leaves from the cloister, but considering she'd only be able to clear a small patch...

Growing a flower at this time of year was difficult, certainly, but it was neither practical, nor pious, nor did it fit particularly well with her speciality. If she was going to use magic to invoke the spring, what would be impressive to the brothers but still within her capacity?

The sister with the caged animal, a dog, came forward and healed a cut on its leg. The next sister was empty-handed. Would she manipulate the weather? She planted her feet in the center of the cleared space, next to a flower bed, and closed her eyes, preparing to work her magic. She raised one hand, and light mist rose from the flowerbed—was she trying to grow a whole bed of flowers? Unbound mages didn't have that kind of power, not in the middle of winter.

A tug in Mellia's chest made her gasp. Just like when Father Glimar had tried to show her how to bond. But where was it coming from? The sister? Father Glimar was on his feet, already striding toward the sister. He took her chin in his hand, and shook her, the motion rippling down her entire body. Her eyes sprang open, and Father Glimar released her as she fell to her knees at his feet. He prodded her with the toe of his boot.

"Drone." He muttered it, but the word was picked up quietly around the comb until it seemed as though a hundred bees hummed in the cloister. The sister stumbled to her feet, but all around, the comb hummed with the damning word. Mellia muttered it under her breath. How dare this sister try to syphon magic from bonds Doloman had not given her? A path opened up in the comb, leading toward the exit from the comb. A drone would never return to this hive or any other.

The sister fled the cloister, her footsteps slapping loudly in the quiet hum. She'd made one mistake and was tossed from the comb. She'd been desperate to prove herself and had reached beyond her means. Mellia had spent time using her magic to make her bonding gifts, so she knew exactly how much magic she could expend without syphoning. But the drone had chosen a task that was too ambitious, in a fit of unbecoming hubris. No, Father Glimar was right. No one was permitted to bond without Doloman's blessing, even momentarily.

The trial resumed. A couple of sisters changed the weather (one made it snow, and the other drew a cool breeze), and another turned a blob of dough to bread (one of the simplest magics, but the brothers seemed to like the bread).

Mellia's name was called, and she stepped forward. *Don't vomit, don't vomit.* Father Glimar fixed her with a hostile stare, took in her little pot, and his brows drew together. Mellia cleared her throat. Should she say something? Explain what she was about to do? No, if she opened her mouth, something other than words might come out. Instead, she curtsied to the brothers, closed her eyes, and focused on the sunlight beating down on the dirt. The handmaid's nightcap grew. She'd put in plenty of seeds, and her pot overflowed with purple bell-shaped flowers.

She opened her eyes. The brothers looked bored. Father Glimar still glared at her as though she'd betrayed his faith in her. Brother Padril looked a bit sick. She'd made more flowers than the other sister… but it still wouldn't be enough, that was plain. But she had no more *supplies*. What could she do?

The brother calling names opened his mouth—

"Wait! There is one more part to my demonstration." Something! She had to do something. The sun glinted off a skep, and a sleepy bee crawled out of its hole. Her feet took her closer while her hands clutched her spring flowers. But could she do this without accidentally syphoning like the other sister had?

Only one way to know. She held the flowerpot close to the beehive's entrance. A murmur rippled through the crowd.

She closed her eyes and let the tension flow from her as she rested her free hand on the outside of the hive, the braided straw smooth under her fingers. A honeycomb glistened inside, which next spring would fill with honey, just inside the cap. She'd be able to extract it easily. The brothers and sisters had fallen silent, but the sharp consonants of an angry whisper reached her from where Father Glimar and the obedientiaries sat.

Mellia took another deep breath and let her magic surround that little spot of honeycomb under the cap. She felt it fill with nectar, as the bees fed from her flowers, then took over and thickened the nectar, the bees working at impossible speed. Yes, there. She opened her eyes, laid the flowerpot on the ground, and lifted the cap off the skep. She cradled it in her hands.

Fresh honeycomb gleamed inside like Doloman's cloak in the afternoon sunlight. She pulled her belt knife and cracked a piece of comb out, the bees dozing again as the chill air hit them. She locked eyes with Father Glimar as she marched to her judges. She held the honeycomb out to him. He jabbed a finger at the comb, breaking through the cap, and brought the finger to his mouth. He nodded once, silently. A babble broke out all around her, mixed with hoots and muted cheers.

The obedientiaries gathered around to taste the honey as well, and Mellia's stomach eased. She'd done it. Pious, impressive, and unique. She would be chosen as the handmaid for certain.

When the obedientiaries were finished judging her honey, Mellia returned the cap to the skep reverently, cradled her flowers, and took her place back in line with the other sisters.

Her heartbeat slowed as a particularly brave sister showed the brothers a blank parchment and an illuminated one, and copied the one to the other flawlessly, and the last asked for a volunteer and made a lock of the brother's hair grow down past his shoulder.

Father Glimar raised his hand, and the comb fell silent. "Thank you very much, sisters, for participating in our trial. We will deliberate and confer with Doloman. Tomorrow at Dolus Lumin, we will share our decision."

Mellia swallowed a protest. She'd have to wait until noon tomorrow to find out whether she was to be a handmaid? She wouldn't be sleeping at all tonight. Father Glimar's piercing gaze landed on her, unreadable. Her fate was in his hands.

8

Alroth

Alroth worked all afternoon with the others to get their livestock collected and inside the houses. Six ewes baaed from the corner of the hall where they were penned, milling around on their straw. What if a dump of snow kept Alroth from reaching Father Glimar tomorrow? If there was a blizzard, then he would be needed here. Alroth tipped the last of the fresh vegetables into the pottage.

No time left to deliberate. He washed, shaved, and put on his nice tunic, a woollen one Selena had made him with the spring shear.

The wind was harsh on his freshly shaven face—he'd grown too used to his whiskers. But he didn't need them to hide his identity anymore, not now that it had been revealed.

The guards at the gate eyed him, and one made a rude gesture, but they let him pass. His boots crunched over the leaves that had blown onto the Grist father's lane. What would he say when he got to the door? The Grist father's manor was far too big for one person. Wasn't he supposed to be pious? Maybe it was more sparsely decorated inside.

Alroth climbed the steps, and the front door swung open. The footman looked him up and down and shook his head. "Do you have a message for the Grist father?"

"No, in fact, I'd like to speak with him."

The footman drew himself up. "Unfortunately, the Grist father is very busy with preparations for the Necrophoresis Ritual."

"I realize that, but it can't wait until after—"

"If you leave your name, perhaps the Grist father will see fit to speak with you after the ritual."

Alroth sighed. Once they knew his name, they would refuse him. His chance to explain evaporated in front of his eyes. "Alroth, of Mill Hamlet. But, look, it's very important—"

The footman shut the door in his face. Trying to press the issue would get guards set on him, and they would take the opportunity to make him suffer.

Who else could he tell? Who else had the authority or the fighting strength to defend the handmaids? A guard eyed him from Iram Square. The last thing he needed was the lordling hearing that the Wolf was trying to warn the Grist father about his plot. Alroth hurried back to Mill Hamlet, head down, back to the cruck.

Del and Kai sauntered into the hall, a gust of biting wind making the sheep baa louder and bolt from the sudden appearance of the loud humans next to them.

"I'm only saying, if you hadn't distracted me, I wouldn't have dropped that split wood on your foot." Del put his thumbs in his belt.

"I distracted you? What was I, standing on my head? I was warning you about that patch of ice." Kai stalked to the fire to warm his hands. "Maybe I should have let you fall on your head, eh? Not that it would change much, amount of brains you have."

"More than you have," grumbled Del, coming to stand beside him.

They fell silent.

"What's wrong?" said Alroth from his seat by the fire. They might be arguing, but their hearts clearly weren't in it.

"This buffoon dropped three split logs on my foot." Kai pointed a thumb at Del.

"And how's your foot?"

"The foot's fine," said Del. "He's whinging, as usual."

Kai glared at him. "My foot is fine. Hurt like Ignis's hearth fire for a spell." He wiggled his booted foot, the scrape across the leather instep evidence of his claim.

They fell silent again. Something else was the matter.

"If the foot's fine, then tell me what's got into the two of you."

They looked at each other. Del sat on the edge of the seat across from Alroth.

Kai clasped his hands behind his back. "We heard something from Drake."

"He told us not to talk to you about it." Del's leg bounced.

Kai frowned at Del. "But we should tell him anyway. What does Drake know about it? He's hardly even here anymore."

"Just get to the point, you two."

Del ran a hand through his blond hair. "Fine, fine. The man here earlier... he's been asking around about a disreputable job."

Alroth sat back. He was still asking even though Alroth had agreed? If the castle guard and everyone knew, surely the Grist father had heard as well. "I know. I took it."

Del grimaced. "What?"

Kai gave Alroth a piercing look.

"I had to. Look, he threatened to burn Mill Hamlet."

"You can't honestly believe that we'll allow you to kill innocent handmaids?" Falkirk stepped into the firelight. They didn't take their eyes from Alroth.

What did they expect him to say? He was giving them the best chance to survive this winter. Did they not see the precarity of their little settlement? Falkirk drew themself up, and Kai retreated behind Del's chair and rested his hands on the back. Del didn't even curse at him to get off. They were worried about Alroth. But they all didn't see what he did; they hadn't seen what he had in his life. Without their settlement here, they would be reduced to begging on the streets. So many among their number couldn't work as Alroth could. When was the last time Del and Kai had managed to keep a day's employment? When was the last time Falkirk had even been considered for paid work? Tarrin was too young, Vernis too old, Selena had been a heretic since he'd known her, some folks had pains that laid them up, some had children to care for, some had histories like his. Together, they could keep their fields and livestock tended, but no one of them could keep gainful employment, and what they needed was actual silver.

If that meant killing handmaids— Alroth sighed. No, they were right about that. His plan to warn the Grist father hadn't worked out, but there might still be another way. He just had to think of it.

"I'm not planning to kill anyone." *I just can't see a way around it yet.*

But he would find a way to save the lives of the handmaids, gain the goodwill of the Grist, and set them all up for a safe winter.

"Sure seems like you do since you took the job," said Del.

Kai smacked his shoulder. "Wolf wouldn't kill innocents."

"He said he took the job," said Falkirk coldly.

A log fell in the fireplace, and the ewes baaed in alarm.

"I don't want to kill them. I'll find another path."

"How do you plan to do that?" said Falkirk.

Alroth shook his head. "We'll get half the payment before. You can use that to move everyone inside the walls."

"Wolf, you can't expect us to take the silver and let you suffer the consequences," said Kai.

They would take the silver. But he couldn't admit that he didn't know what he'd do.

"I don't expect that. There won't be any consequences. Once you're inside the walls, he can't touch our folk."

"It's not worth it, Alroth," said Falkirk. "Either you kill them or he takes his vengeance on you."

They still thought the silver was the point. They'd spent so long chasing coin to keep them safe, but this time it wasn't about that. He couldn't let it be. He'd never be able to live with himself otherwise. If only the Grist father had listened to his warning, he could have stopped the plot in its tracks.

Other folks trickled into the hall from outside, and their conversation was over, at least for the moment. None of them were willing to upset the rest of their hardworking folks. They had enough to worry about with the coming winter without worrying about Alroth's moral conundrum. Five long months until they could plant spring crops, longer until the harvest. They'd be snowed in completely for three of those, and even getting up the hill to town was a struggle. No one used Old Bridge Road anymore, since Old Bridge Keep had fallen to ruin, crumbling into the river. The mill on the Sinu River didn't run once the Sinu froze, and reaching the mill was the only other use for the road. Thus, the road would snow over and wouldn't clear until spring. Sure, they had a few pairs of snowshoes and toboggans to make trips into town, but not everyone could make the trek, and certainly no one from town would come to them.

Falkirk caught Alroth's eye. "We'll find another way to make the coin. Don't do this."

Alroth nodded to reassure them. He had one more day to think of something.

There were no instruments tonight. The wind rattled the shutters and whistled through chinks in the hall. The ewes baaed and kicked their sturdy pen. Etienne was up in town, probably because he didn't want to risk getting snowed in down here and shirking guard duty, and most of their hamlet were in their cottages, tucked in for the storm.

Selena, the mother and babe, two new young ones and their father, Falkirk, Del, and Kai barely filled the hall, even with the ewes taking up one corner. Each time the ewes kicked, it started the babe squalling and set the two young children off. Del sat them on the table and started quietly acting out a silly scene to soothe them while their father leaned his head against the wall behind him and closed his eyes.

Selena took Del's seat across from Alroth. "They got here this afternoon. Been travelling all the way from Trout Lake. No room for them in New Bridge. They were camping outside Upper Gate, but with the storm tonight..."

"We're happy to have them." Alroth stirred the pottage, and Selena passed him a stack of wooden bowls. As he filled them with the stew, Selena tossed a hunk of bread in each, and Falkirk took them to the table, away from where the children were getting rowdier by the moment. A smile stole over Alroth's face as he watched Kai, now having joined Del on the floor rushes. Pretending to be animals? The smaller child clapped their hands. Alroth's ladle scraped the bottom of the pot, and he scooped the last serving into the last bowl.

Three more mouths to feed through the winter.

Three more who couldn't defend themselves if war came to New Bridge. Or if the lordling made good on his threat. But he had another day. They were at least safe for tonight.

The door banged open—the wind?—and Tarrin burst inside. "Torches, from town!"

Full dark had fallen while the pottage cooked. There was only one reason for torches on Old Bridge Road from town at night. To light fires.

Alroth was already on his feet. "Tarrin, tell everyone to gather in the cruck."

The boy darted back out into the storm.

"Falkirk, Del, Kai." But they were already on their feet as well, preparing. Alroth strode to his back room, banged open his trunk, buckled his belt low on his hips, and—one sword. He slid on his cesti. One sword would have to do him. No time for his jack. The cruck had to be secured before the riders reached them.

The father waylaid him as he strode back into the hall. "Give me a weapon. I want to defend this place." He'd been here all of a few hours and was ready to defend them? It didn't matter anyway. Alroth wasn't going to have an untried fighter at his side.

Alroth laid a hand firmly on the man's shoulder. "Take care of your babies." He gestured to the shuttered windows. "Barricade yourselves in the cruck. We'll take care of this."

He joined Falkirk at one of the tables, put his shoulder to it and tipped it on its end, blocking the shuttered window. If the shutters were kicked in, no one would be able to throw a lit torch through.

Folk from the hamlet were hurrying into the hall, the sheep bleating nonstop. They were all scared but calm. They trusted Alroth to look after them. Even though Alroth had let their storehouse be burned down in the springtime, he wouldn't let their hamlet be burned down now. Because a winter without food or shelter was a slow death.

Del and Kai came back through from the bedroom and nodded to Alroth across the hall. They were armed and armoured. He jerked his head at the door, and the four of them converged there.

He turned to Selena. "Bar it behind us."

She nodded sharply and set to organizing the entire hamlet in the little hall.

The icy wind hit Alroth as he stepped outside. If any of their buildings caught, it could spread through the hamlet in a matter of moments. Once their houses were gone, any survivors would freeze to death this very night. They wouldn't let that happen.

The torches were still bobbing dots of light strung down the road from Mill Gate, flickering in the gusty wind. From the way they were bobbing, probably borne by riders. Alroth squinted. There were six torches, maybe eight. Assuming half the party held a torch, maybe a score of mounted folks. And who else could they be besides folks coming for them? No one would be on the road by choice on a night like this. Could they be going to the mill? In the dark? Not likely.

Alroth sighed. This was exactly what he'd been trying to avoid when he agreed to the lordling's job. So who was coming for them?

"Who are they, you think?" said Del. His axe creaked as he loosened it in its sheathe.

"No one good," said Falkirk.

"Don't draw your weapons until we've spoken to the riders," said Alroth.

No light made it out of the barricaded cruck; no moonlight made it through the clouds. Lines of orange firelight from the banked fires in the other houses crept through their latched shutters. Not enough to make out Falkirk's face beside him.

The ground hummed with the drumming of hooves. Alroth loosened his own sword in its scabbard. Would the riders talk with them or begin throwing torches onto the thatched roofs immediately? And what if they did? Would Alroth and his band cut them down? Who were they? A rowdy gang of ruffians from town? And what if the ruffians wouldn't be deterred and Alroth and his band had to kill them? They would be forced to leave. The lord would never tolerate murderers, even living outside the walls as they were. They had to drive the intruders off without killing anyone.

The sound of hooves grew louder on the frozen road, and the first horses pranced into the little square in front of the cruck. The torchlight they brought gleamed off their plate armour, glittering mail hauberks, and matching helms. Castle guard. Mounted castle guard. The lord's *personal* guard? These, they could not kill, no matter what. Not that they were incapable of killing them; he and his band had killed armoured men before, but to kill one of Lord New Bridge's guard? They would be cut down unquestioningly, dangled from the town walls to be picked over by crows, their hamlet razed, along with all its denizens.

Alroth unclenched his palm from his sword hilt, finger by finger, and flexed his hand. What in Bellator's name were the lord's guard doing in Mill Hamlet? Had they come to arrest him for his treason during the Canal War? Or for agreeing to plot against the handmaids? Were they after one of his people? They hadn't asked the mother who her babe's sire was. And the new family who'd arrived today... It didn't matter. None of his people were being dragged away, even if Lord New Bridge himself ordered it.

The riders lined up across from the four of them. If they wanted to toss a torch onto the cruck's roof, they would have to get closer than Alroth and his band. But they could easily reach any other house in the hamlet, and fire would not discriminate. Alroth's heart pounded in his ears. One of the horses tossed its head.

"What have you come here for, after nightfall, during a storm?" Alroth's cheeks stung, and the wind whistled between the huddled buildings, snatching away Alroth's words. Perhaps he should have kept his whiskers, especially at this time of year. Not that he'd predicted being dragged out into the cold during a mounting blizzard.

A guard at the centre of the line removed his helmet. No, not a guard. The gentleman who'd hired him. The one who'd threatened Mill Hamlet. But Alroth had agreed to his unconscionable job, dammit! Why was he here after nightfall brandishing torches anyway?

"I'm glad to see you've made my job easy, Alroth. I feared I would have to smoke you out like a gopher."

Del growled, but the gentleman ignored him.

"You accepted my offer of a generous pile of coin, but my men tell me that you went running to the Grist father's manor mere hours after we spoke." He took in the hamlet in the flickering torchlight. "I suppose I misjudged you. I thought you a savvy mercenary, able to keep to an agreement, but it seems—"

Bang! The shutter behind Alroth rattled in the gust that snatched the gentleman's words. Alroth loosened his hand on his sword hilt where it had jumped at the noise.

"Get on with it then, eh?" Del hollered over the wind.

"Easy," Alroth muttered to him. This gentleman wanted Alroth to carry out his *task*, wanted him so badly he would drag the lord's personal guard out here in the middle of the night in a blizzard to make his point. Maybe to send a message about crossing him. To show Alroth that he had the lord's favour.

If there were a handmaid here in front of Alroth at this moment and the gentleman ordered him to slit her throat or have the cruck burned down with his folks barricaded inside, he would do it. Bile crawled up Alroth's throat. Doloman help him, he would do it. But that wasn't the choice he was being given. And wasn't that a mercy. He still had a day to find a way out for his folk.

"What do you want?" Alroth growled. Any more games, and he might let Del spit the man where he stood.

"I *want* an assurance from you that you will abide by our agreement. I *want* no more skulking around the Grist father's manor house. You *or* your... cronies." He leaned his elbows on the front of his saddle.

That was all? He'd come here in force to gain Alroth's *assurance*? That was far too easy. Breaking his word to a man like this would be the least of Alroth's many transgressions. "You have it. I won't contact the Grist father, and neither will my people."

The gentleman smiled, and Del's leather gloves creaked against the haft of his axe. "You misunderstand. I need more assurance than simple words." He gestured, and one of the guards bearing torches clopped toward a cottage across the square.

Kai's bow protested as he drew, but Alroth grabbed his shoulder. They couldn't attack these men—that's what the lordling wanted—but they couldn't just *let* him burn their houses down.

"Wait!" Alroth shouted over the wind. Thank Hiorach the guard paused. He untied Volnus's scabbard from his belt and handed her to Falkirk. "I'll be your assurance." He stepped forward, head held high.

The lordling looked far too pleased.

Falkirk took the sword. "You mean to go with him? Take his *generous pile of coin*?"

Alroth shook his head. "I fear there won't be any coin for us now. I'll send word to you as soon as I can."

Kai bent his head toward them. "You think they'll leave us be after you go?"

"They will if they want my cooperation." Alroth shrugged. "And it seems they greatly want my cooperation."

"Doloman's boots." Del spat on the ground.

Alroth nodded. “Just get them through the next few days.” He didn’t have to elaborate; they’d know he meant their folk, the children among them.

He crossed the square, and the gentleman nodded to a guard, who, along with three others, dismounted and bound Alroth’s hands in front of him. Snatches of Del’s angry voice whipped on the wind, but either he restrained himself, or Kai and Falkirk held him back as the gentleman’s whole party wheeled and led Alroth from the hamlet.

Where would they take him? Inside the walls surely. Would they throw him in a dungeon? Lock him in a cellar? Try to gain his goodwill with a comfortable room? Surely this gentleman knew that Alroth could easily refuse to carry out his task in the moment, and once the Necro Ritual was done, the handmaids would be safely back in their keep, untouchable. But then what of his folk? The gentleman would surely take his ire out on them, as well as on Alroth. He needed a more substantial plan than simply refusing to carry out the gentleman’s task.

Alroth’s guard broke off from the riders once they reached the castle, and took him toward the great hall, a dark tower looming over it. This was the tower where Alroth had watched corpses dangle, so often that a murder of crows swarmed here every day, hoping for a fresh meal. They hadn’t brought him here simply to hang him; this was also the prison tower. They meant to lock him up.

He ducked under the lintel of a window embrasure and stepped through the opening into a narrow passage that descended to a landing and a door into the prison tower. The warden opened the door and stepped aside, and the guard following Alroth pushed him through into—nothing.

Alroth shouted, landed on his feet on a wood floor, stumbled, couldn’t catch his balance with hands bound together, and fell to his knees. His houppelande cushioned them, and his cesti protected his knuckles, but still, bruises would be in full bloom tomorrow. The warden shut the door, the threshold at almost Alroth's shoulder height. No wonder he had toppled over. There would be no fighting his way out of this tower. The single window was too high and too small to escape through.

Alroth crawled to the wall and leaned back against it. Would they keep him imprisoned here until the Necro Ritual? Would they at least grant him food and water? He worked at the ropes around his wrists. His cesti provided enough protection that he could wriggle them loose without rubbing his flesh raw. He shook his hands out and rolled his touchy shoulder. If the gentleman wanted him to overpower Grist guards and kill six women, he would bring him food and water, which meant opening the door at least once tomorrow. And when they did, what then? They had a four-foot advantage on him. Even with his cesti, they would simply apply a booted foot to his face. He would not make it out of here if they wanted to contain him.

Not only that, but how would he warn the Grist father what was to come? Considering that the lord's personal guard had come to apprehend him, and that he was currently locked inside the castle, could Lord New Bridge be aware of the murder plot? Was he, in fact, the one plotting it? And to what end? It had seemed, in his cramped larder, that the lordling wanted to disrupt the Necro Ritual, weaken New Bridge perhaps, or target the Grist itself, but Lord New Bridge wouldn't want any of those things, would he? He already had his own brother installed as Grist father in New Bridge Hive, how much more power could he gain from installing his own choices as handmaids? As Grist queen?

The logic of a man like Lord New Bridge was beyond him. All nobles craved was power, and there was no understanding men like that.

Alroth turned up the collar of his houppelande against the biting chill creeping through the stone at his back. Surviving the next few days would be enough of a challenge. No need to think about the future or ponder the motives of a grasping, conniving lord. He still had time. Sure, he was locked in a tower with no way to get word out, but he had a whole day to decide what to do when the lordling set him loose at the head of the waterfall. He could always jump over, if it came to that. Better to leap to his death than have to live with killing unarmed handmaids. Once the Necro Ritual was over and he had extricated himself from these plots, assuming he came out of it alive, he would never need to concern himself with immoral lordlings again.

9

Mellia

Mellia had slept after all. She must have, because she was being shaken awake. She gasped and rolled over. Echoes of *drone* chased each other around in her mind. What had she been dreaming? The wide-eyed sister next to her bed shook her again.

"I'm awake, Sister." Mellia cleared her croaky throat.

Pale sunlight crept through the cracks in the shutters. Was it already dawn?

"Father Glimar needs to see you right this moment in the sacristy."

Mellia sat up. Father Glimar wanted to see her. Had the brothers decided who would be granted handmaid status? The sister made no move to wake any of the other candidates. Did this mean they'd chosen Mellia? She threw off her blanket, pulled on her stockings, tied her garters, threw her dress over her head and laced it, followed by her houppelande, which she belted below her breasts. She didn't bother brushing her hair, just threw her veil over it and pinned it in place, poking herself twice with her shaking, half-asleep fingers.

Mellia yawned as she went about her morning ablutions. Was she about to be granted handmaid status? She could stop worrying about being bound to Lord Ainsley, then. Starting today, she could use her magic whenever she wanted to. She would move permanently into the queen's keep with the other handmaids. Maybe she could even help properly with the Necrophoresis Ritual. All the handmaids had such daunting tasks to prepare for it, having another handmaid would ease their load.

Mellia's breath clouded in the still, pre-dawn air, and she tucked her hands into her mantle as she crossed the inner cloister to the riveted sacristy door. Even from within the inner cloister, the sacristy was fortified. The Grist father's cloth of gold raiment was stored there along with other sanctified, jewelled, and golden objects. Even some brothers were not immune to the lure of coin. The Grist guard at the door let her in.

Father Glimar stood in the centre of the room while fanners dressed him in his vestments. The fanners, as brothers themselves, would not hesitate to gossip about anything that they overheard, no matter that they were not supposed to share Father Glimar's secrets. Mellia waited silently until Father Glimar dismissed the brothers, and they were alone.

Ignes prayers couldn't be far off, but Father Glimar had wanted to speak with her before then. Why? Was he working up to telling her that she had been chosen as a handmaid, or working up to letting her down? Would he ever break the silence?

"Sister Mellia. The brothers have deliberated, and unfortunately, your selection is currently in doubt."

Mellia's empty stomach twisted. In doubt? This was worse than either definitive answer. She would have to wait even *longer* to know for sure. But maybe it wasn't totally out of her hands. If her display at the trial hadn't been well received, she could do something else, something better. Whatever the brothers wanted.

"There is a way for you to ensure your selection, my child."

Mellia's chest loosened, and she let out a breath. "Whatever you wish, I'll do it, Father."

Father Glimar nodded. "But you should know it comes with risks. Should you fail, you may not be welcome in the Grist any longer."

Drone. He meant that she would be deemed a drone if she failed.

"You may decline this opportunity, but if you do, I'm afraid the Grist cannot shield you from suitors as a sister."

Lord Ainsley. Mellia took a shaky breath. If she took on this task and failed, she would be a drone, reviled, perhaps unable even to return home to her parents, tossed into the gutter. If she declined the task, she would have to undergo the binding ritual with Lord Ainsley, which she could not countenance, whether or not it took. She had to take on the task, even if failure came with such a heavy price. So she simply wouldn't fail.

She squared her shoulders. "I'm at your service, Father. Anything Doloman asks of me, I will take on and, Doloman willing, triumph."

Father Glimar nodded gravely. "I'm very glad to hear that, child. As you say, Doloman willing, we shall be overjoyed to have you as a handmaid. But Doloman's task for you is not an easy one. Firstly, none must know of it. It is between you and the Golden God only."

Of course. Tasks from Doloman were for the bearer alone. That was no surprise. Mellia nodded.

"I have had a vision. A man locked in the castle. I must speak with him. Free him from his prison and bring him to me in the hive, after the Munis prayer."

Locked in the prison tower of the castle? How was she supposed to get him out? And without letting anyone know? Was Father Glimar assigning her a task he expected her to fail? Did he want her to be caught breaking into the prison tower? What would Lord Ainsley do if she was caught? Refuse to bind her? No doubt she would be deemed a drone if she was caught, for she would have failed Doloman's task. So there must be a way. Neither Father Glimar nor the Golden God would have assigned such a task if they thought it impossible.

Mellia would be in New Bridge Castle today to tutor the lord's children, as usual. Some of the guard even knew her. Perhaps she could use that to her advantage—

Dong, dong, dong. The prayer bells. Father Glimar had to go; she needed to give him an answer.

"Yes, Father. I will gladly accept this task bestowed on me. Thank you for entrusting it to me."

Glimar placed a warm hand on her forehead. "With Doloman's blessing, go forth and bring me Alroth."

The door to the hive opened, and a fanner stepped back into the sacristy. He put the Grist father's hexagonal golden hat on Father Glimar's head, two inverted black triangles standing up like antennae. Mellia curtsied, and Father Glimar swept into the hive for the brothers' dawn prayer.

Mellia retreated from the sacristy into the first rays of the sun slanting into the inner cloister. She wouldn't have to be at the castle until mid-morning, so busying herself helping the handmaids prepare for the Necrophoresis Ritual might take her mind off her God-given task. It wasn't impossible. Doloman would never give her an impossible task.

This man, Alroth, must be important somehow. She'd met him once, when he was guarding the inner ward opposite Etienne, the moustached guard. He'd been serious, vigilant. He'd given her that assessing look, his expression half hidden in his whiskers.

She could get into the prison tower easily enough; even prisoners were allowed Doloman's council, and saying that the Grist Father had sent her wouldn't even be a lie. It was getting him *out* again that would be the challenge. Waltzing through the castle ward with a prisoner would not go unnoticed. Though perhaps if his prisoner status were less obvious... ? But what other status could he have? No doubt his clothes were not fine enough to be mistaken even for a smallholder visiting for the Necrophoresis Ritual.

Mellia barely heard Sathred needling Livine into bickering with her. The Necrophoresis Ritual was tomorrow; no wonder the handmaids were on edge. The day after that, one of them would be Grist queen. Why did Father Glimar want Alroth brought to him? A temporary castle guard? Probably a mercenary. A mercenary. Like the heretic prince. And a friend of Etienne's, the one who had told her that. Was it possible that the heretic prince had been caught and Father Glimar was trying to *save* him?

Father Glimar had said to bring the prisoner to him in the hive, which meant before Dolus Lumin, at midday. Before he announced the brothers' selection for the handmaidship. If Mellia took too long, would she fail simply by running out of time? It would have to be on her way out of the castle after her tutoring, and even then she couldn't linger.

She finished up the flower she was embroidering and said an absent goodbye to Sathred, Livine, and Runas. She would get into the prison tower using her status as a sister, and she would sneak Alroth out... somehow. How hard could it be? Father Glimar was confident that she could do it.

Mellia washed up and crossed the cloister on her way to the castle. But wait. She'd forgotten something—yes, her bee brooch that marked her as Grist. She ran back for it and pinned it on as she hurried through the outer cloister, pricking her finger in the process. This would never do. Anyone who saw her in such a state would wonder what was ailing her. Perhaps here at the comb they would believe she was anxious about the handmaid trial results, but it would simply seem suspicious at the castle where they were ignorant of such things.

She slowed in Iram Square, weaving between the stalls and gawkers around the fountain, who gazed at the golden Doloman statue in awe. Doloman was with her; she needed to remember that. He had set her this task, and He would watch over her as she completed it. Mellia was, perhaps, a bit flushed as she climbed the ramp and crossed the drawbridge to the south barbican, but her pink cheeks could be attributed to the chill wind that had picked up this morning, and not to Mellia's anxiety. After all, this was simply a normal day wherein she was here to tutor little Morgan and Delia. Yes, a normal day. Mellia hurried through the outer ward and across the small drawbridge to the inner gate, where Etienne stood.

He didn't smile as she approached today. Did he know what she was here to do? No, that was impossible. It was only between Doloman, Father Glimar, and her. No one else could possibly have overheard their conversation, and Father Glimar wouldn't have shared such a task with anyone else.

"Good morning, Sister." Etienne was paired with a taciturn stranger today, and he was practically morose. He had been more jocular when they'd been discussing the Grist queen's death.

"Good morning. You seem in low spirits." Mellia paused. She was early for tutoring, her nerves having spurred her to hurry. But surely pausing to speak to a castle guard would lessen suspicion.

"Indeed, a friend of mine, the guard Alroth, has come upon some bad luck, and I fear for his safety." He shook his head. "Alroth doesn't deserve it, either." He pulled himself together. "But far be it from me to burden a sister with my troubles. How goes the Necrophoresis Ritual planning?"

Was he trying to get her to admit to her task? No, he couldn't possibly know what she was here to do. He was simply worried about his friend. Mellia's stomach swooped as Alroth's piercing brown eyes popped into her head unbidden. He'd seemed serious, yes, but he'd been plenty respectful and had looked capable as well, tall, broad, and dexterous... capable of guarding the castle, of course. Good thing the chill wind whistled through the gate into Mellia's face, that way Etienne wouldn't notice how her cheeks heated thinking of Alroth.

"There is plenty to prepare for the ceremony." Mellia's mouth was babbling. "But many hands make light work."

"I'm glad to hear your blessed task goes well."

What? How did he know about her task? Oh, he was speaking of the Necrophoresis Ritual. Of course he was. "Yes, we are all anticipating the Necrophoresis Ritual will be carried off smoothly. If you'll excuse me, I have to attend to the young ones."

"Please, feel free to pass, Sister. Your conversation has brought some light into a boring and grey watch." He flashed his dazzling smile, and Mellia couldn't help but smile back. Even when he was racked with worry for his friend, he was still charming and jovial. What would he do if he knew that she was planning to break Alroth out right under his nose later this morning?

Mellia turned away and swallowed her guilt. If she succeeded, what would become of the guards who let a prisoner slip away on their watch? Especially Etienne, who was known to be friends with Alroth? Doloman would care for them. She just had to trust.

Her tutoring session went on as usual, and Mellia flinched as the two little ones recited the commandments. *No mortal can carve a waterfall by his own hand.* Only Doloman could carve the water's path, as He was doing with hers this very day. Whether she succeeded or failed, it was His will. And if His will was that she be cast out as a drone? What would she do then? Who would take her in? Surely not her parents, not after how they treated her brother. Certainly not Lord Ainsley, who wanted her station rather than herself. Since the Canal War had ended seven years past, work for women was scarce, the returning soldiers having taken all the steady work. Besides, Mellia had been raised a lady, and her skills reflected that.

Stop. There was no sense in pondering what would happen if she failed, because she wouldn't fail. Mellia nodded to Elenta as she chivvied her children away. Tutoring was over already? Goosebumps crept up Mellia's spine and tingled down her arms and legs. She was going to do it. Doloman willed it. He would help her.

Mellia's hands shook as she pinned her mantle with her silver bee pin. She would be admitted to the prison tower. Only Grist wore such a pin, and only those under the direction of the Grist father. She started down the stairs, perhaps recklessly fast, and almost collided with Lord Ainsley coming up.

"Sister Mellia!" He caught her arm, possibly to steady her, possibly to keep her from bolting.

"My lord!" She tried to curtsy on the narrow steps but nearly fell, Lord Ainsley's firm grip all that kept her upright.

"Will you not walk with me?" He half dragged her down the steps.

"My lord, I'm—" What? What was she? What would make him let her go? "Suffering a women's affliction!"

Lord Ainsley recoiled, rubbing his palm on his houppelande, his lips twisted into a grimace. "I will not keep you then."

"Th-thank you, my lord." Would he watch her as she left the castle? Worse, would he walk her out? A gaoler she could perhaps trick into thinking she was permitted to visit their prisoner, but Lord Ainsley would know she had no such permission. "I must be going—"

"Of course. Return to the comb and ensure you are cured of your affliction before our binding."

If she actually *were* suffering from cramps, one of the handmaids could help her. Runas, as the healer handmaid, was skilled at calling down a lagging lunation.

"Yes, my lord." Mellia curtsied, Lord Ainsley's eyes boring into her back as she tried not to hurry to the gate.

Etienne nodded her through. Good. She was free of Lord Ainsley's watchful gaze.

She headed for the prison tower. One gaoler should be easy to trick—

Loud voices echoed from the entrance to the great hall. The prison tower loomed behind, over the hall's roof. How did one even get inside? A sinking feeling pulled at Mellia's stomach. To get in, she would have to cross the great hall filled with lordlings, if the voices spilling from the door were any indication. There would be no way to get Alroth out without the entire hall noticing. If she could even get him out. Where had her fanciful idea of a single gaoler come from? She might as well return to Father Glimar, explain the situation… no. Father Glimar was a regular visitor to the castle. He knew. He knew exactly what he was asking of her. Did he *want* her to fail? Or did he honestly think Doloman would intervene on her behalf?

It didn't matter. She wouldn't fail. She just had to clear out the great hall. But how? She might still be able to get in claiming Father Glimar's orders to let the prisoner speak with a disciple of Doloman. But she couldn't reveal that Father Glimar wanted to talk to Alroth. If Father Glimar had wanted it known that he was rescuing the heretic prince, he would have come himself.

Mellia hugged the wall as a hand cart creaked toward the inner ward. She'd need another reason. Or to avoid giving a reason at all.

Could she still avoid being noticed, somehow? Maybe cause a diversion and sneak Alroth through? But she couldn't cause a diversion while in the cell with Alroth. She'd need help. Elenta? She couldn't get her in trouble again. Who else in the castle would help her? If she told Lord Ainsley it was Doloman's will, he might be pious enough to do it, but she wasn't supposed to tell anyone about her task. And she couldn't chance Lord Ainsley refusing. After all, she was doing this to be free of him. He wouldn't exactly support her bid to relieve him of his chance to be Marquess of Falvair. And she'd already told him she wasn't feeling well. He'd know that for a lie if she approached him now.

A guard might be able to enter the prison tower without scrutiny. What about Etienne? He was friends with Alroth. He'd already told her he was worried about him. But the whole castle knew they were friends. What would happen if he was blamed for the escape? But what other choice did she have?

She hustled back to the drawbridge to the inner ward. Etienne was gone. She'd missed her chance... but maybe the guards on duty knew where to find him. She asked them, trying to look demure instead of demanding, where she might find the big blond guard, Etienne. She had business with him. The two guards exchanged suggestive looks and pointed her toward the southeast tower.

Mellia ducked her head and scurried toward the tower at the other end of the outer ward. What would folks think of her if they were watching her scuttle back and forth across the ward, seemingly aimlessly?

A bawdy song drifted out the door to the tower. Did she dare go inside? Etienne had always been kind to her, in plain view at his guard post, but he was a castle guard, and they were not bound by the rules of etiquette. If she didn't go in? *Drone.* She slipped through the doorway and almost collided with an emerging guard, who scowled down at her.

Mellia drew herself up, the silver bee pin glittering on her breast. “I’m looking for Etienne.”

The guard looked her up and down. “Etienne, eh? I’ve got a bigger prick, and I won’t bore you with jesting the whole ride.”

Mellia stepped back. There was nowhere to go in here; she was backing herself into a corner. “Is that any way to speak to Doloman’s disciple?” It was a risk. He might retaliate.

He scowled and jerked his head at the spiral stairs. Mellia curtsied automatically. Why did she do that? Sisters didn’t curtsy to guards—but he lumbered past, into the outer ward, freeing Mellia to climb the spiral stairs. The bawdy song cut off as she ascended, and a chair scraped across the floor. Mellia emerged into the room just as Etienne turned. They stared at each other. Another guard, sitting by the fire, wolf-whistled. Etienne shook himself.

“Sister!” He grinned at her.

“Trust you to plow a sister.” The other guard sounded more amused than annoyed as he polished off a chunk of bread and pickled fish—the smell was overpowering—and chuckled into it. They all thought she was here for *that*. She should set them straight... but perhaps that *was* a good excuse to get Etienne alone so she could convince him to help her.

“To what do I owe this visit from a sister?” Etienne came to her.

Mellia took his elbow and steered him back the way she’d come, easily making it look like he was leading her. Her training as a lady did come in handy on occasion. Etienne let her lead him back down the steps. “Are you expected somewhere?”

"I'm just on my way to my own cozy little attic room to meet with a luscious"—he glanced at her—"friend of mine. The hive is barely out of my way. I'm happy to walk you home."

"I'm not heading back to the comb, I'm..." The two of them paused, right in the middle of the bustling ward. The kitchen chimney spewed a steady stream of smoke that whipped away as soon as it rose above the castle walls. Horses neighed from the stable next door, and a burst of laughter from the great hall made Mellia jump. Etienne led Mellia to a corner, by the stables, possibly the only quiet corner in the entire outer ward.

"I see Lord Ainsley has unsettled you, Sister." He craned his neck down to speak quietly to her. "I've heard the rumours... Is there anything I can do? I don't want to overstep, of course..."

Of course, it looked to him as though Lord Ainsley was preying on a helpless sister. Etienne thought Lord Ainsley had caused her distress. "No, nothing like that, sir. I'm simply..."

He looked so earnest. She could tell him. She had to.

"Father Glimar asked me to look in on a prisoner here at the castle."

Etienne scowled. Oh, no. She'd made a mistake. He would sound the alarm, drag her off to the guard captain, or worse, Lord Ainsley, and tell him what she'd said, her obvious lie, which wasn't actually a lie, but certainly Father Glimar would deny it. She hadn't been meant to tell anyone. Surely Doloman would punish her for breaking her silence?

"There's only one prisoner."

Alroth. He was trying to figure out what the Grist father wanted with Alroth. And if she was right, then Etienne knew Alroth was the heretic prince. Maybe he thought Father Glimar wanted her to harm his friend? She'd already told Etienne too much, but telling him everything might be the only way to gain his aid.

She stretched up and spoke quietly. "Father Glimar wishes to speak with Alroth."

Etienne scowled again. "And yet he has not come himself." He looked past her at a dog yapping away at the child it was tied to by a rope lead. "You mean to take Alroth to your Grist father, and you want my help."

Mellia wasn't allowed to tell anyone about Doloman's task. But she had told Etienne about yesterday's task, and it had turned out to be a good decision. Maybe it would work again today. "Once he's in the ward, I can get him the rest of the way through town." No one would look twice at a Grist brother in this bustle.

"The guards in the hall embrasure will be your biggest problem. I can take care of it." He smoothed his mustache, nodded, and strode toward the great hall.

Mellia trailed him. *Take care of it?* They crossed the porch and passed into the entryway without drawing notice, passing the chapel door on one side, the passage to the hall on the other. Etienne led her into the serving room, where five servants already took up the bulk of the small space, preparing food and drink for the lordlings stirring in the hall proper. Etienne led her... into the window embrasure? Two guards sat on the window seat dicing, and next to them, a few steps led down to a hidden passage in the outer wall.

"Sister for the prisoner." Etienne gestured to her. "Fetch him to the chapel."

The dark-haired guard shook his head. "He's not to leave the tower for any reason, Etienne."

It was a good plan, but it was falling apart. Mellia stepped forward. "I will go in and speak with him, then."

The guard shrugged a shoulder. "If you like. Just make it quick." He went back to their game.

Etienne thanked the guard and led her through the surprisingly warm passage to a riveted door. He threw out an arm to stop her. “There’s a drop on the other side of this door. Don’t go through, I’ll grab a torch and light the cell for you.” He grabbed one as he spoke, unlatched the door, and drew it open.

The cell was lit by a high window. Mellia squinted into the darkness. Etienne shoved the torch through the doorway, and the shadow of a lump on the floor came into focus. The lump stirred. Thank Doloman, he was alive. The man unfolded himself from where he was curled on the floor and sat up. He shielded his eyes with one hand.

“Alroth?” Etienne leaned further into the cell, thrusting the torch out.

Alroth lowered his arm. “Etienne?”

This man couldn’t be Alroth. The guard called Alroth had been all husky whiskers, making him look like a ruffian. This man could be a lord. Clean-shaven, perhaps a day’s worth of scruff marring his sharp jawline.

But those eyes...

“Help me down.” Mellia scrambled to sit on the threshold.

Both men protested at the same moment.

“Hush, both of you. Do you want the other guards to hear? Now help me down. I need to speak with Alroth.” She turned to the blond guard, Etienne, and muttered, “Grist father’s orders, remember?”

“Fine, fine.” Etienne shoved the torch in a bracket outside the door, plunging the cell into darkness again. He took Mellia’s hands and swung her out into nothingness. Her boots scraped on the wall as he lowered her down, down, until... two strong arms wrapped her body, and a voice breathed in her ear.

“I have you, Sister.”

Mellia froze, molten heat filling her belly and spreading through her veins. Alroth lowered her to the floor—she at least reached his shoulder, or near enough. This was the closest she'd been to a man since the last binding ritual she'd failed. And instead of cold dread pooling in her stomach, fire burned in her blood. Perhaps taking off her houppelande would cool her. Or perhaps she could take off more—

Etienne held the torch over them again, leaning through the doorway, and Mellia pulled away from Alroth's broad chest and pressed her back to the wall below the door, her hands pinned to the cold stone behind her. Perhaps that would stop them from reaching out for Alroth of their own accord. What was happening to her?

She cleared her throat. They couldn't go through the embrasure, not with two guards sitting there. They would notice if three of them came out, or even if Alroth and Etienne switched places. They had to get the guards away from the embrasure.

"I've been tasked with bringing you to Father Glimar." Surely telling the subject of her task was permissible?

Alroth nodded. "Lead the way." Just like that? "I have something I've been meaning to talk to him about."

"You know Father Glimar?" Was that why the Grist father had asked to speak with Alroth? They were already acquainted? Why couldn't Father Glimar simply demand Alroth's release, in that case?

"*Know* might be a strong way of putting it, but I have something to discuss with him."

"Good, then we're in agreement." They would still need to sneak him out of here... "Etienne, are the guards changing soon?"

"Already changed, sister." Of course, Etienne had been on duty before. *Bonds.*

They needed a diversion to draw the guards away. The wind whistled past the narrow windows, catching Alroth's wavy hair. Etienne couldn't mount a diversion from in here, but maybe from outside? In order to catch the attention of the guards in the embrasure, it would have to be close, otherwise some other guards would handle it. But could Etienne go out without her? And what would become of him if he was blamed for the disturbance?

Something in the great hall. Something *not* traced back to Etienne...

Surely Doloman wouldn't begrudge her a bit of magic to carry out His task? Mellia closed her eyes and searched the hall. There were the fires, of course, but she wanted a distraction, not to actually injure anyone. The floorboards were damp and sprinkled with rot in a few places underneath, but again, collapsing the floor would mean injuries. The windows? They were in good condition. The roof? Cedar shingles lay in orderly rows. They were sturdy, except... one shingle was loose, and shivered as the wind groaned past. It would come flying off before winter's end, probably take a few more with it.

"Sister?" Alroth squeezed her arm.

Mellia's numb fingers unclasped her bee pin and turned it toward Alroth, slipping the sharp pin through the fabric of his houppelande and fixing it in place. Still not quite right. His clothes worked. He could keep his head bowed. His work-hardened boots would be fine for a forager... But those thick riveted leather gloves he wore. She reached for his hand.

"What are you about, Sister?" Alroth grumbled and pulled back.

"Brothers don't wear weapons or armour or whatever these are."

"Brothers?"

"Yes. They won't look twice at a brother leaving the castle, heading for the hive."

Alroth crossed his arms over his chest, the bee pin peeking over his forearm. "You're disguising me."

"Of course."

"That won't trick the guards out there." Etienne spoke low. He was listening in.

"Just trust me." She went for his wrist again, where the gloves seemed to be bound, but he dodged her grasping fingers.

Alroth looked way up over her head at Etienne. Something silently passed between them. Why didn't Alroth want to get out of here? As soon as he was within the hive, he would be safe from apprehension by the castle guard. The two of them seemed to finish their silent conversation, and Alroth jerked at the straps of his leather glove, shucking one off his hand, then the other.

"I'm not leaving them behind."

"Here," said Mellia, and hitched up her houppelande and her kirtle to access her pocket hanging from her belt. She braced her feet as Alroth stuffed the heavy gloves in, and he smoothed her skirts over her pocket again. The bulge could be anything from a sewing project to a bundle of food. No one would look twice at it.

"Do I look like a brother?" said Alroth, scowling and crossing his arms.

"Not a bit." Etienne grinned down at his friend.

But enough. Mellia closed her eyes again and found that little section of roof. The wind was already practically howling today. She whipped it into a scream over the battlements, swooping down across the shingle. It rattled but didn't dislodge. She honed in on the one spot, spurred the wind on—the shingle flew off, spinning into the air, swirling off toward the wall. Her screaming wind tore at the others, ripping and tearing, howling in through the hole, shingles scattering now as cries came up from the great hall.

"Up, sister." And Alroth was there, his hands firm on her waist as he boosted her up to the high floor, and she scrambled backward as Alroth hoisted himself out of the cell as well. He and Etienne must have recognized the diversion even if they didn't know that she had created it.

"Just look at the floor and don't speak," Mellia muttered to Alroth as they emerged into the deserted embrasure.

Etienne led the way out of the service room, into the entryway. Mellia followed, the servants paying them no mind. Most hung out the opposite door, watching lordlings bluster and shiver as the icy wind buffeted them. Not all, though. Alroth's escape would surely be the subject of gossip later.

As Alroth stepped into the entryway behind Mellia, a voice drifted past Etienne, ahead of her, from the great hall.

"—leave him unattended? I specifically told you to keep watch." Lord Ainsley.

Fallo's green garters. Her stomach clenched.

"Yes, my lord. Right away." One of the guards was coming. Someone else they might be able to fool, but not the guard, and certainly not Lord Ainsley. Her heart pounded in her throat. They could go back, race back to Alroth's cell, but that wouldn't help them. They could make a dash for the door, but they'd have to pass the doorway the guard was about to come through. Only one other doorway was open to them.

Mellia grabbed Alroth's arm and pulled him past the hanging into the chapel. The hubbub from the great hall was muffled by the tapestry, and the chapel was empty. Mellia pulled Alroth down to his knees beside her, with their backs to the door. She bowed her head, and he followed suit.

Even if they were caught now, even if Alroth's Grist brother disguise didn't hold, she could say that she wanted to pray for the poor prisoner. That might work on a guard. Not Lord Ainsley. Hopefully, it wouldn't come to that. Alroth's thigh was pressed to hers, the heat of it reaching her even through layers of fabric.

"Why are you doing this, Sister?" His husky voice was a low murmur.

"I told you, the Grist father would like to speak with you." She kept her voice just as low. Now wasn't the time for conversation. Etienne and the guard's voices were still audible.

"But why you?"

Mellia blinked at his serious face. Why her? She had inconspicuous access to the castle, of all the Grist brothers and sisters. And she had to prove herself to Doloman so that she could become a handmaid. No one else had a task like hers. And she would succeed.

It sounded like Etienne and the guard had passed the doorway. Now was their chance to escape.

"I'll go first." If Mellia was seen, Alroth could still slip out after she was shooed away. Or marched away, if it was Lord Ainsley who saw her.

Etienne's boisterous voice drifted from the service room; he was likely in the embrasure, pretending Mellia and Alroth were still in the cell. What would he do when Mellia never emerged? With any luck, he had a plan. Mellia beckoned to Alroth, and he followed her through the entryway, onto the porch, and into the turmoil of the outer ward.

The guards at the south gate were always half asleep, and the two of them made it into the barbican and down the drawbridge without any trouble. Once they turned the corner onto Water Street, Mellia fairly sagged with relief.

"Hive Alley is the fastest way to the hive from here." Mellia strode toward the entrance to the alley. But no booted steps followed her. She turned back. Etienne had followed them after all. The two men were talking together in low voices. What were they doing? There wasn't much time. They had to get to the hive before midday. Before Father Glimar's announcement.

They turned to her, shoulder to shoulder. Oh, no. They were planning something.

"I won't come to the hive with you, sister. Not now." Hadn't he said that he had something to discuss with Father Glimar? What was the lout thinking?

"When?"

He shook his head. "I don't know. I don't know when they'll discover that I'm gone. Etienne will… cover for me, for a while, but… I can't risk the Grist father reporting back to Lord New Bridge."

Mellia planted her fists on her hips. "Is that so? What if I report back to Lord Ainsley instead, what then?"

He shook his head. "You won't."

"This isn't the place for this, Wolf." Etienne glanced over his shoulder.

"Too right. Do you have somewhere?"

"My room."

"Let's go."

Just like that? They made the decision? Etienne strode away, closely followed by Alroth. She couldn't very well let them get away. She hurried after them. She had to get Alroth to change his mind and speak with Father Glimar. It was her only chance to fulfill Doloman's wishes and become a handmaid. She'd been so close! She couldn't force him—he could probably tuck her under his arm and carry her like a stick of firewood—but she would convince him. Somehow, she had to.

10

Alroth

"She's still following," Etienne muttered, barely audible over the din on Water Street.

"And she will until I go with her." The glint in the sister's eye had made that clear enough. She wouldn't give in.

"Which you're planning on doing when?" Etienne stepped around a pile of horse dung.

"As soon as you and Falkirk get Mill Hamlet prepared." Alroth waved away a fishmonger trying to foist an eel in his direction. The hazards of the Lower Gate district.

"Give me a few hours, at least, stock the caves."

The sister was practically running to keep up with them, but the longer Alroth was exposed on the street, the higher the chance of someone recognizing him. They may not know that he was an escaped prisoner, but someone was bound to recognize him as the Wolf now that word was out. Impersonating a brother may have got him out of the castle, but there was no reason for a brother to be leaving New Bridge right now. The same trick would not get him outside the town walls.

Hence entrusting his folk's safety to Etienne and Falkirk. Once the gentleman discovered his absence, he would take it out on Mill Hamlet. Which was why he couldn't go to the hive with the sister. There would most certainly be folks from the castle there right now, and he could be recognized. The gentleman himself might even be attending the service. There was no telling where he'd gone after their near brush with him in the great hall. Alroth had to hide away for the moment. After the midday service, he could go to the Grist father and get his aid in stopping the plot to murder the handmaids. Without risking retaliation on his people.

They turned down Hive Street, and the spires of the hive appeared, towering over the town, glinting golden in the late-morning sun. Perhaps the Grist would help Alroth defend Mill Hamlet if they knew what he knew? The Grist Guard was legendary, true enough, but with the death of its queen, the group was greatly disadvantaged. At full strength, they would be a match for the lord's personal guard, but now? Pitting them against one another provided no sure outcome. Alroth couldn't risk it.

The sister still followed them as they turned into an alley. Etienne ushered them into a small foyer, empty but for a worn staircase and a door leading deeper into the house.

"My room is at the top." Etienne kept his voice low.

Alroth started up the creaking stairs. The door flew open.

"Wait just a moment, Etienne! This is too much, even for you." A woman with her sleeves rolled to the elbows popped into the foyer and advanced on Etienne.

"Friends of mine, Filomena." He gestured to the sister, at the bottom of the stairs, and Alroth, halfway up.

"Friends! I looked the other way when you brought lady friends into my boarding house, but—"

"I'm not staying this time. Alroth and Mellia here just need somewhere to rest until the afternoon. They won't cause you any trouble."

"My boarding house doesn't let rooms by the hour, Etienne! I can't let every…" She trailed off, her eye catching on Alroth's chest. The bee pin. She narrowed her eyes on Etienne.

"A Grist brother and sister, Filomena. They just want somewhere to freshen up."

"Why don't they go to the hive, then?"

"That's a wonderful idea—" Mellia started, but Etienne cut her off.

"They're on their way to the hive. You'll see, they'll be off there this afternoon. You know how crowded the comb is right now, all those pilgrims crammed together in one room. I'm offering them my room out of pure piety, madam." Etienne made the flowing gesture of devotion to Doloman. Would his landlady really fall for his shtick?

Her suspicious look didn't soften, but she motioned Alroth and Mellia up the stairs, all the while berating Etienne, who stayed to placate her.

Alroth didn't wait for Filomena to change her mind. He motioned Mellia ahead of him, ignoring her glare, and climbed the creaky stairs, first one set, and then a narrower, steeper set, almost a ladder.

Alroth reached the doorway, which was half full of fuming sister. Her chicory-flower blue eyes narrowed, and her lips thinned in her round face. Spots of pink brightened her pale cheeks—pale with ire.

"Sister, if we could move our conversation inside—"

"I have no intention of going inside at all. I freed you to render you to the hive, and I intend to do so."

Did she not realize he could pick her up and move her out of his way?

He allowed himself a moment to relax his shoulders. Certainly, dealing with an enraged sister would not be pleasant, but at the very least, there was little chance of him being thrown back into prison, so long as he stayed out of sight.

Alroth had barely eaten in a day and slept on a hard floor last night. He was not in a mood to have a row with the pint-sized dragon of a woman who blocked his access to a safe resting place. All he wanted was a meal, perhaps a bath, and to keep his people safe until he could return to them.

The small room, more of a garret than an apartment, had sloped ceilings, two small shuttered windows, and a fire banked in the grate at one end. A table by one of the windows held a cloth bundle from which a delicious scent wafted, and a basin of water strewn with petals sat on a stand by the other.

"I freed you so you could come with me to the hive, not so you could skulk up here."

"Up here is the place I'm least likely to get thrown back in that pit, Sister."

She planted her fists on her hips. "So now that you've used me to get free, you're all selfish designs? I shouldn't be surprised that a mercenary would—"

"I'm not going anywhere until I've eaten and washed the prison grime off me." And until Mill Hamlet was safely emptied. "We'll go wherever you like. After."

Her nostrils flared. The sister moved aside. She could no more *make* him go with her than he could hold back the chill of winter. "Etienne said he was planning... company for the afternoon."

Ah, that explained the petals. He'd prepared for an afternoon romancing one of his lovers. His loss was Alroth's gain. He'd wished for a good meal, and there it was. He unwrapped the fabric parcel to find a bun filled with something delicious, if the smell was anything to go by. The sister crossed behind him and stirred the fire; the thump of two logs landing in the grate must mean that she'd resigned herself to stay.

It would feel good to get the prison grime off his body. Alroth untied his belt and pulled his houppelande over his head as he strode to the washbasin. He'd have to thank Etienne later. The sister made a strangled sound as Alroth unbuttoned his tunic and draped it on the bed, leaving him in just his shirt, braies, hose, and boots. Perhaps she'd never seen a man undress before? She could turn her back if she was scandalized.

The scented water washed away the strange odour Alroth had picked up from the prison floor, and he ran it through his hair as well. His shirt stuck to his damp skin where he'd run the washcloth underneath it. He hadn't left his shirt on to make the sister more comfortable, of course not, it was simply still cold in the room, and leaving his shirt on kept him warmer.

Once Alroth felt slightly more human, he pulled his tunic back on and buttoned it. The fire was crackling by now, and the sister sat on a three-legged chair facing the fireplace, her back still to him. He pulled another chair over from the table by the window, swiped the filled bun, and settled himself across from her. A wool rug warmed the floor beneath their feet, patterned with horses, or perhaps goats. Alroth held a piece of the bun out to the sister, the savoury filling threatening to drip onto the rug. She took it and nibbled at it but shook her head when he offered her more.

Once the bun was reduced to crumbs, Alroth wiped his hands and face on the cloth that had wrapped his meal and settled himself back in his chair. The bells from the hive chimed midday. The sister's head whipped toward the sound, and her mouth fell open, her eyes round and... wet?

Alroth cleared his throat. "Now, tell me why I must come to the hive so very urgently."

The sister fixed her gaze on her own fingers, twisting her skirt in her lap. She shook her head.

"I must not come to the hive?"

She straightened, squared her shoulders. "It's too late. While you were bathing and eating and undressing about the place, my time ran out."

"Midday?"

She nodded.

"You said nothing." She hadn't hurried him along at all.

"I didn't realize how late it was."

She'd been tasked with bringing him to the hive before midday, and yet she hadn't realized how late it was? She was hiding something or perhaps outright lying to him. "I don't believe you. Tell me about your task."

The sister fidgeted, reached into her pocket, and pulled out his cesti. She meandered to the window and put them on the small table where the bun had been. She kept her back to him as she spoke. "I had a task from Doloman. I suppose there's no harm in telling you now that I've failed."

The mystery of the sister who broke him out of prison, just like that, solved. It had been a task set by her god, and of course, as a pious sister, she would never think to question such a thing. Was it perhaps the Grist father himself who had passed on the god's "message" to this innocent sister?

"You may return to your Grist father whenever you wish, Sister. I will not keep you here. I would appreciate if you waited to tell anyone of my freedom until sundown, to at least give me a little time to sort out my next move."

"Why should I do that?" She turned to him, eyes flashing. "When you have resisted my pleas to come to the hive, ruined any chance of—of pleasing Doloman." Curious how she cut herself off, changing the direction of her phrase. What was she trying to hide from him?

"I am sorry that I've caused you distress, Sister. Is there any way I can make amends for ruining your chances of pleasing your god?"

"*My* god?" She frowned.

Ah yes, everyone in Sudra was supposed to be devoted to the Golden God, including him.

"Surely a merciful god would give a pious sister more opportunities to please him." But his words didn't seem to soothe her. To the contrary, her expression turned even more stormy.

"It was my chance to gain— No. There was only one chance, and I just lost it. But perhaps..." She paced across the room. "Why were you locked up?"

Why, indeed. This sister would surely condemn him for his long-ago actions during the war. Why was he so reluctant to see disappointment, even censure, in her eyes? "Many reasons. The simplest of which is that I refused to comply with the whims of a lord."

She pursed her lips but looked him over, perhaps changing her previous assessment of him. "A guard, refusing orders?"

"I am not a guard, Sister. I worked alongside Etienne two days past as a favour." *For the coin* would make him sound like a Locuplean miser. He scratched his cheek, roughening with stubble already.

"If you are not a guard, what are you? Why did Father Glimar want to speak with you?"

"I'm a mercenary." Among other things, but she didn't need to know about the other things.

"Here for the Necrophoresis Ritual and the opportunities it presents. I see."

Did she know about the plot? Surely not.

"A gentleman tried to hire me for a distasteful task, and when I refused him, he threw me in prison." It was near enough to the truth. The sister needn't be burdened with the details.

"A principled mercenary? Will wonders never cease." But she said it under her breath, as though for herself instead of him.

"And you, Sister? What was promised you if you delivered me to the Grist father before midday?" And why had he sent a sister to do such a task?

She shook her head. "It doesn't matter anymore." She slumped down to the three-legged chair, her back bowed. "Please, call me Mellia."

"Sister Mellia, I may still—"

"Just Mellia, please."

"Mellia, then. I may still be able to help you, if you tell me more about your predicament."

She shook her head.

Why did Alroth want to help her anyway? Sure, she'd freed him from the prison tower, which would help him immensely to solve the problem of the murder plot, but she had been acting in her own interests, devotion to her god, and the interests of the reward the Grist father had no doubt offered her for carrying out his task. Alroth owed her nothing. And yet, seeing her slumped there, defeated, he *wanted* to change her back, somehow, to the fiery sister who had bodily blocked him from the room.

He would have to risk showing his hand somewhat. "Does it have to do with the handmaids?"

Her head snapped up, and her wide eyes narrowed on his face. "You know about the handmaid trial?"

Trial? This was something else, but it was something. "What about them?" Perhaps if he could keep her talking, she would reveal something.

"The handmaid trial took place yesterday, and I performed well. But still Father Glimar set me this task as proof that I was Doloman's chosen handmaid." She shrugged. "But I suppose now I've failed. I'm not the chosen handmaid. I'm nothing."

This sister had been so close to becoming a handmaid? That must mean that she was skilled at performing magic. Could she, as Gertie had, mend bones and gashes? Could she destroy a weapon simply by laying hands on it? She would be a formidable ally to have by him, helping to defend his folks. But she would no doubt go back to the Grist after she brought him, too late, it seemed, to Father Glimar. If indeed she still intended to do so.

Alroth leaned forward. "We can go to Father Glimar. We must give Etienne a bit more time to perform his task. But I will gladly go with you."

Mellia shook her head. "As I said, it's too late. I will face the consequences of my failure." Consequences? Was she to be punished because he'd dawdled, as she had pointed out?

"You missed one chance to become a handmaid. Surely there will be others."

"I'm sure there will be." Her voice was flat.

Did that mean she knew the handmaids were to be killed? That she would have more chances once that took place? Was she in league with the gentleman after all?

She stood and brushed the wrinkles from her houppelande where she'd twisted it up. "I should be going. Perhaps if I go now..."

Alroth sprang to block the door. “If you go now, what?” Was she planning to run to the gentleman and tell him what she’d done? Beg his forgiveness? Lead him back here with guards?

The steel returned to Mellia’s spine as Alroth watched her. *Fascinating sister.*

“I may be able to salvage something of my life. You think I’m a silly sister, disappointed not to become a handmaid? Do you know what happens to women on the streets, sir?”

Yes. Alroth knew that intimately. But why was this sister asking him about it? Was she in danger of being turned out? His shoulders rose. Was that her punishment? Being turned out of the comb? Selena herself had been marked as a drone in her youth, the hive’s designation for undesirable Grist, shamed and shunned and left to die. Such was the type of folk who lived in Mill Hamlet. And yet, Alroth couldn’t ask her to come back to the hamlet with him. Intentionally or not, she could bring harm to his people.

He would have to find some way to make her care just as much about the wellbeing of the hamlet as he did, if that was possible. Taking her in wouldn’t be enough; she would have to prove to him that she was committed. The binding ritual? She was a sister, skilled with magic. Surely she would know how to perform the ritual. Having a mage by his side would change everything for him and his people. Now to convince her.

“I’d be happy to keep you off the streets, Sis— Mellia. I would need a token act of fealty, though.”

She planted her fists on her hips. “What sort of act?”

“Are you familiar with the binding ritual?”

She went rigid, turned away from him—but didn’t turn her back. She clenched her fists, her arms loosening. Preparing to fight him? “I am.”

"Then perform it with me. Bind yourself to me as my matron." He resisted the urge to move in closer. She was so skittish, she might bolt. "I swear to you that you will never spend a night without a roof over your head and food in your belly if you but perform the binding ritual with me."

She took two steps back, and Alroth stayed planted in front of the door. Did she think he was planning to force her now? If she wanted to leave, to be turned out by the Grist and live on the streets… it would be a shame, a waste, but Alroth would never force her to accept his help.

Slowly, he stepped aside, leaving the door unbarred. He even sat himself back in his chair by the fire. This was her decision to make. She followed him, stopped a handspan from his knees. She braced one hand on the arm of his chair and leaned forward so their faces were a mere handspan apart. Her sweet breath tickled his bare face, still so sensitive after shaving yesterday. What? What was she— Her thumb brushed his lower lip, and his tongue darted out and licked it. He couldn't help himself. She recoiled, cheeks pink.

She paced toward the door.

He'd scared her away. He had to keep her from leaving. "I couldn't resist, Mellia. Does this have something to do with the binding ritual? I confess I'm not terribly familiar with—"

She barred the door. "I will."

"What?"

"I will complete the binding ritual with you."

Alroth was going to have his very own mage.

11

MELLIA

Mellia must be out of her mind. The binding ritual with this mercenary, this Alroth who was probably the heretic prince in hiding? But what choice did she have? Go crawling back to Father Glimar and let him deem her a drone and expel her from the Grist? Go to Lord Ainsley and give in to his demands to bind her to him?

Mellia couldn't bond. She knew that for a fact. She had agreed to perform the binding ritual with Alroth, nothing more. They would perform the ritual, he would see that she couldn't bond, and his promise would have to stand. He would look after her, at least until she could find a way to feed herself.

But oh, the way sparks had shot down her spine when Alroth had licked her thumb. A seed of hope had sprouted that perhaps this binding ritual would be better than the others, that perhaps it might even be... Surely not pleasurable like the trysts she'd had in her youth. But bearable. Alroth was grinning up at her, perhaps waiting for direction? He didn't seem to know what the binding ritual entailed.

Mellia's cheeks heated. Would she have to explain to him what to do? That would be far too mortifying. The important part was that the source was in control, the mage simply following along.

She had to be sure he would comply even after he realized the bond wouldn't take. "The binding ritual. That's our agreement?"

"Yes. I'll swear to your Doloman, if you like." Did that even mean anything to him? He was still grinning like a fool.

Mellia drew herself up. "At least make an oath you actually believe in."

His smile faded. What did he actually believe in? Now was the time to find out, before they were bound together—not by a bond, which would not take, but by his oath, Alroth's promise to keep her off the streets. Even when she was deemed a drone and turned out of the comb.

He was moving. What was he doing? Sliding out of his chair to kneel on the ground at her feet? Mellia stepped back, but Alroth reached for her hand, and she froze. He bowed his head, dark hair over broad shoulders, his back curving down. Did he want her to kneel with him like Father Glimar? No, he was already speaking.

"I swear, on the health and happiness of those I hold dear, may Ultio raze them to the ground if I break my oath. If you perform the binding ritual with me, I will keep you safe, warm, fed, and cared for until the end of our days." He raised his head slowly, and his serious eyes met hers. A smile curled his mouth again.

Did she look as shocked as she felt?

"What? You think I have no honour just because I'm a mercenary?" His fingers were so firm and warm on hers.

Why did this feel so... permanent? Mellia licked her lips, took back her hand, and retreated to her chair. If he was expecting that she would take a similar oath, he would be disappointed. What would she even promise him? Going through with the blasted binding ritual would be bad enough.

He was smiling again. "What do we need for the ritual? Candles? Water? A hive full of bees?"

Yes, there was a ritual portion that the brothers or the Grist father performed, but they couldn't get a Grist brother to do it. They'd have to make do. "Water."

Alroth strode to the washstand, threw open the shutters, and tossed out the water he'd used to bathe. "Pitcher still has a bit of rosewater. Will that do? It's blessed with an alluring scent."

He was joking at a time like this? A draft reached Mellia from the open window, and she shivered. "Yes, that will do." The water was in a pitcher, which would do for him, but they would need a cup for her, along with the basin. "A cup."

Alroth closed the shutters and paced the room, searching, presumably for a cup. What could they use? It needed to hold water, that was it. Etienne's room was sparsely furnished. If there was a cup about, it was not in evidence. Alroth seemed to have no compunction about rifling through Etienne's things and emerged triumphantly from his wardrobe with a leather flask. He pulled out the stopper and gave it a sniff. He sloshed it about and took a swig. Perhaps Etienne had prepared this for his afternoon's activities as well?

Alroth passed it to Mellia. The embossed leather—in an image of a bird flying over... a battlefield?—made it easy to grip the flask, even though her hands were smaller than Alroth's. These things were always made for oafish man-sized hands. She sniffed the contents. Sweet and cloying with something after. Alcohol? She tipped it and touched her tongue to the liquid inside. Yes, mead. Delicious. And either very pious or very blasphemous, depending on what Etienne did with it.

But they needed the flask to contain water, or at least for Alroth to pour water from the jug into the flask, from the flask into the basin. What a waste of mead. Mellia could go out for a cup, some plain water. But could she bring herself to come back here, climb the stairs, knowing what this room held in store for her? No, she couldn't go, and Alroth certainly wouldn't, afraid as he was of being captured again.

Come to think of it, he was in danger of being captured again anyway! He'd given her his word to care for her, but he could barely care for himself! She was being foolish. She couldn't go through with this. There was no point. Alroth would be caught and locked away or killed for this escape, and she would be left alone in the gutter. She took a swig of the mead, and warmth spread through her chest, down to her belly.

Alroth watched her across the room. "Is the ritual so unpleasant?"

Did he actually care? No, he was making conversation. "I can bear it, sir."

"Please—Alroth. If I'm to call you Mellia, you can do me the same courtesy." He stepped to the empty basin and the full jug, and stretched a hand out to her. "What happens now, Mellia?"

He and Etienne had a plan. Surely, even if Alroth was captured, killed, what have you, Etienne would uphold his oath? And if Alroth really was the heretic prince, *someone* would uphold his oath once he was caught. And besides, no one else was rushing to keep her off the streets. If he was captured, she'd be no worse off than she was right now.

She scampered to the basin and held out the leather flask, her fingers bumping over the battle scene imprinted on it. "Pour from the jug."

Alroth took the jug by the handle and tipped it slowly and gently until a thin stream of rosewater poured from it into Mellia's flask, a cool trickle sliding onto her fingers. The line between Alroth's brows was a testament to his concentration; he wanted to do this perfectly. He stopped a handspan from the top of the flask and tilted the plain pitcher up.

Mellia took a breath and let it out. "May Doloman bind us and bless us with a strong bond."

Alroth's rumble chased her words, and Mellia jumped. "May Prosperitas gift us with a successful union."

Wasn't it blasphemy to call upon the lesser gods during such a ceremony? After all, only Doloman had the power to bestow bonds. There was no taking back what Alroth had said, and besides it *didn't matter* since Mellia could not bond!

Mellia tilted the flask over the basin, and a shining golden stream of mead mixed with rosewater tumbled into it. The scent was sweet, floral, and tantalizing. Mellia couldn't help but lick a hanging drop from the edge of the flask when she tilted it up. "Now you again." She held the flask out to Alroth, whose gaze was riveted on her mouth. Had she really just *licked* the neck of the flask while Alroth watched? They would be doing far more than that soon.

Alroth focused on the flask again, tipped another stream of water from the pitcher into it. His hands held the jug so firmly but so gently. Would he treat her that way too, in a few moments, during the other part of the ritual? A jerk tugged low in Mellia's belly, and she gasped, the flask jostling out from under Alroth's careful pour. Rosewater streamed over Mellia's hands and onto the floor. Still, that strange feeling tugged at Mellia's belly as Alroth tipped the jug up.

"All right?" he murmured.

Mellia nodded. She groped for the stopper and closed up the flask. She laid it on the windowsill and wiped her hands on her skirt. The wool did little other than smear the sweet-scented water—she wasn't wearing her apron, of course. The jug thumped down beside the washstand, and Alroth watched her patiently. He waited for her to tell him the next part of the ritual.

What was she to say? *You take out your...* member... *and put it in my—* She couldn't say such a thing aloud. She cleared her throat. She would make him understand another way. "It's an intimate ritual, the next part." She gestured toward the bed.

Alroth's eyebrows shot up. "Why, Sister, do you mean the binding ritual of the Grist is sexual in nature?"

How dare he make this harder for her than it already was? "Don't call me Sister, and it's not the Grist's binding ritual. It's the mage's binding ritual with her source."

His eyebrows drew down. "Fine then, let's get on with it. Should I turn my back while you undress?"

No one had ever asked her that before. Was he trying to be funny again? "I don't see the point, seeing what comes next."

Alroth wrapped his fingers around her upper arm, drew closer to her, towered over her.

Her heartbeat pounded in her chest, her breathing sped. *Don't pull away, don't pull away.* She made her entire body rigid to keep from yanking her arm from his grasp.

His frown softened, and so did his tone. "We need to talk about this, Mellia. I won't have some vague idea between us of what will happen here. If we are going to bed together, we're gonna talk about it first."

"What?" She turned away so he wouldn't see the horror in her eyes. "I couldn't possibly talk about such things."

"But you can engage in them?"

"*You* will be the one engaging in them."

His fingers fell away from her arm. He took the chair by the fire. She turned a little more toward the back of his head. He bent and unlaced his boots.

Phew. He'd gotten the message. She would simply do as he bid. She unclasped her belt and pulled her houppelande over her head. The room had warmed, and Mellia didn't so much as shiver as she draped her houppelande on the washstand. She crouched and unlaced her own boots. Alroth padded across the room, and the bed creaked with his weight. Mellia's hands shook as she loosened her other lace and stepped out of her boots.

There he was, lying back on the bed, propped on a few pillows, in his tunic and hose. One of her boots had fallen on its side, and her bootlace was swallowed by a crack in the floorboards.

"Mellia, come here."

Her shoulders slumped. Just get through this part, and she would have her protection. She would never have to do this ritual again. Certainly not with Lord Ainsley. She shuddered. Alroth's hand patted the bed next to him, and Mellia climbed up on her knees on the coverlet beside him.

"Here, sweetling."

Sweetling? What was he doing? He coaxed her closer, beckoned and gathered her into his arms until she lay next to him, his arm under her head, the sides of their bodies touching. What did he mean to do with her like this?

She swallowed the question. Enraging him with pointless questions would only make it worse. She knew that very well from her third binding failure. Would he ever speak? Or just pull himself out and spread her legs?

"If you won't tell me about the binding ritual, at least answer my questions, please."

Please? This wasn't right. She should correct him.

"I'll just show you," said Mellia, and scrambled up, slipped a hand under his tunic, his shirt, and pulled the drawstring of his braies, untying the waistband.

Alroth's fingers wrapped her wrist, exactly as she'd imagined. Firmly, but gently. He pulled her hand away from him. What was he doing? This was the binding ritual. Was he changing his mind? She couldn't let him. She slid her other hand up his thigh, but he grabbed that wrist as well.

"Mellia, I don't want you to *just show me*. We must speak of this."

"Speaking is not part of the ritual!" Why was he insisting on making this as difficult as possible, as though it wasn't difficult enough already?

"Either it's part of the ritual or there will be no ritual!"

If he hadn't still been in firm possession of her wrists, Mellia would have scrambled back.

Alroth dropped one of her hands to run his palm over his face and back through his hair. "I didn't mean to scare you, sweetling. But I mean it. You fear me, that much is plain. You think I would force you to perform an *intimate ritual*? You think I would *engage in* intimate acts without your participation?"

"I will participate. I said I would, didn't I?" What was he expecting her to say? That she would happily do those things that haunted her still from five previous times? That she would actively engage in painful acts that made her bleed and ache for days afterward?

Alroth rubbed her wrist with his thumb. Her words didn't seem to satisfy him. "Just answer my questions about the ritual."

"Fine." If he insisted on talking about this, it would just be another awful part of this last time she ever had to do this.

"Is there more to it than simple rutting?"

As if *rutting* were so simple. Maybe for men it was? Her previous potential sources had seemed to enjoy themselves, that was true enough.

"There are rules." She sighed. He was making her speak of it. She picked at a threadbare spot on the coverlet. "The man must stay always above the mage. Water flows from high to low, and so it is with syphoning magic. The mage receives what the source gives her, as with magic. She does not refuse what he offers and takes it without resistance, as the mage will her source's magic—"

"Enough." The tension stood out in his neck. His jaw was clenched, as were his fists.

Mellia nearly fell off the bed in her scramble to put distance between them. She backed to the door, her hands pinned behind her.

Alroth took a deep breath and shook out his hands. "You've performed this ritual before?"

She should say no. She shouldn't tell him that she'd failed to bond before. He would no doubt rescind his promise, toss her out into the gutter. But how did he know that? Would any mage not retreat from such a show of anger at her words.

"Sweetling, I'm not angry with you. Please come back." He reached toward her, made to get up, then seemed to change his mind, and lay back on the pillows and patted the bedspread, as he had before. Was she really supposed to believe he wasn't angry after that outburst? Did he think her brainless?

She shook her head.

"Truly, sweetling, I'm angry at your words, yes, but those words were not yours. If you've done this ritual before, with a man who was following those directives..."

What? If she couldn't bond when the source was following the directives, then she certainly wouldn't be able to when they'd used mead from a flask in the water ritual. He'd found out her deception. He now knew as well that this bond wouldn't take. He knew that she was scrambling to get some measure of protection from him while intending to give him nothing in return.

Alroth rolled off the bed, grasping his braies to hold them up as he strode to the rug in front of the fire and sat in a tailor seat on the floor. "Take the chair."

"What? I'm not supposed to be above—"

"The chair," he growled, his eyes flashing.

Mellia huffed and strode to the chair, lowering herself into it, ramrod straight, and looked down her nose at Alroth.

"Better. Now." Alroth took one of her stockinged feet in his lap and pressed with his thumbs on the ball of her foot, her arch, her heel, massaged the top, the bottom, her toes. As though he knew she'd been run off her feet for days preparing for the Necrophoresis Ritual.

Mellia leaned back in the chair. Even if he was going to do the binding ritual to her later on, what harm was there in enjoying this moment?

"I won't do what the last man did to you." How could he possibly know what the last man did? "I've seen what men do to women... and I will not." His thumbs pressed more firmly before he took a breath and let it out, gentling his movements again. "If we are to perform this ritual, Mellia, we will do it together. None of this refusing to engage in the ritual with me. If there are certain rules, then we will abide by them only as we see fit. If that means the bond doesn't take, then so be it."

So be it, just like that? He didn't care if the bond took or not? But didn't he want a mage bound to him?

"I have promised to care for you if you perform the binding ritual with me, and I will."

Alroth's head was bowed, his dark hair blurred before her as Mellia's eyes filled with tears. He didn't care if the bond took or not. He'd made his oath, and he intended to honour it.

"I've failed before."

Alroth switched to her other foot. He nodded.

"I have found the ritual to be... unpleasant."

His thumbs pressed hard into her arch, but again, he seemed to make an effort to gentle his touch. "It won't be unpleasant with me."

And just like that, heat bloomed in Mellia's center, that tug in her belly back again, pulling her closer to Alroth. He looked up. His gaze practically sparked. Could he feel it too? But he wasn't above her at all right now. He was sitting on the floor at her feet.

His throat bobbed. "May I take off your stockings?"

Mellia nodded. Alroth's fingers brushed up her stockinged leg, under her skirt, under her shift, to her garter, a leather lace tied tight below her knee. He found the knot and pulled it loose, brushed her stocking down, and turned to the other side. He pulled both of her stockings off and laid them aside carefully. Her bare feet now sat in his lap, the scratch of his tunic's wool rough against her skin. What would he do next? Was she supposed to ask him to remove his clothing as well? Or did he prefer to remain clothed?

That moment in the dark cell when his arms had been wrapped around her, their bodies pressed together... Heat exploded in her belly, and it tightened. She wanted that. She put her feet on the floor.

"Stand."

Mirth curled Alroth's lips, but he obeyed her, getting to his feet, still holding up his underclothes. Mellia's face heated. The underthings she'd so brazenly untied. Alroth towered over her now. Maybe this hadn't been such a good idea. What had she wanted to do? Oh, yes.

But his tunic was too scratchy. And she was too short. He'd been helping her down from the ledge, in the cell.

"Take off your tunic."

"As you wish, sweetling." Yes, he was laughing at her. But what did that matter? He was doing as she bade him.

Not how the ritual was supposed to be performed. She was the one who was supposed to do as she was bid. This ritual wouldn't result in a bond anyway, so it didn't matter. She lifted her skirts and climbed onto the chair. He turned back in just his shirt and hose. He must have tied his braies again since he wasn't holding them up anymore. He chuckled when he caught sight of her on the chair.

"Would you like me to bow and scrape?"

"No. Come closer. Hold onto me like you did before."

"Before? In the cell? You enjoyed that as well? I cannot deny you, sweetling." He swept his arms around her hips, and boosted her from the chair, careful to stay in the center of the room so as not to crack her head on the lower rafters. He twirled her around, and Mellia couldn't help her shriek of laughter. He let her down a touch, their bodies pressed together, and nuzzled into her belly, her chest, her collarbone, her neck. Yes, the tug in her belly was spreading higher, broadening, and the heat in her core was turning liquid. He lowered her slowly, and there was the evidence of his arousal as well, pressing into her belly through their clothes.

She… wanted this. The things the other sources had done to her. She wanted to do them with Alroth. She slid her hands to the hem of his shirt. He'd asked before taking off her stockings, perhaps he wanted her to ask as well?

"May I take your shirt off?"

"Yes, please do." His gaze burned down into her as she slipped her hands under the nettlecloth and gathered it up. He helped her pull it over his head. No wonder he'd had no trouble lifting her up and spinning her around—his big shoulders showed not a hint of bone, and his chest and middle were full and muscled. Dark hair bloomed over him, leading in a trail down to the waist of his braies, which he had indeed tied around his hips. Now that she was looking at this expanse of skin, she wanted to touch it with her own. She wanted him to lift her again, but their bodies would be bare. She pulled the lace of her kirtle, loosened the bodice.

Alroth put a hand over hers. "I didn't know what I was agreeing to when we made our bargain."

He was going back on their bargain now? Now that she actually longed to fulfill it? She pulled away. "Now that you know I've failed to bond previously, you don't want to promise me your protection?" And she'd been about to go through with the ritual, perhaps thought it might even be pleasurable, if that was possible.

"You misunderstand. I didn't know that you had been mistreated. I didn't know what the ritual entailed. I didn't—"

"What? You didn't know I was soiled? Scarred?"

He stepped closer, but Mellia was too angry to retreat.

"When we made our bargain, I didn't have any feelings for you. I believed it to be purely mercenary."

She raised her eyebrows. He *was* a mercenary. Were all his actions not mercurial?

But he kept on. "I find myself drawing closer to you, Mellia."

And was that not exactly what she had felt as well? She shook her head. "We had better stick to our agreement."

He nodded, but his smile didn't fade. Did he suspect that she felt something between them as well? No, he had no reason to suspect such a thing.

"If you still want to strip out of your kirtle, I won't stop you again." That grin was back on his face. It turned him from a dour merc to a laughing imp, somehow.

Mellia smiled back and pulled at the lace up the side of the kirtle. And there she stood in her shift and underwear. All it would take would be to undo three little knots and she would be naked with this man, this practical stranger. So why didn't she feel that creeping dread any longer? Even seeing his *member* tenting his braies? Perhaps it would be interesting to take it in her mouth. If she told him to keep still, would he? Would he grab onto her head like the others? How would she keep him from doing that?

"Will you do as I tell you?"

Alroth laughed aloud this time. "I am yours to command, sweetling."

"Sit." She pointed to the bed, and he sat on the edge. If she did this, she would be at his mercy. What if he had simply been trying to put her at ease to get her into such a compromising position? No, she couldn't risk that. If he meant it, he would agree to this stipulation. She swiped one of her garters off the floor and held it out to him.

He quirked an eyebrow. "What could you possibly intend to do with that?"

"Your wrists."

He held them out. No, like that he could still hold her down.

"Behind you."

He crossed his wrists at the small of his back.

Mellia scrambled onto the bed behind him and wrapped the thong around, then tied it. He flexed his arms. He could snap the garter, if he tried. But she would at least have enough warning to move away.

"Now that you have me here trussed up for your pleasure, what do you intend to do with me?"

The tug in Mellia's belly spread upwards again, under her ribcage. "May I..." She gestured to his braies.

"Mmm, you want me at your mercy so that you can mount my cock?"

Mellia's mouth fell open. Did men actually speak this way? He *was* a mercenary, not a dapper lord.

Alroth's grin flashed again. He had been trying to shock her. Had he noticed that she was nervous? "Yes, please, amuse yourself and do as you will with me. I know you'll stop if I say so." His gaze caressed her face, her hair, doing with his eyes what he couldn't do with his bound hands.

Mellia got to one knee before him and pulled out the hastily tied knot below his navel, drew the nettlecloth away from his... *cock*?

He groaned in his chest, and his member jerked. "That means I like it," Alroth mumbled.

None of the others had ever done that. None of the others had ever given her a chance to study them, either. Not since she was young, slipping out to the stables to explore before her first binding ritual failure. Alroth's cock smelled a little of rosewater when Mellia bent closer. He must have bathed himself all over from the washbasin. He was staring down at her. He licked his lips, and Mellia echoed the motion. Alroth groaned again.

"Please, sweetling, don't tease."

Tease? He wanted her mouth on him, right. She unhinged her jaw as much as possible and bent—

"Wait."

She stopped and sat back.

"Not like you think I want it. Just what you want."

What she wanted? Yes, this had been her idea, hadn't it? And what had she wanted? She'd wanted him to stay still, not to hold her down, yes, but she also wanted to know how he tasted, and maybe whether she could make his *cock* twitch like that again. She licked under the head and got her wish. Alroth didn't even try to keep his groans inside, or if he was, then his full volume would disturb Filomena downstairs. If she was keeping an ear out, she might still know that Etienne's pilgrims were engaging in some very impious activities—less pilgrims than lovers.

Lovers? The tug expanded to Mellia's heart. Alroth was willing to rub her feet, let her bind his hands and do as she would with him. He didn't care whether they were bound or not; he refused to treat her the way all the others had. She licked her lips and took him as far into her mouth as she could. His thighs flexed under her fingers, and a stream of epithets rained from him. Mellia squirmed, unfamiliar slickness between her legs.

"Sweetling, please, untie me, I want to worship you. I can't wait another moment to feel you against me."

She sucked on him, and another, more blasphemous stream of curses growled from his chest. A throbbing had begun between her legs. She pulled off. He had asked her to untie him, and she would honour that request. But what would he do when she freed him? Would he be crazed with the passion now burning in his eyes? Unable to control himself? She sat back.

His gaze softened. "I've scared you."

Mellia shook her head, but perhaps he had a little.

"What can I do to reassure you? I'd love to lick you as well, sweetling. You can even grasp my hair. I'll do as I'm told." That grin would break her.

Lick her? Was that done? His warm slick tongue on that throbbing part of her— "Yes. You will."

He chuckled and wriggled and his hands were free. He'd broken her garter? But, no, he was holding it up, still a circle of leather. He'd been able to wriggle free that entire time but he'd stayed tied up because... why? Because she'd told him to. He patted the bed and slid to his knees beside her.

Mellia climbed onto the bed and sat as he had. Perhaps not exactly as he had. Her knees pressed together, and she sat straight.

"May I?"

What was he asking? Did it matter? Whatever he wanted to do, she would like it. "Yes," she breathed.

Alroth held her gaze as he slid his hands up the outside of her thighs under her shift to the bows knotting her underthings. He pulled on one, then the other, until they came free. Now all that held her underclothes in place was her clenched legs.

Alroth's voice rumbled from deep in his chest. "Open for me, sweetling."

Something pulsed between Mellia's thighs, and the heat in her belly surged. She spread her legs, and Alroth's hand brushed up to her belly under her shift, and then down, taking the front of her underclothes with it, baring her to him as he ducked his head into her shift. But she couldn't grab his hair this way to pull him up short if she wanted to. She gathered her shift in one hand, loosened it with the other, squirmed it out from beneath her, and pulled it up and off. Alroth groaned and ducked his head.

At the first stroke of his tongue, she fell back on the bed, one heel coming up to the edge of the mattress to press forward. One of her hands clenched the bedspread, the other flew to Alroth's hair. What was this feeling? This taut ecstasy? It had been so very long... Pleasure at the hands of a man, a source, a binding ritual. Who could have—She gasped. Alroth had kissed her, his lips pressed firmly around her clit. She writhed, and he was welcome to hold her steady if he was going to please her like this.

The tug in her chest wrapped her pounding heart as she tingled, fluttered, and jerked against Alroth's face. Her mouth was open, and a sound was coming out of it, then pleasure racked her body and ebbed, slowly, leaving her wrung out on the bedspread. Alroth pulled back and grinned up at her.

"I take it none of the other rituals were quite like this."

Mellia smiled softly. No, they hadn't been. Not like this at all.

12

Alroth

Alroth lay beside Mellia, pride suffusing him. None of the other sources had brought her pleasure like that, or pleasure at all, by the sounds of it. He tamped down his anger for the millionth time and tried to ignore his raging hard-on.

But Mellia wasn't ignoring it. He'd pulled his braies back up yet again, and she was watching as his cock bobbed inside the tented nettlecloh.

"Do you want to touch my cock some more, sweetling?"

She blushed so adorably. But she also nodded and stroked her fingers down the hair on his abdomen, inside his waistband, and brushed over the head of his cock. He groaned. That seemed to be all he did with Mellia. The sweet, innocent sister. Not so innocent, as it turned out; forced into a worldliness she hadn't asked for. He brushed a lock of hair out of her eyes as she wrapped her warm hand around his shaft.

"Stroke it, if you want to pleasure me."

She did. *Cupidus forebear.* How wonderful it would feel to plunge into her waiting heat. She was wet, wanting, he'd tasted as much... but perhaps her body and her mind were in disagreement. Until she asked him, perhaps begged him, he would resist the temptation to slip inside her, make her gasp and moan and cry out his name—his balls tightened, and he jerked and thrust into her hand as he erupted all over himself.

As his breathing evened out, he opened his eyes. Mellia watched him with a furrowed brow, glanced at his softening cock.

"You didn't... take me."

"I recall you took your pleasure over my face, sweetling. Was it not enough for you?"

She propped herself up on her elbow. "The others *took* me."

He chuckled. She was so prudish—perhaps not surprising for a sister. He stroked fingertips up her arm. "You liked when I spoke of rutting you?"

She rolled her eyes.

Was his sweetling so needy? "I can pleasure you again with my fingers or my tongue, but I'm afraid my cock will need a bit of time to recover." He wasn't so young that he'd be able to perform again this moment. And was that... disappointment on her face? She *had* wanted him in that way.

"If I need to *take you* for the binding ritual to be complete, I'd be more than happy to." He rolled off the bed, and hunted for a rag to clean up, which of course Etienne had in abundance. Was rutting all he used this room for? Alroth wet the rag from the rosewater in the pitcher and wiped himself down. It would have to do until he could visit the bathhouse later. "Perhaps you can come with me to—"

Mellia crouched on the floor, her shift back on, but half laced. Was she looking under the bed? Yes, and was that... whining? Yes, unmistakable whimpering from under the bed. Alroth crouched beside her.

A little creature huddled under there, pale and ghostly... an ephemer? But Alroth hadn't felt anything, they hadn't even properly performed the binding ritual, according to Mellia. But there it was, the little ephemer. And where else could it have come from but a bond? *Their* bond. She crooned to it, and the little creature scuttled toward Mellia's outstretched hand and sniffed her, half curled still in a ball. He couldn't grab the little thing; his hands would go right through it in this state, but they could see and hear one another.

Mellia gathered the ghostly form onto her lap. If she could feel it, then it must be her ephemer. The creature was... a puppy. A shivering, quaking, whimpering little mess. Was that supposed to represent the strength of their bond? A terrified wee pup? Their *bond*.

Gods above, they were bound. The bond had taken. After all Mellia's talk of not being able to bond, there it was, proof that they had. She tore her eyes from the pup and glanced at him, a mix of shock and wonder. She had agreed to Alroth's terms thinking that they wouldn't bond, hadn't she? Well, he would keep his end of their bargain. They had performed the ritual, and he would keep her safe.

By now, Etienne had hopefully secured Mill Hamlet. Alroth could safely venture to the Grist father to inform him of the murder plot against the handmaids. Maybe now that Alroth had a mage on his side, he could work with the Grist Guard to keep the handmaids safe during the Necro Ritual. Mellia could come with him, help him to get in and see the Grist father instead of being turned away as he'd been yesterday morning.

The puppy's barks pierced Alroth's eardrums. What would the Grist father say when he realized that one of his sisters was bound with him, a mercenary, without the Grist's permission? That conversation would subvert the more important discussion they needed to have about the handmaids. And hadn't Mellia said that she had been a handmaid candidate? He couldn't risk taking Mellia with him and the Grist father refusing to talk to him, maybe even threatening to break their bond.

It was decided.

Alroth pulled on his tunic, belt, houppelande, and bare sword belt, and slid his feet into his boots. He sat to lace them, and when he was finished, Mellia watched him, the puppy in her lap trying to chew her fingers, but their teeth kept going right through.

Mellia didn't seem to notice. "You're going somewhere."

"Yes, I have business that can't wait. You stay here. If anyone sees that ephemer..."

"Folk will see it as soon as I leave this room. It's not inconspicuous."

That was true. Which meant that she needed to stay here until he'd sorted everything out. "That's right. So stay here. I'll be back again soon."

"Where are you going?" She scrambled up. The pup fell through her lap onto its little paws on the floorboards and yipped merrily at the edge of Mellia's shift, unable to grip it in its tiny teeth.

"To see the Grist father. I have business with him."

"I have business with him myself. I'll come with you." She pulled her kirtle over her head, and tugged at the lace, snugging it up to her body.

"You won't come with me. You'll stay here, safe, until I come back." He knew best about these things, and she would listen to him and understand that he was doing this for her sake.

She planted her fists on her hips. "Will I, now?"

"I'm your source, and I say you will." He strode to the door.

"*Maga avara sua fons directiones denega.*"

Her strange words made him turn back. Scripture? She was throwing scripture at him? The puppy yipped. His ears rang; his hearing would never be the same with all this yipping and yapping.

"You'll stay here. When I get back, I'll take you somewhere else safe." He lifted the bar on the door and left, her words too muffled to hear through the solid wood. She wasn't planning to stay put. He wedged a scrap of wood in the latch. That would keep her from running off until he returned. She'd be safe and well here, and he could send Etienne for her later.

The babble of the crowd in Iram Square hit Alroth as he stepped out onto Hive Street, and folk spilled from the square along the road, almost to the alley mouth. Pushing his way through the square would take forever; might as well go around. He turned the opposite way on Hive Street, toward Lower Gate. This route would take him past the castle, but there was nothing for it.

After the Necro Ritual tomorrow, all these folk would head back to their homes for the solstice, and New Bridge would calm down again into the snug little town he'd chosen to settle in. He was mostly going with the flow of traffic from Lower Gate up Water Street to the castle, and he made good time, but Castle Street was the opposite. Folk flowed from Iram Square toward the castle, smallholders on their way back from midday prayers at the hive, no doubt.

Folk did seem unusually deferential though. In fact, a well-dressed lordling scrambled out of his way and bowed his head to Alroth. He glared at the lordling. Was he mocking him? Someone else muttered *Brother* and inclined their head as well. Why would they think he was a brother? Did he have a hexiform wrinkle in his houppelande? He brushed it down—his fingers catching on something cold and sharp. No, not a hexagonal imprint, Mellia's silver bee. He hadn't returned it to her.

He would, when he went back for her. No sense in returning now. He waded through the parting crowd, through the Grist father's gate and up the lane. Like yesterday, the footman eyed him at the door, but his gaze caught on the bee pin. His brows drew down suspiciously, but he bade Alroth wait on the step and brought the valet back with him.

"The Grist father has not yet returned from the Dolus Lumin service."

Alroth nodded. "I'll wait for him." He would wait here on the step if they wouldn't let him in.

The valet beckoned, and Alroth followed him into the grand house, over silk rugs and past papered walls into a hexagonal room draped with wall hangings, scenes from the hive's precious scriptures.

The valet left him and shut the door.

On one, a farmer, picked out in shining gold thread clearly intended to represent Doloman, diverted a stream to irrigate his fields. On the next, a river, having carved a path deep into a gorge, and a spectral hand, once more glittering golden, laid over it, as if to protect its flow, or more likely to hold it in place. Beside that, two waterfalls, flowing into one river, the river's feminine face in despair, water bursting its banks and flooding a hapless village. Over the fireplace, Doloman, perpetually woven in gold, pushing a dull man aside as he carved a riverbed with his shining finger.

Alroth took a seat by the fire, facing the door. That was about enough scripture for one day. Mellia had said something to him in the language of the Empire, maybe depicted by one of these tapestries? The tapestry across from his seat showed Doloman, a wound in his side, golden water trickling from it, filling a goose-necked pitcher held aloft by a broad man. A woman with a flared vessel, kneeling at the man's feet, regarded the man with the same awe and reverence that he directed to the Golden God above him. Alroth grimaced. No wonder Mellia's rituals had been horrible if the source took *that* literally.

The door opened. The valet bowed, and the Grist father swept past him into the chamber. He wasn't a stooped old rheumatic man at all; he stood straight, tall, and broad. Should Alroth stand to greet him?

The Grist father didn't give him a chance to scramble to his feet but sank into the chair opposite Alroth.

"Forgive my lack of decorum, child. I usually take a rest after the midday prayers, and my feet will not abide a change in routine." He looked Alroth up and down, his gaze catching on the silver bee pin. "You must be desperate indeed to speak with me, to impersonate one of my brothers."

He knew? And yet he was speaking so gently, so matter-of-factly? Should Alroth insist that that wasn't his intention? He hadn't stolen the bee pin to impersonate a brother... but neither had he taken it off when he had noticed it on his breast. The Grist father sat there in front of him, as he'd wished. It didn't matter how he had come to be here. "There is a plot to kill the handmaids during the Necro Ritual."

The Grist father's face shuttered. "How do you know this?"

"I was approached by a lord, intent on hiring me to bring it about."

"You refused." The Grist father's fingers drummed on the arm of his chair. "Despite a generous payment, I would imagine?"

"Yes." What more was there to say? He'd come to deliver his message. The Grist father looked neither surprised, nor horrified, nor... anything. Could Alroth leave the problem with him? The gentleman himself had said that he would hire someone else to do the job if Alroth refused, and Alroth had clearly refused, what with escaping from where the gentleman had imprisoned him. "Someone else will not be as scrupulous when approached by a gentleman so marked by wealth that his handkerchief has a silver monogram and he wears the latest fashions. A pourpoint that has never seen real harness, I'd wager."

The Grist father nodded. "I believe you're right." He sighed, much too heavily for someone so young. He sounded just like Alroth poring over his small box of coin.

"I'm willing to help you, Father."

Now he did look surprised. "Help me?"

"Defend the handmaids. But I need something in return." Now was his chance to get the status he needed from the Grist to gain access to the safety of the town walls for his people.

"Go on," said the Grist father.

"I need your support for my bid for a place inside the walls of New Bridge."

"A place inside the walls? For yourself?"

"And my people."

"Your people."

"That's right. We aren't safe outside of town."

The Grist father studied the hanging above the fireplace, the Golden God looking down on the source and mage with such benevolence. He nodded. "Your help would be much appreciated. The Grist Guard, though formidable, is weakened without a Grist queen." The Grist father got to his feet. "Once you have proven your support for Doloman's handmaids, you will have more than gained a place for yourself and your people inside these walls. Tomorrow, after the Necrophoresis Ritual, if the handmaids still live, I will find a place for you and yours. Meet us here at the hive at dawn to join the handmaids' guard, you and those you trust."

"I will be honoured."

The Grist father's gaze danced over the bee pin again. "Was there anything else you wished to tell me?"

Did he know about Mellia? It had been her task to bring him here before the midday prayer. The Grist father had assigned it to her. Could he recognize her pin? Could he know what they'd done? Of course not. There were so many brothers and sisters with almost identical pins. Why did it seem better that the Grist father believe

Alroth had stolen the pin than know about their bond? No matter, he would find out in the morning when Mellia appeared at Alroth's side. But when she did, she would not be poised to run from him back to this tall young Grist father. She would stand next to him by choice, not by some accident of a bond that she had not hoped for.

Alroth would take Mellia to Mill Hamlet, show her what a difference she could make in their lives, and she would come around. "No, Father, that was all.

"Tomorrow at dawn, then." He nodded to the door, and Alroth stood. "It might be best"—the Grist father's eyes were flinty—"if you don't prevail, to take the handmaids to safety."

"Of course, Father." He'd find somewhere safe for them. The caves were defensible, if unprepared for the cold winter months. Alroth would keep the handmaids alive, whether by defeating their attackers or hiding them away.

He stepped into the hallway. *By Prosperitas's golden chisel*, he'd done it! All Alroth had to do was keep the handmaids safe tomorrow, and he would have his place inside the walls.

The valet cleared his throat from the doorway, and Alroth took his leave. From the top of the Grist father's front steps, Iram Square still bustled, but the crowd had thinned to a mere throng and no longer a crush. He'd make good time back to Mill Hamlet. He'd apologize to Mellia for shutting her in later. Now that he had the Grist father's backing, she no longer needed to come here and admit her failure. Of course, the Grist father would know that she had failed since Alroth had come so late... Come to think of it, was it not strange that the Grist father hadn't mentioned Mellia? Asked after her task? Perhaps he didn't know that Alroth was the prisoner from the tower. That must be it. His precious god hadn't seen fit to tell him who was supposed to be freed.

He tucked the bee pin into his pocket—a brother would have no call to visit Mill Hamlet—and stole through Mill Gate and down the road toward their knot of houses.

Etienne met him halfway to Mill Hamlet. He clasped Etienne's arm, the other man's firm grip reassuring him that everything was all right. They turned toward the cluster of little cottages, the taller cruck peeking over their thatched roofs, and started down the road.

"I have news for everyone. Gather whoever's around."

Etienne nodded. "I've got them all ready to go, just say the word."

"Good, but we're not running. I'll explain." He jerked his chin at the cruck.

"How is it that you order me around now, little pup?" His broad grin beneath his mustache made it clear Etienne bore no real resentment toward Alroth's leadership.

Alroth shrugged. "You were tired of it, I suppose."

"So tired." His grin faded. "I'll bring them."

They parted ways in the wee square, Alroth into the cruck, and Etienne off to knock on cottage doors.

Ewes baaed, and Falkirk turned from their place standing at the hearth. They looked Alroth up and down. "Didn't lose any extremities, I see."

"Not this time."

"Why did they let you out?"

"They didn't. But let's save that story."

Del shoved Kai over the threshold into the cruck's hall, in the middle of some argument about... vegetables? Alroth sighed. Nothing would make those two get along. He smiled.

More folks wandered into the hall, Etienne bringing up the rear. He nodded to Alroth. Everyone who was coming had arrived.

"I've finally brought the news you've all been hoping for, I know. Since you've been waiting for so long, I won't delay. We have a place inside the walls. We'll be moving in, after the Necro Ritual, once the pilgrims and smallholders clear out of town."

The murmurs and muttering didn't sound relieved. Why in the name of Prosperitas not? Even Etienne had his brows drawn together.

Selena had planted herself by the fire. "You expect us to uproot ourselves, abandon our homes, for that festering pit? And with it already coming on winter?"

Festering pit? Yes, it was coming on winter; that was the entire reason for moving inside the walls!

"I can't go back inside." The young mother cradled her babe—their cheeks growing more round and pink by the day. "My father—" Her voice wavered, and she fell silent.

Falkirk laid a hand on her shoulder. "Don't worry. We'll take care of you." They shot Alroth an uneasy look.

They had discussed this. He and Falkirk had been planning this for so long, before they'd even come to New Bridge. Find a well-defended town and build a life somewhere safe. Hadn't they talked to Etienne about it? Del and Kai? Their plan when they chose New Bridge had always been to get walls between them and... everything. But looking around at their folks, the people they'd taken in and promised to protect and help, not everyone had understood.

"The goal has always been to move inside the walls."

The grumbles got louder.

Alroth raised his hand, palm out. "Do you not remember our storehouse burning down in the spring? Do you not remember last night when the soldiers came to burn our homes to the ground?"

"You sorted that out, Alroth," said a dour-faced man.

Sorted it out? He'd barely escaped with his life!

"Besides, we spread all the vittles put up for winter between the cottages this time, as well as the storehouse. One goes down, we'll still have the rest," A woman with a red nose called out, and those around her nodded.

Perhaps they would have enough food to live through the winter if a cottage burned down, but what of those inside? What if they couldn't get out? What if a true attack came and all of their houses were razed?

He'd have to tell them everything. Scaring them into compliance was low, but if nothing else worked, then so be it. "There have been rumblings of war, folks."

Falkirk's face paled. They hadn't discussed sharing this news with everyone. But what else was Alroth supposed to do to convince them?

He pressed on. "If me and mine are conscripted, where does that leave you? It will only be a matter of time until New Bridge is attacked, and you'll be stuck here, defenceless. You think they'll let you into town once war is declared? No."

"When that time comes, they'll turn us out of the walls, not take us in. Better we have our own place here." Vernis's face was set. Sudra had been spared during the Canal War. None of these folks knew how it was, as evidenced by their nods and agreement with Vernis.

"We've got everything we need right here." Selena's words were greeted with more sharp nods, and it was over. Decided.

What could Alroth say to that? If his threat of war hadn't swayed them, nothing he said would. When war came, they would all be killed, whether Alroth and his mercs were here or not. Five warriors could not defend a knot of cottages with no walls, no matter how good they were. These folks would have to find out the hard way. Once their precious homes were burned to the ground, they would be much more willing to move into the town they reviled.

And then, Father Glimar's word would stand. Alroth had made as sure of that as possible, and it would have to do. As long as he attended the Necro Ritual tomorrow, as long as he kept the handmaids alive, the Grist father would uphold their bargain.

Which meant that he and his mercs were attending the Necro Ritual tomorrow morning. They'd better get prepared.

13

Mellia

Mellia dressed and laced her boots. Alroth had told her to stay put, but he'd soon learn that his word was far from law. She'd slip into the comb, say goodbye to the handmaids, show them her ephemer. The ghostly pup yipped at her heels all the way across the room.

Mellia lifted the bar she'd slammed across the door when Alroth left. She rattled the latch, and it gave a little, but pushed back on her. Was something holding it down? Was there a trick to opening it? Her ephemer leaped through the door, barked on the other side, and leaped back through to chase between her ankles.

The puppy barked up at her and panted.

Mellia closed her eyes and felt through the door. She felt no one, just the empty hallway, the latch, stuck somehow. What was holding the door closed? The landing was bare... There! A wooden shim, lodged in the latch hole, jamming the door from the outside. But Alroth had opened it easily enough—

Alroth.

Mellia's nails dug into her palms as her fists tightened. Alroth had ordered her to stay in here, like the worst kind of high-handed source, but had he been content to treat her like a child or a dog? No. He'd barred her in like a hen in a coop. They had been bound for less than an hour, and he already thought he owned her, after she had freed him from prison, given him her body, *bound* herself to him freely.

Her heart pounded up her throat and nearly choked her. True, she hadn't thought the binding ritual would succeed, but after he'd taken so much care with her during their ritual, refused to treat her as the other sources had, part of her had foolishly hoped that he would keep treating her differently, that they could work together in life as well as in bed. But no. He shut her up here as though she went dormant when he wasn't present, like a plaything that required him to animate it, a tool on a shelf, waiting for his hand to wield.

But she wasn't an object. He was planning to come back, and soon. She wiggled the latch, but the scrap of wood was wedged in with all Alroth's considerable strength. It wasn't budging until he came to pull it out. But wait, she was bound now, a matron in her own right. She could syphon magic from Alroth whenever she wished, but he would feel it if she syphoned from him. He might not recognize the feeling, but he'd figure it out, realize that she was *syphoning without his permission* and come storming back to do who knows what to her. No, she wouldn't syphon unless she absolutely had to. If she could get out without alerting him, she'd have more time to... what?

She'd wanted to go back to the comb to say goodbye, to help with the final preparations for the Necrophoresis Ritual, and then to join Alroth, wherever he was determined to take her. But now... what would Alroth do if she retreated to the comb? Storm in and demand his mage be returned? Drag her away to serve him? Wrench her, as Lord New Bridge liked to do? She stroked her fingers over her ephemer's soft puppy fur, ruffled their ear. Alroth could carry her bodily, sure, but it would be much easier to carry a little puppy.

And of course, she would follow, spectral, silent, and unresisting. She shuddered.

Binding herself to Alroth had been a mistake, a necessary chance she had taken for his protection, but being a drone in the gutter would be better than being wrenched and trapped, ordered around day and night. *Night*. What if Alroth used their bond against her? Bed him or be wrenched out of her body? A man who would bar her in here despite her protests, who would leave her so soon after their bond had formed, would think nothing of threatening her, treating her just as the other sources had, no matter what he'd claimed.

Mellia brushed the tears from her face. Return to the comb, tell the brothers that her bond was unsanctioned, and let them break it. But what if they didn't? After all, would the bond have taken if Doloman hadn't looked on it favourably? They might sanction the bond after the fact or give Alroth some trial to complete to prove the Golden God's favour. And then she would have no recourse.

Who else had the power to help her? The handmaids were busy, Father Glimar was already being swayed by Alroth at this very moment...

Elenta. Elenta would help her. She knew what it was to be bound to an unforgiving source. Elenta would call for Father Glimar and, even if he deemed her a drone, still he would be merciful enough to tear their bond asunder if Mellia asked. And she would beg on her knees to undo this mistake.

Her ephemer licked her hand and whined. She closed her eyes, another three tears brimming over and running down her cheek. Sundering the bond would destroy her ephemer, this innocent little puppy nuzzling into her hand. No, not a puppy. It wasn't a real creature. Ephemers were a sign of the bond, nothing more. She should hate this little thing, as she hated the bond. But how could she when their fur was so soft? Their eyes so big and dark?

She set her ephemer on their feet and stalked to the window. Climbing onto the roof would get her out of here, but what would she do once she was up there? Breaking her bones in a fall from this height wouldn't help her. She'd have to remove that shim.

There was no poking it out, what other tools did she have? Her magic. What could that do? She couldn't move the door or break the shim. But perhaps… the landing had smelled musty. Perhaps, with a little water, she could rot the wood until it was soft enough to break using the latch. *Doloman's eye*, Alroth better not have used cedar.

She charged to the window and the pitcher of rosewater. She sloshed it in the rough earthenware. It would be enough. She took the pitcher to the door and tipped it carefully toward the slot where the latch bar poked through, the shim wedged above it, and poured rosewater over the wood.

The scent hit her, and tears sprang to her eyes. When she'd taken Alroth in her mouth, she'd been so filled with… affection. He'd tricked her into thinking he felt something too with his *sweetling* and foot rubs. Mellia slammed the pitcher back onto the washstand, the water sloshing wildly inside.

She smacked her palm to the door. Her magic made the wood absorbent as a sponge, the rosewater instantly saturating the wood. Sure enough, it swelled and softened, rot taking hold in moments. Mellia slammed her palm into the latch, hard enough to bruise, and the wood squished and disintegrated like ash from a cold hearth.

Freedom. Mellia straightened her clothes and opened the door. Her ephemer leaped around her heels, yapping out its joy at being free of the room—or was that Mellia's relief at being free? She shut the door, smoothed her mantle, and descended the stairs to the foyer. Etienne's landlady peered at her around the corner but didn't confront her as she made her escape.

A crowd still filled Hive Street from the midday prayers in the hive, but the road to the castle was clear, and Mellia took it briskly, her ephemer trotting and panting to keep up. She'd go into the inner ward as usual, go to Elenta's chambers, and wait for her there.

At the corner of Water and Castle Streets, she joined the throng of lordlings and smallholders climbing the ramp to the drawbridge. The Necrophoresis Ritual was tomorrow, and Father Glimar had held a special mass in Queen Arista's honour. No one looked twice at her in the outer ward, and the crowd dispersed, heading mostly for the great hall, but Mellia kept on. She had every right to enter the inner ward.

She drew herself up and approached the inner drawbridge.

"Halt!" The guard at the other side of the lowered drawbridge glowered at her. Not someone she knew. "You must be lost, miss."

"I'm a Grist sister, and I have business with Lady Elenta." She gestured to her chest, but when she looked down, her mantle was smooth and unadorned. Her head seemed to float above her body. Her silver bee pin, the one that marked her as a Grist sister, with the right to come and go from the inner ward, was not there. She'd pinned it to Alroth's chest this morning in the prison tower, and he'd never returned it. No doubt it was helping him gain access to Father Glimar while she had been caught here without it.

"A Grist sister, you say? Any proof of that?"

"I seem to have misplaced—"

Her ephemer growled and barrelled across the drawbridge toward the guard, baring their tiny sharp teeth, small paws pattering on the thick wood. Mellia took two steps after them before the guard levelled his spear at her, and she came up short.

"Never heard of a bound sister before. Get going before I take you in for impersonating the Grist." The glint in his eye confirmed that he was more than willing to do it.

Her ephemer barked around his feet, and he kicked out at the pup, but of course, his foot went right through.

"Come back pup!" Mellia should probably give the little thing a name—*no*. She would break their bond, and the ephemer would dissolve as though it had never been. It didn't need a name since it would be gone before the day was out.

Her little ephemer trotted back to her, tongue lolling, clearly expecting praise for their intimidating performance with the guard. She scooped the wriggling body into her arms and turned. She could still go back to the comb, beg the brothers to help her, ask Dayma to call for Father Glimar, despite how terribly busy she would be preparing for the Necrophoresis Ritual.

"Hold it." A guard now stood in front of her as well, and this one was familiar. "You're the sister who was in here earlier... the one who broke out Ainsley's prisoner."

Orbitus take her for a fool. She stepped back, her boots echoing on the wooden drawbridge. She couldn't keep retreating onto the other guard's spear, but neither could she let this one get his hands on her. They'd tricked him, probably gotten him in deep trouble once it was discovered that Alroth was missing. He'd toss her in prison—or worse.

The pit yawned on either side of the drawbridge, wooden spikes hammered firmly into the bottom. Why had she come here? Back to the place she'd just *broken a prisoner out of*? Even with her bee pin, had she thought she would miraculously escape the blame for what she'd done? Now she would die, spitted on a castle guard's spear or a painfully dull pit spike—

"What exactly is going on here?" Lady Elenta's voice was cold.

Thank Hiorach! Mellia let out a deep breath. She turned.

Elenta stood at the entrance to the inner ward, looking down her nose at all of them. Her eyes widened when she saw the ephemer squirming in Mellia's arms—unmistakably hers. "Mellia and I have much to discuss." She beckoned, and Mellia sidestepped the spear still levelled at her and ambled after Elenta over the stone threshold into the inner ward.

Elenta didn't say another word until they'd crossed the ward, climbed the steps to her chambers, and shut themselves in, alone. "What did you do?"

Mellia let her ephemer go. The pup barked at Elenta's hummingbird and chased it across the chambers and through the wall.

"Whose is it?" Her voice was softer but still carried an edge.

Mellia was betrothed to Lord Ainsley, and Elenta was so excited for her. Should she come clean and tell her that she was bound to a mercenary instead of the rich lord they'd always dreamed of as children? She certainly couldn't tell Elenta it was the heretic prince. She only wanted the bond broken, not Alroth strung up. "Not Lord Ainsley's." True, but vague. "That's why I need to break the bond."

Elenta watched the pup hurtle back into the room, this time chased by her hummingbird.

"Since this obviously wasn't Doloman's will," she added. Regular folks were not supposed to question their bonds. Breaking one, or wanting it broken, simply was not done. Except when it was.

"I should think not." Elenta beckoned one of her ladies from the antechamber and whispered something in her ear. Fetching Father Glimar to break her bond.

"Thank you for helping me, Elenta. It was a mistake." A mistake that had proved that she was capable of bonding. Maybe she could go home to her father after all, once this bond was broken, tell him the good news. Maybe he would have mercy on her, let her have a hand in choosing her next suitor.

Elenta watched Mellia as if she'd never seen her before, two lines between her eyebrows. "I never took you for a putrid Risore."

Mellia recoiled. Not at Elenta's tone, which was more bemused than belligerent. But when had Elenta started using language like that? It sounded less like her friend and more like... Lord New Bridge. Her *husband* spoke to Elenta that way. Sympathy and offence twined in Mellia's breast. Being insulted and abused by her husband didn't give Elenta licence to speak to her that way. But it seemed that it had brought such words into her lexicon.

And what could Mellia do? She needed Elenta's help. She'd wandered into this situation naively and thoughtlessly. Stalking out would get her grabbed by guards. Or seen by Lord Ainsley. She stayed put and kept her mouth shut.

"If you're lucky, Lord Ainsley won't tell your father what you've done, and you can still go home and find a suitor." Of course Elenta was worried about how this would affect Mellia's chances of marrying well.

"It's proof that I can bond, at least." Mellia attempted a smile, and Elenta didn't return it.

Maybe this proof was a mercy. A spark of hope ignited in her. Once she got the bond broken, she would have proof that she could bond. She was too late to be chosen as the new handmaid, but Alroth had gone to Father Glimar as agreed. Would he take pity on her and refrain from expelling her once the bond was broken?

"Apparently, you find ruining your prospects humorous." Elenta scowled at her hands. "I'm just worried about you, Milly. Aren't you worried? Why did you lead a source on? It's not like you." She shook her head.

Lead a source on? Did she think that Mellia had brought this on herself?

"Lord Ainsley might still be willing to look past this." Elenta looked past Mellia and pasted on a smile as a light tread entered. Father Glimar must be here.

Mellia pasted on her most demure look and turned. Not Father Glimar. Lord Ainsley.

Silence hung between them. She had to say something. But why was he even here? Father Glimar could still arrive at any moment. Mellia opened her mouth, but her ephemer burst through the wall and jumped onto her lap. Lord Ainsley looked from her to her ephemer, his jaw flexing.

Mellia's stomach clenched, and she fought to keep the sick look from her face. Would he yell? Hit her?

"Sister Mellia has made a foolish mistake, my lord." Elenta cut through the thunderous tension. "She needs to go to the Grist Father to have it... rectified."

Mellia's ephemer squirmed in her lap. *Rectified.* Elenta hadn't called Father Glimar. She'd called Lord Ainsley. As her betrothed, he was the closest thing to a warder she had—her father was far away in Falvair, and her older brother was long since departed for Orbitus's halls.

Lord Ainsley's mouth twisted into a sneer. "You think that I would parade through town with this—" He cut himself off. Perhaps his piety prevented him from expressing himself fully. "And you believe that I would still take this wrench-a-day she-wolf?" He eyed her doggy ephemer. The slur was apt.

Mellia kept her face firmly frozen. Laughter would not come off well in this moment.He cut himself off. Not to mention that he would no doubt make the expression *wrench-a-day* quite literal if they were bound. A sobering thought if ever there was one.

Mellia could expect to be wrenched *every day* by Lord Ainsley. And he thought she cared whether *he* would take *her* after this. She had no intention of being bound to Lord Ainsley, which was why she'd asked Elenta to call *Father Glimar*. She glared at Elenta, who glared right back, clearly expecting Mellia to prostrate herself, beg for his leniency.

"My lord, I'm sitting right here. And yes, if you want my father's land and title, you will help me break this bond."

Lord Ainsley snapped his fingers and turned on his heel. He expected her to follow? Like a dog. If he was taking her safely out of the castle, past the guards, to Father Glimar, did it matter how he did it? Once she made it to the Grist father, she would convince him to help sway her father, after the bond was broken.

She followed. Mellia had *succeeded* in Doloman's task. It had been late—*too late*—but what did that really matter? Doloman's task had been near-impossible, and she had accomplished it. Father Glimar would already have selected the new handmaid, but surely Mellia's success would be enough to forestall being deemed a drone? Surely Doloman could forgive a little tardiness?

Doloman's face was reflected in Lord Ainsley's profile as he led her across the inner ward. Forgiving was not the trait most associated with Doloman. She trotted across the drawbridge at Lord Ainsley's side, into the outer ward, and turned into the great hall's porch. But he was taking her to Father Glimar. Wasn't he? He had said that he didn't want to parade her through town. Perhaps he would bring Father Glimar to her here. She hesitated on the threshold. Unless he wasn't going to.

Lord Ainsley realized she wasn't following and stalked back to grasp her upper arm and drag her into the entryway. He shoved her stumbling before him into the chapel and pressed her to her knees.

He didn't deign to kneel. What could he possibly be required to pay penance for?

"You think I don't know what you did this morning? Right here under my nose?" His hiss would stay contained to the two of them. She and Alroth had knelt here together while Lord Ainsley berated the guards outside. "And now you come back to shove that *thing* in my face?"

Her ephemer snapped at his pointing finger, and he recoiled as though the furball's sharp little puppy teeth could touch him. Lord Ainsley was right. That left a bad taste in Mellia's mouth. But he was right. Coming to the castle thinking that anyone here would take pity on her had been a mistake.

"You will stay here and ask the Golden God's forgiveness. After Doloris prayer, you will spend the next two days contemplating your wickedness in a tower room. After the solstice, I will return. If you are sufficiently repentant, I will consider granting you a bond with me."

Doloris prayer wasn't until dusk. A laugh bubbled up in Mellia's chest. She shoved it down. What would Lord Ainsley do if she laughed at him? Though kneeling on the hard floor for half a day was laughable. He thought she would endure it for the *prize* of being bound to him? The *prize* of being wrenched every day? Carted back to Falvair, shut up as a lady, bearing his spawn... The giggles burst out of her, and she clutched her belly, tears filling her eyes, no breath left for words.

"I see." Lord Ainsley's words were cold as the wind that rattled the stained glass before her. "I may need to bind you to take Falvair, but there's no requirement to coddle you as I have been. It seems you have rejected my kindness. So be it, vain Risore."

Mellia caught her breath and dashed the tears from her eyes as Lord Ainsley gripped her arm once more. Kindness and coddling. Breaking her bond with Alroth meant this man would latch on to her, determined as he was to gain Falvair for himself. The one source would have her barred in a tower room, the other in a garret. What difference, really, between them?

Lord Ainsley gripped her arm painfully, but Mellia gained her feet. She planted her fists on her hips. Her ephemer yapped at Lord Ainsley's ankles while Mellia glared up at him. What would he do in the face of her open defiance? His fingers flexed on her arm, hard enough to bruise. His head whipped to the stained glass over the trickling fountain. Doloman looked coldly back at them. Lord Ainsley's jaw flexed, and his chest heaved once, twice, three times. His lips moved soundlessly. Praying for patience?

He looked down on her. "Though I'm tempted to leave your discipline to whatever guttersnipe you've bound yourself to, your father has entrusted you to me. If you refuse to attend to your goodness in Doloman's eyes, then I must."

His long fingers wrapped the back of her neck, digging into her skull. He shoved her around and marched her out of the chapel, through the serving room, past the guards in the window embrasure, into the prison tower. He opened the door and shoved her over the edge into the pit where she'd found Alroth. She landed hard on her knee and hip, pain splintering up her leg.

The thunk of a heavy body landing behind her made Mellia turn and scramble back. Why would he come down here with her? Would he try to beat *goodness* into her? He bent and pulled up a ring hidden among the grime and heaved open a trap door. The blackness inside yawned. No windows graced the space below. The close smell of old rot hit Mellia, and she scrambled away from Lord Ainsley's determined approach. There was nowhere to go. He wrenched her arm as he tossed her into the darkness. Mellia landed on her hands and knees in the muck, and the trap door thumped closed. The scrape of a latched sealed her in.

Mellia couldn't see her hand in front of her face, even waving it back and forth. But it was already caked with slime. Her eyes tried to adjust to the darkness, but no light filtered through cracks above; they were all mortared over with grime. She couldn't see the trapdoor above her, let alone reach it. Her magic wouldn't budge the latch. She'd have to be freed from outside. But who would want to free her?

Father Glimar would probably think she had run from him rather than face him and her expulsion as a drone. He would not come looking for her here. Even if Lady Elenta discovered her whereabouts, by rumour if not a malicious comment from her betrothed, what could she do? She had her own wellbeing to think of, and her children. The handmaids would hardly notice one of their attendants disappearing, even on a normal day, let alone with the Necrophoresis Ritual in full swing.

Alroth. Alroth would find her gone from the attic room where he had locked her away. But even he would believe that she had run from him—which was perfectly correct. Would he search for her? It didn't matter. Even if he did, even if he knew where she was, how would he get her out of here? He'd only succeed in getting himself caught along with her.

Was it wrong that a small part of her still wanted him to come? To try? To fight for his bond mate?

Her ephemer barked, and its glowing form ran through the wall, shining a silvery light on the dirt down here, the... bones. Mellia closed her eyes. Her pup climbed over her, barked in her ear, making it ring, and dashed away. As she opened her eyes, they tore out through the wall. Water dripped. They didn't pop back in. Even they had deserted her.

By the time Lord Ainsley released her, after solstice, she'd be weak from hunger and thirst. He'd be able to do anything he wanted to her. Sure, he needed her alive, but no more than that.

Alroth might come for her. Alroth *would* come for her. She would have one last solstice with her sisters, the humming songs, the smell of the beeswax candles, the little treats that Morath was no doubt making right at this moment in the hot kitchen. Even Father Glimar's droning sermon. She would be there for that.

Mellia curled up on her good side on the cold stone floor and tried to ignore the throb in her hip. If it was wrong that part of her wanted Alroth to mount a rescue, it was certainly wrong that part of her wanted him to stay away, stay safe, and let her languish rather than get himself killed for her sake? Yes, that part was definitely wrong. Definitely wrong to fear for the safety of the man who had locked her in a room. A cozy, warm, quiet room, filled with the traces of their binding ritual, their lovemaking. Somewhere safe.

Mellia shivered.

14

Alroth

A few folks remained scattered around the cruck's hall, and Alroth retreated to the bedroom, where he could pace in peace. He scrubbed a hand over his stubbled face. He'd have to shave if he didn't want his whiskers to encroach on his chin and cheeks again. How had he neglected to get agreement from the very people he was trying to protect? How had he spent so long working for something that they just... didn't want? They'd joined on so gradually, built this single old cruck house into a little hamlet over the course of months, and he'd never made it clear that the ultimate goal was not to build a permanent settlement here. These folks had made a home in Mill Hamlet, and they didn't want to leave. It wasn't a stepping stone for them; in fact, many had left New Bridge of their own volition and not only had no interest in returning but were actively against doing so.

Falkirk strode past and perched on the edge of a tidily made bed. "That didn't go quite as planned."

Alroth turned from the horn window. *Not quite as planned.* Yes, that was one way of putting it.

"How did you get out of prison?"

Falkirk wasn't going to let that go, were they?

Etienne chose that moment to appear in the low doorway. "I got him out."

True enough. Obviously not the whole truth, but any discussion of his binding would only distract from the matter at hand. Mellia could wait, safe in Etienne's room. He needed to fill them all in on the plan for the Necro Ritual tomorrow.

"Get Del and Kai. We have a job, tomorrow morning."

Once the five of them were settled around the sleeping quarters. Alroth told them about Mellia freeing him, Etienne jumping in with details every other sentence.

"I wanted a mage for a job, and she agreed. We did the ritual, and now we're bound."

Etienne paled. "You did the ritual?"

"Close enough that it took." Alroth shrugged.

"She ran from you after?" Falkirk didn't quite succeed in hiding the accusation in their tone.

What did they take him for? "I left her."

"You left her right after the bond took?" Etienne twisted his moustache.

"I had to sort things out with the Grist father. I shut her in your room, but she—"

"You shut her in?" Now Kai was glaring at him too.

"Look, all of you. She enjoyed the ritual! She agreed to it, and it was enjoyable, for both of us. I shut her in the room while I went to speak to the Grist father. She's perfectly safe there. Now, don't you all want to know what I was speaking with the Grist father about? This is not a discussion about the binding ritual between the sister and me! We have a job tomorrow morning, and you all need to know what it is. So shut your traps and listen."

"Yes, Wolf. Right away, Wolf." Del faked a deep bow.

"Better." His growl was a testament to his moniker. Alroth outlined the job for them: save the handmaids from being murdered during the Necro Ritual. Get them back to the hive safe, and they would be entitled to a place inside the walls. No one commented that the inhabitants of their hamlet didn't seem to want that place. They all knew what war looked like, especially for those near a walled town. Once the fighting broke out, their folk would change their minds, and they needed to secure their place now before New Bridge was beset by farmers fleeing the countryside.

Particularly if the five of them were conscripted. It wouldn't be the first time, and there was no refusing such a summons. Alroth sat on the edge of his bed and leaned his elbows on his knees. They were talking now about strategy, how to keep the handmaids safe while they performed the ritual. The top of a waterfall was an unusual place to defend.

"So we flee to the opposite bank. What all is over there?" Del looked to Falkirk.

They shrugged. "Pretty much the same as over here. Forest, cliff. No way down back to the road that I know of."

"So then we won't face a threat from there. If there's only one path to the clifftop, why not just guard that path?"

"Unless they plant themselves in advance," said Etienne.

"We could plant ourselves in advance." Falkirk sketched a quick diagram of the waterfall with an end of charcoal.

"And stay out all night at the top of the waterfall, freezing our balls off? No thanks." Etienne stretched out on his seldom-used bed in the corner.

"We're talking about six innocent handmaids here. I think a night sleeping rough is worthwhile." Kai lounged against the wall, but his gaze was fixed to Falkirk's deft strokes with the charcoal.

Del paced between the beds. "Let's find the murderers and get rid of them now. Why wait until they attack?"

"And how would we do that?" Kai finally looked up from the sketch to glare at Del.

"Dunno, hunt them down somehow."

"Very strategic and efficient plan, *hunt them down somehow*. It's a wonder I didn't think of that myself."

Del tromped over Falkirk's charcoal to get in Kai's face. "I forgot your spineless plan of hiding in the woods and freezing to death."

"Enough." Alroth studied the smudged sketch on the floor. However they came to clash with the murderers, there were only five of them. Whoever would be sent to kill the handmaids would know that there were at least Grist guards present, probably a score. Which meant they would come full force, with as many as they could muster. And with the amount of silver the gentleman had been offering, they could muster a whole pile of mercs, castle guard rejects with a drive to kill something. They needed an advantage. They needed Mellia.

"If we set up a guard across the path leading up to the waterfall, we could ambush anyone trying to get up to the Necro Ritual." Falkirk marked the spot on their sketch.

"And leave the handmaids undefended up above?" Etienne rolled onto his side in a token effort to see what Falkirk was doing, but there was no way the sketch was visible from all the way over there.

"The Grist Guard can take care of them." Falkirk drew a bee at the top of the waterfall.

"If that were true, the Grist father wouldn't have bound me to a promise to aid them." They needed Mellia to tip the scales. But how to convince a timid sister to fight? If she didn't want to use magic, he couldn't force her.

"The Grist father can hire some more mercs then, can't he?" Del turned to stalk back across the sketch.

Kai grabbed his arm before he could wreck it again. "No way to know that they'd be loyal. Would *you* be willing to risk the handmaids' lives on that gamble?"

"I'd rather gamble with their lives than with mine." Del glared at Kai, their faces a handspan apart.

A sharp bark broke the silence, the ewes in the hall bleating, their dancing hooves thumping on the packed earth. Del shook Kai's hand off and threw himself onto his bed. The bark pierced the quiet again, and Alroth's ears rang. If he didn't know better, he'd think it was—

A pale shining head poked through the wood of the door, followed by a wriggling body. Its little paws tramped across Falkirk's sketch, not marring it in the least, and it sat demurely between Alroth's feet, tongue lolling.

Alroth reached down to stroke it, but his hand, of course, went right through. "What?"

The ephemer's tail wagged against the floor, and its entire rear end wiggled back and forth.

"That's an ephemer." Falkirk's voice was reverent. "You weren't lying. Your bond is blessed by Doloman."

"Blessed or cursed, what does it matter?" Etienne turned to face the wall. What was with him?

The ephemer took a few steps toward the door, circled, and came back. Its shining eyes looked right at Alroth, and it barked.

Del groaned. "Your matron better be easier on the ears than that thing."

"It's trying to take you somewhere, Wolf." Kai was back to lounging against the wall in the corner.

"Probably your *matron*. Better hop to her summons." Etienne spoke to the wall. Was he jealous?

Whatever. There was no time for Drake's tantrum. "Del, Kai, Falkirk, stay here and plan tomorrow morning, both with and without a mage supporting us."

Etienne rolled off the bed onto his feet. "And I'll come with you."

"With me? Why?" Why would Etienne want to come with him when he'd shown nothing but disdain for the idea of Alroth and his matron?

"Filomena won't let you in without me." Right. Of course.

"Fine." Alroth stepped over Falkirk's sketch and made for the door, the ephemer yipping at his heels. The puppy barked and circled as Alroth crossed to his back room and opened his war chest. There were his two swords, Volnus gleaming, Ictus's hilt dull and cracked. He swallowed and tied Volnus to his belt. He'd be vulnerable without a sword for his off-hand. He bent to the lockbox, used his two keys to open it, the hinge creaking. This coin was supposed to be for building their lives inside the walls of New Bridge. Once they moved in, they would have to pay whatever taxes the lord levied, a sum that would only rise once war was declared. Which meant they needed this coin. But what good would it do if Alroth was killed for want of a sword?

Etienne filled the doorway. "What happened to Ictus?"

Alroth handed over the sheath, peeling hilt and all. "A mage happened."

Etienne harrumphed. "I'd say her source owes you a new sword."

"It's Hasburgen."

"Hasburgen? That Fallo-blessed hack? How'd he get a hold of a mage?"

"Doesn't much matter. His band has three."

Etienne's knuckles whitened on the ruined scabbard.

Alroth counted out the coin he'd need for a passable weapon, locked the box again, and took Ictus back from Etienne. He tied it to his belt. The balance of the two swords centred him. He'd grab his cesti from the garret when he went back for Mellia. He would not be caught unarmed. Whether or not a short sword was available that met his standards, he could defend himself.

Etienne followed him into the hall and out of the cruck after the ephemer, who leaped ahead of them and dashed up the path toward New Bridge. The sun was still a fist and a few fingers above the horizon. There was still time to prepare themselves, get Mellia, and have her back to Mill Hamlet before nightfall, when the gate closed.

The pup raced off the road, toward the castle. Where in Doloman's name were they going? They disappeared through the castle wall. Not leading them to Mellia, then.

Alroth and Etienne passed through the gate undisturbed. At least he had the Grist father's protection for now. First, get a sword. Next, get his mage.

Iram Square was bustling but far less packed than it had been at midday. Carts and stalls filled the square with barely room to thread between them. Surely one would have a sharp blade with decent balance available for coin enough. Volnus and Ictus had been commissions, of course. Back when they'd been hired mercs, earning coin hadn't been a problem. There was always some lord who wanted a battle fought and was willing to drain his coffers doing it, during the war. A fellow merc, Rimaud, had recommended a swordsmith, expensive, but worth every ounce of silver.

No such swordsmith worked in New Bridge. Why would they? The guards were the only armed men in town, normally, and they used old spears made at the farrier's forge like as not. But maybe one of these travelling merchants had taken a blade as payment and was looking to offload it. With just a muttered word to Etienne, the two split up to search the stalls, asked around, and by the time the hive bells rang for Locus prayer, they'd found a serviceable blade that only cost him two thirds of the silver in his pocket. It would be even better with a sharpen, but so be it. He tied it over Ictus on his hip, and the weight pulled him off-centre. He'd put Ictus away when they returned home. *Home.* When they returned to the cruck, obviously.

Etienne joined Alroth as he trudged down the steps, and the ground seemed to recede before his boots as he skirted the trickling fountain. Mellia would be angry with him. He would have to make her see reason. She couldn't be angry once he told her that they were going to save the handmaids' lives tomorrow. He would care for her, as he'd promised, and even care for those she cared for—as a prospective handmaid, she would be acquainted with the current ones. Etienne shouldered by him into the boarding house. Filomena must have been watching for them through a crack in the shutters.

"If you're looking for that *sister*, she's gone. Left just after you, *Brother.*" She sneered the words. If she hadn't known Etienne was lying before, she would have realized when the "sister" appeared trailing an ephemer. "With a fresh little ephemer, no less. I *told* you, Etienne. I don't rent rooms for that sort of putrid—"

"Did she say where she was going?" Alroth's heart pounded. Mellia was gone. Not safe in Etienne's room at all.

Filomena glared at him, but she spoke to Etienne. "I'll not help you find a mage that doesn't want to be found."

She'd mentioned the ephemer, so she was likely telling the truth, but Alroth had to see for himself. He headed for the stairs, Filomena's shrill protest and Etienne's reasonable tone floating after him. Filomena must have seen someone else. He'd barred Mellia in. She couldn't have shifted that shim herself without... magic. He took the stairs two at a time and froze on the landing, panting.

The wooden shim he'd used to block the latch was gone. Crumbs of rotten wood dusted the lever slot and the floorboards outside the closed door to Etienne's room.

Alroth wrenched the door open. A fly startled into the air from the basin by the window, still filled with their mead and rosewater mixture. Nothing else moved. No glimmer of an excitable ephemer, no telltale barking. No furious five-foot-nothing sister to rage at him.

Alroth slunk to the table under the window and hefted his cesti, one and then the other. He slipped his hands into them and wrapped the leather straps securely. A simmering rage built in his gut, heat creeping up from his belly. Was it at Mellia for leaving when he had told her to stay? Was it at himself for leaving her alone? Was she in trouble? He couldn't know until he found her. He banked the fire—Etienne would never forgive him if his room burned down—and strode from the apartment.

When he reached the foyer, Filomena and Etienne's row was punctuated by ear-piercing yips and yaps. Alroth crouched and spoke right to the pup, who quieted and cocked their head. "Take us to Mellia."

With one last shrill bark, the ephemer trotted through the door. They led Alroth, Etienne at his heels, Water Street to...the castle. Mellia had gone to the castle, or been taken there? Outside the walls, the ephemer had disappeared into the castle...into the prison tower.

Why were they keeping a sister in the prison tower? Had they caught her and punished her for setting him free? Or was it the bond? It was unsanctioned. Was someone punishing her for it?

Etienne stood abreast of him, brow furrowed. "I might have been able to get you into the castle, but not anymore, my friend. Not after this morning. I might even be thrown in gaol myself. It's not as though the guards didn't recognize me as the one sneaking you out of there."

Getting into the castle would be challenging, getting into the prison tower would be nigh-impossible, Someone might recognize them if they lingered here gawking too long.

Could Alroth appeal to the Grist Father again to get the sister out? Mellia had said she was to be deemed a drone, expelled from the hive, and why would the Grist father free someone like that? Besides, he and Mellia had an unsanctioned bond. If the Grist learned of it, they were likely to sunder it. He couldn't appeal to the Grist on her behalf.

The two turned as one and trudged up Castle Street to Iram Square and sat on the edge of the fountain. The castle's high turrets spiked over the intervening rooftops. Mellia was in the dank prison tower. She'd gotten him out of there using her wits and Etienne's. Etienne would not be trusted again, and Alroth's wits... if he'd thought to have to rely on them, he'd have honed them more. Could he take out the guards if he found himself in the embrasure outside the prison tower? Easily. He might even be able to get in there, with some luck. But getting out of the castle through the ward unnoticed... They'd be shot through, decapitated, and have their skin scalded off before they made it through the southern barbican. Brute force wouldn't serve him, not this time.

"Any ideas?" said Etienne. He had bought himself a roasted pinecone at one of the stalls, and he pulled off a scale and cracked it open to tip the pinenut into his mouth.

"Is there a more heavily guarded place in all New Bridge?"

"Nope." He tossed the empty scale into the fountain and cracked off another.

"So is there any way we're getting in there?"

"Nope." He offered a scale to Alroth, who waved him away.

They couldn't get in without getting killed. And she couldn't get out; otherwise, she wouldn't still be trapped. Etienne tossed a scale over his shoulder. It fell into the top of the fountain and rode the stream of water into the lower basin, bobbing on the surface. Could Alroth send her the strength she would need to break out of the prison tower somehow? How exactly did their bond work? Without Mellia here to explain it to him, Alroth wouldn't figure it out on his own.

He had only gotten out of the tower through trickery, because of Impietan cunning. He needed cunning of his own.

"I wonder if Lord Ainsley discovered your bond."

"Ainsley?" The name wasn't familiar, but then Alroth didn't keep up with all the various pompous lordlings.

"I heard a rumour they're betrothed."

Betrothed to a lord? Why in Impietas's name had Mellia bound herself to *him* when she could have a lord? Why would a lord be interested in binding a sister anyway? Perhaps she had unusually strong magic? It didn't matter why. Mellia *had* chosen to bind herself to Alroth over this Ainsley. But now the lord had taken her. If Alroth wanted her back, he'd have to fight for her.

"Can you get me an audience with Ainsley?"

"You don't want to do that."

"Oh no?"

"He's as liable to run you through as hear you out, considering who you're bound to."

"He can try." Ainsley killing him and binding Mellia to himself... Alroth's hand went to his sword hilt. But Ainsley wouldn't kill him. No puffed-up lordling could hold his own in a real fight. And Alroth would bring him a real fight.

Etienne trotted at his heels as he strode through the streets, to the castle, up the drawbridge. A guard confronted him at the top, but he brandished his bee pin and growled, and the guard let him pass. The next one wasn't so easily intimidated. He didn't dare draw iron here in the barbican, with at least four nocked arrows staring him down.

"I want to see Lord Ainsley," he gritted out.

Etienne had disappeared from his side, probably for the best. If this bit him on the ass, Etienne would take word back to Mill Hamlet. Shockingly, two guards marched him into the outer ward, and up the steps into the southern tower.

Lord Ainsley looked up from his meal. He sat on a plush window seat.

Him? The Ignis-cursed lording who'd forced him to agree to murder *handmaids* lest he raze Mill Hamlet. No wonder Mellia had chosen Alroth over this Impietas-spawn.

"Come back to save your village from the flames?" Ainsley wiped his hands and his belt-knife on a cloth. "Or have you come for my betrothed?"

Alroth gritted his teeth.

"I'm so very tempted to let you have the Risore." A cruel smile twisted his face. The fucker was talking about *his* matron like that. Right to his face.

"No need to *let* me do anything. We fight, I cut you down. She's mine."

"And why should I fight you? I could order you to dance from the walls with a snap of my fingers, mercenary. No more you, no more bond."

"I think your Grist father might take issue with that. He knows about your little plan." What would he think of that?

Ainsley's eyebrows rose. "And you think he'll give one ounce of mammoth shit about me killing you because of it?" He laughed. The fucker *laughed*.

Alroth faltered. Ainsley wasn't worried about Alroth revealing his plot. What protection could he scrape together? What would make this stuck-up, power-hungry lordling fight a lowly mercenary like him? "That wouldn't get you one handspan closer to binding my *mate.* You think she despises you now?" Surely she did, using Alroth as she had to avoid him. "Imagine what she'll be like when she finds out you ordered me strung up."

Ainsley shook his head. "Considering she came to me looking to break your newly forged bond, I think she might thank me."

He was lying. Mellia had no reason to break their bond. He'd sworn to protect her. A man like Ainsley couldn't resist the allure of power. "Let her watch as you beat me in a duel. I'm a creaky old warrior with a score of old injuries and a rusted old sword." He patted Ictus.

"So why are you so keen to fight me, then?" Ainsley sighed. He was tiring of Alroth, which would not end well for him.

The wind rattled the shutters and a knot popped in the fireplace. Hiorach help him. This wouldn't work.

The door banged open, and the Grist father swept in. "I understand there is a dispute over a bond."

Etienne peeked in around the doorframe. He'd summoned the Doloman-blessed Grist father like a dog. And he'd come.

Ainsley slid to his knees on the wool rug. "The bond is unsanctioned by Doloman, Father."

The Grist father clasped his hands behind his back and looked down on the kneeling lordling. Did he know this was the man who wanted his handmaids dead? Should Alroth kneel, too?

"Who forms bonds, my child?" The father always spoke so mildly.

"The Golden God, of course, but the Grist—"

"Your error can be forgiven. Doloman forges every bond, as a gift to those He chooses."

"But she was promised to *me.*" Ainsley's kiss-ass voice was even more unpleasant than his usual sneer.

"I see. The duel will take place as soon as possible. See that the lady is brought to the lists to witness Doloman's decree." The Grist father turned to Alroth at last. He offered his hand with its glittering gold rings. Behind his back, Etienne mimed kissing the rings.

The Grist father's hard stare beat into him as Alroth went to one knee and pressed his lips to the cold metal, forged with a bee adornment, of course. A duel would be satisfying, but perhaps there was an even easier way.

"Father, this is the lord who hired me." He kept his voice low, for the Grist father alone.

The father's lips thinned. "Thank you, my child. Leave us." He shot the worm Ainsley a glare, but he spoke to Alroth. "I'm sure you have much to prepare for the duel."

He was dismissed. So the Grist father wasn't going to clap Ainsley in irons for treason, so what? Shocking that he would shield a lordling from the consequences of his own actions.

Alroth didn't look back at Ainsley as he followed Etienne out and fell into step with him. He had probably just saved Alroth's life. Again.

Alroth elbowed his friend and gave him the nod. Drake held up seven fingers and raised his eyebrows. Of course the Salus-spawn was still keeping count. Thankfully, he wouldn't need any help winning the duel later today. He'd crush Ainsley with nothing but brute force.

He had, after all, promised to keep Mellia safe. When she'd left Drake's room without his permission, she had made it impossible for him to protect her, but he would get her back, and when he did, she wouldn't run off again. She would stay safely by his side, where she belonged.

15

Mellia

They were taking her to Father Glimar. Finally. She might have slime in her hair, Doloman knows what on her dress, and be trailing an impudent, accidental ephemer, but she was finally going to be free of this Hiorach-cursed bond. She marched across the empty outer ward—strangely empty—and onto the barbican.

Shouts and catcalls drifted over the southern wall. What was going on? It didn't concern her, whatever it was.

The guard flanked her on the drawbridge, where the view over the palisade and outbuildings to the lists was unobstructed. A crowd surrounded the lists, at the far end of the palisade. The throng filled the space around the outbuildings and spilled out the gap in the palisade into the street in front of the castle. They could skirt around, but no, her guards shouldered folk aside, leading Mellia through the gawking crowd, into the palisade. Was Father Glimar in there somewhere?

What was taking place in the lists that had gathered such a multitude? She craned her neck, but most everyone towered over her, and all it did was hurt her spine. It couldn't have to do with Alroth, could it? Please let it not be Alroth's execution. He was a high-handed brute, but he didn't deserve to die. Once their bond was broken, he could go on his way and build a pile of gold bigger than Locuples's fabled sky-brushing mound. It was no matter to her.

Mellia glared at a succession of folks' broad backs until her guards pushed closer to the lists and broke through to the dais. There, a steady gaze bored into her. Father Glimar muttered something to the guard at his side, and in a moment, Mellia was hoisted up into the stands, the guards' hands pinching under her arms. She gained her balance with a strong hand on her shoulder. Father Glimar. Finally, she could tell him all that had happened, convince him that she'd done all she could. Convince him that she should be a handmaid. He towed her to a wide seat and gestured her toward it.

She curtsied. "Father, I hate to disturb you during this..." What was it? A crowd filled the lists, seemingly divided into two knots of people. ". . . event. I understand that Alroth came to you earlier, as required, and I believe that Doloman's will is clear."

Father Glimar turned to her. "Do you, child?"

"Yes. I succeeded in my task. I understand it was too late to become a handmaid, but..."

Lord New Bridge glared at her from Father Glimar's other side. The lists were cleared but for two men. Lord Ainsley to her left, dressed head to toe in plate, the helm tucked under his arm sporting a giant short-faced bear crest. No dents or scratches were apparent in his armour, at least from this distance. Had he ever used it before?

"I don't believe a bound mage can become a handmaid, Mellia." Not Sister. Just Mellia.

Across from Lord Ainsley stood Alroth. His helm was already on his head—unadorned, dented and scratched—but it couldn't be anyone else. His riveted leather gloves covered his hands, and no less than three swords sat low on his hips. His houppelande was gone, replaced by a faded and patched coat. Was it plain fabric? He would get skewered by Lord Ainsley.

Father Glimar looked on impassively. Now was her chance to sway him. Get him to break their bond and end this foolishness. She settled on the seat at his side.

"I've come to ask you to break our bond. This isn't necessary." She gestured vaguely to the lists.

Father Glimar turned slowly, his hard gaze taking in Mellia's soiled mantle, her no-doubt grimy veil. "Of course it is, my child. Did you think there would be no consequences for your unsanctioned bond? *Maga dissoluta sine disciminare adliga.*"

She hadn't *bonded indiscriminately.* She'd believed that no bond would form. Which was why she wanted it broken. "Please, Father, simply sunder the bond. There's no need to kill Alroth. Once the bond is broken, I'll return to Falvair." *And leave Lord Ainsley behind.*

Father Glimar shook his head. "Your source requested this trial. I couldn't deny him Doloman's judgment. Who am I to decide which bonds are His will? *Nemo mortalis cataractam manu sua sculpere potest.*"

No mortal can carve a bond by his own hand.

Lord Ainsley's plate armour glittered in the slanting sunlight, and he put his helm on, the silver-painted bear on top ready to devour Alroth's pitiful faded coat.

"You're going to let Lord Ainsley kill him?" Mellia kept her voice as low as she could. It wouldn't do for everyone to hear her berating the Grist father. But if Lord Ainsley won, she would never be free of him.

"So little faith in your source. *Maga inconstans sua fons dubita.*"

An inconstant mage doubts her source.

But how could Alroth win against Lord Ainsley? They approached the platform and laid their weapons on the table. Alroth turned to Mellia, took the two steps to the edge of the dais, and gave her the same inventory Father Glimar had. Her face heated. To have him see her like this... Alroth dug into his pocket and laid something at her feet, its sparkle contrasting with his dull leather-wrapped fingers. She bent and scooped it up. Her bee pin. Alroth's eyes, hidden deep in his helm, didn't give anything away.

"As the aggrieved party, Lord Ainsley shall choose weapons." Lord New Bridge sounded bored.

Why were they letting Alroth challenge a lord? They could kill Alroth with a word. Which would free Mellia from their bond—and toss her right into Lord Ainsley's hands.

Lord Ainsley chose a longsword, his own weapon, in fact, and a small round shield.

The guard captain brought forth a longsword for Alroth, and it ground with rust as Alroth drew it from the sheath. The guard captain's face twisted into a smirk. He muttered something inaudible over the crowd's roar, and Alroth's shoulders tensed under the woefully thin-looking fabric. The guard captain spat at his feet, and the crowd hooted and hollered.

Should she be glad that Alroth was going to die? Because the knot in her stomach was anything but excitement.

"He doesn't even have a proper weapon." Mellia couldn't tear her eyes from Alroth, hefting the rusted sword, testing the edge.

He didn't take off his studded leather gloves, and no one asked him to. But what use would they be against Lord Ainsley's plate armour? What use would a *sword* be?

Lord Ainsley would kill him. What then? The very act of winning would hand her over to him unquestionably. And once that happened, she would have to undergo the binding ritual with Lord Ainsley. And then what if she failed to bond to him? How would a man like Lord Ainsley view that? As her refusing to cleave to Doloman's will? He would keep trying to make her bend, the duel all the proof that he needed that their bond would form eventually.

"Please, Father, please, don't do this." Mellia slid to her knees before Father Glimar, clutched the hem of his houppelande. "Simply break the bond. Sending me back to Falvair would solve this. No one has to die."

He looked on her coldly, like the Golden God statue in Iram Square, as though Doloman himself surveyed her through his eyes. "It is not my doing, child. Doloman and I were prepared to name you handmaid. Yet you instead chose this path." His gaze rested long on her ephemer. "If you wish to pray, pray that Doloman's will be done today. Pray that He will rectify your foolishness."

Her foolishness? Her foolishness in what exactly? Failing in Doloman's task because a stubborn mercenary refused to listen to her? Agreeing to put herself under his protection instead of being expelled as a drone? Being harassed and tossed in an oubliette by Lord Ainsley?

Father Glimar could try to pin this on her if he liked, but it was not her doing. None of it was. Lord Ainsley had sought her hand, Alroth had practically begged her to bond with him, and she had been *locked in an oubliette* when they'd made this foolish arrangement to battle for her bond without her even being involved. With any luck, both these fools would die and rid her of their high-handed antics.

Mellia's ephemer hopped into her lap, barked sharply, turned around three times, and curled up in the skirt of her houppelande. She sighed and stroked her ephemer's silky ears. No, Alroth didn't deserve death. He'd given her the first tolerable—fine, *pleasant*—binding ritual of her life. For a scant few moments, she'd even thought their bond might be a blessing. Until he'd locked her up, just like Lord Ainsley. Well, perhaps not *just* like Lord Ainsley.

Father Glimar watched her ephemer nuzzle into her sleeve. "It's true, then. A friendly little pup." He reached out, as if to try touching her ephemer. He turned back to the lists.

Alroth and Lord Ainsley faced each other across the field, their weapons bare, the round shield Lord Ainsley had picked looking far too small to protect Alroth's wide body.

Mellia's grip tightened on the silver pin in her hand, the bee's wings digging into her palm. A shout rose above the din, and they began.

Alroth turned in place as Lord Ainsley circled him. His sword wasn't even raised. What was he thinking? He deflected the first blow with his small shield, a sliver of wood flying off and falling into the dirt at his feet. Lord Ainsley swiped at his other side, but Alroth got his shield around to deflect the strike, catching it on the shield's iron-bound edge and bouncing Lord Ainsley's sword off the binding. The lord's sword tip dropped to the ground, and the crowd roared. Why had Lord Ainsley lowered it?

Whatever the reason, Alroth jammed his shield upward into Lord Ainsley's helmeted face and sent the lord staggering. Alroth kept on him, slashing at his side, his legs, his sword arm, the clangs off his plate ear-splitting even over the crowd's wild cheers, and still Lord Ainsley retreated. One more blow that he caught on his shield, and Lord Ainsley toppled into the dirt, relinquishing his shield as he scrambled to his knees. The crowd hollered and catcalled.

Alroth stood over him, and one solid blow to his wrist relieved Lord Ainsley of his sword. Alroth's teeth flashed below his helm, and he raised his shield over his head, sword-point still trained on Lord Ainsley. The spectators were clearly on the side of the lowly mercenary against the high lord. The story of the low-born man binding a mage to him must have spread, and if Alroth could do such a thing, what was stopping other men from doing the same? Of course they were on his side.

Alroth's mouth moved, but he was well out of earshot. Lord Ainsley's face was too hidden to see whether he answered, but Alroth laughed aloud, so presumably he did. *Golden God*, Alroth was lovely like this. How was he so carefree, in a fight where he could lose his life at any moment? Was it wrong to think him beautiful, standing over his fallen opponent, ready to take his life?

He didn't see Lord Ainsley pull his poignard from his belt, raise it, ready to jam it into the back of Alroth's unprotected knee. Even if the duel was called in Alroth's favour, an injury like that wouldn't heal right. And once Alroth was on the ground, nothing would stop Lord Ainsley from going for Alroth's throat. The duel's arbiters, the guard captain and the men sitting by her, certainly weren't stopping him.

Mellia closed her eyes, focused on the poignard, and between one breath and the next, syphoned from Alroth. The poignard hit its mark, the thin blade crumbling to flakes of rust, disintegrating as Alroth whirled and whacked the hilt from Lord Ainsley's hand. Alroth raised his rusted sword. Would he kill Lord Ainsley for his underhanded move?

No. He rested the sword on his shoulder and strode away from the vanquished lord, who bowed his head and pulled his helmet off, spitting blood into the dirt. And then he was there, Alroth, her bond mate, standing before her, before the Grist father and Lord New Bridge.

"The lord has yielded to me, and I will show him mercy." He laid his borrowed sword and shield on the table and swiped off his helmet. He planted his thumbs in his sword belt and looked at each of them in turn: the lord who had agreed to this match, under duress, it seemed;

the Grist father who had accepted Alroth's petition to fight for Mellia; and his bond mate, come to see him defend their bond. The one who'd saved his knee from a crippling blow. Which one would speak, end this match in his favour? Did Mellia have the power to do it?

Father Glimar spoke first. "My child, you have proven Doloman's favour today. As such, let it be known that your bond is blessed by Doloman and by the Grist who serve him."

Their bond was blessed. Any foolish dreams of becoming a handmaid drifted away. She'd never sit snug in the keep with Dayma and the rest. She'd never be free to use her magic alongside the other handmaids. Her magic would always belong to Alroth, her mate, who had the power to wrench her if she used it without his permission.

Lord New Bridge didn't deign to say anything, simply descended from the stands and parted the crowd to return to his castle. Alroth bowed to Father Glimar and gathered his weapons from the table, tying his scabbards one by one back onto his sword belt while well-wishers towed him away. Mellia loosened her hand from the silver bee still clutched in it. She wasn't a sister anymore, by any measure. She would never be a handmaid. She was Alroth's matron. Nothing more.

She held the pin out to Father Glimar.

His eyebrows shot up, but he took it gently from her palm and tucked it into his houppelande. "I'm sure you and your bond mate have much to discuss, Mellia. Both of you will stay in my home tonight, in preparation for the Necrophoresis Ritual tomorrow. The comb is no place for you now, but you may accompany the handmaids to the waterfall."

The comb was no place for her. That had been certain from the moment the midday bells had rung out and Alroth had not been at the hive. If she'd thought otherwise, she'd been fooling herself. It was kind of Father Glimar to offer her somewhere to stay, though, considering

Alroth didn't seem to have a place. They couldn't stay in Etienne's cozy room forever. They would have to find a house of their own. Here in New Bridge? And what would her parents say when they discovered that she had eschewed their choice of husband for a mercenary?

She would follow that train of thought later. For now, she must simply focus on the Necrophoresis Ritual, focus on her bond mate... who was threading through the thinning crowd to the edge of the platform.

He stood there, helmet under his arm, watching her. Her ephemer leaped through her leg and trotted to the edge of the platform, where they barked directly into Alroth's face. He flinched more sharply than he ever had during the duel, and Mellia couldn't help but laugh. He'd face sword blows in nothing but a fabric coat, but her ephemer cowed him.

Two Grist guards appeared behind Father Glimar, and he descended from the platform, Mellia trailing him. Alroth fell into step beside her as they followed Father Glimar out of the palisades and along Castle Street. Every few feet, they stopped so that the Grist father could bestow a blessing on someone.

"I'm glad you're all right," murmured Alroth.

He was? Oh, yes, of course, his mage, safe and sound for him to use. "I am." Was she supposed to say the same back to him? *Was* she glad he was all right? She was bound to him. Bound for the rest of her life now. Their bond was blessed, with no hope of breaking it. Because of his challenge.

Father Glimar bent to lay a hand on the forehead of a small child, who looked up at his Grist father's gilded hat with round eyes.

"I am none the worse for wear, either." Alroth rested his hand on his sword hilt. It seemed a habit, certainly not threatening. Maybe reassuring himself that it was still there, should he need it. But why would he need it against her? "Thanks for that."

Was he trying to goad her into admitting she was glad that he had won the duel? The alternative was certainly unconscionable, but it had been he who had put himself in that position in the first place; he had proposed the duel, wheedled Father Glimar into it, from the sounds of things.

"I knew you would prevail." *Lie*. She'd thought he'd be dispatched hastily by Lord Ainsley. "Where is your armour?" Had he really been so sure of victory that he'd shown up in a plain coat against Lord Ainsley's full plate?

Alroth grinned and patted his faded coat. It thumped, rather unlike cloth. "Jack of plate." He said it as if that was supposed to mean something to her. "The armour is sewn into the lining. You can touch it if you want."

Mellia brushed the coat with her fingertips and pressed them to the fabric. Sure enough, the coat bent strangely, but her finger didn't sink in. He'd been wearing armour all that time? She'd feared for him for nothing. No matter that Lord Ainsley hadn't landed a hit on him, even if he had, Alroth would have been fine. Bruised maybe, but not sliced up or run through as Mellia had feared.

How dare he make her fear for him like that? She stalked after Father Glimar, on to the next supplicant. At this rate, it would be nightfall by the time they made it to his manor. Alroth came level with her.

She didn't look at him. "Father Glimar wishes to house us for the night. I'll be attending the Necrophoresis Ritual tomorrow." Let him try to deny her right to attend. Let him try to drag her away without saying goodbye to her friends, her sisters.

Alroth didn't look at her, either. "Good."

Good? He wanted her to attend the ceremony? "Why good?"

"I have much to discuss with you, but now is not the time." His tone made it clear that he wouldn't change his mind on this, and she couldn't force him to talk.

They lapsed into a silence that hung between them until they were led into Father Glimar's house and upstairs by the valet. He let them know that they were free to use the Grist father's bathing room and showed them to their chamber. Singular. Before Mellia could even formulate a protest, the valet was gone. After all, bound mates shared everything. Instead, she mumbled something to Alroth and escaped to the bathing room. She wouldn't pass up the opportunity to wash the oubliette from herself. She left her soiled mantle, houppelande, and veil with the laundress, at the red-faced woman's insistence, and returned to her and Alroth's chambers.

He left for the bathing room himself, hardly less dirty than her, having washed only the essentials after his stint in the prison tower last night. He'd left his jack of plate behind, and Mellia fingered the scores of metal plates the size of her thumb sewn into the coat. How many times had these little bits of metal saved the life of her bond mate? Not today, perhaps, but the coat was well-worn. He was skilled in the lists, and not in the way Lord Ainsley was, having trained by sparring since childhood. Alroth was efficient, precise, unafraid. Even she could tell as much. Had he fought in the Canal War? Most mercenaries had. In the seven years since its end, many mercenaries had returned to Sudra from their battles in Nordval. By all accounts, the war had been horrifically bloody on all sides. She shuddered. Thankfully, there had always been peace here.

Behind her, the door creaked open, booted footsteps entered, and the door thumped shut. The footsteps trod onto the rug, muffled, then back onto wood, toward her. She was alone with Alroth. Last time they'd been alone... Her chest flushed with heat, and it crept up her neck. Why had she been so disappointed that he hadn't taken her in the way of the others? Would he do so now? Lord Glimar had blessed their bond, which meant that Mellia belonged to him to do with as he pleased, right?

"Some of them need to be replaced."

What? Oh, the coat she still seemed to be examining.

He tapped a plate spotted with red-brown. "Hadn't used this in a few seasons. Sloppy of me to let it go to rust."

Perhaps that was true; what did Mellia know of such things? Finally, she turned to him.

Alroth had left off his houppelande as well; a fire crackled in their very own fireplace, and a tunic would be plenty to keep him warm, just as her woollen kirtle would suffice for her. His hair was damp from his bath, and his face was smooth, freshly shaven. He was handsomer than when she'd first seen him at the castle, shrouded in whiskers. Even more so with the way he was looking at her, as though her face was fascinating. Had anyone ever looked at her like that?

He brushed a lock of blond hair off her forehead. Oh, right. He hadn't seen her with her hair unbound.

He cleared his throat and turned to the fire. "We have something important to discuss. I don't want you to be afraid. I said that I'd protect you, and I will."

Afraid? Why would she be afraid? Of him? She nodded.

"Father Glimar has asked me and mine to guard the handmaids tomorrow."

A mercenary band? What was wrong with the Grist Guard? "Why do they need guarding?"

"There's been a threat to… a threat against the handmaids at the Necro Ritual. My warriors are good. You'll be safe. You'll support me." He frowned at Mellia.

She would have to get used to orders. She was a matron now, a tool to be used by the hand of her source. Mellia had always known that this would be her fate, so why did it rankle? Even though she wanted to help defend the handmaids, and the chance to use her newfound magic was welcome, why couldn't he have asked for her help? A source didn't ask. That was why.

And since he hadn't asked a question, Mellia didn't have to answer. The window in their room was actual glass and looked over the Grist father's garden, toward the Grist Queen's Keep. The handmaids would be there, still feverishly preparing for the ceremony and all the festivities tomorrow, for one of them to be named the next queen, and for one of the sisters to be declared the new handmaid. She could be there helping them right now if Alroth hadn't been so damnably stubborn.

She could be ready to attend the Necrophoresis Ritual, dangerously oblivious to the threat. For surely what Alroth had been dancing around was that the threats were to kill the handmaids. A threat from who? Why? Someone who wanted to send the Grist a message, send a message to all of Sudra maybe.

Mellia's empty stomach churned and grumbled.

"Are you hungry, sweetling?" Alroth's voice was soft. "When was the last time you ate?"

She shook her head. When had it been? "Before our… meeting. Certainly before the oubliette."

Alroth grumbled in his chest. "The oubliette?"

"Beneath the floor of the prison cell." It was dark enough now to make out a light in the high window of the Grist Queen's Keep.

Dayma would be there still, with the Grist queen's husk, fully dried and ready for the ceremony tomorrow. Mellia would not let them be killed. No matter that Alroth had ordered her to help defend them, she would not put them in danger just to spite him.

The door opened and closed again. Alroth's seat by the fire was empty. Why should he stay here with her, now that he'd given her orders for tomorrow? Surely he had arrangements to make with his mercenary band.

And why was that disappointing? Had she wished for him to stay the night with her here? That was silly. Her ephemer, dozing in front of the fire, lifted their head, little tail thumping on the rug when they caught her eye. Mellia sat down beside the little pup, who crawled into her lap. They would evidently need a name now. They had been a surprise, and it was even more surprising that they were not wholly unwelcome. Even if Alroth was prone to ordering her around, like any source would, honestly, he treated her better than he could. Her ephemer wriggled closer into her body. And this little one was an untainted good. The calm and contentment that suffused her knowing that she wouldn't have to part with them was unquestionable. *Mirabi.* A good surprise. As disappointed as Mellia might be that she was bound instead of becoming a handmaid, Mirabi didn't deserve to shoulder that disappointment.

Mirabi lifted their head and barked at the door. A clunk and a curse reverberated through the wood, and Mellia followed Mirabi as they trotted across the room and scratched a paw at the door jamb.

"Move back, little one." Mellia shooed them with her foot and cracked the door.

Alroth wrestled with a tray outside, trying to balance it on one hand to open the door. It tilted dangerously, and Mellia pulled the door the rest of the way open. Alroth looked up, and Mellia ushered him through. She shut the door after him.

Mirabi barked around Alroth's ankles as he settled the tray on the floor in front of the fire; there was no table in their room. Food. He'd clearly scrounged scraps from the meals of the day, a small bowl of pottage, probably from the servant's table, two hunks of soft bread, a wedge of cheese, and was that half a littlefield bird? Alroth waved Mellia toward the tray and made no move to eat himself. Had he brought this for her?

Mellia settled herself on the other side of the tray on the soft rug and dipped the bread into the pottage. She took a bite. Of course it was honey bread, in the Grist father's household. Every meal would have a bit of honey in it, if not every dish. Her stomach grumbled in earnest, and Mellia polished off almost the entire tray, leaving only a couple thumbs of cheese and a bit of broth at the bottom of the bowl.

"More bread, sweetling?" Alroth was watching her.

"No, thank you."

Mirabi snuffled right into the bowl and rubbed their face around, as if they could taste in their ephemeral form.

"Mirabi!" Mellia snapped her fingers at the little pup, who jumped back and ducked into a play bow.

"Mirabi?" Alroth's serious face cracked into a ghost of a smile.

Heat crept over Mellia's face. "I was surprised by them. Weren't you?"

Alroth cocked his head and popped the last of the cheese into his mouth. Once he'd swallowed, he patted his leg, drawing Mirabi trotting to sit by him. "I wasn't expecting you to agree to my bargain. Even to try the ritual. When you bound my wrists and swallowed my cock so beautifully, I felt something." He patted his chest, over his heart.

Had she been blushing before? If so, her face was on fire now. Mellia turned to the hearth, her unbound hair falling to shield her face from Alroth's steady gaze. *Swallowed his cock.* Is that what she'd done? Yes, perhaps she had. And he'd enjoyed it. Both of them had. The power she'd wielded, drawing those sounds from him. Could she do that again? Did she want to? Her body clearly did, the way heat rushed from her face down lower, to her breasts, and lower still to her belly and between her legs to that part that he'd lavished with so much attention.

What was she thinking? She was sitting in Father Glimar's house on his beautiful hexiform rug. She'd eaten his food. How could she be thinking of such things here now?

But were she and Alroth not bond mates? Was it not the most natural thing in the world for them to... couple?

If Alroth wanted to, of course. He would tell her when it was time. She peeked through her hair at him. Alroth swiped a hand toward Mirabi, who barked and jumped back and forth, trying to avoid it—uncaring that the hand would go right through them. They dashed in a little circle and crept closer. Alroth grinned and turned away, looking at the little pup out of the corner of his eye, then swiping out to brush through Mirabi's nose. The ephemer dashed under the bed, barking all the while, then came tearing back, yipping and leaping at Alroth's fingers. Alroth threw back his head and laughed.

"Mirabi." Alroth spoke so low that Mellia almost didn't catch the word, but the look of pure awe in his eyes was unmistakable.

"We'd better settle down if we don't want to keep the house awake. Mirabi, that means you. No more barking." She turned to Alroth. "And you, stop getting them all wound up."

Alroth's grin didn't falter as he bowed his head. "Yes, my lady. I am your humble servant."

Mellia froze, bile crawling up her throat, goosebumps shivering over her shoulders and down her back. He knew? All this time, he'd known that she was a lady? Was *that* why he'd tricked her into binding to him? Was he just like Lord Ainsley, after her lands, her titles? Now that their bond was sanctioned, she was eligible to inherit, and he would be the one to gain her lands as her lord.

"What is it? What's got you unsettled?" He reached towards her.

Mellia was on her feet. How had she gotten there? Alroth knelt before her. Mirabi had disappeared—probably under the bed again.

"How do you know about Falvair?" Her voice was too quiet, too far away.

"Falvair?" Alroth scowled. "The port town? What about it? Sweetling, tell me." He was still pretending. The nerve of him.

How could she have thought he actually wanted to protect a sister—a disgraced sister? No, he wanted a mage, he wanted her lands. Had he been promised Mellia's lands in return for... what?

"What did you agree to do in return for my lands? Your offer was better than Lord Ainsley's, evidently."

Alroth got to his feet, towered over her. "You will tell me what you're on about. Now."

Mellia laughed. "You speak as though you are the wronged party. After you tricked me into giving up my lands to a low-born, untitled mercenary! A marquess is certainly a step up in the world for you. Tell me what you agreed to do. Does it have to do with tomorrow?"

Or was it worse than that? If Alroth was the heretic prince, was he trying to gain a foothold in Sudra... to take his ancestral land back? Falvair would be the perfect place, the closest to Nordval, a deep, protected harbour. What if the plot to murder the handmaids, to send Sudra a message, was *his*?

He claimed that he needed her help to save them, but what if he needed to trick her into helping him kill them? Mellia planted her hands on her hips. "If you hurt the handmaids tomorrow, I swear to you, I will never perform magic for you again."

"Hurt them? I just told you I'm planning to protect them! After all the trouble I've gone to, that's what you think of me?"

There would be no arguing with him. He would never admit the truth, not even after his little slip-up, admitting that he knew she was a lady.

Mellia turned her back on him and went to bed. He must have slept on the rug before the fire, because the sheets were cold when the hive bells woke them before dawn. The Necrophoresis Ritual was beginning.

16

Alroth

Alroth rose stiffly from his place before the fire and rolled his aching shoulder. Not the worst spot he'd ever slept. It was warm, and the rug was thick. Still, his mood was darker than the pre-dawn sky outside the clear glass window. If they were going to accompany the handmaids' procession, they needed to leave now. He pulled on his boots and laced his jack of plate.

The hive bells pealed, loud enough to wake Mellia here inside the walls, next to the hive itself. She stirred in the big feather bed. She'd need breakfast. Alroth went to brave the bustling kitchen and slipped away with two steaming bowls of porridge—drizzled with honey, of course; it was a miracle the laundry wasn't drizzled with the stuff in this fancy manor. When he shouldered back into their room, Mellia was already dressed, pinning her long golden hair under her newly laundered veil.

She turned when he came in and looked him up and down, jaw tight and lips thin. Silently, she motioned to the chair bearing his clean houppelande. He put the bowls of porridge on the mantle and pulled the houppelande over his head. Mellia was still angry with him. Something had set her off last night; she'd said something about her lands, something about that worm Ainsley. Whatever it had been, now was not the time.

Mellia sat to lace her boots, and Alroth turned to his swords, propped in the corner. Ictus would just get in the way today, throw him off balance. So why did he want to bring it along with him anyway? The sword was useless. Destroyed. He tied Volnus to one hip and his new serviceable blade to the other. He left Ictus propped in the corner. Surely Father Glimar would allow him to retrieve it when they returned with the handmaids. If he even wanted to. The blade belonged on a midden heap. He turned from it.

Mellia blew on the steaming bowl of porridge nestled between her palms. She watched him over the bowl's rim, now fully dressed in her belted brown houppelande and veil over her hair, as usual. They were a sister's clothes. He'd have to get her some new ones when they returned. Should he have found her armour, like the other mages had been wearing for the ill-fated mock battle? Mellia would be close to him, likely in the fray. *Bonds.* Why hadn't he thought of that sooner? There was no helping it. He pulled the lace on his jack of plate loose. Her houppelande would protect her from the sewn-in plates biting into her flesh. His gambeson would have to be enough for him. He'd trusted it many times before, when he'd been young and reckless and too poor to afford better protection.

He pulled the jack of plate off and held it out to her.

She glanced from the faded armour to him. "What are you doing?"

"You're about to be in a battle—a real one. I said I would protect you, and I will."

Mellia stared at the armour and made no move to take it. "You'll need that."

"My gambeson will suffice. You'll need it more."

She shook her head. "I can't take your armour."

"And I can't have you fighting beside me in two layers of wool."

"But you can fight that way?"

He patted the quilted nettlecloth layers of his gambeson. "This will turn a blow—at least keep me from being split open."

Mellia took the jack of plate, and it nearly tipped her over. Alroth steadied her and helped lace her into it. The heavy armour drooped on her and would weigh her down, so loose about her body, but nothing would get through it.

"Satisfied?" Mellia planted her hands on her hips, engulfed in the jack of plate.

Alroth couldn't help but smile as he polished off his porridge. He *was* satisfied. Mellia was still angry with him, sure, and they would sort that out, but for today, she wore his colours, and they had the same goal. They'd protect the handmaids, bring them home safe, and then they could sort out whatever was bothering her. A rap on the door made Mellia jump. Alroth opened it.

"If you're ready?" The valet looked past Alroth to Mellia's grumpy form, rounded by armour. He didn't ask, just led them to the lane in front of the house. "Join up with the procession at Upper Gate. They'll be by when the hive bells ring again."

Alroth nodded. Falkirk and the rest were meeting them at the falls. Etienne and Del would have scouted the falls path this morning, having refused to spend the night "on an icy clifftop deathtrap," so hopefully they wouldn't get any surprises during the procession. Alroth loosened Volnus in its sheathe as they threaded through the crowded square, past the comb.

Mellia's gaze lingered on the buildings that used to be her home. Should he say something? It wasn't time to dwell on the past. Besides, she had agreed to bind with him. Even if he hadn't insisted on the ritual, she wouldn't be living at the comb anymore; she had said herself that she would have been deemed a drone. Surely being bound to him was better than expulsion?

They turned onto Upper Gate Street, which was lined with Grist guards. They must have received instructions to let the armed mercenary and strange-looking sister through, because the road had already been cleared, but the Guards let them pass.

Mellia stopped short of the towering archway. "Shouldn't we wait here?"

Alroth shook his head. "If my band has anything to report, they'll be outside the gate. We can wait there."

Mellia trailed him under the raised portcullis and across the ditch, bridged by an embankment. Grist guards were posted out here too, watching the road and the surrounding forest. They must also have been told that there was a threat to the handmaids. None of Alroth's band emerged with a message for him. So it had been a quiet night. If they weren't going to be ambushed, their attackers must have strength, numbers, or some other advantage. At least a score of Grist guards were here to accompany them, and they had Mellia. They would prevail.

The procession came through the gate: the dead queen, carried on a pallet by four guards, bracketed by the six handmaids, three ahead, three behind. Would they make it up the falls path in such flowing gowns? Aemulus save them up on the waterfall.

Mellia stood rigid beside him as the procession passed, and they fell in behind the last of the handmaids. None of them so much as glanced at Mellia. Were they really friends? Perhaps they didn't recognize her in the jack of plate?

Alroth surveyed the forest on either side as they split off from the main road onto the falls path. The way had been cleared, some of the brush and overhanging branches cut back, but still a few brambles reached out and snatched at the handmaids' voluminous skirts. One of them jerked her skirt free, and was that a curse under her breath?

"What's so funny?" Mellia hissed at him. "This is a funeral procession."

"The handmaids aren't what I expected."

She frowned. "What did you expect?"

The cursing handmaid swiped up her skirt and tucked it into her belt, muttering something about Ultio's tarpit, and revealing soft slippers.

"Less cursing."

Mellia kept her gaze fixed on the ground. "Handmaids are people, like you and me."

And I could have been one of them, if not for you. She didn't have to say it. It was true. If he'd gone with her instead of heading to Etienne's rooms, she would be one of them, come tomorrow. Instead, she would wake up in a drafty cruck next to him, outside the town walls, to prepare for a day's work moving them inside the walls—if the folks in Mill Hamlet would finally give up their resistance and agree—

Alroth took a deep breath and scanned the forest around them. The chill wind rustled the last of the fall leaves high above, and he wouldn't hear anything over the crunch of leaves under their feet. At least the mud of the path was frozen enough not to impede them.

The trees gave way all at once, and the broad river stretched before them. Wide shelves of rock lined the shallow waterway. As it passed the crest, boulders divided it, jutting up from the water. The guards surrounding a small flat-bottomed boat came to attention as their procession emerged from the trees. The four mercenaries in their mismatched armour stood out next to the uniformed Grist guards.

The handmaids arranged themselves around the little boat, seemingly unconcerned with getting their feet wet, and the four guards carrying the queen's husk slid it onto the boat. Enough empty space surrounded the husk for a score more corpses. Didn't rich folks usually have a hoard of costly treasures sent off with them? Not his business. Alroth turned his back on the boat and the handmaids beginning their ritual, and he scanned the trees. His fighters did the same, after Del nodded to Mellia and muttered Sister. She didn't correct him. Mellia hovered at his side, neither handmaid nor mercenary. He laid a hand on her shoulder.

"Just be ready to use your magic," he murmured. No need to interrupt the ceremony.

Alroth loosened his sword in its sheath and Volnus as well. His cesti creaked, leather on leather. A snowflake tickled his cheek, then another his nose. He had to convince his people to move inside the damned town walls. But how? They were so dead set against it. Could he bear to retreat inside with those who agreed and leave the rest outside to fend for themselves? It was a logical solution but still rubbed him the wrong way. Maybe if he could convince them of the danger—

There. In the trees. Something had moved.

"Falkirk."

The handmaids faltered behind him, but keeping them safe was the priority, even if that meant disturbing their chant. Falkirk was at his side before the handmaids had even resumed their ritual. Alroth pointed into the trees, and Falkirk drew their bow.

A line of armoured folks stepped onto the flat rocks of the riverbank. Mercenaries. No doubt the ones hired by Lord Ainsley once Alroth had refused him. They weren't in range. The handmaids would be sheltered behind the wall of armoured mercs and guards, even if the attackers had archers.

Mellia stepped up next to Falkirk. "Don't wait for them to get in range."

Falkirk twitched as Mellia's hand rested gently on their elbow. "You better be right about this. Shooting at them when they're so far out of range will just piss them off." They loosed the arrow. It took an attacker in the stomach and stuck there. The man doubled over and went down. The *chink* of mail against stone drifted across the water. Pierced an enemy's mail at three hundred paces? Mellia planted her hands on her hips as both Alroth and Falkirk gawked at her.

"You wanted my help, so I'm helping. You'll catch flies with that." She jerked her chin at Alroth's open mouth.

"How many arrows do you have, Falkirk?"

"A sheaf of broadhead and four of bodkin." They were already pulling another from the quiver on their belt.

"Looks like the broadhead will do as well as the bodkin, with mage help. Keep at it, you two."

Falkirk let another arrow fly, and it took an armoured man in the shoulder—and came out the other side.

Mellia was already improving on her second try. Pride swelled in Alroth's chest.

None of the Grist guards stepped forward. They hadn't brought any archers?

A scream went up from an attacker as an arrow punctured their thigh, and a handmaid looked around, pale-faced, and gasped when she saw the armoured mercenaries wading into the river toward them. Their chant faltered again.

Falkirk and Mellia had already picked off a score of attackers in the few moments it took for the opposing mercs to step into the river.

Alroth drew his swords, and his men followed suit. Etienne unhooked his hammer; Kai hefted a javelin and hurled one through a man's chest, and Del hefted his axe. None of the Grist guards moved. Waiting for an order, most likely. No matter. Now that Falkirk and

Mellia had cut their numbers, only about two score men and mages remained. Mages. They had mages. They'd blended together at a distance, what with their mail, but the mages were there, three of them, hanging back.

Hasburgen waved his mace from the centre of the line. "Alroth! You're on the wrong side!" He laughed. The bastard *laughed*. When he'd warned Alroth about Ainsley, he'd practically spelled it out, told Alroth to send the lordling his way. Apparently, Ainsley had found him.

Kai had run out of javelins, so he nocked an arrow to his elm bow. He loosed it, piercing an attacker deep into the shoulder without Mellia's help. Alroth didn't give their attackers time to close in. He leaped into grappling range of an attacker with a longsword, and pierced the side of his neck with Volnus. Tearing his sword free, he turned to hammer the next man's helmet with its pommel, throwing him off balance long enough to stab up into his belly, the rings of his mail popping apart under Volnus's sharp point.

The others behind him cut through the overconfident mercs. Etienne's hammer crushed mail-clad bodies and rang off plate, stunning the wearer. Del's axe hacked through quilted fabric and leather, and found the chinks in plate. Kai's war bow pierced plate and mail as though it were fabric. Falkirk loosed their halberd from their back and slashed and stabbed from a distance, guarding the others with practised ease.

A whistling in his ear made Alroth raise Volnus by reflex. The mace's blow juddered up his arm to his shoulder.

Hasburgen grinned at him, Gertie at his back. "If you want to switch sides, now is the time." He raised his mace for another blow, but Alroth brought his other sword around inside his guard and jammed it into his belly. Hasburgen's breath whooshed out, but it didn't pierce his mail.

Damned cheap trash. Gertie was the reason Ictus was gone, and Alroth glared at her over Hasburgen's shoulder as he bent to get his breath back.

"Same to you." Alroth watched Gertie. "Is it really worth the money?"

Hasburgen brought his mace up, too fast, and it glanced across Alroth's side. Alroth dropped his cheap blade into the river and pressed his fist to the gash. Damn, he'd become too dependent on his jack. But Mellia was there, pressing a hand to his side. His flesh knit back together in a matter of moments. His gambeson still gaped, but at least he wasn't bleeding everywhere. His ribs ached fiercely. Perhaps they were beyond Mellia's ability to heal?

Hasburgen laughed. "You got yourself a mage!"

Mirabi's high-pitched bark pierced the steady hum of the waterfall.

Hasburgen laughed harder. "*That's* your bond animal?"

Alroth put all his strength behind a thrust up into Hasburgen's belly. The other man blocked it, but Alroth swung with his empty fist and nailed him across the jaw beneath his helm. Hasburgen groaned and staggered back, blood cascading over his chin and neck. Cesti might look like leather wraps, but they could split skin and crush bone if applied correctly.

Gertie stepped forward. She wouldn't get her hands on Volnus. Hasburgen had splashed to one knee, and Gertie stepped around him. "It's not me you should worry about." She jerked her chin behind Alroth as she grabbed Hasburgen under the arms and hauled him up. The other attackers were stumbling away as well, those that could, anyway.

Alroth turned, a knot heavy in his gut.

The Grist guards had drawn their weapons. But instead of a defensive wall around their charges to ward off any attackers that made it past Alroth's mercs, they faced inward, toward the handmaids. How would they defend like that... ?

Hiorach's fiery fingers crushing Impietas's slimy throat! The Grist guards were making sure Ainsley's orders were carried out. No time to wonder why.

The pale-faced handmaids had their backs to the queen's funeral boat. Was that why the boat was empty? Had the Grist father himself planned to house the handmaids' bodies in this funeral boat as well? Then why have Alroth and his mercs here—? No time to puzzle that out. Alroth had been given a task, and he *would* carry it out.

Mellia gasped. She'd finally turned, finally seen the Grist guards advancing on her sisters.

"Alroth?" Falkirk's tense voice cut through the moment that seemed to last forever.

Alroth charged. All he had was Volnus and his cesti, but the Grist Guard didn't have its magic, and there were only... two score here. He punched the back of the nearest one's helmet and broke through their line to the handmaids. He shouldered past, and Mellia slipped by after him. She urged the handmaids into the boat, and they helped each other climb in. At least the gunwales would give them some measure of defence. Alroth planted his feet in the rushing water, his band following suit. The five of them stood shoulder to shoulder.

"I'm out of arrows," Falkirk muttered.

"Same here." Kai had an arrow in each hand. They would work as stabbing weapons in a pinch, but they'd break on the plate the Grist guards all wore.

Etienne wiped his forehead, smearing the blood spatter across it. His hammer was a damned messy weapon. They could take out a few guards. But what was their weaponry against plate? It would take them three, four, five blows to find their targets, and Alroth in a *cloth gambeson* with one sword. He was good, but he wouldn't survive a heavy blow, and five to one was terrible odds. Five blows for each of five men could only equal... dead. They'd all be dead if they stayed to fight. But where could they go?

The guards closed in around them, four men deep, and the defenders had their backs to the boat. They could punch through and run for the opposite shore, but what was over there? Falkirk had said there was no way up or down the escarpment on that side. And if they went back to the main road, no doubt more guards would be waiting for them there, or the mercenaries would have regrouped on the path and would catch them before they even got there... besides, the handmaids in their long gowns and slippers couldn't possibly run over the rocky riverbed, their skirts tangling in their feet.

He chanced a glance back. The funeral boat was solid. It had bottomed out on the crest of the waterfall with the six handmaids and Mellia in there. It wouldn't go over. Not without some help. And if they gave it that help, would the handmaids survive? Would the boat overturn? Better than taking their chances here with the murderous guards.

"Ready to put the queen to rest?"

"What?" Falkirk snapped.

Alroth braced his back on the gunwale and shoved with his shoulders. Falkirk got the idea immediately. The boat edged toward the brink, and the stern lifted ever so slightly.

"In!" roared Alroth, and the five of them vaulted over the sides of the boat, their momentum shoving the boat that last pace toward the edge and over.

Mellia's wide blue eyes stared up at him as the boat tipped and plummeted over the falls.

17

Mellia

They would overturn. At the precipice, the boat's bow crept lower, despite the five armoured fighters who'd just jumped in behind her. The handmaids huddled in the bow while the rapids poured around them to plunge thunderously beneath their drenched knees and white knuckles on the gunwale. Mist obscured the base of the falls. Their light boat would be tossed about like a pinecone, and they would tumble onto the rocks. The funeral boat would follow and land on their heads. They would be crushed. Unless the falls fed into a deep pool. Then perhaps they would be dragged under, the handmaids by their gowns, the mercs by their armour, and drown instead.

The rear corner of the boat ground against the waterfall's crest, and they were free. They needed to slow their boat's rotation, about to tip them out. If only it was a little bit colder today, the waterfall would freeze into a glittering frozen shell they could slide down. It would be steep, but at least it would keep them from overturning onto the waiting rocks. But it was still too warm; winter was weeks away. What was she thinking? She was a bound matron, surrounded by handmaids!

"Freeze the waterfall!" She practically screeched it as the bow pointed to the ground, unmoored and floating, Mellia's stomach lurching at the falling sensation. Dayma's shoulder, tense as stone, pressed to Mellia's, crouched in the boat's bottom, clutching the wood of the gunwale.

"Not the water, the air." Sathred's confident voice cut through the rumble of the water hitting the base of the falls

Of course! Air was more susceptible to magic. They could use the air to freeze the water. Dayma, next to Mellia, went lax, her eyes closed. Mellia did the same, reaching out to the air around them, using her magic. Simple for the group of them. Alroth, on her other side, gasped. The boat crunched into something that gave way. They needed more.

Mellia stilled her mind and reached for Alroth's power. His hand clenched her arm firmly, luckily avoiding Lord Ainsley's bruises. So he *could* feel it. Her magic swept all around them, ahead of the boat. The bow crunched through another layer of ice, the shards stinging Mellia's face and white knuckles, but they had stopped tipping. The next frozen layer crunched, but the boat's flat bottom slid off the shattered ice, sliding steeply down. The mist cleared, revealing a frozen layer coating the pool there, sharp rocks jutting up on its edges.

The bow hit first, launching Mellia's head into Dayma's shoulder. Her teeth clacked together, and she tasted blood. Morath swore. Something cracked. Someone's head? The bow of their boat? It slid across the frozen sheet, the stern plopping into the river as a chunk of ice bobbed by them, and the boat rocked wildly. A sheet of freezing water swept over the gunwale and soaked Mellia to the skin. Runas shrieked, and Mellia shivered beneath the freezing jack of plate. Those two layers of wool were serving her well now, keeping the cold metal plates from her skin, keeping her warm despite being drenched.

A curve in the river hid them from the New Bridge landing. Would the devout waiting there for Arista's passing help them, or would they be like the Grist guards on the falls?

"Come, Sister, let's steer the boat into New Bridge." Morath waved a hand as she spoke, and the boat's bow turned downstream.

"We can't return you, handmaids." Alroth would keep the handmaids from New Bridge? "After that attack..."

"Who knows who else might take the chance to kill you," Mellia finished for him.

"Like, say, some underhanded mercs, looking to make ransom money?" Runas glared daggers at Etienne, of all people. "I'd rather swim." She straightened, but before she could dive over the side, Etienne grabbed her around the middle and tossed her over his shoulder.

"We are the ones who can steer this boat." Dayma waved, bringing the boat closer to the right-hand shore, where New Bridge's landing was just visible through the trees.

"Wait, Dayma, they're right. Archers could pick us off from the walls—" Morath took her shoulder.

"You too?" Sathred crouched in the bow. "I'm with Runas. Especially if these people are going to wrestle us to the ground—"

"Ouch!" Etienne let Runas free. "We agreed that you wouldn't bite me anymore, Rune!"

"We also agreed—"

Thump!

The boat jerked, making them all scramble to hang on. Etienne barely saved Runas from going over the side, not by choice this time. The river was low, and plenty of rocks lurked just beneath the surface.

"I think this impromptu abduction counts as extenuating circumstances." Mellia had only a few moments to convince them to let New Bridge pass. They were within sight of it now. "Circumstances where your own guard were trying to murder you." Now that the Grist Guard had turned on them, it was clear that they weren't safe with the Grist.

The little boat jerked toward the landing and back again, one gunwale dipping low in the water before the boat righted itself. Their argument continued in the river's currents.

"Sisters, stop this!" Adding her power to the tug-of-war wouldn't help.

The boat carved left, and water poured over the gunwale. One of the combative mercs cursed and shrank back from the icy tide.

She would have to syphon. She used a passing current to distance them from where Father Glimar glared, his face unreadable as he watched a boat full of mercenaries float jerkily away with the handmaids—and among them his future Grist queen.

The boat carved back toward him, and they rose on a swell, then tipped to tumble down the other side. The gunwale next to Mellia was a hairsbreadth from going under—it would swamp the boat. The handmaids in their dresses and mercs in their armour would drown, here in the channel. There wasn't time to syphon. They needed less weight on this side of the boat. Mellia slid onto the gunwale and dumped herself, ass over teakettle toward the chilly river.

Alroth shouted and clutched her skirt, but it was wet and slippery, and she was wearing her weight in armour. She collided with the water in a deafening splash. She tried to move her arms and legs, her face upturned, reaching for the surface, but where even was the surface? Her skirts were soon saturated, the jack of plate dragging her inexorably down. Of course, this was one of the deepest parts of the river. She couldn't have fallen a hundred paces further on where she could practically stand up at this time of year. Wasn't she far too calm for a person being dragged to the river bottom?

The panic slammed into her chest and kicked her heart into a gallop. *There's no air down here!* Her limbs flailed wildly, and her bum hit the channel's bed, rocks grinding under her, the armour's plates jamming into her back. She scrambled into a crouch and pushed off, but she barely hovered above the rocks, and her kicking feet soon slammed into a heavy rock as the current tugged her along, the impact screaming in her toes and ankle. If only she didn't have Alroth's armour weighing on her. She yanked at the jack of plate's lace, but the leather was swollen with water, and she had no weapon to cut it.

The boat had already been swept far past her, toward New Bridge. Even if she was going to die down here, she could help Alroth keep the handmaids safe. She gathered one last current, and sent the boat flying downriver, past the landing, away from New Bridge.

She was actually going to die down here! Her lungs burned, aching to take a breath. No one was coming to save her. She summoned the currents. Maybe they could lift her? But they just pushed her downstream. No current flowed upward to tap into. She blew the last bubbles from her mouth and gasped in water. One last effort. She gripped Alroth's power. There had to be an eddy that would lift her. She just had to find it—

Every part of her body was tearing. Not her skin tearing open, but her *self* tearing from her bones, from her muscles, from her very liver and heart and—

She floated up through the water, popped up like a twig, kept rising until she stood on the even surface. Through her ghostly pale hands, the water rushed beneath her translucent feet. Her skirts were dry, the jack of plate light as milkweed silk. A piercing bark rent the air. The funeral boat was a blob down the river, past New Bridge's landing, past the Sinu River's mouth. Mellia willed herself there, and there she was.

Mirabi's little brown body wriggled in Alroth's grasp. They were trying to jump over the gunwale toward her, while Alroth wrestled them down onto the deck. They might be able to swim in the water, but where would they go? Mellia willed herself onto the funeral boat, and soon she was sitting comfortably, hovering over the Grist queen's husk. Mirabi hopped into her lap and nuzzled her face, their wet nose colder than ever before.

Everyone in the boat was staring at her.

"What happened?" said Mellia—or she thought she did. No sound came out of her mouth. Of course. She was an ephemer. Alroth had wrenched her.

He'd felt her syphoning magic from him, and he'd cut her off. He couldn't have known that wrenching her would save her life, could he? Still, he'd cut her off. Jerked her leash like an errant cur.

Alroth stared up at her, almost as pale as she was. He'd thought her dead. How long would she be in this form? Unable to touch anything, interact with anything, speak or be understood? Mirabi licked her fingers and nibbled on them affectionately. No one could touch her like this, except Mirabi.

Alroth shook himself. "Now that that's sorted out, we have to keep these handmaids safe."

"*These handmaids* are sitting right here listening to you. We have to get back to New Bridge." Runas's tone brooked no argument.

"We go back there, you're dead, handmaid." Alroth's growl made it clear he was just as determined.

"If not New Bridge, where will we go? This is hardly a vessel fit for the lake." Dayma's straight back pressed to the gunwale.

"Bridge." Falkirk muttered it to Alroth, but Mellia had no trouble hearing.

"There's a village, downriver, we can get you all to shore and spend a few days, get our bearings. Find out who all is trying to kill you." Alroth was all business.

"The safest place for the handmaids is the Grist Queen's Keep," said Runas, glaring not at Alroth but at Etienne.

"I assure you, we know the safest place for the handmaids better than you all. You've been out of the world for what, twenty years?" How could he know that about Runas?

"But why did the Grist guards attack us?" Morath said. "They've sworn to protect us. It must be a mistake."

Alroth glared across the pyre Mellia sat on. "It's no mistake. Father Glimar himself asked us to defend you. He knew there was a threat."

"And we should believe you, why?" said Sathred. "From where I'm sitting, you have kidnapped us."

"Sathred..." Morath touched her arm.

Runas glared at Etienne still. "She's right. Maybe they were trying to stop you from doing exactly what you just did! Kidnap us and take us—"

"And if we were trying to kidnap you? What could you do about it?" Etienne's perpetual smile was gone. Good thing Mellia was ephemeral, or she would worry about being on the bier next to these two.

"Enough, Drake." Alroth spoke firmly, but he didn't shout.

Etienne huffed and turned his back on them.

"Like it or not, we're the ones going to get you out of this boat." Alroth waved at the shore, spinning slowly around them as they were swept along. Without a rudder, nothing kept the boat pointing downstream.

Mirabi hopped up and barked in Alroth's face. He glared at the little pup, who ran the length of the bier, heedless of the husk, tore back, and leaped onto his lap. Oh, the way her bond mate's eyes softened when he looked at Mirabi.

Mellia opened her mouth to support her bound mate, but nothing came out. She waved her hand in Dayma's face.

"Mellia has thoughts." Dayma looked unimpressed. She must know that Mellia was about to side with Alroth... the source that she wasn't even supposed to have. Dayma and the others hadn't known about Alroth, maybe until the moment he'd wrenched her and Mirabi had become corporeal. The last they had heard, Mellia had been desperate to become a handmaid. She'd explain the strange turn of events when she actually had words. Now, she had to figure out how to tell them Alroth was right.

She pointed to Alroth, then pointed down the river.

"She wants us to throw this horse's ass in the river and head back to New Bridge."

Mellia huffed silently at Dayma and pointed back to New Bridge, crossed her arms in an X shape, and shook her head, mimed getting stabbed.

Runas grinned. "If we don't go back to New Bridge, we'll die."

They were definitely doing this on purpose.

"I believe she means that the mercenary is correct in his assessment, and we should continue down the river to their encampment. If we return to New Bridge, we're in danger of being killed." Livine was dead serious.

Runas rolled her eyes. "Yes, thanks, Livine."

Dayma sighed and turned to Mellia. "There's no convincing you to give up this foolishness?"

"Even if we wanted to get back to New Bridge, how would you propose we do it?" Etienne tossed over his shoulder. "Paddle with our feet?" He really couldn't help himself, could he?

"And in this." Sathred held up a hand, letting a score of snowflakes fall on it and instantly melt.

"You, too?" Runas glared at her.

Sathred shrugged. "I know when I'm outmatched."

Dayma settled in the bow with a huff. Etienne tipped his head back against the bier and closed his eyes.

Alroth slipped up carefully to sit beside Mellia on the slab next to the husk, staring across the bow. Mud Island drifted by. At least they hadn't got hung up there.

"We'll catch ourselves at the old bridge."

"There's nothing there except the ruins of the keep." Dayma addressed Alroth. "Where will we sleep?"

Falkirk answered. "There's a village, other side of the old bridge from the keep. Not walled or anything, but it'll be warm, and they'll have food and shelter enough for us."

They lapsed into silence.

Morath broke it. "Where will we land, then?"

"Why?" growled the soaked merc. The fair one who she'd caught bickering with the tall dark one as the comb entrance. He fingered the axe on his hip.

"You'll need us to land the boat safely. No rudder."

"And how will you do that?"

"The same way we've been avoiding collisions with rocks beneath the surface. Or hadn't you noticed the lack of jolting?" Livine glared at him.

"You can see beneath the water?" Falkirk sounded half sceptical, half impressed.

"Anyone can do it if they know how. I can teach you, if you like." Morath blushed. "The point is, we can direct the boat, at least a little bit. Especially away from rocks."

Falkirk showed her the island, visible now around a point. A crumbling keep towered over the near side, practically falling into the water, the rest looked overgrown and rocky. They really wanted to land there? But Morath and Livine didn't question them, just guided their flat-bottomed craft in to the pebble beach around the far side of the island.

An arching bridge towered over them, one footing reaching into the water, bisecting the smaller arm of the river behind the island. It was half crumbled away on one side so that the bridge narrowed dangerously in the middle, the parapet missing. But if they could get across, it would let them climb from the island to the top of the sheer stone riverbank, which they'd never be able to climb otherwise.

The blond merc and Alroth leaped into the icy water and dragged the boat up the beach, rocks grinding on the flat bottom. Morath and Livine chattered something about exploring, tucked up their skirts, and headed up the hill to the keep. Sathred, Dayma, and Runas headed for the bridge. Dayma and Runas stumbled over the sharp rocks, but Sathred's steps were sure. Her sturdy boots were serving her well.

"Shouldn't we send Arista off properly?"

Mellia was the only one close enough to hear Alinace's words. She was still tucked into a corner of the boat, her damp hair plastered to her head under her translucent veil. Mellia crouched her ghostly form beside her friend, and Alroth turned back for her, leaned his arms on the gunwale. Mellia gestured to Alinace. Mirabi hopped off the bier and crawled into the handmaid's lap.

Alroth cleared his throat. "It's been a hard morning." He glanced at Mellia, who nodded to him to keep going. "We should get all of you somewhere warm."

Mellia pointed forcefully to the queen's husk. Her dress was probably all that held her corpse together at this point. Her trip down the river had hardly been peaceful, as intended.

"You want to send off the Grist queen?"

Alinace glanced up at Alroth through her lashes. "If it's not too much trouble."

"Of course not. You come on out of there, and we'll get it—her—sorted out."

Alinace clutched Mirabi to her chest as Alroth helped her rise and step out of the boat on shaky legs, Mellia unhelpfully ephemeral on her other side. He gestured the two bickering mercs, Del and Kai, over from where they were already at each other farther up the pebble beach, and the three of them shoved the boat off. Alinace closed her eyes, probably trying to keep Arista's funeral boat in the centre of the shallow stream. Arista passed under the bridge and was swept out of sight.

Alinace kept her eyes closed. Mirabi barked and wriggled in her arms. When her eyes opened, a small smile lit her face, and she set the pup down. "There you are, little one. You want to explore? Your aunties went up the hill. I bet if you run, you can catch them!"

Mirabi tore up the hill after Livine and Morath. Dayma and Runas loitered at the top of the hill, at the near end of the bridge, seemingly unconvinced that it would hold them at all. Sathred was already halfway over, following Falkirk. Etienne had wandered up the beach past the bridge. What a merry troupe they made, everyone in various stages of annoyance.

The snow fell into the river and all around them, melting as it hit the stony ground, but that wouldn't last. Soon, the bridge would be slick with it. They needed to cross now before it became a problem. Mellia floated after Mirabi. Livine and Morath didn't have time to explore the island.

By the time she caught up with them, mimed her concerns, and drew them back to the bridge, the whole expanse was wet with melted snowflakes. Mirabi dashed across, easily navigating the narrow spot where the bridge's wall and a patch of walkway had tumbled into the river below. Mellia would be safe as well, ephemeral as she was.

Kai and Falkirk waited at the bridge's end. "Let's go, before the whole thing freezes over." Falkirk took Morath's elbow, and she let them guide her up onto the bridge. At the narrowest part, they urged her to go first. Morath's shoes might be slippery on the slick stone, but she never wavered. She turned back to say something over her shoulder, and Falkirk's boot slid. Morath grabbed their arm to steady them, and they regained their footing, clear of the treacherous section.

Kai turned to Livine. "Our turn."

Livine nodded. "Morath didn't slip because she was sure of her footing. If you put your weight over your foot, it'll be less likely to slip out from under you, you know." She demonstrated leaning forward over her front foot.

Kai shrugged. "Falkirk just needs new boots. Come on."

Livine trailed him up onto the bridge, and they crossed, Mellia hovering after them.

Halfway across the bridge, as Livine was crossing the narrowest section ahead of her, shivers racked Mellia's body, as though she could feel the chill wind in her wet clothes. Both Kai and Livine had passed the narrowest point without issue. Mellia locked eyes with Alroth, just on the other side. Maybe she would have been fine. If her lungs hadn't returned to her filled with choking icy water, and the sharp throb in her ankle hadn't pitched her sideways. Mellia stumbled forward, clutching the intact side of the bridge, the jack of plate wet and weighing her down, her sopping skirts around her knees, protecting them somewhat from the icy stone. When had she hit her knees? She gagged and spewed water that ran between the bridge's stones, freezing and slickening them further.

"Easy, sweetling. That's right, cough." His hand was firm and warm on the back of her neck, beneath her frozen hair and veil.

Mellia gasped in a rough breath, coughed—her throat must be tearing open, the icy, snow-filled air needling into her raw flesh. Mirabi whined and wriggled between their bodies. When the coughing stopped, Mellia's breaths coming steady but ragged, Alroth stood before her, steadied her.

"Can you make it, sweetling?"

Mellia straightened, winced as pain lanced up her ankle, and Alroth cradled her in his arms, surefooted on the slippery bridge. Three more steps, two, one... He set her on her feet once the bridge widened back to its intact size and tried to work the jack of plate from her shivering body. He swore and pulled his knife, cut the swollen lace. Her belt knife would have served just as well. Using her eating knife that way had never even entered her head. Her sheltered life as a sister was over.

Alroth pulled the freezing metal-lined coat over Mellia's head and untied his belt.

"Don't put it on." It came out between chatters of Mellia's teeth. Her woollen mantle and houppelande would keep her warm still—at least warm enough to keep from freezing, but Alroth's houppelande was thinner than hers.

"Hush, sweetling."

Who are you to tell me to hush? But her chattering teeth wouldn't let the words come out. Alroth pulled off his houppelande and handed it to her to keep it off the damp ground. She held it away from her drenched body while he pulled the jack of plate over his head and put his belt over it to keep it shut now that the lace was ruined. He took the houppelande—shouldn't his belt go over that too?

He threw it over her head. The warmth wouldn't come through all her wet layers, but she turned up the collar and pulled it close around her neck. Alroth's warmth wrapped under her stiff hair and kept it from dripping cold fingers of water down her back.

"It's not far. Can you walk?"

"Come on, man! We're freezing our— Oof!" Del's admonition was cut off by Kai's elbow to his ribs.

Alroth still watched her, waiting for her answer. She rotated her ankle. No, she couldn't walk on it. Until it was healed. She called Runas over, and Arista's healer made quick work of patching her up, ankle and lungs both.

She nodded to Alroth. Trying to talk might make her cough again. Or burst into tears.

The rest of the party waited on the other side of the bridge, snowflakes collecting on the shoulders of their houppelandes and mantles.

"Finally," said Del and stalked on up the road. It had once been paved, but stones had come loose from the edges and now they were more hinderance than help. The day had darkened, the snow blanketing the sides of the road and reducing visibility to a hundred paces in front of them. If they'd been hoping to return to New Bridge on the road, that was no longer an option. This snow was settling in to be a big dump, and everything would be snowed over until spring.

Until spring. They would be stuck out here until spring. Alroth had said it wasn't far. He'd mentioned a village out here. At least they were headed somewhere warm. Alroth's sure steps at her back kept Mellia putting one frozen foot in front of the other. As long as she kept shivering, she wouldn't freeze. She opened and closed her hands rhythmically, tucked inside her mantle and Alroth's houppelande, her fingers alternately numbing and tingling.

Perhaps being snowed into a tiny village wasn't ideal, but surviving was, and staying out in this storm would kill them sooner rather than later.

The *village* of Bridge was more a string of old cottages, some of which were overgrown, but smoke poured from a handful of rooftops, and firelight flickered from the cracks in their shuttered windows. Alroth led them to the largest house in the village and rattled the door. A hook hung above it, as though there used to be a sign there. The door seemed to be latched inside.

"I've got it." Falkirk disappeared around the side of the building, and they all waited in the icy wind until the door swung open.

They brushed the snow from their clothes and stomped it from their boots. The handmaids gathered on the far side of the fireplace while Alroth's mercenaries bunched together on the other. Alroth did a quick round of introductions. No one introduced the handmaids. Kai and Del fought over how best to stack the tinder until Etienne shoved them out of the way and got the fire going. Falkirk threw two logs on, and they crackled and sparked. Mellia hovered close to the hearth.

Morath heaved a sheet of canvas off an old couch, and Runas helped her drag it closer to the fire. Sathred steered Alinace, who was shivering, onto it, and Dayma sat next to her and wrapped an arm around her shoulders. Livine sat on the hearth. She pulled her portable desk from her pocket, thawed her ink wither magic, and began writing in her logbook.

Falkirk popped back in, snowflakes dusting their head and shoulders. "I'll have food and shelter ready for you all soon… It might take some work to get it to rights, but I'm sure if we all..." They seemed to take in the handmaids' fine clothes.

"Thanks so much, Falkirk." Alroth gripped their shoulder. "You've already done plenty just with the fire."

"Might take a bit to get the rooms ready."

"Of course, we'll all pitch in," said Morath. "Just show me around, and I'll sort it out."

"And dirty your fine dresses?" Falkirk looked her up and down.

Morath blushed and looked down at her own silks. She laughed. "You must think I'm very fine!" She held out her work-roughened hands. "I'm not afraid of a little elbow grease. Please, just think of me as plain Morath."

"Fine, plain Morath, let's see the state of the rooms..." Their voice trailed away as they led Morath up the staircase.

Rooms, a fire, shelter from the snowstorm. They had survived. Yes, the Grist had turned on them; yes, they were probably still in danger, but they couldn't do anything about that until they were fed and rested and warmed. Mellia held her stiff hands out to the fire. Thank Doloman for the fire. *It wasn't Doloman's doing, it was your bond mate's.* Her bond mate, with whom she'd be spending the night. Was that shiver anticipation or dread? Just cold. It must just be cold.

18

Alroth

Now that they were here, safe from the storm under a cozy roof, the tension bled out of Alroth's shoulders. They had survived the day, they'd survive the freezing night. As long as Mellia didn't shiver right out of her skin.

Alroth went to the hearth, where Mellia and the writing handmaid held a low conversation. It didn't seem to be slowing the handmaid down, though; her pen worked over the parchment in quick strokes. How had she learned to write so fast? Any merc band worth their salt had a ledger, but the entries were figures and markings, not the long phrases this handmaid was writing. How much did it cost to keep her in blank books and ink?

Mellia glanced over her shoulder at his approach and fell silent. She pulled off his houppelande, now soaking, and they both watched it drip onto the floorboards.

A smile twitched at Alroth's mouth. What a day. What a fucking *day*! He dropped the houppelande to the floor with a slithering smack and burst out laughing. No one joined him, but why in Hiorach's name shouldn't he laugh? This morning, he'd been worried that they would all be dead by sundown. Now they'd escaped the

Impietas-cursed Grist guards along with the expected mercenaries; the snowstorm would keep anyone from following them for weeks, if not months, and they were all *still alive*, the only real measure of failure, after all. As long as the handmaids lived, the Grist father's promise held. And he'd seen them pass, hale and hearty, with his own eyes.

"Excuse me, but what is there to laugh about?" The sharp handmaid—Etienne's pet—clutched the curly-haired one closer into her body and glared at him.

"We're all still alive, handmaid. Any day that ends like that is enough to laugh about for me." Alroth grinned at her harsh look.

"And we have you to thank for that, I suppose." The tall curvy one stood next to the couch, her red hair just visible beneath her blue-and-silver veil.

"Me and mine, that's right." He gestured to his folks, who had bunched together and gone silent, watching the handmaids. When had this battle line been drawn between the two groups? Alroth scowled. "We're going to have to get along, staying here together all winter. Don't start off on the wrong foot."

"*Don't start off on the wrong foot.*" The severe one drew herself up. "After you disrupted the sacred Necrophoresis Ritual, tossed us over a waterfall, and kidnapped us?"

Kidnapped? Alroth opened his mouth to snap at this uptight, presumptuous handmaid, but Mellia beat him to it.

"That's enough, Dayma. We all saw the Grist guards turn on you. None of us were getting out of there alive if it hadn't been for Alroth and his people." Her teeth had stopped chattering.

Dayma shifted her glare to Mellia. "We will talk later." Her gaze flicked to Alroth and back. Had Mellia had a chance to see her friends—her sisters—before this morning? Likely not. They must be wondering how the two of them had come to be bound.

The sharp handmaid on the couch cut in. "Talk as much as you like, I'm not sleeping under the same roof as *them*." It sounded like the handmaid was talking about all the mercenaries, but her glare was only for Etienne. Ah yes, the one with a special hatred for Drake.

"What, you don't remember the last time we shared a roof?" Etienne's smile was cutting.

"It's because I remember it that I will not repeat it. I understand why *you* would be eager to."

Mellia cut off Etienne's retort. "That's decided then. Handmaids will stay here. Mercenaries, elsewhere. I'm sure there's a barn or a spare room somewhere in the village."

Del rounded on him. "Alroth, you're not going to let your matron kick us out! We saved their Fallo-cursed lives, and now they're banishing us to a drafty barn?"

Alroth shrugged. "The inn is big, but not big enough for all of us." There were plenty of abandoned houses here, perfectly good, if a little overgrown and in need of a little plaster. They could patch them up once the storm died down.

The handmaid Morath led Falkirk down the stairs, chattering over her shoulder. She was still talking when she got within earshot.

"There are six rooms up there, so we'll have to double up, but..." She trailed away as she took in the standoff.

"Six rooms. Perfect." Etienne's nemesis gathered the curly-haired handmaid and stalked up the stairs, the uptight one marching after.

Morath looked to the tall handmaid. "What did I miss?"

"The fighters will find another place to sleep."

"That seems so silly. Come up and see, the beds are a good size—"

"Runas wasn't comfortable sharing a roof with them." Mellia's voice was soft.

"Oh. Runas. Right. Well, then..." She glanced between the remaining handmaids and the mercenaries. "I'll go help them clean." She scampered back up the stairs.

The fire crackled.

"I'll see Yasmine, rustle up some food." Falkirk stalked away.

"What did you do to that handmaid, Etienne?" Del didn't bother to keep his voice down. "She'd condemn you to Orbitus's tender care in a heartbeat, eh?" He elbowed Etienne, whose hand flew to his hammer grip.

Kai seemed to realize at the same moment as Alroth that this was perhaps the one topic Etienne would not joke about. He stepped between Etienne and Del. "He didn't mean anything by it, Drake."

"I did mean something—"

"No, you didn't, you Doloman-possessed Sarilla spawn! Take a look at the man. He's about to bash your Stultitian head in with his big-ass hammer." The two of them pulled out their fists.

Alroth sighed. Mellia shrank back behind the recently vacated couch as Del took a swing at Kai, narrowly missing an upholstered chair.

"Not in here!" Alroth roared. "You'll turn the furniture to kindling!" Their cruck's furnishings were solidly built for a reason—that's all that survived these children of Turbatius.

"They can't very well fight in the blizzard." *What?* The bookworm handmaid hadn't even looked up from her writing, let alone backed away from the fistfight.

Etienne chivvied Del and Kai out the door, muttering something about finding a sty to sleep in.

The tall handmaid looked back and forth between Alroth and Mellia. "Livine, let's go clean up our rooms."

Livine sprinkled sand over her filled page. "Is there a hearth in there, because I'm not done—"

"Let's go and see, shall we?" The tall handmaid hooked her arm in Livine's, who barely managed to close her inkwell and slam the portable desk shut as she was marched away.

The fire crackled. Alroth picked his houppelande off the floor and spread it on the hearth.

He cleared his throat. "I guess we'll be taking the last room. Won't be nearly as fine as the one we had last night—"

"No. We won't be. You can't stay here, Alroth. Not with the handmaids blaming you for"—she gestured to the inn—"this. They won't be comfortable."

Comfortable? It might be good for them to be a little uncomfortable after their cushy lives in the hive, being waited on hand and foot. Would they be *comfortable* burning the firewood the mercs chopped for them? Or eating the food they made?

"I don't care much if they're comfortable or not. I said I'd protect you, and I will." The handmaids were innocents, and they would be protected too, but they wouldn't get the kind of *comfort* they were used to, not by any stretch.

Mellia got to her feet, planted her fists on her hips. "You don't care if they're comfortable? Well, I do. I care very much. These women have been taken from their lives, ripped from their duties and their callings at the whims of ambitious men. Did they deserve that, after all they've worked for? Do they deserve to be here, in the backwoods, removed from everything they value? Thrust into the protection of a man who doesn't care a bit for their comfort? No, Alroth. I won't let you take this from them, too. The handmaids deserve their own space. They deserve not to be forced to share with grimy mercenaries, who can't keep their hands from enacting violence for the span between mealtimes!" She gestured at the door where Etienne, Del, and Kai had disappeared.

Etienne was never like that. The handmaid Runas brought out the worst in him. As for Del and Kai, they fought, but they never hurt anyone else, not ever. Why couldn't they keep their fists to themselves while the ladies were around? Maybe it was better to have them out of here, where they could all have a little more breathing room. Him included. He turned on his heel and stepped into the blizzard.

His men's footprints were already filled with snow, but Alroth didn't need to follow them. He turned toward the edge of the village, the way they'd come, past a few more lit cottages to a dark one. He kicked the snow away from the door until he could open it enough to slip inside. He tripped over a stool in the darkness and slammed his knee into the table, but the kindling in the fireplace was still set up, just as he'd left it, the flint and tinder dry in a box on the mantle. He struck sparks from the flint and blew them to life on the tinder, then stuck it into the kindling.

He shivered. Perhaps he shouldn't have been so quick to leave his houppelande behind. The wet from his jack had seeped into his gambeson and straight through his tunic and shirt while they were inside in the warmth, and his clammy skin made him shiver. But this fire would warm the hearth soon enough.

Back here for the winter. Alroth pulled up the little stool and sank onto it, his sigh clouding in the still air. Not that it was much warmer here by the tiny fire, not yet. Last winter, before they'd built Mill Hamlet, the others had stayed at the old inn, Ignis's Rest, but he'd needed his own space, and this had been it. Just a little smoky cottage, out past the other lived-in houses. Let him go watch the barges on the March River whenever he wanted.

The bridge had seemed safe enough last winter, when it was just his own life in the balance. Perhaps he'd gotten used to where to put his feet. It had served him well today, though. That moment when Mellia teetered over the edge... He scrubbed a hand over his scratchy face and worked his chilled hands open and closed. It was already warming up in here. If he wanted a sister—almost a handmaid—to bed down here with him, he'd have to spruce the place up.

The bed behind him needed fresh straw. He'd emptied the tick before they left. There was no food in the place. He'd need at least a little something if he was going to keep his matron here. More firewood. The thatched roof was covered in snow by now, so would keep at least until the spring melt. He laid a few logs on the merry fire, grabbed the empty tick, and ventured forth into the storm.

Word had gotten round by now that there were guests arrived in the blizzard, and the tithe barn was busy, despite the weather. Del was already filling ticks with fresh straw, using an unnecessary amount of force. Etienne scooped up two freshly filled mattresses—one for each shoulder—and marched them away.

The granary, just next to where Del was working, was only partly full. At this time of year, it should be overflowing, ready for winter. What had happened to the harvest? Already, this would have been a lean winter in Bridge, but with twelve extra mouths to feed? Someone came to stand next to him. Yasmine.

One grey curl peeked out from her plain veil, light against her dark-brown forehead. "The Grist wouldn't help us with reaping this year."

"Did they say why?"

She shrugged. "Do they ever? Doloman was punishing us."

"I would have come to help you." Alroth gestured to Del. "We all would have."

"You had your own fields this year, Wolf."

And they'd all agreed that Bridge would be fine without him. But look at them now. They'd been willing to starve before asking for his help.

"I should have stayed."

"If you're trying to make me agree with you, you're wasting your breath. You were passing through. Helped some while you were here, but you don't belong in Bridge any more than those fancy ladies you brought with you. You want to stay and help? Fine by me. But don't get stuck here."

Alroth nodded. Grabbed a full tick from Del and stitched it up. It was downright relaxing, plying the needle and necton thread. Imagine if he could go the rest of his life stitching fabric instead of flesh. Though now that he had a matron, he could stitch flesh back together with magic. Heal folk from the inside.

Once the last tick was sewn up, Alroth found Etienne hovering around the end of the barn, with the cheese.

"You and Del. Is it going to be a problem?"

They both stared at the stacks of cheesecloth-wrapped wheels.

"No."

"And the handmaid? Will that be one?"

Etienne turned a sparking gaze on him. "If she makes it one."

Was it possible that Etienne didn't see how different he was since he'd exchanged barbs with her in the funeral boat? Either way, Alroth couldn't bring it up without getting clocked. He and Etienne might have passed the brawling phase, progressed to more temperate natures, but the handmaid seemed to take Etienne back to the Drake of their youth. The one who'd used his intimidating size and weapons skills to pull Alroth from the gutter and lead all of them to war, back when they were foolish enough to think the silver would be worth the bloodshed.

"I'm not talking about her. I'm talking about you."

"Your matron is smarter than you, Wolf." His grin was back, but there was no life behind it. "Keep the queen bees well away from us. Wouldn't want any other slips like yours. Could have a whole host of nattering mages trailing us when we head back to New Bridge." He clapped Alroth on the shoulder and strode away.

A whole host of mages. And why not? If the handmaids were bound to them, they could be safe from whatever schemes the powers in New Bridge were drawing up. But the way they'd kept half the room between them in the inn hall made it clear enough that they disliked each other. He had all winter to change their minds, lead by example, him and Mellia. He hefted a basket of provisions onto his back, and the tick over his shoulder, and strode into the blizzard.

He wrestled the mattress back inside the warmed cottage and brushed the snow off the tick before it could melt and soak the thing. By the time the bed was made and the food stocked, the dim light was beginning to fade to true darkness. Time to fetch his matron.

19

Mellia

After Alroth left, Mellia went to Sathred's room. All the handmaids were busy clearing away dust, shaking out blankets, and moving furniture around.

Mellia shut the door. They couldn't stay here. New Bridge was too close; they'd have to go somewhere else. Somewhere the Grist couldn't easily reach them. Where would they be safe? Falvair would be a safe trip, even this time of year, and her parents wouldn't turn the handmaids away. If she could get Sathred to agree with her, the others would follow. The most important thing was to get them away from the volatile mercenaries. Away from the men seemingly lined up to use them as pawns.

Sathred watched her from across the little room, the doors of the wardrobe hanging open. "What happened, Mellia?"

Happened? "I don't know why the Grist guards—"

"The mercenaries. You're bound."

Oh, that. "Yes, I am."

Mirabi chose that moment to trot through the closed door and hop onto Sathred's bed. They trotted up to the bolster and back down to the foot, then looked back and forth between Mellia and Sathred, panting.

"You were going to be a handmaid." Was that hurt in her voice?

Mellia sighed and sank onto the bed. The straw in the mattress gave way, and she sank down, nearly to the floor, with a squawk. "We'll need new ticking."

Sathred didn't move, arms still crossed over her chest, face impassive.

"It was a task from Doloman."

"Binding yourself to an untitled mercenary?"

"No." She could share the whole chain of events with Sathred, but what right did the handmaid have to it? "It doesn't matter how it happened. We can't stay here."

"No, we can't."

"We'll go to Falvair."

"Falvair?"

"My father is the marquess."

Sathred pursed her lips.

"They tried to kill you, Sathred. All of you. You saw it as well as I did."

"Yes, I did." She turned to the shuttered window, ran a hand down the crack between the wooden panels. "How would we get there, in this?"

"Barges run up and down the March River all winter. If we can get back to the river, we can convince one to carry us. We can make it to Falvair that way. I'll ensure your safety."

"On your lands. That's right."

Mirabi jumped into Mellia's lap.

Mellia stroked their soft ears. "Tomorrow, if it's sunny, we'll clear the bridge. All of us together can do it." Coax the sun to melt the snow and ice on the bridge and dry it, make it safe to cross.

Mirabi nuzzled at her hand. Alroth would never go with her, leave his people behind. But maybe that was for the best. She needed to go back to Falvair. Now that she was bound, she could take some of the burden off her father. Alroth was... he wouldn't make a good marquess, with his swords and his mercenary tendencies.

"I'll tell the others."

Mellia nodded as Morath burst in, straw stuck in her hair, veil askew, silky dress tucked into her belt.

"Hand over your mattress." She was already ripping the coverlet off as Mellia jumped up, Mirabi clutched in her arms.

The little ephemer squirmed out of her grip, floated to the floor, and barked, jumping back and forth at Morath's feet.

Mellia took the other end of the mattress and helped Morath wrestle it out the doorway and down the stairs. Tomorrow, they would leave. Why go to all this trouble? Then again, if Alroth and his fighters realized they didn't intend to stay, they would stop the handmaids' escape. They would want them to stay here for the winter, surely. They had to pretend, just for the moment, that they were going to stay. And Mellia would have to pretend that she planned to stay with Alroth too, if he came back tonight to find her. It would be fine. He could spend another night on the floor nearby her bed if he so chose. And that's where he'd remain.

She and Morath took care of the straw ticks, emptying the old straw dust onto the midden heap and handing the empty ticks off to the dark, serious mercenary Kai. He seemed calm enough now, without Del around. But who could tell when he'd pull out his fists again?

Etienne brought the full ticks back to the inn, one on each shoulder, and he and Kai dragged them back upstairs to each of the handmaid's rooms. There were only six. Mellia would have to find somewhere else to sleep. Alroth would find her somewhere.

Mellia paused, mid blanket tuck. Would he expect her to sleep next to him? Would he want to be intimate with her? And did she want that? It didn't matter. He'd left. She could sleep in Dayma's room. It was warmer with two to a bed anyway.

"What's wrong?" Morath shook out the coverlet and tossed it over the bed.

"Just thinking about sleeping arrangements."

"You're welcome to bed down here with me. We wouldn't leave you to freeze, Mellia."

They each smoothed their own side of the coverlet.

"I know, I was—"

Etienne poked his head into the doorway. "Dinner's ready."

Morath paled. "I didn't help with dinner. I should have been down there. Did Falkirk do it all by themself? I have to go apologize—"

"Easy there, handmaid. Falkirk has it well in hand." Etienne's grin was back, now that Runas was nowhere to be seen. She hadn't opened her door for her mattress when Etienne had brought it up; she'd waited for him to leave to scurry out and kick it bodily through the doorway while he was downstairs.

Morath was already hurrying past Etienne, probably down to the kitchen to apologize to Falkirk for not being everywhere at once.

"Ah, you found the instruments!" Etienne stepped into the room to swipe a horn and a drum from the washstand. He dusted them with his sleeve and bowed Mellia out into the hallway ahead of him.

Mellia led the way to the landing.

The place had filled up since they were down here with the ticks. Chatter floated up the stairs along with a tantalizing scent. Benches were filled with curious Bridge folks. Dayma was already daintily eating a bowl of pottage, and Sathred steered a dazed-looking Morath to the seat next to her, her own bowl steaming in her hands.

Etienne gestured to a free spot at one of the tables. "Save me a seat, Sister. I'll get us some vittles."

"I'm not a sister any—" she called after him, but a few curious heads turned in her direction, and she fell silent.

Getting to know Etienne over dinner was nice, even if all he did was talk about Alroth. How he'd been the best merc to have at your back during the war, how he'd taken over the merc band when they came over to Sudra, and—this had to be pure embellishment—how he'd single-handedly ended the Canal War. Etienne dodged her question when she asked how one man could possibly do such a thing, and moved on to a more recent story, from Bridge, last year, before they'd gone upriver to New Bridge.

They'd been out checking snares and looking for maybe a glyptodon they could cart back to Bridge when they'd glimpsed something much bigger in the bushes.

"I think I must have shrieked like a little child and clung onto Alroth's arm." Etienne squeaked at the top of his low register in demonstration.

Mellia couldn't help but laugh. The story must end happily since they were both still here to tell it. But in the moment, it could have been a sabre-toothed cat, a dire wolf, or even a titanis. One of those huge, toothed beaks lunging from the bushes right at them... Mellia shuddered.

"Alroth thought it was a peccary, not the worst, but they can still tear you up some with their tusks..." Etienne kept talking, but Mellia didn't take in his words.

Alroth shouldered through the door. He scanned the room, nodding back to a few of the folks who saluted him with tankards. His gaze caught on her and locked. He strode to their table and took the seat across from her and Etienne.

Alroth swiped his half-empty bowl. "Lots of curious folk here in Bridge. Are they bothering you?"

"Not at all." Some had come over to introduce themselves, but none had bothered her. "They seem to know you here. Etienne was just telling me—"

"The one with the peccary." Etienne looked altogether too pleased with himself.

Alroth glowered. "If it *had* been a peccary, I would have saved your sorry skin."

Etienne could barely contain his guffaws long enough to answer. "Yes, tackling me into the bushes was the best defence against a charging wild pig."

"Better than being gored." Alroth focused on his food.

Had he really tackled Etienne into the bushes? Saved his life?

"It would have been if you hadn't tossed us into a stand of stinging nettle." Etienne thumped the table jovially. "Thank Paratus I was wearing my gambeson with the collar."

"You barely got stung. I'm the one that got a face full of the stuff."

Mellia flinched. A face full of stinging nettle was no laughing matter. Wild nettle spines could blind a person, cause scarring that would never fade.

Etienne sobered. "Barely missed your eyes." He turned to Mellia, all trace of humour gone. "He'd have saved me from a goring, no mistake about that. No matrons around Bridge to patch me up from such a wound, either." He gave Alroth a sly look. "But still, you should have seen his face when that badger poked its delicate little nose out of the bushes."

"Badger!" It hadn't been a peccary at all?

Etienne mimed looking furtively around the room like a frightened badger. "I thought Wolf was going to skin the thing for scaring the daylights out of us!" He slapped his knee and crowed.

Mellia didn't bother to contain her laughter anymore, and a smile even tugged at Alroth's mouth.

"I would have skinned it too if your hollering hadn't startled it off." He jerked his head at Etienne to keep going. He knew what came next, obviously.

"On the way back to the village, Alroth is leaning on me, moaning about the nettle, and I'm gallantly supporting my saviour, when we turn a corner in the path—and there's not one, not two, but a whole herd of peccary! Right there in the path! Just staring at us!"

Mellia gasped. One peccary could be irritable and charge a person, but a herd? Parents with their young would trample you to death for looking at them sideways. "What did you do?"

"What *could* we do? We looked at each other, drew our weapons, and charged them before they could charge us."

Two men charged a *herd* of peccaries?

"Brought home enough pork to last the season." Alroth scraped the last of the pottage from his pilfered bowl and shoved it back at Etienne. "Least we could do for the village that took in some rough-around-the-edges mercs, no questions asked."

They'd risked their lives to bring Bridge food? There was no way that Bridge would have been able to pay them for the pork. They could have retreated, run the other way, gone around the herd. But they'd been out hunting for food, and they'd brought some back, injured or not.

"And lucky you, Yasmine got you healed up so you don't have a mess of nettle scars on that ugly mug." Etienne twirled his moustache.

Alroth pushed back from the table. "That's about enough stories for today."

Was he uncomfortable with Etienne telling her about his heroism or trying to forestall her protests that he was not ugly, not in the least? Should she say something like that? She wrapped her hands tightly around her empty bowl.

Alroth reached for her, his palm up. They both watched his hand, Etienne mercifully silent. She put her fingers in his warm palm. Did he really have somewhere for them to sleep? Separately, of course.

"Where are we going?"

"I have a place, I told you." Had he told her? He'd just disappeared after their fight.

Etienne grabbed both empty bowls off the table. "Cozy little cabin it is, too. Good night, Sister." He inclined his head and strode away in the direction of the kitchen, collecting dishes as he went. To wash up? Who were these men she'd found herself tied to?

Mellia made to pull away from Alroth to grab his houppelande, still drying by the fire, but he tightened his grip on her fingers. She held his stare as a hint of fear clouded his face. "I'm just fetching your houppelande."

He nodded and let her go.

The houppelande was nearly dry, and Alroth put it on before they braved the storm again. The wind was at their backs, and Mellia huddled close to him as he broke a path for her through the snowdrifts. Stripes of light streaked the falling snow through the shutters they passed, even the dim firelight far brighter than the enveloping darkness of the blizzard. The wind had died a little, but it would pick up again once night truly fell.

His cottage looked like all the others: a squat little thatched thing, needing a good coat of whitewash, firelight flickering through the seams in the shutters. Snow had drifted in front of the door, and Alroth scraped it away with his boots before pulling it wide and ushering Mellia in. She banged off her boots and stepped inside. The cabin was small—one room—but cozy. The bed was opposite the fireplace, and between them stood a table and two stools. The small horn windows were shuttered, and the underside of the thatch high above flickered with firelight.

Alroth came in, shut the door, and stirred the fire—in a proper hearth—tossing on another couple of logs. "Used to be a manor here, so they say. Built a little house around the chimney, the only part still standing. But the hearth warms the whole room, even in the depths of winter."

More firewood sat by the fireplace. A pot hung on a hook, away from the fire for the moment, already filled with snow to melt, for their morning porridge, perhaps?

And the bed. It looked freshly made. Had he changed out his own straw ticking, just as she'd done for the handmaids?

Alroth was still poking at the fire, though it didn't seem as if there was any need. He turned to her, looked up from his crouch by the hearth, his face in shadow. Should she invite him to bed? Turn him out?

A piercing bark broke the silence building between them, and Mirabi burst through the wall, yapping their tiny head off.

Mellia gasped, her heart beating practically out of her chest, and sighed it out. "Mirabi! Where have you been?"

The pup rolled over and showed their belly. How could she resist giving them a pat? She crouched and rubbed their soft pink skin, their puppy belly warm under her chilled fingers.

Alroth had left his jack of plate by the fire to dry, and he flipped it over so the faded fabric was up, the muscles in his shoulders working under his tunic—the armour was heavy. When he turned back to Mellia, he froze. He'd caught her watching him. Mirabi whined, and Mellia resumed her petting.

Hopefully, she wasn't blushing, after getting caught ogling him.

"I put fresh straw in the tick this afternoon. No bugs, that I could see. Should be warm under the covers, once..."

Once what? If she hadn't been blushing before, she was now for certain.

Alroth cleared his throat. Was that a blush creeping up his neck as well? "I'll sleep here by the fire, like last night." He licked his dry lips.

"Our bond is sanctioned." She stood up, ignoring Mirabi pawing at her skirts.

"It was sanctioned last night as well." He scowled. Was he annoyed that she'd made him sleep on the floor last night? Except that she hadn't made him do anything. She'd gone to bed, and he'd chosen to stay away. But that had been because they were in Father Glimar's house, hadn't it? "Your will is still your own."

How dare he say that straight-faced? "Like it was my own when you jammed the door shut on me?"

Alroth loosened his belt, and Mellia tamped down her flinch. He just slung the belt on a chair back and pulled his houppelande over his head. "To keep you safe. Just until I returned."

Mellia didn't answer. How would he justify his actions?

"If you had stayed put, you might not have ended up tossed in an oubliette."

He was blaming *her* for ending up tossed in that dank hole? Mellia kept her reaction contained, just raised her eyebrows mildly.

"And I might not have been roped into a duel with a lordling in full harness."

Roped into it. Is that what he thought? She'd had nothing to do with that duel, hadn't even known about it until the castle guards had dragged her to the lists. It was laughable, him trying to blame her for it.

"So perhaps next time you'll do as I say."

And there it was, her opening. "Do as you say."

"That's right." His heels were dug in now. Perfect time to pounce.

"Follow your directions?" Just a little more...

"To the letter."

"Join you on a dangerous job wearing heavy armour into a tiny boat that gets tossed over a cliff?"

Alroth blanched, having fallen neatly into her trap. He didn't have a leg to stand on when it came to telling her what to do. She had accomplished far more acting on her own decisions than by following his inane orders. So why was he chuckling? Did he care so little?

"Is that amusing to you? I almost died today, more times than I can count."

He sobered. He took a long stride toward her and dropped to his knees, close enough to touch. "And you saved all of our lives, at least twice. Helping Falkirk, freezing the waterfall, leaping out of the boat—" His words seemed to catch in his throat. A sob shook his shoulders. He'd been worried about her. Genuinely worried. Was that why he was being so peccary-headed and Stultitian? All the fight went out of her. He couldn't keep doing this, trying to keep her safe by controlling her, but it couldn't hurt to reassure him. Besides, she would only be here until tomorrow.

She combed her fingers through his hair, and her thumb swiped at a tear on his cheekbone.

He addressed the packed-earth floor. "To lose you so soon after our binding..." He wrapped his arms around her and pressed his face into her middle.

She swallowed down her guilt. She could pretend that she wasn't leaving tomorrow, just for tonight. She couldn't let him know her plans, and it would be easier if she played along: They were bound together, never to part. "You think I wasn't worried about losing you? When I saw Lord Ainsley in plate armour, and I thought you—" She took in a shuddering breath. The words had gone in an act and come out real, somehow. She hadn't known about the jack of plate, not until after. That tightening in her gut, that lurch of terror when Lord Ainsley's blade had gone for him; the split second before he'd blocked it. A tear trickled down her cheek.

He looked up at her, earnest, certain. "I'll stay by the fire. I've slept in worse places." His face lightened. "A lady like yourself is used to feather beds, I'm sure."

There it was again. The reason that she had to leave. How had she forgotten that this was a mercenary? A mercenary—perhaps even the heretic prince himself—who had tricked her into being bound to him, tricked her into giving him her lands and titles. Had she thought it a good idea to sleep next to this man? He absolutely should sleep by the hearth. It was far too easy to remember his worry, his tears, that damnable peccary story of Etienne's, and forget what he'd done to her.

"That's probably best." She pulled away.

But he didn't let go. "Wait. Sweetling, wait." He must have caught the murderous rage in her glare, because he sighed and released her. There was no door to slam between them. He followed her as she stalked to the other end of the cabin, toward the cozy bed he'd made for her.

Mirabi dashed back and forth between them, yapping and nipping at Mellia's hem.

"Please, sweetling, hear me out." And if she did? What would he say? More binding lies wrapped up in sweet truths? She could tease them apart now. She knew what to watch for. Might as well let him have his say.

She whirled, her fists planted on her hips. "Talk."

He sat on the bed. Closed his eyes. Took a deep breath. Coming up with exactly what she wanted to hear, no doubt.

"I want you to come home with me. We won't stay in the cruck, not unless you want to. I want privacy so that I can make you moan my name whenever the mood strikes us."

Did he think that would sway her in his favour? One orgasm and he thought she needed him. Though it had been a delicious orgasm. She huffed, but he kept on.

"I want you to teach me about our bond, sweetling, so that we can heal folk, help the crops grow strong, make sure that if the Grist don't come, folk don't starve. Keep people safe when war arrives at our doors. I don't know what your life has been, before you were a sister, if you were a lady or a laundress. Mine has been hard for a long time. Drake—Etienne—and the rest are the only ones I could rely on..." He looked at her, finally. That had been the truth part. "I'm not used to trusting folk. But I'd like to try. If you'll let me." And there was the lie. If he'd trusted her, he wouldn't have tricked her.

She had to hear him say it. She had to hear him admit what he had done. "Just tell me that you didn't know about Falvair." Would it be worse if he kept lying to her? Or worse if he admitted it?

He locked eyes with her. "I didn't—I *don't* know about Falvair."

Lying, then. She sighed. "Lord Ainsley wanted to bind me to him for my lands and title. Since my brother... I'm the heir. Or rather, whomever I'm bound to is the heir."

His mouth fell open, and he wavered on the bed, bracing himself with one hand on the coverlet, his face pale enough to show a pink scattering of scars down one side.

"You really didn't know." He couldn't be pretending, not like this. Was that... fear in his eyes?

Alroth closed his mouth. Wrestled his expression under control. Was it possible he didn't want lands, titles? Was that why he'd run from his princely duties in Nordval and become a mercenary? Would he break their bond now just to be rid of all the responsibilities that came along with her? She could run the marquessate; that had been her plan anyway. But she would only get the chance if she was bound.

"Alroth." Mellia knelt in front of him, between his knees. She cupped his cheek, and his wild eyes met hers. "I'm sorry I didn't warn you. I didn't want..." What had she wanted? She'd wanted him to bind her because he wanted *her*. But that had been exceptionally foolish. He barely knew her. He'd bound her for her magic.

"You didn't want me binding you for your lands. Your titles. Like Ainsley."

Like all the others. The men who'd wanted to inherit, who thought of her as a mere inconvenient addition to their true goal.

"Fuck, sweetling. I'm sorry."

What did he have to be sorry for? Oh, yes. Poor rejected mage. Of course. "Now you force your pity on me?"

Was he... smiling? "I grew up on the streets of Munificast, if you'd like to give me the same."

That must be a lie. The heretic prince was a noble from Nordval. But if he wanted to pretend, she would, too.

Just pretend. For tonight. Pretend she wasn't leaving tomorrow. And since she was, they had to make the most of tonight. "We don't have to talk about any of that. Not right now."

The wind howled across the chimney and rattled the shutters. As good an excuse as any to share the bed.

"Let's focus on keeping warm." She rose and untied her belt.

Alroth's voice was gravelly. "I don't think undressing will keep you warm, sweetling."

She smiled as she pulled her houppelande over her head. "You aren't telling me what to do again, are you?"

"I wouldn't dream of trying. I'd be wasting my breath."

Now he was getting it. She untied the lace on her kirtle. Alroth kept his hands on the bedspread as she pulled it over her head. She shivered in just her shift and stockings.

"Do you want me to..." He gestured at the fireplace.

She shook her head and reached for the laces of his tunic.

"Do you want to tie me again?"

Mellia's fingers slowed on the lace of his tunic, and he took over and eased it off, tossed it on the floor to join her pile of clothes. *Did* she want to tie him? Would she let him take her unrestrained? Was she willing to endure that?

"Sweetling, what are you thinking? I know you've—in the past..."

"Had tragic and horrible experiences?" Is that what he thought of her? A nervous maid who'd never found pleasure with anyone before? Certainly, her binding rituals had been terrible, but did he think he was the only one who'd ever made her come?

"Yes. I don't want to be one of them." His stubborn streak was coming out again.

"Then don't be."

He ran a hand over his face. "You're not making this easy."

"And it should be easy for you."

"I want it to be easy for *you*. But I can't do that for you unless you tell me how." He sounded annoyed, but it wasn't really annoyance, was it? He was afraid. He was afraid that he would hurt her, that he would fail to keep her safe, protect her, even from himself, as he'd promised her.

"No, I don't want to tie you, Alroth."

His eyes widened. Was that the first time she'd said his name since they'd been bound? She ran her hands up his sides, under his shirt, her fingers exploring the texture of his scars. He closed his eyes and let her pull his shirt over his head.

He caught her wrist. "Tell me." His eyes burned into hers.

"Why don't I show you?"

He shook his head, the fear obvious in his eyes now that she'd noticed it. "You're not afraid I'll hurt you?" *Like the others.*

She cupped his cheek. "If I tell you to stop, will you stop?"

His brow furrowed. "What kind of—" He shook his head. He knew what kind. The Lord Ainsley kind. "Yes, of course I will. But what if you don't tell me to stop?"

"Then don't stop." She pulled the drawstring on his braies, untying the knot and pulling them down.

His hands skated up under her shift, and it was off, over her head. He tugged the ties on her underwear, the fabric falling to the floor. He threw back the covers on the bed, and Mellia straddled him, nothing between her slick heat and his hardening cock. With one hand on her back and one under her bum, he slid them fully onto the bed. Mellia rolled so that he was next to her, nudged him to settle into the cradle of her thighs.

His breathing was ragged now, his heavy cock twitching between them. "Are you sure you don't want to be on top? You'll have more control that way—"

"I trust you, Alroth." One day, they would do it that way, one day she'd tie him down again, one day... As long as she was pretending they would be together for always, there was no reason not to imagine what they might do together.

Alroth rolled on top of her, and he was there, so close... "I want to hear you telling me you're enjoying yourself."

"Hmm?" She ran a hand down the muscles of his back, spread her legs a little wider.

"I need to hear your words, Mellia." He was serious. He wanted her to talk while he was inside her? "I won't—feel *comfortable* doing this otherwise."

Comfortable. The word that had sparked their fight. Maybe now he understood what she'd meant? Was he admitting that he'd been wrong? Maybe coming as close as he ever would. A laugh escaped her. "Fine, yes, I'm enjoying myself. I would be enjoying myself more if you would stick your cock in—"

Mellia gasped as he slipped a finger inside her and groaned.

"Yes, good, but your *cock*, Alroth."

"I'm working on it, sweetling." He slipped in another finger and stroked her. He'd done this before, many times.

Was he trying to make her beg for his cock? He wouldn't dare do something like that... No, he wasn't being stubborn, he was being careful. Carefully spreading her wetness around her clit, making her gasp and moan another affirmative. Mellia reached down and wrapped a hand around his cock herself. If he was too nervous to do it...

"Wait, sweetling. You have to listen to me, too."

Mellia huffed, but he slipped away from her, working his way down her body. She hissed out another *yes*. He was going to lick her, stroke her with his tongue, as he had during their binding. She clutched at his hair as she writhed under his tongue, a steady stream of affirmations tumbling from her lips now—if he stopped she might cry—until her back bowed and she was coming under his tongue again.

She heaved in a breath, another. "Now your Hiorach-blessed *cock*, Alroth."

"Mmm, yes. Now my Munificus-blessed cock." The god of bounty. He was so damned arrogant—

And he was inside her, his Munificus-blessed cock. She chanted *yes* under her breath, and he chuckled into her neck, kissing it, sucking, maybe leaving a mark, as he thrust long slow strokes with a little snap to his hips at the end. Was she still talking? Was she *breathing*?

"Still enjoying yourself, sweetling?" he murmured.

She heaved in a breath. "I'm enjoying *you*."

He shifted and found the perfect angle, the perfect speed, the perfect everything, and time ceased to exist. Her world shrank down to their joining, their perfect pleasure, the sounds she was making no longer affirmative, no longer anything but harsh air from her lungs—her whole body on fire, every muscle locked, then writhing, twisting pleasure that washed over her, and his name. He made her moan his *name*. A small part of her recognized that as embarrassing, but the spasms still racking her, spreading to him now, pushed that away until it was distant and unimportant. She could look forward to having this for the rest of her life.

She opened her eyes, looked up at the thatched ceiling. The rest of her life, until tomorrow.

20

Alroth

Alroth had done this before. Obviously. It was not possible to be a mercenary, a soldier, and not have camp followers hanging off you. And as a young man, he'd taken them up on their offers. He knew what sex felt like. He knew the forms. It seemed Mellia did, too. But they had been setting their own steps tonight.

They'd fallen asleep after making love—the first time he'd ever considered fucking anything to do with love—and Alroth woke up to mad barking.

"Mirabi..." His voice was like stone grinding together. He rolled out of bed and shooed the ephemer away from his feet. Might as well stir the fire and get the porridge cooking for their breakfast. He shivered with goosebumps now that he was out from under the woollen covers, but he'd crawl back in once the porridge was started. Maybe they could *make love* again before breakfast. A grin spread over his face. With any luck, the whole winter would be like this. Just the two of them in their cabin, Orbitus take the rest of their party.

Mirabi brushed against his legs, and he scooted the pup away from the fireplace. Ephemers probably couldn't get singed, but just in case.

He poured wild rice into the pot and swung it into the fire, then stumbled back toward the bed, Mirabi tripping him up underfoot. Were they bigger than they'd been last night?

He crawled back under the covers and kissed Mellia's shoulder, then the mark on her neck that he'd left last night. *Shit.* He should've asked before leaving it there.

Mirabi hopped up on the coverlet, walked over Alroth's legs and ass and up his ribs, little paws digging into his bones. He groaned, and Mellia's eyes opened, a smile already curving her lips.

He winced. "Your ephemer has sharp little paws."

She looked askance at him, then to Mirabi. "Come here, little one." She reached for her ephemer, wrapped her arm around them—and pulled it right through.

"Mischievous little pup." Alroth waved a hand toward Mirabi—definitely bigger than last night—and his fingers came a bit too close, grazing the pup's soft fur. He froze. He couldn't touch Mirabi, they were Mellia's ephemer. Only a mage could touch their own ephemer, and only if the creature chose. It must have been his imagination.

Mirabi hopped around the bed, bowing and barking, trying to play with Alroth's waving hand, jabbing him in the kidney.

"That's enough, Mira." Mellia sat up and reached for her ephemer again, but it seemed they were feeling ornery, because her hand passed right through again.

The pup crawled up the bed, right onto Alroth's chest as he rolled to keep his poor kidney from another prodding, until they were almost nose to nose. Their breath huffed onto his cheek, and they licked a long wet stripe up Alroth's face. He swatted playfully at the ephemer, and his hand connected with soft fur over a thick skull.

Mellia gasped.

It wasn't his imagination. He could touch Mirabi.

"What's—"

Barking cut off Mellia's dumbfounded question, but not from the ephemer on the bed. The patter of paws on the packed-earth floor, the huff of breath from a dog hopping off the ground, and another ephemer, almost a copy of the first, crept across the bed toward the first one.

The first ephemer whipped around and pounced on the second, growling playfully. Soon they were on the floor, tearing back and forth around the small room.

Mellia looked just as shocked as Alroth felt. Whose ephemer was playing with Mirabi?

"You have an ephemer." Mellia sat up to watch as one pinned the other on the floor by the bed.

That couldn't be. Only mages had ephemers. An ephemer let you perform magic by syphoning from a bound mate. He couldn't perform magic, so why would he have an ephemer? But he had touched the little pup. Not so little anymore. Where Mirabi had been, just last night, a squirming puppy, they'd grown lanky with adolescence, long fawn-like legs and narrow body, yet to fill out into a proper dog.

The other was the same. The same pointed ears, long nose, fluffy but sleek fur.

"What will you name them?" Mellia smiled softly at him.

How was she accepting this so calmly? Had she known this was a possibility?

"We don't even know it's mine. I can't have an ephemer. Sources don't."

Her smile didn't waver, if anything it got even softer. "I didn't think I could have an ephemer either, remember?"

The two ghostly dogs jumped on the bed and climbed Mellia and Alroth, licking their faces, before dashing off again.

Mellia threw off the covers. "Look at them together." She hunted up her clothes while Alroth watched the translucent forms weave through the wall and back inside again.

He had an ephemer. His own ephemer. Mellia was right: He would have to name them. If Mirabi had been a wonderful surprise, then his ephemer was a baffling one: Mirandus.

He tried it out. "Mirandus."

"Mirabilis and Mirandus." Mellia crouched next to where the two pups now lay collapsed by the fire and scratched Mira's ears.

Hopefully, she didn't mind that he'd used her ephemer's name as inspiration.

"I like it. Mira and Miran. They should be similar." She turned to him, a lock of her unbound hair framing her face. "Two halves of our bond."

Goosebumps traced up his arms and around the back of his neck. Alroth threw off the covers and hunted down his own clothes. Mellia was already stirring the pot when he finished, and he clasped her around the waist.

"No need for that, sweetling. I'm fully capable of making your breakfast."

Mellia raised her eyebrows at him and took a seat by the fire. Would she sit there and watch him? He rooted in the provision basket for the gourd of maple syrup and laid it on the hearth. Over in the corner, it was cold enough that they could be here all day and never pour a drop of syrup out.

"I'll be taking stock of the village's provisions today, with Falkirk and the others."

"Do you think there will be enough for all of us over the winter?" A crease marred her forehead.

"Don't you worry about it, sweetling. We'll take care that you're all fed."

The crease didn't go away. "You should let us help. We can..." She shook her head, looked at her hands in her lap.

There was nothing wrong with her not being able to help. No one expected the cosseted handmaids to work around the village, go out hunting, and whatnot. He would gather the mercs, and they'd make a plan to supplement the village's stores. It would be challenging in all this snow, but doable, especially so early in the winter. The fauna would be fattened for the winter, good pickings, whatever they found.

Mellia didn't protest again, and after they ate their porridge, Alroth reached for his houppelande. He pulled it over his head to reveal Mellia doing the same.

"Where are you going, sweetling?"

"Not that it's any of your business, but I'm going to the inn."

She should stay here where it was warm and safe. He opened his mouth to protest and closed it again. Was this not exactly what he'd done after the binding ritual? He could order her to stay, but he couldn't force her to remain here. It *was* his business, as her protector. But what harm could it do for her to go to the inn? She was already bundled up by now anyway.

Mellia followed him out into the snow. The sun was fully up, glinting with almost blinding brilliance off the smooth layer of white over the village, paths and rooftops alike. Alroth squinted against the bright and set to breaking a trail past a few other houses, toward Ignis's Rest.

Mellia could check in with the handmaids while he continued on to the tithe barn. At the inn door, she stretched on tiptoe to feather a kiss on his lips but smiled and dodged away as he made to deepen it. A shadow of sorrow flickered over her face. She turned and disappeared through the doorway, shutting the door firmly behind her.

"Hey! Someone's made more than friends with his matron." Del catcalled as he emerged from a small hut, probably abandoned before they'd claimed it, smoke now curling from the thatch.

Kai trailed him, head down.

"That's the idea. You'd do well to follow my example." Alroth clapped him on the back as he joined his trail to theirs, heading for the tithe barn.

Kai gave him a piercing look. "Trick a mage into forming a bond with me?"

"No one tricked anyone. Let's get inside and see what we're dealing with."

Kai didn't press the issue, just motioned Alroth ahead of him into the tithe barn.

What they were dealing with was a big problem. He'd been right yesterday, talking to Yasmine: They didn't even have enough here to feed the village for the winter, let alone twelve more mouths. Wild rice, corn, a pile of squash, dried fruit, and beans—but not enough for the number of people it was to feed. They'd have to supplement—or ration. Had they been planning to hunt? None of the villagers had the kind of skill needed to hunt in the winter, not last year when they'd left. Had they been planning to ration all winter? That wouldn't be necessary now that Alroth and his band were here.

"I know a few likely spots for snares, and we can take down a bit of game in the next few weeks." Alroth nodded to himself.

"The nettles should be harmless by this time of year." How did Kai always keep a straight face no matter what came out of his mouth?

If only it had been him with Alroth that day, the story would have died before it had even taken root. Damned Etienne and his flapping jaws. Though Mellia had seemed enthralled by the tale, thought him a hero for saving Etienne. Drake had spun the yarn to look favourably on Alroth. He wasn't always so generous. Etienne had seemed miffed when he'd first learned of Alroth's bond, but now he was trying to get Alroth in Mellia's good graces?

They sorted out the hunting parties—Del and Kai with Falkirk, to keep them from killing each other, and Etienne with Alroth—and got on their way. They'd be able to find deer trails easily in this snow, though it would be tiring to follow them, even with the snowshoes they all strapped on.

There wasn't much time for discussion in the woods as Alroth followed Etienne along a deer track, but they stopped to set a snare on a rabbit run and take a rest.

"Why did you tell Mellia the peccary story yesterday?"

"She toss you out in the cold last night?" Etienne took a swig from his firebird flask.

"You didn't have to make me out as a hero."

Etienne shrugged. "You got yourself in a mess. Who am I to you if I don't help you clean up after yourself?"

Alroth had got himself in plenty of messes before, and Etienne sometimes helped him out—sometimes left him to slog through the quagmire alone. This seemed different. Perhaps it pained him to think of Alroth's bound mate hating him as that handmaid did Etienne. Though the circumstances were different, since Etienne and the handmaid weren't bound. "Does it have to do with that handmaid? You two seem—"

"We seem nothing. Are we hunting or chattering like hens?" He tucked away his flask and turned back to the deer trail.

Etienne did practically nothing *but* chatter like a hen, most of the time. Alroth would have to ask Mellia about it, since Etienne was as hard to crack as a hickory nut when he didn't want to talk about something.

So at their next rest, Alroth talked about himself. "Mellia's the heir to Falvair." He flattened the snow around his boot.

Etienne crowed with laughter, probably scaring all the game for ells around. "You're a marquess? How does it feel to be a pompous, stuck-up—"

"All right."

"—useless, foppish—"

"Drake..."

"—self-centred, lily-handed noble yourself now?"

Alroth deserved it, with the number of times he'd ribbed Etienne for his noble birth. But that was in their youth before he'd realized how solid Drake was under his admittedly vain exterior.

"Shall we retire to the hearth? The gale is quite biting today, don't you agree, Lord Falvair?" Etienne grabbed his middle and bent over, guffawing.

Alroth smacked his shoulder. "Yeah, it's hilarious." He stalked a few paces down the path, and Drake hurried to catch up.

"Falvair, eh? No wonder Ainsley wanted her."

"Yep." Falvair would be instrumental in a war. And very lucrative. With both the harbour and the shipyards—

Alroth stopped. The deer tracks ended. In a spatter of blood. A print with a deep oblong toe next to a smaller one, brown dirt churned up from the claw imprints... titanis. A terror bird, this close to Bridge?

Drake stopped beside him and whistled. "Think two cosseted nobles like us can take it out? Could be dangerous, this close to Bridge."

Alroth should say no. They'd need their whole band to take down the wily, vicious bird, as tall as Etienne with a beak that could break a shield in one lunge.

But he wasn't saying no. Despite Etienne's jesting, they were anything but cosseted nobles—they actually cared about folks other than themselves. A terror bird in Bridge would find its own storehouse of morsels for the taking. Doors and shutters wouldn't keep it out. They couldn't let it overwinter here.

Alroth picked out the prints leaving the clearing. "Went that way."

"Just like that? Thought you'd fight me a bit more." Drake's puzzled expression cleared, and he brandished his spear. "Let's get us a beak!"

They began by making the travois. If they wanted to bring home a carcass almost as big as Alroth, they'd need it.

Alroth followed the tracks, each as big as his two spread hands, out of the clearing. He'd make Mellia a down pillow when they brought the carcass back. The trail of broken branches and deep prints in the fresh snow made it easy to follow, around Bridge. Maybe the titanis was keeping its distance from humans for now, but that might not last. In the dead of winter, when it started to get desperate, its hunger would override its fear. And once Alroth's band left... the Grist wouldn't defend Bridge, not with Yasmine in charge. He shouldn't be surprised they'd refused to help. The village followed an unbound mage who openly used her magic, and the Grist would never—

Crunch. Crack.

Alroth froze. The crack of another bone splitting rent the frigid air. Maybe a deer bone, being cracked by a beak as long as his arm? He loosened Volnus in her sheathe and crept forward. Etienne had left the travois back in the trees and appeared silently at his side. They should go back for Falkirk or Kai. A war bow would make this much easier. Etienne had the spear he'd made from a sturdy stick last winter. That would have to do. They snuck around behind the terror bird, its beak busy tearing at the deer it had brought back to its nest. Making it impale its own head on the spear was the way to go. Alroth motioned for Drake to hand it over, but he shook his head. He wanted to be the hero? Fine.

Alroth sheathed his sword and strung his hunting bow. The arrows would only aggravate the titanis, but they would get its attention. Maybe he could shoot its eye, if he could get its head up. He whistled, and the terrifying beak snapped up, the long throat bobbing as it swallowed one last chunk of deer entrails.

Alroth drew, sighted down the arrow, and let fly—just as the bird straightened. The arrow took it in the leg, and it screeched. Alroth's ears rang, and he drew Volnus as the massive predator barrelled toward them. Not that his sword would do much, but it was better than his cesti. Besides, if this went to plan, Drake's spear would be all they needed.

The titanis didn't have much space to pick up speed, but Etienne held his ground as the huge bird closed on him. Etienne's motion as he shifted his weight hid the spear he had braced on the ground. Or that was the idea.

The titanis dodged the sharp spearpoint and lunged with its hand-length talons, raking Etienne's ribs and side. He shouted—it must have pierced his armour. *Fuck.* It was focused on Drake, who clobbered its beak with the spear. The terror bird shrieked again, drew its head back to impale Etienne, and Alroth pounced, wrapping his arm over its neck and slashing through its throat with Volnus.

The huge bird bucked and rolled, its hot blood steaming as it spilled over Alroth's arm. If he got more distance, he'd be in range of those massive claws and wickedly sharp hooked beak. The pool of blood in the snow squished under Alroth's boots as he staggered with the bird's last buck. The titanis toppled to the ground. So did Etienne.

Alroth dropped his hold on the carcass and stumbled to his knees beside Drake. Blood leaked between the fingers he clenched to his side, and his face was ghostly pale.

"Can you walk? We have to get you to Bridge."

Etienne shook his head. "Even Yasmine can't..." He passed out.

Fuck! Yasmine couldn't, but the handmaids, Mellia, could. Alroth plunged into the brush and came up with the travois. He slung it under Etienne, hitched the poles under his arms, and got moving.

They weren't far from Bridge. They would make it in time. He stuck to the path. Going off would risk getting hung up in a thicket. Twice, he had to shove his way between trees just too narrow for the poles. Sweat poured down his back, even in the chill air. Drake had saved his life so many times. What was it now, five? Six? He would return the favour, and he would be that much closer to balancing the scales between them.

Scales that could never truly be balanced. Etienne hadn't just saved his life, he'd given him a life worth living. Footsteps crunched the snow, just audible over Alroth's laboured breathing, and he called out. Voices drifted to him.

"There you are, Wolf. What did you and Drake get? Find something good—" Del peered around him. "Fuck. Kai! It's Drake!"

Del and Kai took his place on the travois, and Alroth burst through the trees and made straight for the inn where the handmaids would be sitting by the fire waiting for them. He didn't even bother to take off his snowshoes as he burst in the back door.

"Mellia!" He clattered across the kitchen and banged open the door to the hall. It was empty. Even the fire had burned low. They weren't here. Must have left just after the mercs had. Gone... somewhere. Could be anywhere. He would never find them in time to save Etienne.

Del cursed as he and Kai wedged the travois in the door. "Falkirk's gone for Yasmine, but..."

Yasmine wouldn't be enough.

"They're not here." Alroth hauled on the travois, and it popped through the doorway.

Wherever the handmaids had gone, they would have left tracks in the snow. Miran joined him as he stalked out the back door and circled the inn. The tracks from the front door were obvious, even if Miran hadn't dashed that way and barked. They'd gone back to the river.

21

Mellia

It didn't take much for Mellia and Sathred to get the other handmaids on board for their plan. They'd go to the island, wait for a barge going downriver, and get the captain to take them to Falvair. Even a barge could make the journey, sticking to the shallow shoreline of March Bay, and who wouldn't want to earn the favour of the Grist and the Lord Falvair by helping them out?

Only Mellia and Sathred had proper boots, so they broke trail for the handmaids in their lovely slippers—and still got boots full of snow before long. The wind whistled across the unprotected bridge, high above the freezing river and jutting rocks. Snow had gathered on the narrow section; they just had to get across this final time, and they would never have to make the treacherous journey again. But one slip would be all it took.

Better to take a few moments to clear the snow off than risk slipping. At least the sun was out, and they could use magic. Mellia surveyed the snowdrift next to Sathred. The last thing they needed was to melt the snow and have it turn to ice on the cold stone. But heating the stone would take a lot of magic—maybe more than they had—since stone had an impractically low magic affinity.

She said as much to Sathred.

"We'll work together. Don't syphon." Sathred meant *Don't syphon and alert your source that you're using magic.*

The other handmaids huddled on the bridge, Morath blowing on her hands, and Runas dancing from foot to foot, trying to keep the blood flowing in her toes.

"Focus on the air in the snow." Sathred closed her eyes, and the drift deflated.

Mellia did the same, the stones growing slick with slush. *Just don't freeze.* But a layer of ice was building on the stones. She could syphon and warm them, but then would Alroth catch them before they were safely sailing away?

Mellia opened her eyes. The cleared patch of bridge glittered with black ice.

"We'll just have to be careful," Sathred muttered. But her furrowed brow showed she was aware that she and Mellia had made it worse. Snow was slippery, but the black ice they had made would dump them all in the river.

They could turn back. Go back to the inn and try again another day. But every day they stayed risked more snow, a deeper freeze that might even put an end to the barges on the March River.

Livine sidled up to Mellia's elbow, Morath and Alinace trailing her. "Why did you cover the bridge in ice?" She sounded puzzled rather than annoyed.

"They didn't mean to." Morath edged forward and ran her embroidered toe over the slick stones, getting no traction at all.

"Well done, comfort handmaids." Runas stalked forward. "I thought you were supposed to be good with sunlight."

They *were* good with it. Otherwise, there would be a pile of slush instead of a clear bridge.

"Not all problems need to be solved with magic." Livine pulled out her portable desk. "Hold this." She shoved it at Alinace, who dutifully took it.

"Ah yes, record their blunder for handmaids to come." Runas just couldn't help herself, could she?

Livine dug in her pocket and came up with—a bag. "Move aside, please." She elbowed Morath out of the way and crammed her hand in the bag, pulled out a handful of sand, and tossed it over the ice. Sand, for finishing pages before turning them to keep her ink from smudging. She tossed a layer of sand over the ice, shook the last of it from her bag, and stepped onto the slippery stones. She tested her weight gingerly, then with more gusto. It held. "It's still slippery, so watch your feet. Centre your weight over your foot like this." She leaned forward, demonstrating, her silk skirt blowing around her legs.

Livine crossed slowly; Sathred sidled up behind her. As soon as there was enough width, Sathred stalked around Livine. "I'm going to hail a barge." She strode down the bridge and down the rocky beach, skirting drifts and favouring shallower patches, making good time in her boots as the handmaids shuffled across the slippery bridge. Hopefully, by the time Mellia got the handmaids to the other side of the island, a boat would be waiting to take them to Falvair.

Mellia followed Runas across after Alinace, Morath, and Dayma. They clumped together on the other side of the bridge until Mellia led the way, following Sathred's tracks around the end of the island. The pebble beach suffered the worst of the wind, but as a result, much of the powder had blown into drifts that could be circumvented, making their progress winding but less of a slog.

A round tile-roofed building squatted at the end of the island, nestled in the trees just off the beach.

"That was probably Bridge's temple." Livine had caught her looking. "It was likely built for the pagan deities, before the Empire brought Doloman's teachings to Sudra."

Hundreds of years ago, before King Lorthran, Queen Olena, and their Loyalists had been driven out of Sudra to Nordval and settled there. The heretic prince's ancestors' gods. Alroth's gods? Was that why their bond had taken?

A barge drifted by, heading downstream. Had they not seen Sathred trying to hail them, or had they refused to take the handmaids? Mellia passed the end of the island. Sathred chatted to a barge captain. Ah, she'd already secured the passage they needed. No wonder she'd let the other barge pass. Mellia strode faster, leaving the slippered handmaids to pick their way around the sharpest stones.

"I'll get you into New Bridge by the noon bells, don't you worry." The captain nodded, looking as though his thin neck might snap right off.

New Bridge? Mellia would set him straight. "We're not heading—"

Sathred cut her off. "That's wonderful."

What? Why was Sathred agreeing to go to New Bridge?

"The Grist father will be so grateful."

Mellia grabbed Sathred's arm. "We agreed we were—"

Sathred shook her off. "Are you coming or not?" She took the captain's hand, and he boosted her over a narrow strip of water onto the deck. Their ox waited on the opposite bank to pull the barge up the river to New Bridge, its breath puffing in the chilly air.

A growling bark rang out from the end of the island. Mira? But no, Mira barked back from Mellia's side. Miran. Alroth. He'd discovered their flight already. Sure enough, he rounded the end of the island at a ground-eating pace, Falkirk and Kai on his heels. The mincing handmaids were quickly overtaken.

"You coming?" Sathred snapped. "Or staying with your bond mate, who marks you like a prize tarand." She jerked her chin at Mellia's neck.

Mellia's hand flew to it. Alroth had made a mark? Sathred would leave without her if she didn't hop aboard this moment. Her bond mate was almost here, his eyes wide and desperate, and his houppelande darkened with dirt... or was it blood? What had happened? Was he injured?

Before he could grab her, Mellia turned to Sathred and shook her head. Perhaps if the barge had been on its way to Falvair, she would have gone. What was there for her in New Bridge?

The captain looked from Sathred to the determined bloody mercenary descending on his barge, but before he could express any misgivings, his barge was swept away from the shore, from the rock where Mellia perched. Sathred turned her back.

They couldn't go back to New Bridge, and Mellia couldn't let the handmaids go back there, not until they determined that it was safe.

Alroth stopped a pace before her, made almost of a height by the rock she perched on. "You stayed." He looked shocked. Not pleased, but who would when they were covered in blood? "I need you."

He *needed* her? Her? Mellia? Why? What could he possibly need her for? Or was it... affectionate? Did he *need* her the way poets needed their subjects? A smile crept over her face. Did he really care for her that much?

"Drake—Etienne is wounded. I need you to heal him."

Oh. He needed her magic. Of course.

Runas, who had planted her feet and was in the midst of smacking Kai's hand away, froze.

"We ran into a terror bird in the forest—"

Runas's mouth would make a sailor blush. She tucked up her skirt and broke into a run, up the beach, cursing out the mercenaries and their egos that dwarfed Locuples's mountain of treasure. Kai jogged after her, and Mellia and Alroth hurried after them. Falkirk and the rest of the handmaids, slowed by their silks and slippers, trailed behind.

"What happened?" Mellia huffed as she narrowly avoided turning an ankle on the uneven stones, even in her boots. How was Runas making such good time in her flimsy slippers?

"We were afraid the bird would hunt in Bridge." He shrugged. "We went after it. Should have gone back for the others, but..."

But what? They were too egotistical, as Runas had said? Something about that didn't fit with the Alroth she knew. Though, admittedly, she'd only known him for a few days. He wouldn't risk Etienne's safety recklessly, without reason. Clearly, he wasn't telling her everything. But that could wait. "What are his injuries?" If the titanis had pecked him, he might already be dead. Had he been wearing armour?

"Raked with the thing's talons, along his side." Alroth mimed clawing his ribs. "Got through his armour, but how deep..." He let out a puff of breath. "He was alive after the trek from the woods."

The trek from the woods. As though Alroth had somehow dragged him back to Bridge from wherever the titanis had attacked him. Wait, was Alroth planning to go back there alone to hunt it?

"Take more of your fighters if you go back." Why had she said that? What did it matter to her if Alroth was hurt—or died? Except she was thankful it hadn't been him mauled by a terror bird.

"Back?" A grin split his face. "Don't worry, sweetling, I brought it down." He gestured to the blood coating his houppelande. "Once Drake is healed, I'll take some folks to fetch what's left of the carcass.

Might get Drake his beak, at least. He's been hankering after one for years..."

If Etienne survived.

Runas and Kai were already over the bridge, Runas on Kai's back as they disappeared into the trees toward the village. No wonder they'd made better time than the other handmaids. As healer handmaid, Runas would have Etienne healed up by the time Mellia and Alroth reached Bridge. Then Runas would kill Etienne for giving her such a scare.

Mellia swallowed the lump in her throat. If it hadn't been for Etienne, she never would have met Alroth, they wouldn't be bound, she wouldn't have Mira. She wouldn't even have participated in the handmaid trials. She'd be set to be bound to Lord Ainsley.

"Hey, sweetling, he's come back from plenty worse than this." Alroth nodded, as though reassuring himself. They climbed the arch of the bridge from the island side. "You handmaids did good work clearing the bridge. Made it safer for us."

Thank Hiorach he was changing the subject. "We almost didn't. It was lucky Livine had sand in her pocket."

"Sand? She carries around dirt?" Alroth followed close behind as Mellia's boots ground on the sand in question.

"She uses it for her writing. To dry the ink."

"Carries around dirt to dry ink." He whistled. "Impietan handmaid."

Livine *was* clever. They would have been stuck right here without her. And they would make it back to Etienne faster. The track back to Bridge was thoroughly packed down, just a bit slippery, now that it had been trodden by so many feet. Hopefully, the handmaids in their slippers would have an easier time on their return trip.

The inn's glazed window sparkled with the firelight within. Mellia slipped through the inn door, Alroth at her heels. She put a finger to her lips. They didn't want to break Runas's concentration. Etienne was laid out on a table, his armour and shirt gone, the gashes on his side revealed. Mellia pulled off her mantle as sweat beaded on her forehead. Del paced in front of the fire and stopped to poke it. No wonder it was sweltering in here. But Etienne might need it if his body was distressed.

Mellia tiptoed to Runas, hunched over the table, her hands outstretched, almost touching the wounds, which still oozed black blood. Yasmine stood across from her. Her jaw was set. She must already have done all she could and now stood arms crossed, watching Runas's progress intently. The handmaid was using her magic—all of it, it would seem—and still, the wounds weren't closing.

"Runas," Mellia breathed.

She opened her eyes and shook her head, a tear glistening on her lower lashes.

Mellia took the spot beside her on the bench. "Tell me what to do. I have—" She jerked her chin at Alroth, who had planted himself at the foot of the table after unlacing his snowshoes.

Runas guided Mellia's hand over Etienne's torso. "Here. It won't fully heal. I can't— Even with all my power, it opens again."

Good thing Mellia had more power. She locked eyes with Alroth, and he nodded. She'd use as much of their power as she could before she turned herself ephemeral.

She closed her eyes. Runas had found it. That was the deepest part, where the raptor claw had dug into Etienne's liver. She focused on the smallest spot she could to be most effective with her power. She used her magic, watched it stitch together, Etienne's body healing that one little spot, weeks' worth in a moment.

"You're doing it." Runas's voice probably didn't carry past the two of them. "I've got the skin and muscle."

The three long gouges knit back together and didn't open again.

"That's... great, mages." Yasmine's voice was low as well. "But he lost so much blood."

Etienne *was* pale. His breaths were shallow. Maybe they'd been too late after all.

Clang!

Del had tossed the fire iron on the stone hearth. Alroth stormed across to him, grabbed him by the scruff, and dragged him out the door. The silence after it slammed remained tense.

"Lor isn't going to die." Runas reached for him again, this time laying her hands on his chest. Her breathing slowed, and a tug pulled at Mellia's chest.

"Stop, handmaid." Yasmine's voice was steely.

Runas growled low in her throat. She didn't stop. Whatever it was in Mellia's chest tugged harder. Runas was looking to syphon—from whoever was nearby.

"Without a bond, it won't help, handmaid." Yasmine rounded the table and hauled Runas backwards.

Runas roared and lunged for Etienne. She couldn't help him, but Mellia could.

She stepped in Runas's path. "Tell me what to do."

Runas only wasted a moment shaking Yasmine's hands from her. "His bones. Not all, just the hollow centre. When they've lost blood, it's their bones that help."

Bones. Runas whirled and took up Del's track in front of the fireplace.

Mellia closed her eyes. Bones running down his arms, legs, hips... Runas was right, the bones were... not hollow but spongy in the centre. Using magic on them would help Etienne's blood? Runas knew more about healing than any of them. Mellia grasped Alroth's magic along with hers and syphoned.

Etienne's skin lost its pallor. The door opened behind her and closed softly, letting in a chill. His breathing was still shallow. *Keep going.* The bones were, somehow, working. Why were her own bones aching?

A hand closed over her shoulder, big and gentle. "That's enough, sweetling. Let the others help." Alroth drew her away. Let the other handmaids gather around Etienne. The ache in her bones faded. She'd almost wrenched herself, trying to use more magic than she had. Alroth had stopped her. He didn't let her wrench herself, not even as punishment for running away, not even to help his best friend. He could have stopped her from running with a simple wrench. But he hadn't. He'd come after her himself.

Runas hovered near Etienne's head.

"Rune." Etienne's whisper had Alroth pulling Mellia into his—now blood-free—chest.

"Thank you, sweetling."

She'd saved someone's life. She'd used their bond to do something... good. Alroth had pulled her back from tipping over into an ephemer.

And Runas was spitting insults at Etienne as he tried to sit up. She stalked up the stairs, and her door slammed as he tried to go after her. Kai's hand on his shoulder was enough to keep Etienne down.

Sathred had betrayed Mellia and left them all behind to return to New Bridge. But they still couldn't stay here all winter. The handmaids needed to get somewhere safer. And Mellia needed to get to Falvair, take over the marquessate from her father.

But next time they would be better prepared. The handmaids gathered by the fire to warm their wet and half-frozen feet and dry their sodden skirts.

Let Alroth think they'd given up, that she was happy to stay here with him. That would make it easier to get free when the time came. When they tried again, the handmaids would have proper shoes; they'd take warmer clothes. They'd make them themselves if they had to.

22

Alroth

Etienne was safe. He would need more rest, but he would live. And Alroth's bond mate had done it. Her magic was powerful, just as he'd hoped. He could use it to help so many people. The handmaids were half frozen, but they had come back. If their band had more mages, imagine how much more they could do. Runas on her own wouldn't have been able to save Drake as Mellia had. Surely all the handmaids would want to bond now that they'd seen the difference it could make to their power?

Once they had established that none of the handmaids had frostbite, Alroth left them by the hearth with Mellia and gathered his mercs in the kitchen.

"I want at least one of you in the inn hall at all times. We don't leave the ladies alone again."

"We're guarding them like prisoners?" Kai leaned against the counter, but tension hardened his shoulders.

"We're keeping them safe, Kai. We already lost one..." And who knew whether she'd make it to New Bridge? What if something happened to her? Father Glimar would still hold to their agreement, wouldn't he? It couldn't be helped. "If you can, get to know them a little bit. See if any are looking to bond."

Drake laughed humourlessly. "Handmaids? That'll be the day. Glyptodon will fly before a handmaid binds herself to a lowly merc."

Alroth grit his teeth. Mellia was practically a handmaid, and she'd bound herself to *him*. The lowliest merc there was. When she'd been desperate and out of options.

Etienne's raised eyebrows dared Alroth to deny it.

"And you are sitting here because a sister decided to take a chance on the gutter rat," Alroth ground out.

Etienne scowled, ready to berate him for referring to himself that way.

"Against her better judgment." Del tipped back in his chair, as if he thought Alroth wouldn't shove him over. Which he wouldn't. He was leader of these ruffians. He had to set a good example.

"Be that as it may, it sure would be handy having more bound mages around, right?" He settled for lightly punching Del's shoulder.

The mercs grumbled their assent, but they clearly had no intention of mixing with the mages.

Etienne stood and stretched. "Right, then. I'm ready to fetch my titanis beak." He wobbled and grabbed the nearest chair back.

"You mean *my* titanis beak?" Alroth elbowed him—gently. "It was my kill."

"Only because it was distracted by chewing on my innards!"

"It barely scratched you."

"I looked Orbitus in the eye for that beak!" His cheeks were pink, and his moustache was puffed up like an affronted cat.

Kai rolled his eyes and strode to the back door. "We'll bring it back, old man. Sit your ass down." He unhooked a set of snowshoes from the wall, and Alroth joined him.

Del huddled with Kai and they spoke low together—too low to catch, even nearby as Alroth was—shared a look, and Del rummaged in a chest and came up with a playing board. He slapped it down in front of Etienne. "You'll be busy anyway, getting your ass whooped."

Etienne glared from Del to Kai, then at Alroth. He knew exactly what they were doing. Being stuck here while everyone else was busy was his nightmare, but he took the seat and grumbled something about Del's favourite dagger. If he needed stakes to make it more interesting, Alroth would get Del a hundred daggers. At least it would keep Drake sitting still and resting.

Alroth followed Kai out into the glaring sunlight, their snowshoes letting them tramp over the deep snow, back to the travois in the yard. The travois coated in Drake's lifeblood. Alroth picked up the poles with shaking hands. Kai grabbed his arm, stepped in front of him.

"You did it, Wolf. He's safe."

Alroth closed his eyes, tried to keep breathing. He didn't deserve Kai's reassurance. If he hadn't agreed to go along with Drake's reckless plan, if he'd insisted on going back for more folks to back them up, Etienne never would have been in so much danger. But he'd let Drake goad him into taking a stupid risk. He deserved to feel this shaky sick knot in his stomach.

He opened his eyes and trudged past the low inn-yard wall, into the woods. Kai huffed and followed in blessed silence. The others might not see it, but they needed more mages. What if it had been him hurt instead of Drake? Mellia wouldn't have been able to syphon from him to heal him. As it was, she'd almost wrenched herself to save Drake.

They followed the drag marks and deep black holes Drake's blood had made in the snow back to the titanis and hid in the trees. In their absence, anything could have come to pick over the corpse—dire wolves, scimitar-toothed cats, even a short-faced bear—but all they found was a giant stork and a couple of coyotes they easily chased off. The titanis's belly was ripped open, and its eyes were gone, but the feathers had been protected by the snow, and Drake's coveted beak was still intact.

They sliced up the carcass in silence and took a rest back to back. A scavenger could appear any time. They didn't need another injury. The giant stork eyed them from the trees but stayed well back.

"How did you and Mellia bond?" Kai's shoulders shifted against Alroth's back. So he *was* interested in binding a handmaid.

Good thing he couldn't see Alroth's grin. He got it under control and tried for a neutral tone. "We did the binding ritual. Pouring water, saying some words, then we made each other come."

Kai jerked him around, scowled at him. "Mammoth shit."

Alroth shrugged. "Not my idea. Mellia told me that's how the ritual is done."

"That's all." Kai turned back around, and so did Alroth. "Poured some water?"

Alroth explained the water pouring, repeated Mellia's words to Kai. *May Doloman bind us and bless us with a strong bond.* But Alroth had added something, hadn't he? *May Prosperitas gift us with a successful union.* He didn't tell Kai about that part. Maybe that was why Miran had appeared, why the bond seemed to have latched on to him as well as Mellia.

Miran burst out of the woods and barked in Alroth's face. A howl echoed through the trees. Dire wolves.

"Better get moving." Alroth clambered to his feet and rolled his sore shoulder. Hopefully, the offal they were leaving behind would keep the wolves busy while they dragged the rest of the carcass away.

Kai brushed snow from his mantle. "They're close, too. Like the titanis."

"Yep. We'll have to get Yasmine hunting more deer around here, keep the pickings slim for the beasties."

They each took one pole and dug in their snowshoed feet. The cold air burned Alroth's lungs as they laboured through the trees, blessedly devoid of any more howls. Miran appeared again, Mira at their side. Kai stopped, and the pole slipped from Alroth's mittened hands. He swore and picked it up again.

"Two ephemers." Kai cocked his head. "Yours?"

"Yep." Alroth pulled on the travois, and Kai kept on as well. Did Kai think him a mage now? Did he expect him to start doing magic? He wasn't a mage; he wasn't weak. He had the strength to defend himself. Protect those around him. No magic required.

They stuck the carcass in the tithe barn and washed up in the bathhouse before returning to the inn hall, which was packed with people. The handmaids, Etienne, Del, Yasmine, and a passel of townsfolk filled every bench and lined the walls. Was the whole town here?

The handmaids had set up a loom, and Mellia stood before it, her magic making finished cloth pour from it, almost faster than a handmaid could let out the warp from the loom weights and another could fill the shuttle.

Del strode over to them. "Got them some fleeces from the tithe barn, and look at that. Months of work in an afternoon. And they're not even bound. Just regular mages, like anyone. Livine said she'll teach us once they're done."

Teach them? But they weren't mages. The idea was to *bind* mages, not *become* them.

"I bet you could do the same as your bound mate there." Del elbowed him.

Weave fabric? Using magic? The knot in Alroth's gut bubbled into fury. "You won't catch me using magic."

Del ignored him, babbled about using magic to cleave armour with his axe or some such nonsense. Kai looked at him sideways, and Alroth glowered. Just because he had an ephemer didn't mean he was a mage, playing about with magic when there was work to be done. He threaded past the rapt townsfolk into the kitchen, where he found Falkirk cooking alone. All those magic-obsessed folks out there and not one could lift a finger to help them make the food they would all eat.

"Brought back most of the titanis's meat." Alroth pulled his knife and set to peeling sunchokes.

"Good." Falkirk sliced salt meat and tossed it in the stew pot.

"Drake?"

"Fine." They grabbed another hunk of salt meat. "Well enough to flip the board after the fifth time Del beat him at draughts."

Good. Drake was recovering; soon the handmaids would have proper clothes, and who knew? Maybe Kai would succeed in binding whatever handmaid he'd taken a fancy to. Maybe the healer, Runas, would even come around. She'd been worried enough about Etienne when she'd heard he was injured. Surely that meant she cared for him. And she'd helped save his life. Surely he would bind her, if only in appreciation for that.

"What are you planning, Wolf?" Falkirk had put down their knife and spread their hands on the table.

Alroth shrugged.

"Not still convinced the rest of us will bind handmaids, are you?"

Alroth couldn't hide his grin as he shrugged again.

Falkirk leaned toward him over the table. "Bonds are not to be entered into lightly. Just because you got lucky with Mellia doesn't mean the rest of us will—or even want to." They lowered their voice even further. "We're not *yours*, Alroth."

What? Why would they think that he considered them *his*? What did that even mean? They were people under his protection, but they didn't *belong* to him. Obviously. But just as obviously, having more mages in their band would help everyone. Why were they all struggling to understand something so simple?

Or had Etienne told them his bond with Mellia had effectively made him a noble? Maybe that's what was bothering them. "I haven't changed, Falkirk, even with lands and a title. I'm still just Alroth." He shifted under their sharp gaze.

"You haven't changed. Maybe I have." They turned their back and dumped the meat into the stew pot, and when they turned back, their face had cleared. "Tomorrow night is the solstice. You think Yasmine has anything planned? They probably don't have enough supplies for a feast."

Fine. If they wanted to change the subject, there was nothing left to say about the mages anyway. Alroth couldn't force anyone to bond, nor would he want to. But he could make sure they got to celebrate the solstice tomorrow. "We can do more hunting. Don't worry about food. Let's make sure Bridge has a solstice festival fit for the handmaids." They might be used to more comforts, back in their keep, but the mercenaries weren't without revelry, especially on the most festive night of the year.

Mellia slipped into the kitchen, their ephemers barking around her legs. She took in his knife, still busy with sunchokes, and smiled. "That would go faster with magic."

Falkirk harrumphed.

Alroth's face must have drawn storm clouds, because Mellia's smile faltered. Alroth didn't want to argue. "The solstice is tomorrow night."

"That's right." Mellia pulled her belt knife and reached for a sunchoke.

Alroth let her. "I'm sure you handmaids are used to a big to-do with candles and feasting. We don't have much out here, but we can whip something up. With your help."

"I'd love to, Alroth. I'm sure the handmaids are anxious for something familiar after... everything." She was so *sweet.*

"I'll take you over to the storehouse after dinner, and we can arrange everything with Yasmine."

Mira and Miran barked and wrestled, Mira pinning Miran and quickly getting pinned themselves, Mira belly up on the kitchen floor. Falkirk didn't comment on the two ephemers, thankfully.

"I'll go talk to her." Alroth wiped off his knife, sheathed it, and dumped his sunchokes into the stew.

The gawkers in the hall had broken up, and the uptight handmaid, Dayma, was measuring the mousy one with string, a long strip of fabric laid out on the table. Someone had cleaned up Drake's blood.

Del, Kai, and Etienne sat by the hearth with Yasmine, and Alroth joined them. Tomorrow would be a day of cleaning, then they would keep fires burning all through the longest night, mages and mercs alike.

23

Mellia

Alroth left Mellia alone with Falkirk in the kitchen. They stirred the pottage, having made no effort to gawk at the handmaids' magic like the others.

"Not interested in watching the show?" Mellia peeled the last sunchoke.

They shrugged. "It's hardly entertainment, watching wool processed. My mother taught me as soon as I could walk." They sawed the top off a squash.

Mellia wandered to a basket of dried beans in the shell and popped open a pod, let the beans inside tumble into the pottage.

"So you do use your hands for something." Falkirk kept their eyes on the squash, scooped the seeds out, and put them aside.

Was that why they were so dismissive of the handmaids' magic? They thought the handmaids never did any hard work? "Our magic is only as good as our skills. Magic neither spins a strong thread nor a consistent one until the mage has the skill to do so."

Falkirk nodded but didn't respond, chopping and peeling the squash while Mellia shucked beans by hand. She could use magic, even for this, but they were right: Sometimes repetitive manual tasks were soothing. Not everything had to be about magic.

Alroth strode back into the kitchen, Del and Kai on his heels. "There you are, sweetling. The handmaids are asking for you."

"Can see why," said Del. "The way you did that sheep wool." He mimed combing unreasonably fast.

Kai rolled his eyes. "She looked nothing like that, you twit."

"Think how much firewood I could chop!" said Del.

"The mage has the powers, not the source." Alroth's amber gaze sparked across the kitchen as he said it.

Alroth had an ephemer. Did that mean that he could use magic too? Syphon it and use his skills to chop firewood, hunt for food for them? Maybe Del wasn't so far off. But it was Alroth's to share, not hers. Mellia and Alroth's bond had only been sanctioned when it had walked the line of blasphemy by performing the ritual without a Grist brother. Now they were far past that. Having a second ephemer, let alone wielding magic as a source, was utterly unacceptable in the Grist's eyes.

Mellia shelled one last bean and laid the basket aside. She brushed her hands on her skirt. "I had better get back to the weaving." She nodded to Falkirk, who nodded back without looking up from the next squash they split with a whack.

Only one fleece remained to be combed when Mellia returned to the inn hall. Morath had finished the header and had begun warping the loom yet again. Dayma had gone back to spinning as Alinace combed. Livine had retreated to the hearth with her logbook, but no one admonished her for shirking. Runas wound wool from a spindle shaft to the loom's shuttle with her magic. A pile of yarn hanks sat stacked in the basket where the fleeces had been. Time to weave.

Runas handed Mellia the loaded shuttle and began loading a second one. Morath stepped back from the warped loom, and Mellia syphoned again: *Pull the shuttle through, beat the weft, move the heddle forward, pull the shuttle through, beat the weft, move the heddle back...*

Alinace wound the woven fabric onto the beam as it poured from the loom, and Dayma let the warp slowly out from its bundles on the weights. Morath handed Mellia one loaded shuttle and then another until the warp threads were exhausted. Then they warped the loom again. What would have taken days without magic took them one afternoon.

Dayma took over for the cutting, sewing, fitting... Mellia had never been any good at those, and using magic would just make a mess of it much faster.

Alroth and Yasmine sauntered to her table. "Ready to plan the solstice, sweetling? If we wait any longer, we'll lose the light."

Shouldn't a handmaid do this? Mellia was just a sister—not even that anymore. None of the handmaids looked her way. Besides, she was the one who'd agreed to try to salvage this celebration. At the comb, there would be a feast, fires roaring all night, candles burned to hot pools of honey-scented wax, scripture readings—Doloman's triumph over Cupidus was a favourite—humming and Grist dances. Plus, a service in the beautiful hive.

The handmaids and sisters didn't attend daily prayers like the brothers, so they weren't inured to the beautiful glass, the sparkling pink granite floors and pillars, the golden altar cloth, and the sweet smell of beeswax that always permeated the hive.

But they couldn't have any of that here. Mellia nodded and followed Alroth and Yasmine to the tithe barn in the centre of the village. It was the best kept structure in the place. Its stones were freshly whitewashed, and the roof was tile, if a little mossy. It must be left over from when the village was a bustling town, back before the water rose and Bridge Keep became half submerged.

Yasmine waved them through between the wooden bays, pointing out corn, dried fruit, nuts, squash, and beans. At the end, by the cheese, was the wool clip, fleeces piled neatly, easily enough for a score more kirtles. More folk than she'd thought must live in Bridge with this many fleeces piled here from the spring shearing, and yet none of them were worked. Perhaps the Grist had come for shearing time?

Mellia peeled a fleece back to look at the cut side. "The Grist brothers do good work. Hardly any seconds on these fleeces."

Alroth loomed beside her. "Brothers had nothing to do with it. We left here just after the spring shearing."

Before sowing and long before the harvest. Was that why there were so many fleeces and yet so little food? Alroth had mentioned something about a food shortage, now that there were twelve—eleven—extra mouths to feed this winter.

"It doesn't seem right that we didn't help with the harvest and we're eating all the food. Making the folk who live here ration..."

Alroth strolled back down the length of the barn. "They would have been rationing anyway. The Grist see no profit in helping Bridge, so they don't."

Profit? The Grist brother foragers were not in it for profit. Naturally, they took a tithe from those they worked alongside. How else would the hive sustain itself? But they served these communities, especially those unable to support themselves otherwise. Since the war, there were significantly fewer able folk to work the land, the Grist brothers ensured that everyone had enough to last the winter. Except, apparently, in Bridge.

"Have they tried asking for help? I'm sure if the Grist knew of the predicament of the folk in Bridge—"

"Enough, sweetling." Alroth crossed his arms, looked down at her. "If the village could have secured the Grist's aid, they would have. The picture you've woven of the Grist is a pretty one, to be sure. I envy you your faith."

Faith? He thought it was mindless devotion to the Grist that made her believe such things? She'd lived among the brothers for years. They were good men. They cared about the folk they shepherded. She'd heard them speak many times of the villages they had helped. And the tithes they'd returned with.

Uncertainty squeezed her chest as she followed Alroth to the shelf of candles. They *did* boast of the size of their tithes. Was Alroth right? Did the Grist only forage in villages that could provide them with a profitable exchange? Surely Father Glimar didn't know about this. He would be dismayed to learn that his brothers were being so greedy; he cared for the folk of his forage. *Like he cared for you.* The small voice in her head couldn't be denied. He'd cared for her, sure, but had that been because she was useful to him?

The candles were all tallow. "Where will we celebrate? I hardly think the townsfolk want us taking up their inn hall." There was work to be done and no use mulling over past slights.

Alroth waved away her concern. "We'll all celebrate together. I'm sure folks will be glad to hear real scripture."

Yasmine nodded. "We'd love to celebrate with you. I know our little Bridge isn't what you handmaids are used to..."

Mellia shook her head. "I'm not a handmaid."

"Of course. Sorry. You'll see, we're not without means of celebrating ourselves, though, Sister."

I'm not a sister, either. Contradicting Yasmine again would make her seem ungrateful. As would moping about the tallow candles on the shelf. Yasmine assured them that they could use anything they wanted from the barn and left them to it.

"What's wrong, sweetling?" Alroth had noticed her dissatisfaction with the perfectly serviceable candles.

She squared her shoulders. "Just trying to think of how many candles we can use. If the whole town is there, would they begrudge us a score to light up the hall?"

Alroth grumbled in his chest.

Was that too many?

He swept about twenty candles into the basket.

Not too many, then.

"We'll hunt up some deer and make more." Just like that.

Guilt choked Mellia. If she had her way, they would be gone within a week. But Alroth would still be here to care for the people of Bridge. She chose a few ingredients, and Alroth collected them all in his basket. There was no honey, but they could make a reasonable spread of solstice treats with maple syrup. They'd be... almost the same.

"I guess you have honey all the time at the comb." Alroth hitched the basket onto his back and led the way out of the barn. The winter sun was touching the horizon, even though it was still early.

"On holidays, yes. We have eighteen beehives around the hive and comb. Including the one in the wall of the hive itself."

Alroth's jaw dropped. "You sit for services with a bunch of bees?"

Mellia tried not to laugh. "It's closed off from the inside of the hive. But there's a glass pane where you can see the bees building their combs." She bustled back into the inn hall and plastered a smile on her face. They would celebrate, thank Doloman for his bounty this year, thank him for Mira. For keeping the handmaids and the townsfolk safe from the icy wind and darkness.

She gathered the handmaids in the hall, and they made their plans.

Morath rooted in the basket from the tithe barn. "No beeswax candles?" She pulled out a tallow candle in each hand.

"Of course not," Runas snapped. "Does it look like there's a hive in this village?"

Morath blushed. Few things drew the Grist's ire like a beehive tended by a work-a-day person. Not quite as bad as wearing gold, but close.

They worked by firelight, saving the candles for tomorrow, speaking in hushed tones. The wind rattled the shutters. They were so lucky to be safe and warm inside on the second-longest night of the year.

Alroth came to coax Mellia to bed, but she sent him off—they had work to do. He smothered his hurt look, took in the companionable atmosphere of the handmaids, and went off to bed, Mira and Miran trotting at his heels.

Falkirk sat up with them, over by the hearth, removed from the six handmaids—five handmaids and Mellia, rather—working around the table in the dim, flickering light. Was the merc there to guard them? Make sure they didn't run off again? Leaving now would be a great way to freeze to death.

"Are you ever going to tell us about your binding, Melly? I heard there was a duel for your hand."

Runas rolled her eyes. "She had a roll in the hay with a handsome mercenary and stumbled into a bond. Who hasn't?"

"Rolled in the hay with a handsome mercenary, or stumbled into a bond?" Livine raised her eyebrows.

"If you don't want to hear the story, Runas, why not tell us about *your* history with a handsome mercenary?" Morath poked her arm.

Runas went red, then pale.

No one should have to talk about their painful binding history—Mellia certainly didn't want to talk about hers. But her binding with Alroth hadn't been painful. "I rescued him from the castle prison." That took their attention off Runas. Good. "He knew about the plot to kill all of you. I think that's why he was locked up."

Falkirk's whetstone rasped against their blade.

"You think?" Alinace's doe eyes went wide.

It *was* shocking that she'd let a criminal bind her to him. Or it should be. But Alroth didn't seem like a criminal. He'd risked his life to save the handmaids against not just Grist guards but other mercenaries he'd seemed to know. And Father Glimar had wanted him freed. Surely the Grist father wouldn't have wanted an actual criminal broken out of prison. But the Grist guards had attacked them. Were they acting against Father Glimar's wishes or...

"It doesn't matter. Your bond is Doloman's will." Dayma didn't look up from the cookies she was cutting out.

The others murmured their assent. Doloman's will. Her tasks had been Doloman's will. Her binding failures had been Doloman's will as well. Then was Alroth's ephemer Doloman's will? Was the handmaids' being here Doloman's will?

They all crept up to bed soon after. There would be plenty of work to do tomorrow, and the celebration might well last until dawn tomorrow. Mellia took Sathred's room, slipped into the cold bed. Maybe she should have made the trek to Alroth's cozy cabin. His bed would be warm, and the ephemers had gone with him. She rolled over. She would see Alroth in the morning. It was better this way anyway. Better not to get too attached. They'd celebrate the solstice here, but now that the handmaids had warm clothes, they would be off to Falvair after Doloman-grat. After burning through half of Bridge's supplies with their festival.

Alroth and Yasmine had assured her that it was all right, but how could it be? They would have to find a way to replenish them before they left. Tomorrow.

Growing plants was no problem at all, and with her newfound syphoning ability, she would be able to take a seed from germination to fruit-bearing easily. Perhaps not fifty seeds, though. And where would they keep them in the winter? They'd have to stay inside, but they would still need sunlight to grow, wouldn't they? Mellia shook her head. She would need to find out more about growing plants before she would be able to grow food with magic. Alinace was the most likely handmaid to know how to do such things, since she was the companion handmaid. But her purview was mostly flowers and medicinal herbs, not vegetables.

She'd ask someone in the morning. Alroth might just pat her and tell her not to worry her head about it. If he did, she'd ask someone else. Mellia drifted off, and when she woke, her feet were still frozen. Without the hive bells, it could be almost dawn or midnight. But her eyes wouldn't stay shut, so she rose and crept downstairs.

Falkirk puttered around the kitchen. Kai came in the back door as Mellia shut the hall door softly behind her. The meat he was carrying hit the counter with a thud.

Falkirk turned from their place on the hearth where they'd been poking at the fire. "Can we help you?"

"I'm just looking for Alroth." Alroth would know about growing plants.

Kai looked up from the meat he'd begun cutting from the bone.

"He's hunting." Falkirk stood, their tone making it clear that she should come back when Alroth was there. But Alroth had dismissed her when she'd suggested the handmaids could help.

"Who's the most knowledgeable farmer around here?"

Kai scowled.

Falkirk leaned over the long counter. "Why would a handmaid be interested in farming?"

Why were they treating her so suspiciously when she clearly only wanted to help? She planted her fists on her hips. "I'm interested in making sure the folks here don't starve this winter, just the same as you. Now you can either tell me how corn grows or tell me to go to Orbitus's cursed domain, only stop the glowering and glaring."

Kai glowered harder.

"Turning wool into cloth is one thing, but growing food?" Falkirk shook their head.

Rage bubbled in Mellia's gut, tingled up through her body. But she wouldn't give in to it. The best way to deal with these doubting mercenaries would be to show them. But in order to do that, she needed a farmer. "You'd rather people starve?"

Kai tipped the meat, bone and all, into the pottage. "No. What do you need to know?"

Falkirk glared at him and turned their back, stirring the pottage vigorously.

Mellia sidled to the counter and leaned on it, opposite where Falkirk had been a moment before, as Kai methodically cleaned the counter and knife.

"When we use magic, it doesn't make things appear and disappear. To grow a plant, which by the way, I have done in the past," she tossed this over her shoulder at Falkirk, "the plant needs to be healthy to have a hope of growing on its own. It needs to be planted in soil, get proper light and water, just as it normally would."

Kai nodded. "So to have a stalk of corn bear ears, you have to treat it as though it was growing in a field." He sighed. "I think you'll be disappointed, Sister. Corn only flourishes when surrounded by other stalks. Those at the edge of the field never thrive."

Her heart sank. "I certainly can't grow a whole field."

"Potatoes can grow in a bucket. Maybe that's more feasible for you." Falkirk poked at the fire again.

They were being unkind, but what they said was true. A bucket of potatoes. Mellia would start there. "Where are they kept?"

Kai raised his eyebrows. "Tithe barn."

Falkirk couldn't resist adding their opinion. "You'll still need soil to grow them. They're packed in sand for the winter."

She'd need to thaw some, since the ground was no doubt frozen. Warming it, once the sun came up, should be no trouble for her magic. "Where's the soil?"

"Outside, under half an ell of snow." Falkirk waved to the window.

Kai shrugged. "I'll show you." He turned to the back door.

The path to the storehouse was narrower around back of the inn, but still passable. Kai trailed her to the tithe barn, and she gathered a few seed potatoes in her pocket, at Kai's direction. By the time they stepped out into the light, the sun edged over the horizon. Kai stopped inside the low wall of the inn yard and gestured to the ground, a patch of snow that looked like any other. Hopefully, there was good soil there, and it wasn't the midden she was about to thaw.

A shaft of dawn sunlight fell squarely on one patch that Kai had indicated, and Mellia reached into that spot. It would be easier when the sun was high, but she'd still be able to do it. She selected about a bucket's worth of ground under the snow and syphoned from Alroth, letting the sun beat on that spot.

Kai muttered an epithet next to her. The snow had melted in a neat circle, dampening the earth, and Kai sifted the loam through his fingers. He looked at her in awe.

Mellia smiled. "Where's that bucket?"

Folks joined her in ones and twos. A couple handmaids, a few townsfolk, and Etienne, Del, and Kai. Yasmine was the first to push up her sleeves and grow a little leaf on Mellia's potato plant. After that, others came forward, Morath and Livine took over a couple more buckets Mellia started, and soon they had a handful of potato plants flourishing in the freezing air.

Some of the townsfolk had bonds, proper ones with a mage and a source. Those mages got the hang of growing the plants quickly, accustomed to the household magic they used daily to boil water, dry clothes, and make bread rise. One of them grew a carrot from a seed, another a little tomato plant. It wouldn't bear fruit—not yet—but it was a start. None of them seemed concerned that the Grist forbid such use of magic.

They hauled the garden buckets into the inn hall, ranging them near the hearth to keep warm. Magic might be able to keep them warm enough for a few moments outside, but they would freeze like any other plants if left there alone.

There was no sign of Alroth as the short day wore on. Mira curled up among the plants by the fire, and Etienne was coaxed to rest again while Del and Kai went out to help gather evergreen boughs for decorations—a heretical tradition, but not one of the handmaids complained. Runas stayed in the kitchen with Falkirk while Etienne instructed Mellia and Morath where to sit the candles around the hall. Del popped in and took Morath aside. She glanced at Mellia, announced that she was needed elsewhere, and bustled out. They were plotting something. For the solstice?

"I never thanked you properly, Sister. You saved my life." Etienne leaned on the mantel.

"Without Runas, I wouldn't have known what to do. And I'm not a sister."

Miran burst through the wall, barking madly, and Mira's tail thumped on the floor.

"I suppose not. What do I call you, then? She-wolf?" He said it jokingly. But if Alroth was Wolf, then it was fitting that she be dubbed as such. And unlike when Lord Ainsley had said it, Etienne imbued the word with admiration rather than contempt.

A shaft of sunlight slanted through the window. The day was fading already. The shortest day. The inn hall would fill with folk soon, for the handmaids' service.

Miran settled with Mira on the hearth after a brief tussle through the plant buckets—thank Turbatius they couldn't actually knock into them.

"I think She-wolf is more fitting than Sister."

A smile curled Etienne's mustache. "You might be right about that."

The door burst open, and a nest of green spines and biting fresh scent came rustling through. Bunches of cut pine, spruce, and cedar boughs, tied with woody vines, paraded in, and Dayma and Livine gathered to admire them. Del, Kai, Morath, and Alroth each carried an armful, and they set to arranging them around the hall, not too close to the candles. Mellia took her own bunch, and there was Alroth, watching her. He closed the distance between them.

"Where should we hang this one?" Mellia's voice was soft, somehow.

"You tell me, sweetling."

She led him to a cozy corner and climbed onto a chair while he passed her the bunch to tie up. He offered his hand to help her down, and she took it, his fingers warm and strong in hers. She didn't let go once her feet were safely back on the ground.

"I have more." Alroth pulled something from his pocket, held it out to her. Another candle? Why was this so— The scent of it hit her as he brought it up to face height. Beeswax.

Dolomgrat with her brother, back in Falvair. Almost ten years her senior, Delphus had always taken the time to dance with his kid sister, made sure she got a taste of the honey-laced sweets, let her stay up as long as she liked on this longest night. More often than not, she'd fall asleep at the table and wake to him gathering her and carrying her up to bed.

Mellia opened her eyes. Alroth watched her, proffered the candle.

"Where did you find this?"

He shrugged. "I knew you wanted one."

Mellia laid the candle on the table, drew Alroth down, and kissed him.

24

ALROTH

Mellia was kissing him. *Kissing him.* She liked the candle, it would seem. Hunting down the beehive, climbing the sappy tree, even the sting he'd endured from the bee that had crawled up his sleeve was worth it, for this. He wrapped his throbbing arm around her waist.

Falkirk had told Del how much Mellia and Morath wanted a beeswax candle, so he and Del had scoured the trees for a honeycomb while cutting boughs for the inn hall. The bees were so sleepy he only got the one sting.

The look on Mellia's face when she'd smelled the sweet beeswax, all the tension falling away. Better times. No doubt in her beloved hive with the sisters and handmaids, rich honeyed food, prayers and beautiful glasswork. He couldn't give her any of that. But he'd brave a million bees to see that look again.

Mellia pulled back, smiling, and cradled the tiny candle Morath had helped them make. She approached the hearth, surrounded by... potted plants?... and put the candle in the centre of the mantelpiece.

The handmaids gathered around the hearth; Etienne stayed on the couch where they had settled him; Falkirk leaned on the wall by the kitchen door; and Del and Kai stood by the windows where the sun dipped below the treetops, casting long shadows of the bare branches, reaching through the snow toward their cozy inn hall. The townsfolk filled the benches on the other side of the room.

Livine opened a tiny book and adjusted her magnifying glass. The coin the Grist had spent on that handmaid could have fed Bridge for years. Livine read in Eichian, and the handmaids and Mellia responded. The townsfolk and the mercs were quiet, listening. A child whined and their parent drew them into the kitchen. Someone cleared their throat, and still, the prayer droned on. When Del dragged a chair noisily across the floor, Livine fell silent. She glanced around the room at the glazed faces, at Mellia, then at Kai.

"None of us speak Eichian, handmaid." Del spoke kindly—as kindly as he was able. "Might as well be chicken cheeping to me."

Livine flushed. She looked back at her tiny book and furrowed her brow. "Um, the Golden God, may He bring back the sun, shines his light on all penitents... like a... bee flying from flower to flower, carrying His word..." She huffed. "Do you all want me to read this?" She flapped the priceless book at the room and scanned the faces around her. Surely they were all expected to endure the scriptures on Dolomgrat?

"Maybe a more suitable festival would be... ?" Runas trailed off, raised her eyebrows at Morath, who glanced at Alroth.

"Of course!" Morath hurried to the kitchen, Falkirk trailing her. Alroth's other surprise.

Morath emerged holding an earthenware bowl, the whiny child and parent grinning in her wake. Falkirk slipped out, hands in their pockets. Morath held out the small wood spoon to Livine.

Livine spoke some Eichian over the bowl and took a spoonful. She stuck out her tongue, dripped one droplet of golden honey, and closed her eyes as she savoured it. She gave one to each handmaid in turn, one to Mellia, then surveyed the townsfolk.

Would they share the blessed honey with the Bridge rabble?

Livine grinned and beckoned Del and Kai. The Bridge folk took their turns with the blessing, with mixed reverence and jocularity.

Mellia beckoned Alroth over. She thought that a blasphemer like him was worthy of Doloman's blessing? He got on one knee so that Livine could lay a shining droplet on his tongue. Sweet, warm. Like his bond mate's soft gaze on him.

Mellia pulled a spill from the mantel and lit it in the fireplace, brought it to the beeswax candle's wick. She held it there until it took and moved on to the tallow candles on the mantel. She shook the spill out and tossed the end in the fireplace. She carried the beeswax candle and to him. "There are plenty of spills on the mantel. Can you light the rest of the candles while I do this?"

Shouldn't the handmaids— But she'd asked him. She needed to do *this*. Whatever *this* was, he nodded. Lighting a mess of candles was no hardship. While Livine gave the last stragglers their honey drops, and Alroth lit the candles, Mellia took the beeswax candle around, wafted the sweet smoke onto any who wished it, with a brief prayer.

Del and Kai brought out the horn and drum they'd left behind in the spring and started up a soft tune. Etienne picked up the melody, humming along, and Alroth joined him. The cozy warmth of their inn hall almost overshadowed the darkness, now fully fallen outside the windows. The longest night of the year had begun. May Doloman watch over them.

After the candles were lit, prayers said, and the honey doled out, the children lined up for a second round of blessings, and Etienne claimed a second one on account of his still recuperating. Del and Kai struck up a lively tune. Etienne knew the words to this one and joined in, along with his nemesis, Runas, who stood as far from him as possible while their voices blended perfectly together.

The floor was cleared for dancing—Alroth's cue to duck into the kitchen. Where he found Falkirk cooking, skirting more plants around the kitchen hearth.

"Why are there plants in the kitchen?" He bent for a closer look. A potato plant. Inside the inn.

"Your matron grew it." Falkirk's voice was carefully neutral.

So the magic Mellia had syphoned from him hadn't all been for cloth making. She had used some to grow plants. He fingered the clump of little leaves. She'd tried to mention something the handmaids could do to help with the food shortage, and he'd quieted her. Was that why she'd done this behind his back? What if she'd been less forceful? He might never have known she was capable of this. What if she could make more? Enough to keep Bridge through the winter?

He swallowed down his guilt at how he'd dismissed her. If she was serious, she shouldn't have let him shush her so easily. And she'd waited for him to be out cutting boughs to do this furtively.

"She grew all this?" He gestured to the hall as well.

"No, she was teaching everyone." Falkirk scooped out a spoonful of stew and tasted it. *Everyone.*

Alroth and Falkirk put together a lovely dinner in silence. Having a separate kitchen left them with plenty of elbow room, but only snatches of conversation—and laughter—reached them from the inn hall. The cruck had been open, children and animals underfoot, Del and Kai always in the way... so why did he long for it? The peace and quiet was relaxing. Not having to worry about the Turbatius-cursed uproar while they cooked was a blessing.

"I'll go for the bread," Alroth grumbled to Falkirk. The bakehouse was just across the square by the tithe barn. He strapped a basket to his back and stalked out into the snow.

Big clumps of snowflakes fell softly through the encroaching darkness as he crossed the square, and he opened his mouth and caught one on his tongue.

"Aren't you too old to be doing that?" Yasmine smiled as she fell into step with him.

Alroth's face heated at having been caught doing something so childish, but at least he hadn't been caught eating a handful of the stuff swiped off the ground. He shrugged.

"Your matron does good work."

Alroth nodded. "The weaving was very impressive."

"I meant with the planting." She held the bakehouse door open for him.

Miran chose that moment to burst out of a snowbank and yap around Alroth's feet. He nudged the raucous pup away and unslung the basket from his back.

"Your matron's ephemer is attached to you." A smile pulled at Yasmine's mouth.

His matron's ephemer. Right, they hadn't told anyone about his ephemer. He didn't correct her.

Yasmine followed Alroth into the sweltering bakehouse. The sweet smell of bread had Alroth taking a deep breath, and his stomach grumbling. He piled his basket with round loaves, and Yasmine filled a cloth, and they went back to the inn.

Alroth brushed the snow off and went into Ignis's Rest by the front door. A shout greeted him, with calls of "Bread!" and proffered bowls. Del and Kai were resting, along with the dancers. They would probably pick back up after dinner, play and dance through the night.

Mellia watched him from where she sat with the doe-eyed handmaid on the couch. Mira lay at her feet and raised their head, spectral tail thumping on the floor.

Livine, Morath, Etienne, Del, and Kai were huddled around the hearth. A tin cup of water sat next to the fire. What were they doing? He'd have to get closer to see. Del crowed and raised his fists high in the air in victory.

"Told you I could do it. Easy as anything. Don't know what you handmaids are all high and mighty about."

Mellia smiled. "There, you see? I knew you could do it."

"What did you do, Del?" Alroth growled.

They all froze, then turned one by one.

"He made the water in the cup boil." Kai seemed most unfazed.

Had Etienne ever looked at him guiltily before?

Mellia rose and smoothed her skirts. "Morath, Livine, and I were teaching everyone the basics of magic today."

"That right?"

She gestured to the plants around the hearth. "You're welcome to join us."

Join them in learning magic? Magic was the province of mages, not men. Del had said it was easy, and that right there was why. Did Alroth really need to learn when he had Mellia? No. He might have an ephemer, but he was no mage.

He turned on his heel and went back to the kitchen to help Falkirk, who clearly had the sense to stay away from the magic lessons.

"They still at it out there?"

"The magic?"

Falkirk nodded.

"They are. Del boiled some water. Fat lot of good that'll be to us."

"Thank Quies. One more round of moaning and whining that he couldn't get it because he was too manly for magic and I'd have decked him."

Ah, so it hadn't been as easy as Del had made out. Would Alroth be able to learn magic without lessons? Mellia would instruct him, like a child. His jaw clenched, and his scalp tightened. No. His matron teaching his mercs was one thing, but he was the one taking care of her, not the other way around.

Etienne wandered in and filched a loaf of bread. "Fight with your lady love?" He deftly hollowed out the loaf, and Falkirk scooped pottage into it.

"What makes you say that?" Alroth grabbed his own loaf and scooped a chunk out.

"You're in here with us." Falkirk filled Alroth's trencher, then another of Etienne's.

"I'll see her in my cabin soon enough."

His two mercenaries looked at each other.

"What?"

"With Sathred gone, there's a free room here at the inn." Falkirk kept their voice neutral, relaying a fact, nothing more.

Irrational rage bubbled in Alroth's gut. "My matron won't be sleeping here on her own when I've made her a bed in my cottage." Maybe it wasn't all rage. Would Mellia prefer to stay here at the inn without him? The fire in the cottage would have burned low by now. He'd be able to see his breath as he entered the shadowy room. Maybe Miran would curl up next to him on the cold bed like last night. He clenched his jaw. He *wanted* Mellia to sleep next to him, and not just so they could *make love* again tonight. Why did that make his anger boil higher? She hadn't even refused him yet.

"Careful, Wolf." Etienne paused to lock eyes with Alroth. "You'll drive her off. Mages are skittish."

Alroth lifted an eyebrow. Mellia? Skittish? His eye caught on the plants by the hearth. She had been skittish when it came to using their magic, at least while Alroth was around. She'd seemed to have no trouble syphoning when he was out. And why was that? Did she not trust him? The anger was back, like a fist in his middle. After all he'd done to make her feel safe, still she didn't trust him. What more could he do? Did she want him to be a mage like her? Doing magic instead of dirtying his hands properly? Did she want him to be a proper lord, passing off the unpleasant work to others? *Never.*

The others carried the food out to the inn hall while Alroth bolted his in the kitchen with Falkirk. Were they hiding in here like him? Once he was done eating, washing up, and had beaten Falkirk at two games of draughts in a row, he had no more excuses to hide away from Mellia. Not *hide away*. He wasn't avoiding her. He just didn't want to dance. He wanted to keep Falkirk company.

They all gathered in the inn hall again as the splash of the Milky Way faded in the sky and the eastern horizon's stars winked out. The children had long since dropped off, and some of the adults too, slumped over tables or curled on chairs. The handmaids stood by while the candles were snuffed, and Livine intoned a translated prayer of thanks for the sun, now in evidence. The light would return, even after the longest night.

Mellia leaned on a chair back and yawned as she snuffed the beeswax candle. It was late, and she would be tired. Unless Alroth *wanted* her to retire to a room here at the inn, he would go to her now and drag her to his cottage if necessary.

Mellia turned, smiled at him. "Don't you think it's time for bed?" She had one fist planted on her hip, the other still braced on the chair.

"You don't want to... ?" He jerked his chin at the stairs.

"No, Sathred's bed is occupied. I said I didn't need it..."

"Good." His shoulders dropped, his touchy one aching from the tension he'd been holding there all night. He stuck his head into the kitchen and nodded to Falkirk, who lifted a brow and began to tidy the game pieces.

"I'll win back my beans another night." They swept Alroth's winnings back into the jar of dried beans.

Mellia led the way through the light dusting of snow—it had already stopped falling—back to their dark little cottage. The two ephemers, ran ahead, doubled back, circled behind Alroth, and barked. Mellia laughed, and Alroth's heart leaped into his throat. *Cupidus's eye*, if only he could make her laugh like that.

By the time Alroth had stirred the fire in the cottage to keep them warm in the night, Mellia was already in bed. He undressed down to his shirt and braies and slipped in next to her. She snuggled into his side, natural as could be.

"The folks here are good at magic."

"I heard you had them growing plants and whatnot." He couldn't quite keep the censure from his tone. "Del seemed to get the hang of it. I guess he's more mage than I thought."

"He was trying all day. It just takes practice. For anyone." She fell silent.

Miran jumped on the bed, turned around twice, and lay down with their head on Alroth's foot.

Mellia sighed. "Are you planning to learn to wield your power?"

"The man aims the mage. The mage does the magic." He'd meant it as a compliment, but she gasped as though he'd said something hurtful.

She rolled away from him and curled up.

No *making love* tonight, then.

Alroth lay on his back while shadows danced on the thatch overhead. She really wanted him to learn to use magic? To syphon? That was *her* purview. Shouldn't she be glad he wasn't trying to take it from her, the one thing that she could do that he couldn't?

In his dream, he chased the ephemers through the forest, but they left no tracks and kept disappearing, dodging behind one tree and coming out from behind another until he was so turned around that he called out for Mellia—

The ephemers' barking woke him. The other side of the bed was cold. Mellia was already dressed, stirring the porridge for their breakfast. Her back was to him, but he could still make out her words in the near-silent cottage.

"Hush now, little ones. Don't wake the big strong source, too good for magic."

A bark in response.

"I know you want him to syphon, but he's far above the likes of us."

Ah. That's what had got her going last night. It wasn't that he was *too good* for magic. It was just that he wanted her to feel useful. And how could she feel useful if he was just as able to syphon as she was? He'd set her straight—

"Too afraid of being labelled a mage to even admit he has an ephemer."

Afraid? "I am not afraid." He'd meant to speak gently, but his voice came out a growl from sleep.

Mellia's attention snapped to him. "Of course you're not. Come have breakfast."

They ate in silence. She clearly hadn't changed her mind, but the more he protested, the more she would think him *afraid* to admit to having an ephemer. He just didn't see the need to announce that he had an ephemer to the whole town. They needed to trust him and follow him, and sources were just easier to depend on than mages.

They finished up and marched into the late morning sun. Everyone would be half asleep from their festivities and late night. Alroth shivered as his breath clouded the still air.

A bleat and a curse came from around the back of the inn as they approached.

"One of the sheep must have got out." Alroth led the way around the side of the inn. As they rounded the corner, Del's and Kai's voices reached them.

"I don't know anything about it. You're the one with all the answers."

Was Del afraid of a sheep?

"All the answers? I'd think a magic expert like you would be able to handle this without trouble."

A sharp crack and curse followed.

As soon as Mellia and Alroth rounded the corner of the inn, their meaning became clear. Two ephemers clopped between Del and Kai, curving horns lowered as they ran at each other and thumped together with a bone-jarring crack. Bighorn sheep. Ephemers. Two ephemers. They'd convinced two of the mages to bond with them! This was more than Alroth could have hoped for.

Mellia stormed forward. "What have you two done? If anything untoward has happened with the handmaids—"

"Leave off, Ultio-spawn!" Del spat.

"It had nothing to do with the handmaids." Kai didn't take his eyes off Del.

Ephemers without handmaids? "Then where did you get these ephemers? Whose are they?" Alroth gestured to the sheep, who were lining up to take another run at each other. A light hand on his arm stopped him, and he turned to Mellia.

She raised her eyebrows at him and nodded from Del to Kai. Did she mean… they were bound to each other? But that was impossible. Neither one of them was a mage. Did they even know how to do the ritual?

But Del was running his mouth. "We didn't think it would *work*, by Stultitia's cracked spindle. We were just playing around…"

Kai huffed but didn't say anything. Not just playing around according to him, then. Alroth had told him how to do the ritual, but with a handmaid. He'd done it with Del?

If he and Mellia had been able to bind themselves together with rosewater and a meady flask, barely acquainted as they had been, it was no surprise that Del and Kai had had such an easy time forming a bond. They'd been lovers for years, on and off, as they did, and friends for even longer.

"Having two ephemers isn't unheard of." She spoke briskly and glanced at Alroth. Would she tell them about Miran?

He cut in. "Let's get inside before we all freeze out here." He chivvied them through the back door into the kitchen.

Word travelled fast in Bridge, and by the time lunch was over, everyone seemed to know about Del and Kai's ephemers. They got more than a few congratulations and claps on the back. So the villagers were open to having two ephemers, even though the Grist were not?

Mellia watched the two bighorn sheep butt heads as she finished her meal. Mira sat at her feet, but Miran was nowhere to be found. Mellia turned to Alroth. "Would you like to help me with the potato plant today?"

"I'm sure you can handle the magic. You can syphon from me without fear."

"Actually, the pail is too heavy for me to carry out into the yard. But I'm glad to know you won't cruelly wrench me on a whim." She didn't look glad. She was practically glowering.

He shoved the pail out the door into the sun, and Mellia poured a stream of water into the pot as she bent over the plant and closed her eyes.

The small leaves grew slowly at first. Then the slight tug of syphoning pulled at Alroth's belly, and the leaves spread and rose taller, another stalk came up, then another, until the pail was overflowing with potato plants. The tug lessened and faded away.

Mellia dug through the pail, oblivious to how dirty her hands were getting, and pulled out a potato about as long and wide as her hand. "See what you could do if you'd only try?" One potato a day wasn't likely to feed the village, but he should encourage his mage.

"Well done, sweetling."

Her smile disintegrated and turned to a scowl. "I'm so glad you approve." She tossed him the potato, then brushed her hands on her skirt, doing nothing to dislodge the dirt around her nails. "Take that and the pail back inside so the plant doesn't freeze out here. She turned toward the yard's exit.

Was she going somewhere? "Where do you think you're off to?"

She rounded on him. "Where do I *think* I'm off to? I don't think, Alroth, I know. I'm going to the temple by Bridge Keep, and I don't require your leave to do so."

She made to turn back around and escape, but he grabbed her arm. "You *do* require my leave. Don't you recall the last time you did something so foolish? You ended up locked in an oubliette. If I hadn't fought for you, you would be bound to that prat, Ainsley."

She went stiff under his fingers. "Get your hand off me."

Mira growled at him, hackles raised.

Could she use magic to light him on fire? He dropped her arm. Better not to find out. But he still wasn't letting her go across to Bridge Keep. A storm was in the clear air this morning, and she'd be trapped out there. What kind of source would he be if he let her go into danger? He stepped in front of her, blocking the break in the inn-yard fence.

Mellia's knuckles were white where she planted them on her hips. "Don't you remember the last time you tried to stand in my way?"

"Don't *you* recall last time you defied me?" Keeping her here was for her own good, and she needed to learn not to question him. She would see, once the storm rolled in, that he had been right. She might even thank him.

Mira barked and snapped at his leg, and he automatically kicked out, even though he knew that Mira couldn't touch him.

Mellia turned on her heel and stalked back into the inn. Alroth sighed. She'd come around. He hauled her potato plant back into the kitchen by the hearth and trudged out to the inn hall.

"If you're looking for your matron, she's shut herself in Sathred's room upstairs." Livine barely looked up from the game of draughts she played with Falkirk.

"I wouldn't go try to talk to her, though, if I were you." Falkirk leaned back in their chair and crossed their arms. "Whatever you've done now, doesn't seem like Mellia wants to talk about it."

Alroth threw the potato at Falkirk and turned away.

"Where are you going?"

"Hunting, before the storm breaks."

Miran hung their head as they trotted at his heels.

25

Mellia

Mellia slipped out the front door of the inn. Livine and Falkirk had promised not to tell Bellator-cursed Alroth where she'd gone, so with any luck, she'd be back before he realized that she wasn't where he'd left her.

If he insisted on ordering her around, he would soon discover he was wasting his breath. Better he learn sooner than later. Not that there would be a later. Once Mellia discovered how to break their bond, she was leaving. Del and Kai's binding had given her the idea: Maybe the old temple would have the answers the Grist hid from them on how bonds were formed and broken.

Because Del and Kai's bond could not be explained by the Grist's teachings. Even if they performed the ritual perfectly, such a thing should not be possible. It took a mage and a source to bind together. Neither Del nor Kai struck her as a mage. But the temple had been there before the Empire conquered Sudra and drove out the old gods. Could there be something there that might explain the surprising bond between Del and Kai? And her strange bond to Alroth? The man who locked her up, ordered her around, and... hunted down beeswax for Dolomgrat. And dismissed her magic as a domestic pastime, not worth learning.

Since the handmaids' reckless flight, the wind had blown powdery snow onto the track across the village toward the bridge, island, and keep beyond, but it was still clear enough to tread. The sun warmed Mellia's face. She'd make it there and back with no trouble at all.

The wind had whipped snow into a drift against the intact parapet. The pristine slant of snow reached from the top of the wall across the deck to the crumbling stones and the long drop to the river below. She'd been able to clear it once with Sathred and the other handmaids. Could she do it herself? The sun was a bit less warm today.

She focused in on the air trapped between the snowflakes. Air was more susceptible to magic than water, so that would yield better results and might not require syphoning and alerting Alroth. She planted her feet on a sturdy part of the bridge and used the sunlight on the snowdrift blocking her path. The snow melted to slush, and steam rose from the suddenly warmed snow at the edge of the bridge. The water pattered into the river below, slow moving as it was this time of year. The way was clear. And she hadn't even had to syphon. *Perfect.*

Mellia hummed as she crossed the wet stones, sticking as close to the wall as possible. No reason to chance a gust of wind throwing her off balance and tossing her over the edge. She shuddered and concentrated on the path trodden through the snow on the other side. The bridge sloped down on the island side, and Mellia kept a hand on the icy stone wall to steady her feet. A patch of ice could easily be hidden under the snow. Though she had passed the point of tumbling into the river, a slip could still mean a painful topple onto her rear or her head.

Once she stepped from the bridge onto the island, she took a deep breath. She was here, and she was about to explore a temple, maybe unsullied by the Grist.

Unsullied? Certainly, she was not and had never been terribly pious, not since her brother, anyway, but the Grist brothers were fundamentally well-intentioned. For all that they had conquered Sudra, not much had changed when they did. They introduced the Sudrans to Doloman's light and the binding ritual, but her people had worshipped Doloman before their arrival; they just hadn't been able to form proper, righteous bonds without His blessing.

So what was a temple to the old gods like? What had it been used for? If there were no binding rituals and no Grist masses, why did they need a temple? Mellia climbed the hill toward the keep. The dark stone stood tall on one side; before the river rose and washed the other side out, it must have been formidable, larger than the Grist Queen's Keep in New Bridge. The round, squat temple's mossy tile roof had mostly survived. The door had partly fallen in, and Mellia put her shoulder to it and squeezed inside. She tripped down—the building was taller than she'd guessed; the plants outside had overgrown it, and soil had collected over the years to half bury the building.

A shaft of sunlight filtered through the winter-brown vines latticed over the hole in the roof and onto the roof tiles scattered on the ground dusted with a frosting of snow. The walls still blocked the wind, and Mellia's eyes adjusted slowly to the dim light after the brilliant sunlight reflected off the snow outside.

Inside, the temple was not round, but octagonal. Half-faded paintings decorated the eight walls, and carved statues, larger than life, sat in each corner—their heads knocked off and left in the dirt covering the soil-encrusted flagstone floor. Mellia's hand flew to her mouth. This was a *temple*. These statues must be of the old gods. And someone had knocked the heads off them, one by one, each and every—no, not every one.

The remaining intact statue was a dour man with traces of gold glinting in the folds of his cloak. Doloman. They'd left Doloman intact. Could that mean that whoever had desecrated this temple had been a devotee of the Grist? But the Grist hadn't *forced* anyone to worship Doloman, they'd simply explained that he was the highest of the gods and—*Stultitia's gnarled fingers—explained* that Doloman was the only god worth worshipping... and the people of Sudra had embraced Him unquestioningly? How much of a fool was she?

Mellia bent to turn over the head of the next statue, wiped the moss and dirt from its face with her thumb. The severe features were not unlike Doloman's, but the statue above her held a flame in his hand, seemingly without being burned. Ignis. And there, on the other side, a woman bent over a small bundle she held in her arms, a stand of carved mushrooms sprouting from her shoulder. Dolor. And on the other side of Doloman, the statue's fingernails were pitted, as though they'd once held gemstones that had been pried from the sockets. Locuples, then, who showed off his riches through his glittering bejewelled nails.

The others were unfamiliar. A statue with bulging muscles and breasts under a rough-spun tunic; a curvy statue with willow whips curling all around her, perhaps instead of hair? An empty dais, only the statue's bare feet still standing. Mellia turned over one of the stones littering the ground in this corner—a woman's body parts, legs, breasts, arms, and the curve of a hip, though the crotch seemed to be stomped to gravel, as was the face. She took a shuddering breath.

No. The Grist had not taken Sudra peacefully. This proudly naked goddess had stood across from Doloman. Could she have been... his equal? Doloman's winter solstice festival was perhaps reflected in a summer solstice festival, overseen by this mysterious goddess, not a second ode to Doloman, as the Grist proscribed.

She needed to put this statue back together. Leaving her here in the dust was unacceptable. There must be a way to restore the reverence this high goddess had inspired before the Grist had come and stomped her into the dirt, taken everything lovely and unique about her and destroyed it, mangled it beyond recognition. The sand that had once been a powerful deity grew speckled with the tears that flooded Mellia's eyes so she couldn't even see the shards of the goddess her fingers collected into the cradle of her skirt. Her fingers found the texture of hair, smooth skin, was that the dip of a dimple? Maybe the small curved tip of a finger or a nose.

Mellia's back bowed, and she hunched over the precious shards of stone like Dolor over the stillborn child in her arms. But unlike her husband Orbitus, god of death, Dolor was also the goddess of rot and decay, and—as the mushrooms that always graced her shoulders attested—ripening and moving out of grief to the next stage of growth. Heat tingled through Mellia, boiling up from the base of her spine, up through her belly, into her chest. She straightened. Set her jaw.

The Grist destroyed people's lives. She had known that ever since they had killed her brother. But all this time, she'd thought her family the exception. That sometimes the Grist made such difficult decisions by Doloman's will. But this was a temple of her people and had been here long before the Grist came over the mountains with the Empire and crushed Sudra's gods—*her* gods—to dust.

She had found her answer. Del and Kai had formed a bond because the Grist might deny the power of all gods but Doloman, but even *they* couldn't destroy the gods' influence. They could tear apart the statues, erase the memory, kill anyone who—like her brother—revealed their deception, but the gods lived on through people like Del and Kai, Falkirk, even Alroth. Even her. Because it was clear now. Doloman had not blessed her bond with Alroth. She studied each headless deity in turn. Their bond had been blessed by one of the other gods. There were so many more than the Grist would ever admit to. The eight statues, yes, but the walls were covered with paintings, too.

Each painting overflowed with deities, in the midst of every activity imaginable: household tasks, outdoor work, caring, fighting, singing, travelling, telling stories, and yes, fucking. The gods were not, as the Grist painted Doloman, dour and beyond reach. They were here and all around. There was no need to beg contact with the gods through a Grist father or brother when the very act of spinning or fetching water or sailing could bring a person closer to the gods. No wonder the Grist had tried to destroy them.

Mellia brushed the shards of the unknown goddess off her skirt. That was not her. The goddess, whoever she was, still watched over Mellia and her people, even two centuries after the Grist had smashed her likeness. Mellia's heart swelled. If she called on the nameless goddess, she would answer.

Mellia bent and plucked a piece of granite that fit in her palm with the texture of the unknown goddess's hair and slipped it into her pocket. She was not forgotten. Mellia would make sure she never was.

She climbed ungracefully out the narrow gap in the door. It had started to snow while she was inside, the bright noonday sunlight having changed quickly to dark clouds and a canopy of falling flakes. The path from the bridge into the village would quickly fill with snow and make her trek back miserable. And the bridge. She gasped, heart pounding. In a snowfall, even her magic couldn't clear the bridge. She hurried down the hill and emerged from the trees onto the shore by the bridge. Yes, snow collected there, and a small drift was forming where she had melted a way earlier.

She stepped onto the bridge, and a strong arm wrapped her waist and pressed the air from her lungs. Alroth had found her.

"I knew if I hung around long enough, I'd catch a handmaid." Not Alroth.

Mellia hollered and thrashed, but her captor's arm just tightened more.

"I'll admit, I doubted I'd find anyone skulking around this island. I'll have to apologize for doubting the Grist father."

The Grist Father? To have contact with the Grist father, this must be a Grist brother.

"Father Glimar won't be happy when he hears you treated a handmaid so abominably."

"I don't think he'll mind, actually."

Mellia screeched in frustration as the brother bound her wrists behind her back. "I have magic. Your bindings won't hold me."

The guard chuckled. "I have magic, too, handmaid. I suppose you wouldn't know that, though. We have a new Grist queen."

A Grist queen? Who could that be? All the handmaids were in Bridge, except... Sathred.

And she'd known where to find the handmaids.

Sathred had betrayed them to the Grist. And now the Grist were here. And one of them had taken her captive. In a blizzard.

26

Alroth

Alroth had to talk to Mellia. She'd been in the other handmaid's room all afternoon, and she hadn't eaten since their tense meal this morning. He prepared a tray for her and mounted the stairs, shaking off the admonishments of the handmaids, and Falkirk, for some reason. He knocked on the door.

No answer.

"It's Alroth. Your husband."

She was angry with him for keeping her from going to her temple, that was plain. But she could at least tell him that directly.

"Won't you at least let me in, sweetling?"

Silence.

He shifted the food tray to one hand and knocked again with the other. If she wouldn't open up, he would have to break down the door. She could not stay up here and starve herself out of spite for some slight about him preventing her from going out in a snowstorm and getting herself killed.

"I'll take you to the temple tomorrow." They could go together. That way he could help her across the bridge. There would be snow, but he would keep her safe.

Still no answer.

"You can't be angry that I didn't let you go out in a blizzard and freeze to death, sweetling. I swore to protect you, and I will."

Why wasn't she at least answering?

"If I don't hear a word from you, I'm coming in." He tried the latch, and the door swung open. It hadn't been latched at all. The room was empty. Mellia was gone.

He fumbled the tray. Pottage ran across the floor as the trencher tipped over and rolled upside down; the cup of water washed the gravy from the roast littlefield bird he'd hunted under the bed; and the little mound of potato he'd made her from the one she'd tossed him this morning thwacked onto the floorboards.

If she wasn't here, where was she? *The temple.* She had gone to the temple.

She'd lied to him, made him think she was going up to a safe, snug inn room, and she'd gone out... The wind rattled the shutters, and a stream of snowflakes hissed through a crack between them. The freezing, deadly blizzard had started, and Mellia wasn't here. She was in a rotted-out temple. On the other side of a treacherous bridge.

Alroth strode from the room, leaving the mess on the floor. He practically leaped down the stairs and bent over the bookish handmaid, Livine, one hand on each arm of her chair.

"Where is my wife?"

The handmaid looked up slowly from her book. "She said not to tell you."

"She told you to lie to her husband on her behalf, and you agreed?" He pounded one arm of the chair.

The mousy handmaid on the couch next to them jumped and whined, but Livine didn't so much as blink. "My friend asked me to cover for her when her *overbearing and controlling* bond mate tried to exert an influence on her disproportionate to his role within their relationship."

What the fuck was that supposed to mean? Saving her life was overbearing and controlling now? "She didn't think me so *overbearing* when I saved her from falling to her death from the bridge."

Livine glared at him, batted his arm aside, and stood. She tucked her book under her arm. "I think you know where she's gone."

"And you just let her go in a blizzard. If she doesn't come back"—Alroth swallowed past the lump that jumped to his throat—"it'll be on your head."

Livine paled, but she didn't relent. "This could have been prevented if you had told her there was a storm on the way instead of ordering her to stay."

Fuck. Why did it hurt worse that Livine was right? If he'd taken the time to talk to her, to explain his order… He was wasting time. Every moment, the bridge would become more treacherous, and Mellia would get colder. He strode toward the door.

"Wait, Alroth." Falkirk stepped up. "You can't go out in this."

Alroth glared at them. They had hidden Mellia's scheme from him just as much as the handmaids had. Hadn't they noticed a blizzard was brewing out there? Why hadn't they stopped Mellia? But, it wasn't their responsibility to care for her; it was his. Alroth was the one who had failed, so he was the one who had to make it right. "You going to stop me?"

Falkirk shook their head and stepped back. "If anyone can safely cross to the island right now, you can."

Alroth must look fearsome indeed to make Falkirk recoil. He snatched a pair of snowshoes from the wall by the door and slung them on his back. He wouldn't need them on the way there, and hopefully not on the way back, but Paratus knew it was better to have and not need than to need and not have.

Falkirk appeared at his elbow and thrust a hood at him. They had seen him like this once before. There was no stopping him, so they were trying to equip him to come back alive. Just like last time. Alroth took the hood and inclined his head to his friend. He pulled the woollen hood over his head and snugged it around his scratchy face. Falkirk nodded back, and Alroth stepped into the howling wind.

Tiny ice crystals pecked at the exposed skin around his eyes, and he tucked his mittened hands into the warm folds of his houppelande to protect them from the wind. He squinted through the snow, mostly whirling in eddies, not really falling at all. He would need the snowshoes sooner than he'd expected.

He passed the cottages, their strips of light filtering faintly through the storm around him, and he could barely make out the glow of his own banked fire between the shutters. Miran burst through the cottage door as he passed, barking sharply, and blending into the storm around him, almost like the dream where he'd been chasing the ephemers through the forest. He would find Mellia. She'd be cold, huddled in the temple, shivering, but alive and well. Her clothes were plain and sturdy, and she had magic, should she need it.

But she hadn't used the magic, or if she had, he'd missed it. His heartbeat was steady, and his middle, where the tug of syphoning seemed to pull, was quiet. He deepened his breathing and focused on stepping carefully in the gathering snow. Still nothing from their bond. She would use her magic if she was in danger. But maybe not. Maybe she didn't want to alert him by using magic. She thought he was still ignorant of her lie, and she knew he would seek her out at the inn if she syphoned. But surely she wouldn't let that stop her if she was truly in danger?

He paused, pulled his hood lower over his eyes, and strapped on the snowshoes, his fingers almost frozen by the time he had them tied. Miran circled him, dipping their nose into the snowbanks and whining. They knew that Mellia was in danger. They must. The going was easier with the snowshoes, but would it be enough to let him cross the bridge? He'd done it in the snow and ice before, but never with such strong wind. The gusts would be howling past the cliffside, ready to toss him from the bridge's open parapet. But he wouldn't let it. If he died, so would Mellia, out in this cold with nowhere to go.

Alroth emerged from the trees. No telltale sparkle of fire reached him from the island, though it might be obscured by the swirling snow. That didn't mean that Mellia hadn't started a fire. He took a breath and stepped onto the bridge. As he'd predicted, the wind picked up and tried to pluck him into the air. He hunched and steadied himself against the icy wall. Miran dashed over the bridge, barking, then back to him, tangled around his ankles and toppled into the snow. Alroth gripped their chin in his hand and looked them in the eye.

"No. You trip me up here, and we're dead." He gave the pup's face a gentle shake to punctuate his words, and they huffed. He let them go, and they trotted across the bridge, much more sedately, to pace just on the other side of the narrow stretch.

Alroth took a deep breath. If he took off the snowshoes, his gait would be narrower, give him more leeway to stagger a step, but he would be liable to slide right over the edge. He kept them on and bent to keep himself out of the wind behind the wall as much as possible. Three more steps until the worst was over... two more... last step... He let out a sigh as the bridge widened out, and he ruffled Miran's ears.

"Good dog."

Miran panted and barked, leaped in front of him again, and dashed off into the snow. They didn't leave footprints to follow, and a pang hit Alroth. What if he couldn't find them again? That was absurd, though. Miran was always disappearing for long stretches of time and popping up again later on. They would come back. They would.

Alroth climbed the hill toward the temple. He'd passed it often on his rambles over the island, but he'd never been inside. The gap in the door was narrow, and he was not. Besides, it seemed sacrilegious somehow to break into such a place. Not for a sister, of course, but for a blasphemous lout like him. He reached the temple, his breath panting through the stiff frozen fabric covering his mouth and nose. At least it kept him from inhaling sharp little snow needles, but it smelled like wet sheep and shed wool into his mouth.

The door had been bent open a little more, enough for Mellia to slip through, but certainly not enough for him. There were no marks in the snow around the temple, so hopefully she was still inside where it was sheltered. Then again, marks in the snow would last a mere blink in this wind. The keep loomed over the trees behind him. That was the only other place that Mellia would go to seek shelter. He'd check here first and then head that way.

He crouched and peered through the crack in the door. "Mellia, I'm here. Come on home with me and get warm, sweetling."

Fear pinched his gut with every gust of wind that didn't bring Mellia's answer floating out of the temple.

Bark! Alroth startled and leaped to his feet. *Miran.* They were back, but not for long. They dashed toward the keep. Could they be leading him to Mellia? Mira had done it before. He listened at the temple door for another two heartbeats and strode after Miran through the snow.

Up the hill toward the forbidding black stone of the keep he toiled, his snowshoes letting him take long slow strides over the snow. The crumbling keep walls would at least protect Mellia from the wind, though the roof had long since caved in. She would have been more protected in the temple. Why had she left it? Unless she never made it there in the first place. But the gap in the door had been wider than last he'd seen it. Was he leaving her? Was she too weak to call out to him? He could kick in the temple door… but that seemed the sort of thing that would incite the gods' rage for the rest of a man's short life.

Before Mellia, he'd never worried about such things. Did he believe in the gods' power now? Their bond had to come from somewhere, and who could make such magic possible except the gods?

Alroth crested the hill, and the keep's arched entrance loomed before him. The wind moaned through the ruins, and Alroth shuddered. Hopefully, no spirits haunted this place. The story of Bridge was not a happy one.

He passed through the second archway into the inner keep and was knocked sideways off his feet into the snow. His head cracked off stone, and he blinked the stars from his eyes. An enraged scream reached him over the wind, but a man loomed over him now, weapons in hand, frost coating his reddish beard. If Mellia was here, this man had found her as well. He had to get to her, keep her safe—

No time to think of Mellia. She was still alive and was more likely to stay that way than he was, unarmed. For Paratus's sake, why would he have brought weapons with him? Who would have thought he'd need them in an Ultio-cursed snowstorm?

It wasn't useful to curse what he didn't have. What he did have were snowshoes tied to his Sarillian feet. Bare fists would do little against the long dirk his opponent held, but at least Alroth wore his trusty gambeson under his houppelande, and his fists would be numbed by the cold, so any injuries would bleed but little.

He lumbered to his feet. He dodged a strike with the dirk and staggered sideways, already tripping over his snowshoes. He wouldn't be much for dodging. He caught himself with a foot on a snowdrift, his snowshoe granting him purchase on its crest. That was a blessing. Without it, he would be knee-deep in icy-cold powder. He leaped forward and got a hit in on his opponent's middle. Pain shot up his arm. Without a cestus to protect his fist, he had overestimated the blow's effectiveness. The other man grimaced and slashed at his torso, opening a chilly hole in his houppelande. But the blow didn't get through his gambeson. Alroth grinned back and stepped forward again. Thankfully, his possibly broken fist was half frozen. He struck out again, and the other man lurched back, staggering into the snow-drift. His foot caught in the snow, and he stumbled to his knees. *Aha. That* Alroth could use to his advantage.

He advanced on the kneeling man, Alroth on the drift while the other man floundered and sank in. Alroth kneed him in the nose, and the dirk flew from the injured man's hand and vanished in the snow. Alroth grinned, taking his advantage.

"Where's the lady." His voice came out raspy and muffled behind his hood. He ripped the man's helmet off and tossed it aside to sink into the snowbank with his dirk.

Blood streamed from his nose, and his answer came out garbled. He was unarmed now, but there was still no turning his back on the man.

A screech made Alroth turn—and duck under a blow to his neck from behind. There were two of them.

The bleeding man behind Alroth cursed, but as the unarmed opponent, he was less of a concern. Alroth had the high ground atop the snow drift, but the man he faced now had a halberd. With long enough reach to keep him out of the deeper snow his compatriot was mired in.

What could he possibly do with his bare fists against a halberd? With his cesti, he would get inside the man's guard—a halberd was worse than useless for grappling. But without? One blow from the gauntlets the man wore would cave Alroth's face right in without a helm. If he could find the dirk in the snow, he stood a chance...

If only he'd brought Volnus and Ictus with him—he dodged a swing from the halberd—well, just Volnus now, since the mage had destroyed Ictus.

There was a way to disarm a man without taking his weapon. Magic. Alroth had an ephemer now, and besides, Del had performed magic before the bond had formed between him and Kai. Miran popped out of the snow and harried the man behind Alroth. *Good.* Hopefully, Miran could distract him long enough for Alroth to try this.

He dodged another halberd swing and focused. How did one use magic? The blade was the thing to destroy. He concentrated on that and imagined it dulling and rusting away. *Come on, come on... fall apart!* Miran barked, and he grasped at the thread of Mellia's power. *Rust, damn you!* The snowflakes landing on the blade would dampen it.

A halberd blow struck Alroth in the side, and he grunted, doubling over. Orbitus take useless magic! Mellia appeared, crashing into the guard from behind, who whirled, long enough for Alroth to kick the back of his knee with the sharp edge of his snowshoe and take him down. The guard swung the halberd for Alroth's legs, but the suddenly rusted blade sheared off and fell into the snow by Alroth's snowshoe. Alroth lunged at the other man, took him to the ground, hefted the rusted halberd head, and slashed it across his opponent's throat.

The life drained from the man's eyes as he clutched the lifeblood spurting into the snow.

Alroth turned. There was still another man. A man who wasn't looking at him but at the rusted blade in his hand. Then past him. A bark reached Alroth from somewhere over his shoulder, but Miran was at his side. Doloman's teeth, this man was putting it together. He could plainly see their two ephemers together. He couldn't be allowed to live.

Alroth advanced on the wide-eyed man, the rusty halberd head digging into his palm.

"Alroth!"

He turned toward Mellia's voice. There she stood, hands bound behind her, pale, with red spots on her cheeks, but seemingly unharmed. He hefted the magically rusted blade. She'd done that. Miran barked a warning, but by the time Alroth turned back to the dead man walking, he had slipped out through the archway.

"Fallo's green garters, woman, what?" He rounded on Mellia.

She stood her ground. "You were going to kill Brother Padril."

"Damned right I was, and I still am. He saw Miran." And he would take the story back to the Grist. They would come for the handmaids, and when they did, they would come for him too—and Mellia. Alroth stalked toward the archway. If he followed now, the brother's trail would be visible, and in his snowshoes, he could catch up easily.

"No, you're not." Mellia stepped into his path, blocking the archway.

"Out of my way, woman." He could shove her aside, but with her hands bound, she might crack her fool head open.

She didn't move.

"You want him to go running to your precious Grist father and tell him about us? Do you think he'll sanction our bond with two ephemers the way he sanctioned the first? Would you have me go into the ring with your lordling again on your behalf?" Did she have any concept of the danger they were in? Had she ever been in real danger in her life before this very week?

"I didn't—" She coughed and spat into the snow. Red.

Alroth's heart froze in his chest. Mellia was not unhurt. He'd seen this before. A blow to the chest and the breathing went pink and foamy, red, gasping, drowning in blood while he stood helplessly by and watched.

He'd let his matron get hurt. Mellia was dying.

27

MELLIA

Mellia's breath was fire. She fell to her knees, only saved from cracking her head by Alroth's gentle arms. He snapped her bindings with his bare hands and leaned her back against him. Pain lanced up her side as he cradled her body.

She was injured, her side. She closed her eyes, tried to find the place within her body, but with every inhale, her concentration was shattered by the lancing pain. If she hadn't known it would be excruciating, she would have roared her frustration.

She couldn't heal herself. She couldn't focus when every breath screamed for her to cough but coughing tore her apart.

"You have to—" She couldn't get a sentence out. Any more and the lurking cough would overtake her. But she couldn't *breathe*. "Magic." She laid Alroth's hand lightly on her side where something was stabbing into her, even though there was no wound.

"Shh, Mellia."

Was he crying? Over her?

"Magic," she whispered, the word's hiss melding with the snow over the ruins. Mira barked and whined. They pawed at Mellia's skirt and nuzzled under her arm on her uninjured side.

"I—I couldn't do it, before. I don't want to break you." Alroth's voice had become small, timid.

"Focus." It was all she could say. She wouldn't be able to speak again, not even a whisper. He would have to do this. Or not. She could drift away right now. The chill seeping into her bones from the cold stone beneath her beckoned. Perhaps it would be fine to die like this. Mira whined. Leaving Mira would be hard, but what else did she have?

A face floated into her mind. Not someone she'd seen before. A naked woman, kind, strong, robust. A woman who could stand next to Doloman—or against him. The destroyed goddess from the temple. *Hiorach's fiery fingers*, Mellia couldn't die. She had to tell the others about the temple. She lifted her heavy lids, gritted her teeth, and clutched Alroth's hand to her broken body.

"Now, husband."

A cough racked her, her bones grinding together inside, and Miran growled from their place beside Alroth.

But something was happening. Her next breath didn't stab her quite so deep; the fire in her lungs burned low and faded to embers. The pain was lessening, and her next breath had lost its rattle. The taste of blood faded from her mouth, and the stabbing in her side dulled to a throbbing ache. Alroth heaved in a breath and shuddered it out.

Mellia coughed, the lancing pain sharp, but nothing like the grinding of bones from a moment before. She spat blood onto the snow and took a deep breath. She coughed again, but this time it was easier.

She wasn't healed, not fully, but she was no longer dying. That was an improvement. She squeezed Alroth's hand where she still held it to her and let it go.

"Can you stand?" Alroth's breath was warm on her face.

Mellia's teeth chattered as she nodded.

Alroth dragged off the hood that wreathed his head and pulled it onto her. His warmth seeped into her ears and cheeks and made them tingle painfully.

Alroth saw her wince. "Still hurt?"

"Yes, but it's... manageable." She made to sit up and fell back against him.

"Can you make it back to the village?"

"With your help? Yes."

He guided her gently to her feet and supported her good side as they trudged through the snow. Alroth had snowshoes on, but Mellia just had her boots. She couldn't hobble all the way back to the village like this. They would freeze before they even got to the bridge. If she wanted to live, her pride would have to take a blow.

"Alroth." Mellia had to stop, unable to walk and speak simultaneously.

"Sweetling?" Ah, so she was *sweetling* again and no longer *woman*.

"Will you carry me?"

"It will hurt to be jostled..."

"It hurts now."

Alroth nodded and gently hitched her into his arms. He was right, the jostling at each step did hurt, but still Alroth was faster than her hobbling self. When they left the trees' shelter behind, a gust of wind made Alroth stagger a step. The far side of the bridge was cloaked in snow, obscured to brief glimpses of trees.

"I'll have to put you down, sweetling." Alroth's breath was warm on her face.

Mellia nodded.

He set her gently on her feet. "Wait here."

Their ephemers were silent as they trotted across the bridge, circling each other and pacing on the other side, their luminescence hardly discernable from the swirling snow. Mellia leaned toward the edge, the water far below also hidden by the storm. Snowflakes cocooned them, the narrow section of bridge beneath their feet, their entire world. Alroth unstrapped one snowshoe and knelt, sweeping the snow off the bridge with it, making a path for them. It would fill again within moments, but it was better than the drift that had been there, ready to tip them over the precipice.

Alroth put his snowshoe back on. "You go first. I'll be right behind you. I won't let you fall."

Mellia almost asked whether she could wear the snowshoes, but she could barely walk; she'd never be able to lift the shoes with each step. She crept onto the crumbling section of bridge, hugging the wall, hunched against the wind. A gust buffeted her, and Alroth steadied her hip from behind, pressing her to the wall until it ebbed. She watched her feet, step after step. They would make it. They'd get back to the inn, and she would tell the handmaids about the temple, and when the weather was better, they could all go back together. Livine would copy the paintings and sketch the statues into her logbook and—

Mellia's foot slipped out from under her, and she tipped sideways, toward the endless drop. She gasped, pain shot up her side, and she instinctively hunched, taking that last stumbling step toward the drop when warm hands shoved her hard toward the parapet, and she staggered into solid rock and landed on her knees in the snow.

Alroth.

She looked back as he disappeared over the slippery stones. His wide amber eyes disappearing in the blizzard. He'd pushed her to safety, but shoved himself backwards into swirling snow. The ephemers barked wildly. Miran howled. Alroth would land on the rocks and ice five ells below. Mellia couldn't heal him, not from that, not when she was half frozen and her ribcage was recently smashed in. But she wanted to save him. The wind was strong. Could she use it to slow his fall? Her magic wouldn't come. Miran's howl rang through the dull snow.

Miran.

Mellia didn't deliberate, she didn't wonder how to do it, she just pulled. She wrenched Alroth. She opened her eyes, and there was Miran, mostly black with splashes of cream, white underside. A darker version of Mira. They were still here, Mira and Miran. Which meant that it had worked. Alroth was alive. Ephemeral, but alive. She'd wrenched him. Mellia had wrenched her source. She scorned sources who wrenched their mages as cruel and selfish, and now she'd done it herself.

How could she humiliate him like this? He scorned mages. Would he have preferred to die rather than be wrenched? Would he hold this against her? After he'd finally used magic to save her, he was repaid with this. How long would he be ephemeral? Would his mercs see him this way when they got back to Bridge—

Bond and Grist. Alroth was *ephemeral.* Mellia had to limp all the way back to the village in a blizzard. If she stayed here, she would freeze. How long until Alroth became corporeal again? Could she make it back through the snow without him? Alroth, silvery and translucent, hiked across the bridge with no regard to the snow. He crouched by her and tried to say something, but obviously she couldn't hear him.

Miran nudged her with their nose. She had to stand, to move. The path back to the village stretched in front of her, but it was barely discernable, and fast filling with snow. She was just as likely to flounder and collapse in a snowdrift. If only she could send word to the village. Maybe they could come and help her back.

Alroth. He would have to go on ahead and bring back help. He would have to let everyone see him in this form. Could she ask that of him? The alternative was freezing to death in a snowbank.

"Alroth." Mellia spoke toward the ground. He couldn't argue with her, but if she saw the look on his face, she might not have the nerve to keep going. "I need you to go to the village, get a sled for me."

Miran growled.

"Don't argue with me. We both know I can't make it back to the village right now. In your condition, you can get there between one heartbeat and the next. Go and get a sled." *And if no one will come, at least you won't have to watch me die.*

Alroth tried to touch her cheek, his bright fingers slipping through her skin. He nodded without hesitation, even though he had to know what it meant. He pressed his fist to his heart. *I swear.* His form swept away. Mira curled up on one side of Mellia, Miran on the other.

"Aren't you going to go with him?" Mellia nudged Miran with her elbow, and they huffed out a breath. Stubborn, just like their mage. The idea of Alroth as a mage was so dissonant. Everything Mellia had ever been taught about mages and magic had been scrambled and overturned in the past few days. Alroth's ephemer, Del and Kai's bond, the temple. None of that made sense with the Grist's teachings, but she'd seen it all with her own eyes. The solid ephemer beside her was undeniable, their quiet breathing pressing their side rhythmically against Mellia's hip.

When the guard had taken her to Brother Padril, she'd thought perhaps he could be reasoned with. But he'd attacked Alroth, ignored her protests. And he was on his way back to Father Glimar to tell him about Miran. He'd seen Miran and Mira together, there could be no mistake. He would have no trouble piecing together that the ephemers belonged to the two of them; how many mages could there be out on a remote island in a snowstorm? And he'd gotten away. Alroth had wanted to kill him for good reason. Their lives were forfeit if they returned to New Bridge. Once Father Glimar learned of their two ephemers, he would apprehend them as soon as they entered the town walls and make an example of them. Even having protected the handmaids wouldn't save Alroth now.

And Del and Kai couldn't go back to New Bridge. They would end up like her brother. More deaths on her conscience. No, that wasn't right. It wouldn't be on her. It was the Grist. They were the ones who had decided that natural bonds were forbidden. They were the ones who insisted that devotees deny what their eyes could plainly see: That men could be mages just as easily as women, that *anyone* could be a mage. Not only that, but a bond didn't consist of a mage and source; in fact, in a bound pair, either one could act as mage or source. They could work together. When one of them was unable to use magic, the other could step in and support them with their own power.

Why would the Grist deny them this knowledge?

Doloman loomed over Mellia, and she startled back, His golden eyes boring into her. But no, nothing was there. It was just her imagination. Doloman, the Golden God. The god of anger worshipped by the Grist, by all of Sudra, for the last two centuries. Sometimes, like now, Doloman had Lord New Bridge's face. Always cold, angry, ready to mete out punishment to any who he deemed to have mis-stepped. But why should he be the one to determine who deserved punishment? There were seven other major gods and countless household gods. The Grist had elevated him above all others and decreed that it was the natural order.

It was not, and Mellia would no longer pretend along with them.

If she survived the day. She'd stopped shivering, which didn't bode well. Mira and Miran both had their tails over their noses and were half covered with snow. Mellia herself must be half covered. Her breath kept the small window of her hood open, but the swirling snow had covered her drawn-up knees and probably her shoulders and her head as well.

Maybe, when she didn't make it back, the handmaids would make the journey to the temple in better weather and find what she'd discovered. They all knew that she'd wanted to look in at the temple when they'd been on the island with Sathred. Sathred, who'd become Grist queen and sent guards to... what? Kill them? Bring them back to New Bridge? Perhaps simply find them and report back? Mellia's eyes drooped, and she caught her head falling forward.

The warmth at her side vanished. Miran was ephemeral again. Alroth would come for her.

28

Alroth

Alroth was a terrible source. When he passed through the inn door—unable to open it—Del and Falkirk took one look at his translucent face and scrambled to get a sled from the inn yard. If he hadn't slipped, stupidly tumbled over the edge of the bridge, Mellia wouldn't have had to wrench him, and she wouldn't be sitting in the freezing snow right now. That moment, waiting for his body to crumple on the icy river rocks—

When his flesh had felt torn from his bones, he'd thought that he'd hit, but no *that* was how it felt to be wrenched.

Feeling returned to his body as Del drew the sled around the side of the inn. Alroth took the sled's rope from Del and picked up the pace. His snowshoes ground into the fresh powder.

When they reached her, Mellia's breath had formed a frosty patch on the outside of the hood. As long as the mist kept up, she was still alive. She didn't open her eyes when Alroth lifted her onto the sled, and her breath clouded the air far too seldom. The two ephemers stayed stuck to her sides as Alroth took up the sled's rope again and dug his snowshoes into the rapidly deepening drifts.

Should he take her to his cottage? No, she was still injured, and Runas would know better than he did how to help her. She would help her. Mellia would be fine.

And if she wasn't fine? Alroth wouldn't have to worry about being a Locuplean marquess, about having an ephemer, about learning magic... but he wouldn't have Mellia either. He'd never see that wonder in her eyes, never kiss her soft lips, never be on the receiving end of that glare. He swallowed the lump in his throat. He wouldn't have her magic, which was obviously the most important thing. Miran huffed.

Alroth cradled her and shouldered into the inn, where the handmaids cleared a space in front of the fire and pushed the couch in close. They nattered about this or that magic healing method, finally deferring to Runas, who stood over Mellia and closed her eyes.

Alroth took off his snowshoes and paced to the kitchen door and back again. Feeling tingled back to his hands and his feet as they warmed.

"Will she recover? I tried to heal her, but I don't know what in Sarilla's name I'm doing." He should have let Mellia teach him when he'd had the chance.

"There's a weak spot in two ribs. She's cold. She'll live." Her glare added *No thanks to you.*

"What happened?" Falkirk's voice was neutral. They wanted information, nothing more. They weren't accusing him of failing Mellia—even though he had.

Still, Alroth couldn't keep the defensive note from his voice. "Grist guards. Two of them. Killed one, the other got away."

"They know where we are."

"They already knew that. They know about..." Alroth jerked his chin at Miran, ephemeral again now that Alroth was corporeal.

Falkirk could have admonished him for putting everyone in danger, but they just nodded. "They'll be coming for you."

"Tomorrow." Alroth scooped Mellia up and carried her upstairs into the chill, empty bedroom.

Someone had cleaned up the mess he'd left on the floor. The bed was fresh, equipped with a warm blanket. Alroth laid Mellia in it and took off both their houppelandes and boots. He took off his gambeson and lay down next to her, gathered her close, and pulled the fluffy blanket over them. The room had no fireplace, but this would be the best way to warm Mellia.

He traced a hand up and down her kirtle-covered back. She'd saved his life. She could have let him fall, been rid of her overbearing and controlling bond mate. Was he really so unreasonable? He'd ordered her to stay away from the temple without telling her why, that was true. But she'd gone with him willingly to his cottage; he hadn't forced her to do that. He'd wrenched her in the water, but that had saved her life, even she'd admitted that. But she'd been dragged under by the jack of plate he'd insisted she wear. Hell, the only reason they were bound at all was because he had proposed it to her—after refusing to go with her to see the Grist father, as she'd asked, the task she'd been assigned by Doloman himself, or so she believed. If he'd gone with her, would she be a handmaid now? And what did that make him, that he'd kept her from what she'd desired most?

Or would the handmaids be dead? What would Father Glimar have said to him had they met, as he'd intended? Would he have said the same thing he'd told Alroth later: Protect the handmaids? Or would he have echoed Ainsley and asked that Alroth kill them in Doloman's name? Was he behind the Grist guards' betrayal after all? And *why*? Why did Ainsley want the handmaids dead?

Alroth shook his head and kissed Mellia's hair. He would never puzzle out the motivations of a fancy nobleman like Ainsley. He had full harness, any weapon he could ask for, and a day filled with empty hours for training, and yet he'd probably only lifted a dulled blade with an over-flattering tutor. He had more wealth than Alroth would ever see, yet he wanted more. Typical. When he couldn't use coin and influence to get his way, he used brute force and threw Mellia in a dungeon. Ainsley only wanted Mellia for the power that she could give him. Power that she could confer onto Alroth. Maybe even enough to keep his people safe.

Salus's glowing white forge. Mill Hamlet. He could do nothing about Mill Hamlet. But with the handmaids safe in Bridge, the Grist father would have to honour his pact with Alroth to let them inside the town walls. That was certain. Were they safe, hunkered down inside with the food they'd put up for the winter? Or had they been attacked in retaliation for Alroth taking the handmaids over the waterfall? What exactly had the handmaid Sathred told the Grist father? Something bad enough that he'd sicced his guard on the defenceless hamlet? Alroth had sworn to protect them, and look at him now... snowed in in Bridge, taking it on faith that they were taken care of.

Mellia snuggled into him. Alroth's eyelids drooped, and he let them. A marquess could protect them. Give them lands and keep them from having their hovels burned down. Such a shame that nobles were heartless Impietas-spawn, the lot of them. Mellia's soft breathing and warmth lulled him to sleep.

In Alroth's dream, Mellia rode out to the meadow where he was building something, a ship maybe? Sunlight glinted off her golden hair and her brilliant grin. She admired his work, wondered whether it would be big enough. *There are scores of them, after all.* Alroth turned, and the gods stood there: Ignis with soot on his cheeks, Munificus with his basket of fruit, Locuples with his gemstones and jewels, Aemulus with her fabrics, Orbitus and Dolor with the stillborn child, and so many more. The ship was for them. But where were they going?

Bang bang bang. Alroth was up and stumbling toward the door almost before he'd opened his eyes.

"We've got Grist." Etienne's serious face was lit by the grey dawn slanting through the horn window at the end of the long hallway.

"Where from?"

"Coming down the river. They've landed on the island. I think we got there around the same time, just after the storm died down this morning."

"How many?" Mellia's voice at his elbow made Alroth jump. She'd been near-silent in her stocking feet.

"A score. Nothing we can't handle."

Mellia shook her head. "We're in on the planning this time."

"I appreciate the offer, Sister, but—"

"It wasn't an offer, and I'm not a sister. The handmaids are in on the planning."

Etienne looked to Alroth. The handmaids knew nothing about the world. They would only slow the process down... and every time he'd excluded Mellia from his plans, ignored her protests, or tried to give her orders without justifying them, she'd been hurt or nearly killed. He nodded. Etienne glowered but didn't argue. He turned on his heel and thumped down the stairs.

Alroth shut the door, his breath clouding the cold air of the bedroom. "Get dressed, sweetling."

Mellia shook her head but reached for her houppelande. "You call me that so much, is it working?"

"Working?"

"Have you convinced yourself I'm sweet?"

Convinced himself? She *was* sweet. She was a sister, almost a handmaid. She'd saved his life. She'd... made his fighters find their own sleeping arrangements. She'd tried to trick him into swearing to protect her even though she'd thought she couldn't bond. She'd lied to him and deceived him so that she could go to the temple yesterday. Did she defer to Father Glimar? Yes. Did she often stop arguing with him when he tried to placate her? Yes. But perhaps she didn't want to waste her breath when she knew he wouldn't listen. He'd refused to let her and the handmaids help with the food shortage, so she'd gone behind his back. Perhaps she was right. Mellia wasn't sweet. A smile curled the corners of Alroth's mouth.

"Not sweet, then. Stubborn as a mule." He bent over her as she sat to tie her boots. "Wily as a fox." He kissed her neck. "And patient as a spider in her web."

Mellia swatted him away, but she was grinning. "And you are silver-tongued, Wolf."

A thrill shimmered through him. Had she ever called him that before? He shoved his feet into his icy cold boots and pulled on his houppelande. He belted it and caught Mellia watching him. She'd seen him kill someone in cold blood yesterday. She'd stopped him from killing the other Grist brother. But she wasn't pulling away. She'd called him *Wolf*.

Alroth went to the door to their chamber. "If the Grist are already on the island, we don't have much time to defend the bridge. There won't be time to explain everything to the handmaids or answer all their questions. You'll have to sort that out once we're gone."

She made no move to leave the room. "I will have to sort that out once you're gone." Mellia's voice was flat, and those damned fists were back on her hips.

"You all will stay here while the fighters deal with the Grist." Alroth swung the door wide, a gust of warm air wafting in from the hallway. The fire didn't warm the whole inn, but plenty of heat found its way up here and stayed put under the rafters.

Mellia didn't answer. She was saving her arguments until they were all together. She knew a losing battle when she saw one, and she had determined that she would be better served fighting him in front of the others—with the handmaids as backup. How had he not seen this before? She brushed past him without arguing, and he grinned at her back. Sly woman.

Muted voices drifted up as they descended the stairs. Etienne's low growl, his handmaid's curt response, murmurs from the others. Almost a full score, gathered around one long table. Mercs on one side, handmaids on the other.

They all looked up as Alroth and Mellia reached the inn hall floor.

Morath snatched Mellia's hand. "Mellia, tell them we have to fight. We can't just run away and leave the people of Bridge to suffer the Grist's anger."

"That's right. We can't run away," said the proper one, the one who was good with a needle. "We'll simply confront them and force them to return us to New Bridge."

Runas turned on her. "And what? Be killed for our trouble? You might recall that the Grist guards were the ones trying to murder us on that waterfall. I can't let you just walk into that trap."

"Let me? Last I checked, you weren't Grist queen."

Mellia cut through the chatter. "No, but Sathred is, and she doesn't seem bent on protecting us."

Grist queen. They had a new Grist queen. Which meant that the Grist brothers had magic, right? Not as much as he and Mellia, not as practised as the handmaids, but still. They were well trained to use magic in combat. But his mercs had fought for their lives more times than they could count, and they were still standing. They didn't need magic.

They could fight off a score of Grist brothers if they got to the bridge first and guarded that. The brothers would be most vulnerable as they crossed, and they were wasting time explaining things to the handmaids.

"We'll go and keep them from crossing the bridge. They might have magic, but that won't help them." No need to discuss this at length, because that was the best course of action.

Etienne nodded. "But first, Falkirk and I will bond with some handmaids so we have magic, too." His smouldering gaze fixed on his handmaid nemesis.

She made a rude gesture in his direction. "You won't need to bond with anyone since it's folly to fight the Grist Guard. We'll go home to Nordval, and they won't have any reason to attack you. Don't worry, you don't have to come with me. I know how much you hate—"

Etienne cut in. "Generous offer, but Alroth is the one making the decision, and he said no Nordval."

Alroth made to cut off their bickering, but Mellia beat him to it.

"We're not going to Nordval."

Runas gave her a betrayed look, but she continued.

"We're going to Falvair."

Etienne grumbled as his handmaid shot him a cutting smirk.

Mellia squared her shoulders. "I can see to it that you're all safe while we sort out this mess with Father Glimar. I'm sure it's a mistake anyway." But she didn't sound sure.

Carting the handmaids off to Falvair wasn't a terrible idea: It would get them out of the way. There was no need to return to Nordval where folk would know him as the Wolf, where they had fought and killed for a decade...Falvair was the best option. But what of the people of Bridge? The handmaids could leave the mercs here to defend the village, but then what if the Grist chased them? They'd be defenceless.

His fighters couldn't be everywhere at once. Better that the innocents all stayed together.

"So we're fighting, then? Seems a waste when we could just give the Grist what they want." Del tossed a dagger into the floor, yanked it out, and tossed it again.

"Give them over to be slaughtered? I didn't know you were a cruel bully as well as being a daft, brainless weasel." Kai's voice was even, but their two bighorn sheep were lining up to charge each other through the table. "We draw them away from the handmaids. They won't like Del's and my bond."

"Fighting a score of magic-wielding Grist will be suicide." Livine didn't look up from her logbook. How could she have so much to write in there all the time? "There are only five of you. That's more than two to one, and they have magic."

"We have magic." Del tossed the dagger again, and it thunked into the floor almost to the hilt.

Livine slapped down her pen. "You have been training with it for two days. The Grist guards will have a combined experience of decades. The odds will be slanted decidedly against you."

"Some of us don't care if the odds are against us." Del yanked the dagger out. "I still say hand the mages over."

Everyone started talking at once.

Alroth raised his hand, and the chatter died away. "We defend the bridge. Handmaids will stay put. That's final."

Mellia didn't say anything, but she was doing it to save her breath again. She was not for this plan any more than Runas was.

"Just stay put? We can help!" Morath was on her feet.

"Wolf says stay put, you stay put." Falkirk cut in from their place in the shadows by the kitchen door.

"While you and the others risk your lives? We're supposed to just stay sitting by the fire and what? *Sew*?"

"You're *supposed* to follow orders. Wolf has kept us all alive a hundred times. I suggest you let him keep you alive, handmaid." They slouched into the kitchen.

Morath paced to the kitchen door as though she would burst through. She let out a feral yell and paced back to the fire.

The atmosphere in here was getting too tense. They needed their wits about them for this fight.

"Not sew, handmaid." Alroth stepped into her path. "Care for the villagers."

Morath narrowed her gaze on him. She knew he was trying to placate her. Would she be placated anyway? She dropped onto the couch by the fire and crossed her arms in a huff.

Del and Kai bickered over what weapons to take with them as they shouldered out the door to arm themselves. Runas scampered up the stairs, probably eager to be released from Etienne's presence. The proper handmaid had her head bent to Mellia, but their voices were a low murmur. Livine picked up her pen and settled herself on the couch next to Morath, towing the mousy handmaid with her.

The mousy handmaid hadn't spoken up at all. He'd probably only heard a handful of words from her in all the time they'd been here together, and that was only when Mellia drew his attention to her. Her ability to disappear in a group of people was uncanny. He shook his head. He needed to get back to his cottage, get his jack and his weapons, get to the bridge before the Grist guards crossed it.

The handmaids would stay put. He had to believe that; otherwise, he would be too distracted to keep his fighters safe. Mellia *would* stay where he left her this time. She had to know that he was counting on that from her. Besides, she couldn't get to Falvair without crossing the bridge that they would be guarding. No Grist would make it across, thus she would be perfectly safe here. They all would.

Alroth stalked to his cottage and armed himself. Miran followed silently, cocked their head, stared at him as he laced his jack of plate, as he tied on his sword, and as he strapped on his cesti.

"You learning to be my squire?" He ruffled the pup's ears, barely bending to do it. They were taller *again*.

Drake and Falkirk waited in the shadow of the tithe barn, talking quietly.

"Where are the Turbatious twins?" Alroth checked the direction of their cabin, but no bickering voices drifted on the light breeze. Falkirk blew on their hands. Fighting in the snow always left them with half-frozen fingers. Mittens didn't play well with bowstrings.

"We'll have to go without them. The Grist get over the bridge, we'll be overrun." Falkirk tucked their hands back in their houppelande.

"We need Kai's bow. I'll go check—"

Clang!

Weapons. A shout went up from... the other side of town. How had the Grist got around without anyone sounding the alarm? No prints marred the snow in the direction of the bridge; their tracks from last night had been swallowed up in the flurry, and Etienne's from his scouting this morning were a single track of light snowshoe prints.

Clang!

No question. The three of them broke into a jog at the same time, rounding the inn toward the sound, toward Del and Kai's cabin, toward... the road from New Bridge.

Not snowed over. Cleared down to its ruts. And currently occupied by a complement of Grist guards. But *how*? The handmaids had melted some snow, that was true, but a small patch on the bridge was nothing compared to the *entire road from New Bridge.*

The guards were playing with Del. They could easily have overwhelmed him. Instead, they warded his furious axe-blows with magic and their halberds. *Clang!* Del roared his frustration.

Kai and Etienne caught Del's arms and hauled him back as the guards parted and two figures wreathed in gold stepped forward. Father Glimar and the handmaid Sathred. Grist Queen Sathred, rather. Mellia had said the Grist queen was powerful, but to bring spring to leagues of roadway? And why was she here? Wasn't the Grist queen supposed to be locked in the Bellatorian keep?

But she wasn't locked away, she was standing here, threatening Alroth's mercs. And the handmaids. The guards would still come for them from the island. They needed to defend the inn; defending the town was impossible now.

"To the inn yard," Alroth snapped. The low wall wouldn't provide them much protection, but at least the gate might give them a bottleneck in which to pick the guards off one by one and keep them from being surrounded.

They retreated, even Del. The guards followed, but leisurely, knowing that they would prevail. Alroth and his fighters might hold them off, for a while, but Livine had been right—she was right infuriatingly often—and the five of them couldn't stand against a score of Grist guards.

They could—and would—defend the inn, but the guards would overwhelm them eventually. They'd be taken and their use of magic discovered. Del and Kai's ephemers would be discovered. They would be made an example of.

"Keep your magic to yourselves," Alroth muttered.

"What? We can take them, Captain." Del hefted his axe again, as though he hadn't just been brushed away like a buzzing fly.

"You heard me. No. Magic."

Del cursed, but he would comply. As Falkirk had told the handmaids, they had survived this long by listening to him, and they would keep listening. The Grist guards didn't bother shooting at them. They ranged themselves outside the low wall, halberds at the ready.

Falkirk drew and loosed, but their arrow turned to dust before it reached them. Why didn't the guards destroy the mercs' weapons? Use magic on their bodies, hurt them—kill them—from afar? The mercs couldn't defend against magic, and the Grist had to know that.

Kai loosed a shot, but a hole opened in the guards' line, unnaturally fast, and his arrow stuck harmlessly in the ground. Why weren't they approaching? Were they going to kill the mercs? Capture them? Why didn't they get on with it?

A torch shot from behind the guards' line, flew end over end onto the snow-covered thatch of the inn roof. It should have fizzled in the snow, but it didn't. The fire caught, leaped, spread, up the thatch and down, hissing and steaming as it met the snow layer, but not slowing.

"They're going to smoke out the handmaids." Falkirk's voice was oddly detached as the flames raced down, smoke clouding the bright sky, heat rolling off the inn, making the very air dance and waver.

"Sarilla's golden petticoats," Drake muttered. Then he was gone, lunging for the kitchen door and into the flaming inn.

"Drake!" Alroth hollered—but Etienne had already leaped into the billow of smoke that poured from the doorway.

Alroth's eyes watered, and he gasped and coughed. They couldn't stay in the yard. They would choke, they had to move—into the arms of the Grist guards.

"Wolf, we can use our magic, clear the air." Over the crackling flames, Kai's voice was as urgent as he ever got. But Alroth couldn't let them condemn themselves to the same fate he would undoubtedly suffer.

Alroth shook his head and stumbled toward the waiting Grist guards, hacking, falling to his knees, the hem of a golden houppelande glittering through his clouded vision as his arms were jerked behind him, shooting pain through his shoulder, and he was bound.

29

Mellia

Mellia watched Alroth turn without a word and stride out the door of the inn. Maybe he thought giving her one last kiss would be too much like a goodbye? He was overestimating his fighters' strength.

"Sathred, at the very least, doesn't want us dead." Dayma was still trying to convince herself that there had been some kind of mistake, that the Grist, whom she'd toiled for thanklessly for years, didn't want them all dead, no doubt for some advantage.

But what advantage? Sisters could marry, but handmaids belonged to the Grist for life, and their lands, too, in the absence of other heirs. If the current handmaids were dead, Father Glimar could choose six sisters from powerful families to ascend in their place. Sisters who were heirs, like Mellia. Their parliament seats would go to the Grist as well. Why install a puppet lordling when they could control the seat directly? It would be an advantage maybe even Father Glimar couldn't turn down.

Why had it taken her this long to realize that Father Glimar was no different than Lord Ainsley: They wanted her lands. Nothing more.

In the end, it didn't actually matter *why* the lords and Grist wanted the handmaids dead. They weren't going to change their minds because the handmaids begged for their lives. The only one who might be able to forestall them was Sathred, the Grist queen, but she would be locked safely in the queen's keep for the rest of her life now. She had influence as the head of the hive, but she had to work through the Grist father, since she was not permitted to see anyone but him and the handmaids. She wouldn't be able to help them.

But Alroth and his mercs would fail. Even if they defended against this attack from the island, the Grist could send more guards, even more hired mercenaries of their own. There were only five fighters in Alroth's band. In spring, they could be easily overwhelmed by forces on New Bridge Road. Once they were dead, nothing would stop the Grist from killing the handmaids. Which meant they had to leave, no matter what Alroth said. The road out of Bridge was impassable now, after two huge snowstorms. Mellia and the handmaids had melted a little snow here and there, and if the sun was shining brightly could manage a little more, but they could never thaw their way as far as New Bridge, let alone beyond it to Trout Lake and farther, to Falvair. The March River was the only route out of Bridge to March Bay and Falvair. And now it was guarded by the score of Grist guards Etienne had seen, along with who knew how many more coming down the river from New Bridge. And Alroth, who wouldn't simply let them leave.

Now that the mercs were gone to fruitlessly defend them and get themselves killed in the process, the handmaids needed to reconvene. Mellia gathered them all at the table: flouncing Morath, straight-backed Dayma, hunched Alinace, Livine, immersed in her logbook, and Runas, come down from her room the moment Etienne was gone.

And they were all looking to her. A lowly sister, with five *handmaids* answering to her. Just last week, she'd been begging them for hints on how to win a place among them, and now she had saved their lives, lives that she still held in her hands. The mercs wouldn't save them again.

The Grist couldn't reach them once they made it to her parents' land. Her pious parents might defer to the Grist, but they wouldn't permit the slaughter of handmaids.

"We'll go to Falvair. My parents will give us succour. They're pious enough."

"You can't honestly be suggesting that we sail March Bay on a barge in winter to escape the Grist, who may not even mean us harm." Dayma was always haughty, but an edge of fear peeked through her eyes.

"We can't take that chance, Dayma. The guard who captured me certainly meant me harm, and he thought I was a handmaid. Once we're safe in Falvair, we can send a message and sort this all out. Would you risk your life to prove me wrong?"

Livine looked up from her logbook. "The likelihood of the Grist guards trying to kill us on the waterfall and then capturing Mellia and still not being hostile to us is infinitesimal. I certainly wouldn't bet my life on it." One of Del and Kai's ephemers wandered through the far wall of the inn hall, straight through the table, and lay down at Livine's feet. She stared at it, scribbled in her logbook, and continued. "If we can get to the island, taking one of the Grist's boats would be the easiest."

"And crewing it with whom?" Dayma snapped.

"I can sail," said Runas. "But getting to that boat will be nearly impossible. Even without the guards, the bridge to the island will be treacherous."

"With any luck, the Grist will have it cleared by the time we get there." Morath swept lingering crumbs from the tabletop.

"And they'll be guarding it, if they have." Dayma paced to the window, her steps so light she could have been floating.

"So we help the mercs to clear out the Grist and then grab a boat. Seems simple enough." Morath was forever thinking things seemed simple.

Helping the mercs was a good idea, and maybe they would even have a chance against a score of Grist guards. The six of them, plus Alroth, Del, and Kai, all with magic. It could work. As long as the Grist hadn't sent more guards down the river since this morning.

"How can we help them?" Alinace's voice, as always, was practically a whisper.

"We have to try." Morath clapped Alinace on the back, and she winced.

"Just as I did on the waterfall. We can make their weapons faster, blow arrows off course. Destroy weapons." And heal their wounds. But hopefully it wouldn't come to that.

Morath nodded, practically clapping her hands; Runas gritted her teeth, resigned to fighting.

"It's simple enough, really. Protect the mercs and weaken the Grist guards." Now Livine was oversimplifying. Mellia had successfully helped Falkirk with their shots on the waterfall, but it hadn't been as simple as all that. There was no time to argue. The mercs would be at the bridge already, guarding it or crossing it.

"Collect anything you can't stomach leaving behind. Dress warmly." Sunlight streamed through the horn window by the door. They would have a chance of melting snow and ice today. Even if the Grist hadn't cleared the bridge, they would be able to.

The handmaids dispersed, with varying levels of purpose, to ready themselves for the coming fight. Maybe it *would* be better for them all to keep out of the way. After all, the only fight they'd ever been in had ended with them all hurtling over a waterfall, almost to their deaths. But how could they just sit here and let the Grist kill the mercs, probably them as well, and burn Bridge to the ground? How could they sit here and let others die for them?

They couldn't. The six mages gathered outside the inn, Livine trailing behind, talking to someone through the doorway.

"If they see you, they'll know about Del and Kai's bond. You'll get them killed. Just stay here." She slammed the door, as if trying to keep a cat inside, and one of the bighorn sheep ephemers wandered placidly through it. Livine huffed and turned her back on the stubborn thing.

Mellia stroked Mira's soft ears. Miran sat at her other side. Both of them had put on some muscle. How fast did ephemers grow? Were they supposed to grow at all? They no longer looked like gangly pups, and their pawprints in the snow were as big as Mellia's palm—maybe even bigger.

Shouts echoed from the direction of the bridge. No more lingering.

Mellia set off, following the mercs' trampled path toward the tithe barn. Morath squawked behind her. She'd stepped off the path and had sunk into the snowbank up to her knee. Runas and Livine grabbed her under the arms and hauled her back onto the trail. Single file only. Snowshoe prints marked the compacted snow they could traverse.

Morath grumbled and stomped her snowy foot, brushing clinging flakes from her hose. "I just wanted to talk to you, Mellia."

Dayma hushed her. "Keep your voice down."

"The snow will muffle it." Morath waved dismissively. "Mellia, how will we find the mercs? What if they're hiding for an ambush?"

"They'll find us if you don't shut your trap," Runas grumbled, sounding almost like Etienne.

Morath cursed and slapped at something, probably Runas poking her.

Mellia rounded the last bend in the path, a gap in the trees revealing the snowy bridge. The mercs were nowhere to be seen, but on the other side, a handful of Grist guards worked to shove snow over the broken edge of the bridge. Four more toted long planks between them, climbing the slippery far side of the bridge. So they meant not only to clear it but to widen it. That would make it harder for the mercs to pick them off as they crossed, harder for the handmaids to blow them over the edge with rogue winds or tip them over with slippery ice.

But it would make it easier for the handmaids to slip across to the island. Mellia waved the handmaids to a stop behind her to avoid being seen. Were the mercs on this side of the bridge, waiting in the trees? Or were they somewhere on the island waiting to sneak up on the Grist guards?

Sarilla's petticoats. Maybe they shouldn't have come. But one way or another, they had to get across that bridge, grab the Grist's boat, and get to Falvair. Let the Grist lay their planks and clear the way for the handmaids. They could hide in the trees until the Grist guards passed. But if they reached Bridge, they would burn the village down looking for the handmaids; they knew the handmaids were here, from Grist Queen Sathred's very lips. But the mercs wouldn't let them get that far. If the mercs were here, they would protect Bridge.

Mellia took a single step toward the trees and sank into the snow past her knee. *Ignis's icy windowpane!* Morath and Runas hauled her back, yanking her boot from the deep drift. The snow around the bridge was pristine. The mercs couldn't be hiding in the trees; their tracks would have been immediately obvious. Where were they? The handmaids could help the mercs fight off the Grist guards, but they couldn't keep the guards at bay *by themselves*.

What if... what if the mercs had crossed to the island, waited for the Grist to leave their ship, and then sailed off and left the handmaids to fend for themselves? They were mercenaries, after all. Why should they care about the handmaids? All they had done was cause the mercs trouble. They'd have been hoping for an easy, lucrative job, protecting the handmaids on the waterfall, and instead they'd stumbled into a plot to murder everyone there. They'd never been paid, and their lives were at risk.

Abandoning the handmaids at the first opportunity just made sense. And if they were truly on their own, what should they do? Going off the path wasn't an option in this snow, and the thumps and scraping coming from the bridge meant that the Grist guards were setting their planks in place and would soon be coming straight for them. Should they hurry back to Bridge and hide? Give themselves up?

Mellia turned back toward Bridge. The trees hid the town, but smoke curled up into the still, clear air from a score of hearthfires. They couldn't hide there and let the villagers take the brunt of the Grist's wrath. If the mercs really were gone, there would be no one to protect the villagers from the trouble the handmaids had brought down on their heads. A new plume of smoke joined the others, thicker and blacker than the rest. Had the bakehouse oven just been lit? No, the plume turned into a pillar of smoke. Something in the village was alight.

"Back to Bridge!" Mellia chivvied the milling handmaids back toward the village.

They grumbled but turned and perked up as they too saw the smoke. The trip back to Bridge took only a few moments, hurrying along the slick, snowy trail, all of them seized with the urgent need to find out where that smoke was coming from and maybe fight the fire—though magic was far more suited to stoking fires than dousing them.

It was the inn. Across the square, the flames leaped from the thatched roof and climbed the whitewashed walls. Someone had known that the handmaids were staying there and had tried to, what? Smoke them out? Burn them alive? That would be fitting, considering the Grist's punishment for any who flouted their laws.

Villagers stood in the square, watching the inn char, the roof fall in, nothing to be done about it. The snow covering the neighbouring roofs kept the sparks that drifted over from catching, thankfully. Someone stumbled out the inn door. Etienne.

Mellia slipped through the snow to his side and knelt by his prostrate form. "What happened? The fire..."

"Sister! You—" His gaze snagged on Runas, who had come to stand behind Mellia, arms crossed.

"Stultitian-headed fool. Why did you go in there?"

"You were supposed to be inside, as you were ordered." Etienne brushed ash from his sleeve and coughed.

"It's a good thing we didn't follow your orders, then isn't it?" Runas turned her back on Etienne.

"We were coming to help you at the bridge. Where were you?" Mellia offered a hand to help Etienne to his feet. "The Grist guards are probably across the bridge by now." They should find somewhere to hide. But where? They'd be putting the Bridge folk at risk—

"Doesn't matter," Etienne wheezed.

Why didn't it matter? And who had lit the inn on fire?

Etienne jerked his head at the corner of the inn. Alroth stumbled around, hands bound behind him, followed by the rest of the mercs, and... Grist guards. But how? They'd been setting up the bridge just now, and the snow had been pristine! There was no other way into the village. They were *snowed in*.

Finally, around the corner of the burning inn came Father Glimar and Sathred. Grist Queen Sathred. She melted the snow in front of her steps to nothing in the sunshine. Was she doing that with magic? No, it wasn't possible. She'd cleared the road from New Bridge all the way here? And what if she had? There could be an army of Grist guards waiting to destroy the village, take them captive... kill them all.

"We found them around the other side of Bridge. Don't know how." Etienne stepped between Runas and the approaching Grist. "We didn't stand a chance."

They had to run. They could still take the Grist's ship, get out of here—Grist guards came through the trees on the path to the bridge. Blocking the way. They'd never get through.

Mellia squared her shoulders to Father Glimar. "This is Doloman's will? Handmaids slaughtered by Grist guards sworn to protect them?"

Behind him, Sathred crossed her arms, glared at Glimar's back.

"Of course not, my child." He was still doing that *my child* stuff. "But you know that heretics must burn." He fisted Alroth's hair, jerking his head up.

Alroth winced. Mira and Miran growled from their places, flanking Mellia. Denying it would be futile. Or did he mean that he knew Alroth was the heretic prince? She had to know, even in front of everyone.

"Why did you tell me to fetch you Alroth?"

"It was Doloman's—"

"*You* wanted me to bring him to you after you found out the heretic prince was a mercenary." She cut him off; if she heard him say it was Doloman's will, she would use magic to seize his heart.

Etienne cursed, Runas gasped, and Glimar's lips thinned.

"You think *this* is Prince Lorthulus?" He shook Alroth by the hair again. "This is nothing but a mercenary the prince pulled from the gutter, willing to do anything for a little coin. Even stab his captain in the back, or didn't he mention that?"

Alroth started to speak, but Glimar cut him off. "Don't worry, mercenary, I delivered the coin we agreed on."

Coin they'd agreed on. How many times had Mellia thought the same thing? These were mercenaries. Concerned only with getting paid. So why was her stomach a clenched fist? Why was there a lump in her throat as though Alroth had betrayed her?

If he wasn't the heretic prince, if he wasn't trying to help his people somehow, if he didn't have a plan beyond making silver, even if he didn't want her just for her title like Lord Ainsley, she was still just a means to an end. A more efficient way of generating coin. Would he hire out her magic? He'd talked about crops and healing, but if he didn't have people back in Nordval, if he was just a mercenary for hire, then surely he meant for her to use her magic that way, too? *His* magic. And he could wrench her if she refused.

"Now. I can be reasonable. These heretics here, I can't relinquish"—he gestured to Del, Kai, and Alroth—"but the rest of you may go."

Del and Kai? Had they been foolish enough to use magic in front of the Grist?

Livine called out. "Pardon me, Father, but what evidence of heresy to you have against my mate?" Her *mate*?

Glimar glared at her, but she stood her ground. "You mean to say one of these ephemers is yours?"

The sheep at her knee bleated as Livine nodded.

"And the identical one? You can't expect me to believe that you have two ephemers in a Doloman-blessed bond."

"I know whose they are." Dayma stepped forward. She would betray them, dead set on trusting the Grist as she was.

Etienne must have thought the same thing, since he grabbed her arm and pulled her back. Runas kneed Etienne in the thigh, and he grunted and let Dayma go, glaring down at Runas.

Dayma continued. "When the Grist guards turned on us during the Necrophoresis Ritual, these warriors protected us."

"And thwarted Doloman's will," a Grist guard growled.

"Be that as it may, I was... thankful." She looked down, an embarrassed blush rising to her cheeks.

She was... lying... ? She was lying to the Grist father, surrounded by an army of Grist guards. She put out a hand and made an excellent show of petting the sheep's head.

"And me," said Livine, gesturing to the other sheep, clopping around Del.

The Grist Queen looked back and forth between the two handmaids. If anyone could tell that they were lying, it would be her. She'd known these handmaids far better than any Grist guard. But she was silent, as were the other handmaids. The villagers had retreated to their homes, hopefully barred the doors and waited by the back to escape if the Grist lit their homes afire. No one contradicted the handmaids' claims.

"Then we've no interest in the rest of you." Sathred spoke with regal authority. She turned to Alroth. "This one is the heretic. Give the handmaids back their mates."

The Grist guards complied—they didn't wait for confirmation from the Grist father. They cut Falkirk, Kai, and Del free, and Falkirk and Kai helped Del stumble across the square to the handmaids and Etienne. Leaving Alroth alone with the Grist.

Glimar stared Mellia down. "They won't stop you." He jerked his chin at the Grist guards. His gaze flicked past her to the handmaids and mercs behind her. They could fight. They could try to get Alroth back. But for what? He'd gotten his coin, along with more than he'd bargained for. Miran and a heretic's brand.

Once he was dead, the bond would be broken, as though it had never been. She would be in Falvair, and she could tell her father what Ainsley was like and beg him to choose a different suitor.

"Sweetling." Alroth's voice was choked.

He'd lured her into thinking he was more than just a Locuplean mercenary, with his silver tongue and his beeswax candle. No. She was not sweet. She was not *his* anything. She raised her chin and parted the Grist guards before her.

30

Alroth

Alroth's neck pinched, his scalp screamed, and his shoulder ached. Slushy snow seeped through the knees of his hose as they pressed into the half-melted ground, as Mellia's form retreated, followed by Del, Livine, Runas, Dayma, Kai...

Falkirk, Drake, and Morath didn't move. Why not? Did they *want* to die? Falkirk had been disarmed, but Etienne fingered his hammer grip, and Morath stepped closer to Falkirk.

"*You* should be grateful I don't throw you on the pyre as well." Was the Grist father talking to Morath?

Drake answered. "No one is going to burn."

"Your word isn't law here. Not now." What was that supposed to mean? Why would Etienne's word mean anything... ?

Mellia had thought Alroth was the heretic prince, descended from lost Sudran royalty. Perhaps he might have daydreamed such a thing when he was a child, but Alroth was nothing. Born and raised in the gutter, he'd only amounted to anything because Drake had plucked him up. The prince *would* be about his age. And Mellia had said he was playing at being a mercenary. Could Alroth know the heretic prince without realizing it? It was laughable, a boy born in a barn cavorting with a blueblood. Maybe Etienne knew this Lorthulus. He came from Nordval nobility himself and would be of an age with the prince. *Aemulus's moss-green smile.* Etienne. The heretic prince.

"Free him, and I'll take them to Nordval. You'll never see them again." Etienne's usual playfulness was gone, replaced with a bone-deep exhaustion.

A bird trilled, and bare branches rattled.

The Grist father nodded. "The ship is waiting, just over the bridge."

Alroth's hands were freed, and Etienne and Falkirk hauled him to his feet.

"What are you doing, Drake?" Alroth ground out.

"Saving your life, *again*. Can't have you catching up to me." They marched him past Morath, who fell in behind them.

"You're taking handmaids." And the Grist father *wanted* him to.

No good could come of the heretic prince absconding with Sudra's handmaids. Didn't Etienne see that more hung in the balance than Alroth's pitiful life? How could he live with himself if he let Etienne do this?

"Drake, think about this."

"What's to think about?"

How could he be so cavalier?

"Falkirk, you're going to let him start a Stultitian *war*?"

They shrugged. "They'll start their war either way. At least this way, you live."

Alroth couldn't let them do this. He'd have to stop them taking the Grist ship, stop them going to Nordval. He rolled his aching shoulder and picked up his pace.

The Grist guards were following them. Leaving a bit of distance, but they were taking no chances. No doubt they already had folks in Falvair and Dolomast waiting to kill them if they changed course, not to mention New Bridge. The Grist wanted them in Nordval, and they wanted Etienne to take them.

So Alroth just had to stop them going—or stop Drake.

By the time they reached the bridge, Mellia and the others were disappearing around the end of the island. Someone had laid planks across the ruined section, and they made quick work of crossing. Etienne paused to help Alroth tip the planks into the foaming water below. No need to make it easy for the Grist to follow them.

The Grist's ship would be close by, big enough for a score of Grist guards, big enough to get the handmaids to Nordval, as the Grist father wished.

Their party rounded the island, and sure enough, the cog bobbed in the current, anchored in the channel. A large sailing vessel. A skiff had been hauled up the beach, guarded by two Grist guards, who leaped to their feet at the sight of the approaching mercs. The Grist father didn't want to make it *too* obvious that he'd let them go.

Del and Kai stalked ahead, unarmed. Alroth swallowed a curse and surged forward, but they had things well in hand. Kai slammed his hand toward one man's sternum, and he fell to one knee, gasping for air. Del crumbled the other man's halberd with a gesture, ripped the empty pike from his hand, and slammed it into his nose, snapping the man's head back before he crumpled to the ground. They had been practising their magic.

"Stop!" Alroth bellowed, and Del paused, his shoulder to the skiff's transom. "You can't take them!"

Del shoved the skiff into the river, and Kai hopped in. Runas dragged the mousy one in, and Kai unshipped the oars in their oarlocks. Mellia clambered over the transom.

"Let's get away first, then we'll talk." Del was being far too reasonable. Alroth must seem like a wild man.

He splashed into the shallow water and grasped the bow. "He's trying to start a war."

Mellia glared from the stern of the skiff.

"The Grist father. If you take them to Nordval, he'll use it to start a war."

Drake reached them, pale-faced. He wasn't fully recovered from nearly dying. "Which he'll start by killing us all if we stay. Kai, go on."

Etienne might be right, but then at least they would have *tried*, for Bellator's sake.

"You want to help him along?" Were they all content to save themselves and damn so many?

Livine and the other who had spoken up for Del and Kai climbed into the skiff.

Kai craned around to look at him. "Move, Alroth." Not *Captain*, not *Wolf*. Just plain Alroth, from the gutters.

Heat bubbled in his belly. "Or what?" They'd followed him into battle, where they could be spitted, and followed him back to Sudra, traitor as he was; they'd even left him to die when he'd told them to, but now they were turning on him? "How will you live with yourselves?"

"I'd rather live with myself than burn on a pyre." Del splashed toward him. "You think they bought the story about the handmaids?" He jerked his chin at Livine and the other one. "We stay, they burn us all."

He was right. *Ignis damn him.* And yet, wouldn't that be better than living with the knowledge that innocents were dying in a war they'd helped the Grist start?

For the first time in his life, Alroth raised his cesti against someone he loved, someone who was practically a brother to him. He hit Del where it would hurt, the upper arm. His eyes went wide, then hardened. Del rammed his shoulder into Alroth's middle, his boot sliding on the loose stones and muck of the riverbed. They splashed into shallower water, and Del wrenched his bad shoulder. Alroth grunted, the whoosh of the boat gliding off hit him harder than Del ever could. Del and Drake pulled him up, dragged him back onto the sharp rocks.

He coughed. "You can't go, Drake. Or are you just a selfish prince after all?"

Etienne's face went blank, hard as stone. "Maybe I am selfish. Maybe I'm tired of living in the ass end of nowhere. But in Bellator's name, Wolf, it doesn't matter. The war will start, with or without us."

They kept saying that, as if it made a difference. Would they be the ones fighting, dying, when Sudra attacked Nordval? At least if Etienne wasn't with them, the Grist father couldn't blame the Loyalists, couldn't attack them. He swiped the intact halberd from the beach where it lay next to the downed guard and swung at Etienne.

But the halberd rotted and cracked as it made contact, splintered. Alroth whirled toward the water, the skiff bobbing next to the ship, handmaids climbing up the side onto the deck. One looked right at him. The slightest one, with a brown mantle, not undyed like the others.

"It wasn't her, Wolf." Del gripped his shoulder. "It was me." He sucker-punched Alroth, who fell to his knees again.

Alroth was worthless. He'd attacked the man who had given him a chance at living, saved his life, what seven times now? Del was right to beat him down. He couldn't even keep his own loyal men from starting a war. And a small part of him... didn't even want to. He wanted them to live. *He* wanted to live. But what did that say about him? What kind of terrible monster did that make him?

The skiff ground on the pebble beach. Hands tried to coax him in, but he roared and threw them off.

"Wolf, please, we have to—"

A volley of arrows clattered onto the beach around them, two glanced off his jack.

Drake and Del both cursed.

"Leave me, cowards. Save your own skins." Alroth didn't deserve their love or their care. Best that he be left behind.

"We can't just—" Drake shook his shoulder, but Alroth jerked away.

Del yanked Etienne, who stumbled. Not at full strength. "If he wants to stay and burn, I'm not burning with him. *Come on.*"

Splash. Splash. Splash. They left him there. Going to Nordval to start a war that would overtake them. Raze Nordval and—

A gold hem swept toward him, stopped next to his soaked knees.

"Were you planning all this with Ainsley?" Alroth spoke through clenched teeth. Had the Grist father set them all up from the beginning? From the moment Alroth had shown himself at the castle guard tournament, or maybe from when he'd shown his face in New Bridge last spring. Had he set up Mellia to be bound to a monster, one way or the other?

The Grist father shrugged. "It doesn't matter."

Someone scampered up the ratlines; another couple followed more slowly, and the sail unfurled.

Alroth clenched his cestus-clad hands. They always forgot to disarm him completely. What did he have to lose by fighting back now? Everyone he cared about was gone.

The Grist father bent to say something in Alroth's ear, and he took his chance. He slammed his head up into the Grist father's face and crashed a fist into the stomach of the nearest Grist guard. The guard had a knife to his throat in a heartbeat. Good. Make it quick.

But the Grist father held up a hand. "Not yet."

A shudder worked through Alroth's shoulders and down his back. He hung his head. Couldn't even secure a quick death for himself. A growl rumbled from his left. Another from his right. Why were Miran and Mira still here? Shouldn't they be with Mellia?

Mellia. Headed unknowingly into war. Nordval would suffer. She would have nowhere else to go. He'd been there. He knew what became of unprotected women... but he could keep her safe. They'd run away together, far from the blood and the screams and the acrid smoke.

He took hold of their bond and wrenched.

31

MELLIA

Alroth, Mellia's *bound mate*, helped the Grist guard muzzle and bind Mira. Miran snapped their teeth around Alroth's leg, drawing bright blood, and he let them. How could he do this to all of them? How could he do this to *her*?

Mellia had been a handspan from escape, finally, to a land where she could be free, when that tearing, burning had jerked her from her body. She floated silently now, ineffectual, watching her Mira thrash at their bonds on the cold stone beach. Her heart cracking open.

They tied Alroth up too, though he didn't resist and followed placidly when Father Glimar led him, head bowed, over the bridge—new planks had been found—Mira slung over the saddle of a placid mule. Even the mule's staunch nature couldn't completely dull their fear, betrayed by their rolling eyes. Mellia drifted after them, tugged along as the distance widened between her and Mira. If Alroth had been telling the truth, the Grist's war would start when they brought back news of the handmaids being taken to Nordval. And Alroth would burn.

How could he have kept her from safety after everything? What could have possessed him to drag her back into danger when they were so close to being free of the Grist's influence? Did he not understand that he would be killed? Burned on a sacred pyre? Whether she was or not, his life would never be spared, not without an intercession from Golden-fucking-Doloman himself!

Now that the road was cleared to New Bridge, they would be back there by noon, and by dusk, Alroth would be tied to a pyre in the square, under the gaze of Doloman's statue, a place she wouldn't willingly go for all the gold in Locuples's hoard.

Gold. Did Alroth... expect to get paid? Was he dragging her back to Lord-fucking-Ainsley? Is *that* why he hadn't let her go with the handmaids? Father Glimar had said that he had betrayed his own captain for coin. Alroth hadn't tried to deny it, and he was a mercenary. What else would drive him to do such a thing?

The same thing that drove him to battle a herd of peccary for a poor, starving village. But no, that had been Etienne's story. A man who was clearly trying to get Mellia to accept Alroth's bond and use her magic to their advantage. And it had almost worked.

Coming back to herself this time wasn't nearly so dramatic as the last time, when Alroth had saved her life. Mira snarled, passing through their bindings, and streaked off into the forest. Mellia's feet sank into the half-frozen mud. That was all.

They put Mellia on a horse, even left her hands unbound, and tied its lead rope to Father Glimar's mount. Alroth was tied behind a guard's horse to stumble along, while Sathred rode in front, dealing with any drifts that had blocked the road since she'd cleared it, which had been when? After the storm yesterday, certainly. The Grist guards on foot were soon left behind, along with Alroth.

They rested about halfway to New Bridge for the horses and a bite to eat. Mellia sidled over to the Grist queen.

"You're out of the keep."

She nodded. "They needed me to clear the road."

"And when we get back?"

Sathred gave her a sharp look. "They won't need me anymore."

"I'm surprised your new handmaid didn't come with you." The one Father Glimar had chosen when Mellia had been *with* Alroth. Making the gravest mistake of her life.

"There's no new handmaid. Glimar never chose one."

Never chose one. Mellia hadn't been too late. Father Glimar had said that he would announce the new handmaid at the noon bells, so when Mellia had head them pealing, she'd assumed...but perhaps she'd been wrong. She'd still had a chance. Had Father Glimar been waiting for her after all? Was he *still* waiting for her? Her lands *were* important—No, she couldn't still have a chance to become a handmaid. But hope bloomed in Mellia's chest unbidden.

Once they were back on the road, there was no time to speak. And what would Mellia say anyway? They emerged from the trees near the Sinu's mouth. The millworks stretched across the river, New Bridge Castle guarding it. Smoke rose from the hillside below.

As they crossed the millworks, followed the road toward Mill Gate, they passed a patch of blackened ground. Had this always been here? Ash floating in the air made Mellia sneeze and blink, the acrid smell of burnt thatch far too fresh. This had burned down recently, whatever it had been. Far too big for a bonfire, and there, a chimney still stood, and a clay jug of something. Storehouses?

She called to Father Glimar, a few paces ahead. "Was there a fire?"

He slowed his horse, let hers come level with his. Sathred and her guards kept on toward Mill Gate.

"Your betrothed burned it down in a fit of pique."

Betrothed? Lord Ainsley.

Pique had led him to burn down buildings? "Over what exactly?"

Glimar gave a thin smile. "He was outmanoeuvred."

Outmanoeuvred. She'd left him. Alroth had won the duel, and then he'd spirited her away. If she'd just married him, this wouldn't have happened. These buildings, supplies, wouldn't have been destroyed.

"Come, Mellia. Now that you're back here, we have things to discuss."

Her heart leaped. Now that the old handmaids were gone, Sathred needed a whole new cohort of new handmaids. And he wanted Falvair. Yes, he was going to make her a handmaid. So what if it was only to gain her lands? Being a handmaid would be better than Lord Ainsley. And what other option did she have? The goddess's face floated through her mind. She clenched her fist around the textured granite in her pocket. She had to do this. The goddess hadn't saved her from being wrenched, and She wouldn't save Mellia from Lord Ainsley either. And hadn't Mellia always wanted to be a handmaid anyway? Her stomach churned.

Father Glimar led her horse up the hill, through Mill Gate, and around the back of the comb. He swung to the ground, held her horse's bridle, and offered her a hand. But his eyes were solemn. As they should be for a solemn moment like making her a handmaid. She matched his expression, and swung down from her mount, muscle memory from years of riding as a girl carrying her steadily to her feet.

She followed Father Glimar through the builders' hall into the cloister, a string of brothers straggling after them. Sisters too, in the cloister. Father Glimar climbed to the low dais, still in place from the handmaid trials, though the awning and chairs had been cleared away. The chill wind ruffled his hair, and his gold rings glinted. Two of the obedientiaries joined him, the grizzled guard obedientiary and the fanner obedientiary with long hair—the one who had dismissed her when she'd burst into their conclave, a lifetime ago. He couldn't dismiss her now. She'd proven herself twice over, proven her magic. Father Glimar had ordered her brought back here, had Alroth wrestle Mira into submission to get her back here. She squared her shoulders. She'd face this with her chin up.

How would he tell her? Would he grant her the handmaidship right away, or would there be more trials? Would he ask her to accept it or simply grant it to her? Would there be a ceremony in front of everyone? Either way, she'd be safe here in the comb. Safe and shackled to the hive. No Ainsley. No war. And no Alroth.

A fist clenched in her middle. Alroth would be dead. Not sitting by her chair, rubbing her tired feet. Why did that sweet illusion have to come to her *now*?

"Sister Mellia." Glimar's voice carried throughout the cloister to everyone gathered to witness this moment. "Your conduct the past week has hardly been usual for a Grist sister."

But it was commendable, right? Following Father Glimar's instructions, carrying out Doloman's tasks, saving the handmaids.

"Even less so for a handmaid. Binding a treasonous mercenary in an unsanctioned bond after rejecting five lords."

Rejecting? Was he implying that she'd *chosen* to fail the binding ritual five times? "Bonds are Doloman's will, Father. I'm a slave to His plan." *Just as you are.* She kept the censure inside, though. Unease was building in her. Annoying him now would be a mistake.

Father Glimar's sharp gaze turned to her. His mouth tight. "Nevertheless, I can't permit your... abrasive influence in the comb any longer."

Not in the comb. He was sending her away. That couldn't be relief flooding her. That made no sense. Once Alroth was dead, he would give her to Lord Ainsley. The man who had burned storehouses to the ground in a rage, tossed her in an oubliette *for her own good*.

She hit her knees on the cold dead grass. "Please, Father, not Lord Ainsley. My father will listen to your advice. Please choose someone else." Everyone was still there, watching, but Father Glimar was the only one who mattered. The one who held her fate in his hands.

He shook his head. "Not Lord Ainsley. You would have to beg him to take you now at any rate." He turned back to the comb. "I deem you a drone, Mellia." He sighed.

If she didn't accept Ainsley, he would deem her a drone?

With Alroth dead, the rest of the mercs and handmaids gone, she couldn't be a drone. Where would she go? What would she do?

She flexed her fingers in a fold of her mantle. She nodded, the frosty thatch of grass wavering with tears. If refusing him made her a drone, then... "All right. Once Alroth is gone, Lord Ainsley will bind me."

Slow footsteps crossed wood and dirt to her. Father Glimar's hand rested on her head. "No, my child. He won't. Drones are not fit for lords to bind."

He meant... he meant that she was a drone *now*. His word made it so. The Grist Father had said it. *Drone.*

The whisper carried through the cloister, passed by scores of throats. *Drone.*

Breath rushed into her lungs, then out again.

Drone.

Her nails dug into wool.

Drone.

Father Glimar's hand left her head.

Drone.

Did she even have a body? Yes, her heartbeat thudded. She opened her eyes.

Father Glimar might have given up on claiming her lands, but Lord Ainsley still needed her to get Falvair. If she reached him fast enough, he might still agree to take her. Father Glimar's declaration had made her a drone, but if Lord Ainsley would deign to speak on her behalf, he could protect her. He wanted Falvair. Maybe enough to defend her. But she would have to move quickly.

She stood—she still had legs after all—Father Glimar said something, but what did it matter? She was a drone, and the Grist wasn't for her anymore. The crowd parted before her, as they had for the handmaid hopeful who had pushed past her limits at the handmaid trials. Mellia crossed the empty guest hall, solid granite tapping under her boots. The icy wind hit her as she stepped out in front of the hive. Her cheeks numbed within moments.

Doloman looked down on her disapprovingly. But then, he always had. She reached the castle, and no one stopped her from crossing the south barbican into the outer ward. A dog barked and scratched at the kitchen door. The pilgrims, the lordlings, they were all gone home after Arista's funeral, no doubt spreading the story of the heretic prince kidnapping the handmaids to every corner of Sudra.

Where was Lord Ainsley? Was he even still here? She asked a castle guard, who pointed her to the southern tower. She climbed one turn of the spiral stairs, and Lord Ainsley rose when she entered. Perhaps she should have knocked.

His shoes had pointed toes, in the latest style. What would convince him to agree to their union? Falvair. And...

She fell to her knees at a man's feet for the second time today. She bowed her head. His floor was solid wood, no rug to cushion its bite.

Mellia cleared her throat. "My lord. I've come to beg that your lordship accept my oath to be bound to you, along with my hereditary lands and titles."

Lord Ainsley shifted, spoke mildly. "You are already bound, putrid Risore."

She could swallow the insult. The alternative was being a drone, ousted from the hive and family. On the streets. Even Elenta wouldn't help a drone. "My bond mate is sentenced to death, my lord."

"Ah, a heretic's mate. Precisely what I wish bound to me." He grabbed her hair through her veil and wrenched her head up, made her look at his stone-hard face, his flinty eyes. "Not even the promise of Falvair could make me bind you to me, crude, wrench-a-day she-wolf." He didn't kick her, not really, but his foot sent her sprawling sideways, and her ribs throbbed. "Remove yourself before I call the guard to remove the heretic drone from my chambers. And I won't ask them to be gentle."

Mellia scrambled back to her knees, bent, kissed the hem of his houppelande. "Doloman—"

His fingers closed on her arm and dragged her to her feet. "Keep the Golden God's name from your drone lips." He knew? How did he know? "Out."

He shoved her backwards, and Mellia stumbled against the wall. Ainsley wouldn't change his mind. He wasn't trying to make her prostrate herself before him. He wouldn't toss her in an oubliette just for a few days to teach her a lesson this time. She fled.

Mellia slunk down the spiral stairs. What now? The last thing she needed was for Ainsley to discover her lurking here and toss her to the guards. She left the castle. Skirted the palisade, her feet taking her unthinkingly to Iram Square, back home to the hive. But it wasn't home anymore. She stood frozen by the cold rim of the silent fountain, Doloman's hulking form overshadowing her.

News of her being a drone would reach her parents before she could. And they would do to her what they had to her brother. Leave her to burn. Mellia had tried to convince him to run, to hide that part of himself, but he'd smiled sadly at her, called her a kid, and gone to her parents. He'd known. When Delphus had entered her parents' hall, he'd known Father Limosa would sway them into disowning him, leaving him to burn.

Her parents saw Doloman like this statue. Disapproving, larger than life. But there was another goddess, his equal. Mellia had seen Her. Seen her destroyed remains. Doloman was here, a gilded statue as tall as the hive, and She was gone, even Her name forgotten.

Mellia clenched her fingers around the cold granite in her pocket. It wasn't fair. It wasn't right. But it was fact. Doloman's power always won.

32

Alroth

Alroth had never been so thankful for his cesti. His bound wrists would be skinned and bleeding by now if not for the solid leather wrapping them beneath the bindings fixed to his wrists. This time, the tug of the lead as he stumbled forward left no room to work them loose, and even if he did, the score of Grist guards at his back would be on him before he could stumble into the snowbanks lining the road from here to over the horizon.

As it was, his mercs' betrayal stung more than his wrists. Did they understand what they'd done? There would be no peace if they, and Nordval, took the blame. Father Glimar wanted war with Carille, and Alroth had handed him the perfect excuse to attack and look like the wronged party. It would start with a small force, rallied to rescue the handmaids, but even after the handmaids were returned—if they were—the warmongers would find some other wrong requiring revenge on or repayment from Nordval.

At least he would be able to check on Mill Hamlet, before they reached New Bridge. Father Glimar had seen with his own eyes that the handmaids were safe. Etienne had even done exactly as he'd ordered. They had given the Grist father no excuse to break his word. He would settle folks inside the walls. Alroth could give them that, even in death.

And Mellia... Mellia would be free of him. Free to become a proper lady. Ainsley might be stuck-up, pompous, and shite with a sword, but he was rich, and folk listened to him. He would keep Mellia safe better than Alroth could, certainly safer than she would have been in Nordval with Drake and the rest in the midst of a war. He'd made the right choice, set her free of a useless heretic like him. Her return to Ainsley and her life as a lady would be his last gift to her; he'd sworn to protect her, after all.

They stopped for a rest by a swift-running stream, still open even in the frigid air. None of the guards made to bring him a drink. His guard wrapped his lead rope over a tree branch like a horse and left him there—unguarded. But he wouldn't get far in the deep snow off the path, and they could easily track him until he broke his ankle in a hidden crevice or froze to death once night fell. Might be a cleaner death than burning. They wouldn't let him escape the pyre so easily. He worked carefully at his bindings, loosening them bit by bit.

A brother approached him. Not armed with a guard's halberd but with a dirk at his hip. The red-bearded Grist brother who'd gotten away from the island, the one who'd taken word of Miran back to the Grist. The Grist brother offered him a cup of water, swiped from the icy stream. Alroth took it in bound hands, careful not to show how loose they'd become.

"You defended your mage against me."

Alroth shrugged. "I swore to defend her."

"And you don't break your oaths?" He must be referring to Captain Julius.

"Only if they need to be broken." Alroth drank the cold water.

The brother nodded. "I'm the outriders' obedientiary for New Bridge Hive." Was that supposed to mean something to Alroth? "I'll be sent to sue for the return of the handmaids. I want you to know, no matter what the Grist say, not all of us want war. I'll do my best to broker peace."

"Why bother telling a dead man?" Alroth drank the last of the water and handed the wooden cup back.

The brother took it, passed it from hand to hand. "So you can go to Orbitus knowing that someone is looking out for your people. For the regular folks."

Why would a Grist brother, even one with a fancy title, care about reassuring a heretic? "You don't think I'm a heretic."

"No, I know you're a heretic."

"Then why?"

He shrugged and sauntered away. Was *that* supposed to mean something to Alroth?

Alroth's guard untied his lead from the tree, and they were moving again. He focused on his breathing, favouring his Miran-bitten leg instead of mulling over the brother's words.

They would pass Mill Hamlet, and when they did, hopefully Alroth would at least glimpse Selena or Vernis, get a nod from them that everything was all right, even if the guards refused to let him stop. If his folks refused to move inside the walls—stubborn old peccaries—they had everything they needed in Mill Hamlet, for now.

Before they'd even reached the Sinu, the smoke reached them. As they crossed the millworks, the scorched earth where Mill Hamlet had been stood out against the pristine snow. But that didn't make sense. He'd done what the Grist father wanted. He'd secured protection for his people.

But he'd sworn and oath to Mellia, hadn't he? To protect her lest his people be brought down. And he wasn't protecting her now. He wasn't even capable of that.

A single rider emerged from Mill Gate as they left the millworks and approached the impossible charred hamlet. Ainsley. Alone. He reined up in what used to be the square, and the Grist brought Alroth to stand in the ashes across from him.

A cruel smile twisted the lordling's face, and he leaned on the front of his saddle. "What do you think of my work?"

Alroth dropped his loosened bonds and leaped at Ainsley, his cestus-clad fist swinging up and catching him on the chin. Ainsley's head snapped back, and Alroth got one more hit in on his thigh before three guards wrestled his arms behind him. His shoulder pulsed with pain.

Ainsley worked his jaw back and forth, rubbed his chin. "Such behaviour is not very becoming of the Marquess of Falvair. But then, grovelling at my feet was not becoming of Lady Falvair. either."

Mellia. Grovelling at the feet of this worm?

"One would think that after your little escape resulted in *this*"—he waved a careless hand at the ashes of people Alroth had sworn to protect—"you would be more eager to please me."

Alroth spat on his tunic. He'd been aiming for the lordling's face, but his horse was tall. It would do.

Ainsley sidled his mount forward and kicked Alroth in the face. Held as he was, he couldn't even duck the blow. His nose streamed. Blood.

"Did you know that your little mage has been deemed a drone by the Grist? And she begged me to take her, as if you were already a pile of blackened bones." He sighed as though Alroth's death was exceedingly inconvenient for him.

Mellia had bound herself to Alroth to avoid becoming a drone, and somehow, she'd been made one anyway? Alroth had agreed to this lordling's demands, and still he'd burned Mill Hamlet. Alroth had sworn to protect Mellia, and yet she was out there, shamefully unprotected. Not even this man-shaped peccary would agree to keep her.

"Here's what we'll do, Lord Falvair. I'm sure you don't want to burn to death, so I'm giving you a better option. You fighters all have these romantic notions of dying in battle, so I'm willing to give you that. Another duel. I kill you quickly and cleanly, with a sword in your hand."

What was the catch? Why give Alroth the chance to kill him? And he'd already rejected Mellia, so why duel for her hand?

"You said you don't want Mellia."

Ainsley's lip curled. "Not a duel for your Risorous mate. Your title: Marquess of Falvair. You don't want it anyway. You want a quick death. I'm taking *pity* on you."

Ah, so this wasn't a question, exactly. Ainsley had decided. If Alroth was foolish enough to think that he could refuse, he would be tossed in the lists and summarily slaughtered so that Ainsley could take his title. And if he renounced the title? Without it, he would be burned at the stake—by all accounts, a horrible way to go. There was no way out for him, but maybe he could still help Mellia.

"Take Mellia as your mate."

Ainsley eyed him as if he were a particularly large hairy centipede. "I'm mortified. Did I give you the impression I was *asking* you?"

"You will ask. Otherwise, I'll renounce your precious title."

Ainsley dismounted. Alroth's arms were still firmly pinned behind him. All he could do was stand there as Ainsley prowled toward him.

"You would burn to spite me? Join your precious Mill Hamlet in the ashes?"

Absolutely. But it wasn't about that. It was about Mellia. All he had left in this world. He lifted his chin, looked down on the lordling who held both of their fates in his hands.

"No. Not to spite me. It's worse than that." His eyes glinted. "When will you learn not to parade your weaknesses in front of me?" He nodded to Alroth's guards, and they shoved him to his knees. "Beg me, like your mage, Lord Falvair."

Alroth bent his head. Beg like a mage. If that's what it took, then he would do it. Hadn't he healed Mellia like a mage when she was on the brink of death? He had made it through that, and he would make it through this. "Please, care for—"

"Please *who*?"

"Please, *my lord*, care for Mellia when I no longer can."

"Why won't you be able to care for her, Lord Falvair?"

Alroth swallowed the bile that crawled up his throat. He would have to say it. But if it would save Mellia from the streets, he would. "Once you've killed me."

"Of course, my dear marquess. Once I've watched the worthless life drain from your eyes, I'll bind your precious mage to me, no matter how long it takes."

Every muscle in Alroth's body spasmed. He wrenched free of two of the guards, but the last grabbed his bad side as he lurched to his feet, and yanked his bad shoulder half out of the socket. He roared, but Ainsley turned his back on Alroth and vaulted onto his horse. He wheeled and trotted up the path to Mill Gate. Alroth collapsed back to his knees. His bad arm hanging loose at his side. It was done. Mellia would be safe. Bound to *that*, but off the streets, living the life she deserved, as a lady.

Ash blew into Alroth's eyes. He coughed as it whirled into his mouth. Ash that used to be homes, food, livestock, and people. Selena. Vernis, Tarrin. The father and his two children, come to them for protection. The desperate mother and her beautiful baby, rosy cheeked, plump, and smiling. Burned like he should be burned. He'd made his last deal with Ultio for the one person left he could protect. The one person he hadn't completely failed. And he wouldn't fail her this last time. He would play his role for Ainsley, die at his hand, pass on the title he'd never really had. Secure his mate the protection she so longed for, the marquessate she deserved.

He blacked out.

33

Mellia

Mellia had done her best to complete Doloman's tasks. And still, she was here, perched on the freezing edge of a deserted fountain, a drone, her bound mate a heretic. Her bound mate, who had sworn to protect her, drone or not. Sworn a binding oath. And instead, even he had betrayed her, wrenched her, taken her ephemer captive, forced her to stay. And once he was dead, who would protect her then?

"You're Alroth's matron, eh?" The red-faced laundress who had cleaned her clothes last time she was here hauled a basket of washing to the fountain.

"For now." Mellia couldn't disguise the contempt in her voice, and why should she? The man had sold her out.

"If you need a hand, you let me know. That Alroth took in my niece, heavy with a bastard child as she was." She dunked a shirt in the freezing water. "I went out to visit them before the snow flew, and there they were, happy and healthy, red-cheeked babe and laughing mama sitting by the fire. Doted on by a score of hard-boiled fighters, if there was one, I swear it."

Alroth had taken in her niece? The half-score fighters must be Alroth's mercenaries. How could they take in a baby? Didn't they live in cramped apartments like Etienne's?

"Out to visit them where?"

"Mill Hamlet. Fixed up the old cruck out there, built a few more little cottages between them. Hard-working lot, no one can deny them that." The laundress sprinkled soda on the shirt and scrubbed. "They took in Vernis, too. He came back from the war not quite right. Being in town didn't agree with him—used to get into tavern brawls, stab a man just for looking at him sideways. Out there, he waved me inside and hosted me, sane as you please."

Mill Hamlet. Maybe they would take her in, if she was willing to work. Even without Alroth, she could help with her magic.

Mellia turned to the laundress. "Could you take me there? To Mill Hamlet?"

The laundress gave her a long look. "Burned down, right before the solstice." She gestured toward Mill Gate, icy wind flinging water drops from her hand.

Burned down. The charred patch on the road from the millworks. It hadn't just been empty mill outbuildings and storehouses, but cozy cottages and a cruck where a baby thrived with rosy cheeks. A baby who was now nothing but ash.

"I'm so sorry." Maybe she would murder Ainsley. After all, was being a murderer worse than being a drone? He hadn't burned down a few storehouses in a fit of rage because she was taken, he had retaliated against Alroth by slaughtering innocent people connected to him. And she'd *begged* him to bind her once Alroth was dead.

Alroth, who had taken in the laundress's niece. Supported a volatile, traumatized old war veteran. Who'd sworn to protect her, drone or no. Who'd rubbed her tired feet and brought her a beeswax candle and bonded with her when she'd thought it was impossible. She swiped a freezing tear from her cheek.

He'd wrenched her, and they would have words about that. Once she saved him from the pyre.

But first, an apology. The path from Mill Gate to the ashes of Mill Hamlet was still clear from Sathred's work, and Mellia's strong boots kept her from slipping as she strode down the sloped path.

Very likely no one had bothered to put the spirits here to rest, to dedicate them to Orbitus. She couldn't do a big Necrophoresis Ritual for them, but at least she could say a few words, draw the gods' attention to welcome them into the Vita Maris, the spirits' ocean. She picked her way between the ashy rectangles, foundations of cottages, to the middle of the hamlet. A chimney stood over there, likely the cruck's chimney. The cottages would have had open hearths, with no stone parts to survive the fire. No evidence that anyone lived here, besides the folks they'd left behind in New Bridge.

Even if no one else cared to remember, Mellia would. She crouched and gathered a handful of ashes. She wouldn't be able to get up to the waterfall in all this snow, but she could at least send them off in the Sinu. She paced down the road to the millworks and leaned over the edge, downstream, downwind. She mouthed a prayer and released the handful of ash. It exploded out from her hands, floated for an instant, and drifted down, landing silently in the rushing water, carried away to the March River, Lake Val, and the faraway sea.

Maybe one day someone would do the same for her, a lonely drone. She swiped a handful of snow from the millworks' parapet to clean the soot from her hands, and turned back toward New Bridge, because where else could she go? Perhaps she'd kill Ainsley. She still had Alroth's magic, after all. She could manage it, even perhaps from a distance—but not from this distance.

A lone figure climbed over the stile, over the low wall on the far side of Mill Hamlet. They didn't turn up the road toward Mill Gate, either. They shuffled through the ashes of Mill Hamlet, bent to rummage through. Stealing from the dead. Mellia stalked up the road back toward the charred graveyard.

The skinny young man drew himself up as Mellia covered the last few ells to the square.

"What business?" he called.

"I could ask the same of you. I was putting these folks to rest as well as I am able, but you seem determined to disturb what little peace they've found." She planted her fists on her hips.

The youth scowled. "Putting what folks to rest?"

Mellia gestured at the ash surrounding them. "The unfortunates who lived here."

"No, my lady, none of us died. Who're you looking for?"

None of them died? Then where had they gone? How?

"I'm... looking for help."

"Just let me carry out my business, and I'll help however I can. Don't you worry." He puffed out his chest—no doubt his best Alroth impression.

Mellia bit her lip to keep from laughing. The youth was dead serious, and she did need his help. But the bubble of joy swelled in her chest. They'd escaped Lord Ainsley's wrath, somehow.

He rambled over the remains of the cruck, kicking at the ashes until he crowed. "It's here!" He hauled on something buried in charcoal, and Mellia joined him. Together, they unearthed it: a lockbox.

"Didn't have a chance to grab this when we left. Besides, Alroth took the keys with him. Gotta have it when he comes back."

Mellia swallowed her guilt. She was a large part of the reason he would never come back. But she couldn't tell this fresh-faced young one that. She helped him strap the heavy box to his back, and they set off over the stile and around outside New Bridge's walls. A path was already broken through the snow, but by the time they reached the road emerging from Upper Gate, Mellia was gasping for breath.

"Why didn't we just go through town?"

"Never been in there. Full of guards and stuff anyway." He lived so close to New Bridge, but he'd never been inside? Perhaps one of the Mill Hamlet adults would explain why they hadn't fled inside the town walls when their hamlet caught fire—was set alight, rather. Surely the comb, at least, would have taken them in when Lord Ainsley burnt down their homes.

They left the road near the waterfall path, heading for the cliff face, and the youth took the lockbox off to shimmy through a crack in the wall.

"Selena!" he called into the darkness.

Mellia followed him—what choice did she have?

An older woman called back. "Tarrin! Who is that? Who are you, girl? Looking for shelter?"

"No, matron. I'm here on Alroth's behalf—"

"Come on in." She looked Mellia up and down, stepped back, and beckoned Mellia farther inside.

The cave was warm and dry. Sheep baaed in a pen in the corner, but the floor was clean and well swept. Folks ranged around, some on pine-bough beds. An open fire crackled away, and the older woman coaxed her over and sat beside it herself, holding out her hands toward the flames' warmth.

"Speak, girl. What news of Alroth and the others? I know it can't be good. Otherwise, they would be here instead of you."

How to tell this woman that they may never be back? That they were being blamed for kidnapping handmaids? That Alroth had been branded not only a traitor but also a heretic? Dripping water echoed from a side passage.

"You're Alroth's mate?" Perceptive woman.

Mellia nodded. "That's right." She sighed. Might as well get it over with. "The mercenaries are on their way to Nordval. They won't be coming back."

The old woman poked at the fire. "Wouldn't have thought they would leave us high and dry with war on the way, but that's what mercs are like, eh?" She gave Mellia an expert side-eye. She didn't believe it; she was simply testing to see whether Mellia did.

And Mellia would have agreed, this morning. Now? "They didn't have a choice—the Grist didn't leave them one. And Alroth is here in New Bridge. But he's in trouble." Her voice broke. *Fuck*, she didn't want Alroth to be killed. Once she told this woman about it, it would be more real somehow. Could she even get the words out?

"I'm sure our revered Grist father had nothing to do with that?" The older woman sniffed.

Mira sidled through the cave wall, past the sheep, and shoved their head under Mellia's hand. They were tall enough to head-butt Mellia's belly now without stretching up. *Revered* was hardly the word she would use for Father Glimar. "The Grist don't rule us all."

"Ain't that the truth. I heard tell you were a sister for a while. What changed your mind?" The older woman studied Mellia this time, her face in shadow.

True, she had never chosen to be a sister, as some pious folks did. But she had believed that the Grist could keep her safe, that Father Glimar could protect her and help her. But she didn't anymore. What had changed her mind? The way Father Glimar had tried to manipulate her? The way they had threatened her accidental bond with Alroth? She slipped her hand in her pocket and pulled out the hair-textured stone of the smashed statue. The temple. The older woman eyed it but didn't reach for the chunk of rock.

Mellia wrapped her fingers around the cold stone. "Doloman might be the Golden God, but he's not the only deity. The Grist would have us believe that—would force us to believe it."

"Have forced us, sure." She waved at the seat across from her. "Have a seat, former sister. Arista used to talk about the household gods sometimes. Before she was Grist Queen of New Bridge, of course. She wanted to bring them back. Idealistic she was, once. But you know, the Grist queen's words are smothered by the Grist father's voice. Not much she could do, locked in that tower." She gestured to the fire, which leaped and sparked. That was magic.

"How did you know Arista?" Had she been a sister once too?

"We were handmaids together. A long time ago." Her gaze was distant on the fire, as though looking back through it to her youth.

Mellia's heart hammered. A former handmaid. How was that possible? Handmaids were supposed to be cared for the rest of their lives by the Grist. But this one lived out here in a damp cave outside the town walls with a herd of sheep. And she knew about the household gods. Did she know about the Grist destroying the temples? The very memories of the gods they disapproved of?

"What did she tell you about the deities? Was there a beautiful woman?" That smashed statue haunted her. The strong, calm face of the goddess from her dream shouldn't remain nameless.

"Reverentia." The older woman smiled. "The only one who could match Doloman in power, strength, and wits. The old Grist father heard Arista utter her name once and beat her bloody. Once she was queen, he didn't need to do that to keep her quiet anymore. He got the knack of wrenching her into silence—whenever she wasn't locked away."

Mellia shuddered. That was to be Sathred's fate. Power and yet no power. The voice of Doloman and yet censored and gagged by the Grist father's whims. Arista had lived her whole life that way, because even when Father Glimar became Grist father after his cruel predecessor, surely he used the same tactics. Unless Queen Arista had given in by that time, become the docile Grist queen required of her. Would the same thing happen to Sathred? Something similar was already happening to Elenta, under Lord New Bridge's thumb, afraid to exist without his permission for fear of that tearing feeling of having her soul ripped from her very bones. Which was why Mellia had to escape Alroth, right?

Perhaps she could be like this woman: leave the Grist and titles behind and have a simple life. Alone. "I see why you never let a source bind you."

The old woman's grey eyebrows lifted. "Who says I didn't? If you're fishing for a judgment of Alroth from me, you'll catch a megalodon. But I'm sure as his mate, you're already acquainted with his many flaws, so I'll give it a rest and skip the syphon for the magic. He would give his own life to keep his oath to protect us, and you, I've no doubt. Most of us here would be dead or destitute without him. Some can't work, some got turned out. Some are on the run, like Alroth. He raises folks up wherever he goes. The Grist don't like that too much, in my experience," she finished dryly.

Stultitia's gnarled fingers twisting fresh nettles on her cracked spindle! Mellia had chosen to leave him behind, flee to Nordval, and let him be burned as a heretic. She hadn't even tried to intervene. And unless she did something, he still would be. But what could she do?

Kill Ainsley, free Alroth, threaten Father Glimar, none of that would accomplish what she actually wanted: build somewhere safe for her, for Alroth, for folks like the mercs, for the handmaids, for folks like these. Like her brother. If she could get back her title to Falvair, she would have a chance to shape it into such a place. But how could she do that?

Father Glimar had washed his hands of her when he made her a drone, and Ainsley certainly wouldn't help her. These folks couldn't bestow a title on her, so who could? Her father would follow whatever the Grist decreed, which meant she needed to sway the Grist's decision. Not the Grist father, the Grist queen. Sathred.

She was no friend to Father Glimar, and she had power. The Grist couldn't contradict her, not outright. But she was locked back in the queen's keep, and Mellia was no longer a sister permitted to enter the keep on a whim. But if she could get into the keep—and get Sathred out—before Alroth was killed...

"You're plotting something." Selena looked altogether too pleased at the prospect.

"You don't know a way for the Grist queen to escape the queen's keep, do you?"

Selena grinned and told Mellia how she and Arista had slipped out and back into the keep, back when Arista was a new queen.

Selena helped Mellia prepare: lent her snowshoes, mittens, and a spare mantle, and Mellia returned to New Bridge Hive. Hopefully for the last time.

She skirted Father Glimar's manor to the keep's high wall. Selena couldn't be remembering correctly. The wall Mellia was supposed to scale stretched up, its tall windows high off the snowy ground. The hive sat to one side, the queen's keep to the other, and this passage, slightly lower than both, certainly, but three times Mellia's height, stretched between them. The passage allowed the Grist queen to reach the hive for special ceremonies without leaving the keep. On the other side lay the Queen's Garden with its unguarded entrance to the keep.

But the entrance was unguarded for a reason: Climbing this passage wall was impossible. Maybe with Arista's magic Selena had managed, but...

Snow drifted against the wall, drifted up to the windowsills, collecting in the juncture between the keep and the hive. A breeze swirled powder into the corner. Maybe her power would be enough.

Mellia took a deep breath and held her hands out in front of her. The breeze gathered the snowflakes and set them in the corner. She syphoned a little more magic from Alroth and opened her eyes. The snowdrift grew as she watched, the powder climbing up the mullioned window, almost to the eaves. The thread of magic wavered, and Mellia stopped. The last thing she wanted was to use too much power and become ephemeral now. The gap between the top of the snowbank and the corridor's roof was still sizable, but she could scramble up with the snowshoes.

She lumbered forward, almost tripping over her own feet. It was secluded enough here that she didn't need to rush for fear of being seen, and the manor's windows were out of sight. The only ones who could see her would be in the queen's keep, and Sathred would hopefully realize that they were on the same side. Mellia made it halfway up the snowbank before she slid backwards.

She dug her hands into the snow—thank Doloman for the fur mittens Selena had foisted on her. It stopped her backward slide, but to move forward she would have to... what? Crawling on her knees just made her sink into the snow. She needed to stay on top of it to reach the roof.

She jammed one foot forward, digging the toe of the snowshoe into the snow, then the other. The snow compacted under her feet, but she was no longer sliding. She stepped up again, kicked into the snow, stomped it down this time, and made herself a little step. She was up past the windowsill, now relying on the snow that she had gathered into the drift. It was looser, sinking as she stepped and packed it down. The cold air burned Mellia's lungs, and her legs screamed for rest. The hallway's eaves loomed overhead. Would she make it to the top before her lungs or her legs gave out?

She lifted one foot, then the other, her legs burning from lifting the heavy snowshoes, but she finally took the last step to the top of the drift. She panted and clutched the edge of the tile roof, at about her shoulders. The gap between the drift and the eaves hadn't looked nearly so wide from the ground.

How in the name of Prosperitas was she supposed to hoist herself onto the steep tiles? The snow gathered up here was about as deep as her arm was long, the edge of the tiles just peeking out where the sun had melted the edge of the snowdrift. Could she use magic to help her again? What exactly would she do? The snow wasn't moving; there was no sunlight to melt it, and wind would only sweep away the snow she'd gathered.

Mellia bounced on her snowshoes, hopped as high as she could... ridiculously. She rose a handspan off the snowdrift and thumped back down on her snowshoes, packing down the snow under them and making her lose even more height. If she could pile more snow beneath her feet, that might give her the height she needed, but the only snow she had was on the roof. Bringing it down on her head wouldn't help.

Her magic must be able to do something. Of course. She might not be able to alter the snow with magic, but she could use Alroth's magic on herself. She pulled off her mittens, icy wind biting her fingers, and clumsily untied the snowshoes and pulled her mittens back on, flexing her fingers inside the fur to bring the feeling back.

Deep breath. She could do this. She reached for Alroth's magic again, syphoned it into her legs, bent and—Alroth's magic cut off abruptly. Had he wrenched her? No! She couldn't be ephemeral right now. She loosed her hold on the magic, but it was too late to stop her jump. She pushed off from the ground, energy pounding through her muscles, propelling her upward off the snowshoes... What? How? But she was high enough! She got a booted foot onto the slippery tiles, and it held as she scrambled up, panting.

That hadn't been her magic—Alroth had cut her off. Mellia craned her neck, the windows of the Grist Queen's Keep staring down at her, empty but for the twitch of a curtain. Sathred had helped her. Sathred was on her side. This plan would work. It had to work.

Mellia scrambled over the corridor rooftop, knocking snow down the other side in an avalanche into the Queen's Garden, in deep shadow from the garden wall. She'd made it up, now to make it down. There wouldn't be any guards at the garden entrance to the keep, but there certainly were on the other side of the far garden wall in the hive. Alerting them would be the end of this. *Get down without making too much noise.* There had to be a way.

"Careful up there, Mellia." Sathred's murmur almost made Mellia slip right off the rooftop. A shadow wavered in the garden below.

Sathred had come to meet Mellia in the garden. If only Mellia could get down.

"Hang on." Sathred's shadowy form rustled, and the nearest tree creaked and groaned, a small branch that reached toward the rooftop thickening and lengthening, reaching right for Mellia. It grew until it brushed the eaves next to her. How did Sathred do that? Trees didn't grow in the winter, no matter how much one urged them. "Quickly. It'll freeze and crack in a moment."

Mellia scrambled onto the limb, wriggled her way to the trunk, and climbed down the ladder of branches until she dropped into the snowbank at the base of the tree. Sathred had not only made the tree grow; she'd changed the very season around the branch, she had to have. Was that really possible? How much power did the Grist queen possess? No wonder the Grist father always kept her on a tight leash. She was more powerful than a hundred bound matrons like Mellia.

"Why do you think I came all the way back here?" Sathred said, as though reading Mellia's realization in her stunned face. "Handmaids are nothing compared to the Grist Queen."

Obviously, that was true. But at what cost had Sathred gained such power? "And Father Glimar? You enjoy having him holding your leash?"

Sathred eyed her coldly. "I could wrench him with a thought."

"But he could wrench you."

Sathred shrugged. "If he wanted a swarm of angry bees to attack him, he could." All the brothers' ephemers.

Wait, Sathred could wrench Father Glimar? Did that mean... the Grist brothers had the same type of bond with the Grist queen that Alroth and Mellia had? Two ephemers? And yet, they called it heretical and intended them to burn. This was wrong. All of it. Doloman's will it may be, but he was not the only god. He was not even the greatest god. The powerful goddess from her dream matched him in every way. *Reverentia. Reverentia.* They had destroyed her statue, punished those who so much as said her name, wiped her from every record, but she was a goddess. Try as they might, Reverentia would live on.

All the more reason to make sure Mellia's plan went smoothly. And the next step was to recruit Sathred. Giving Sathred what she wanted would be the way to win her over.

Mellia brushed snow off her skirt. "What if you didn't have to speak through Father Glimar?"

"The Grist dictates that the queen stays in the keep. You know this, Mellia." Sathred turned to the keep, and Mellia followed her.

"And yet, your orders to the Grist guards were followed without question. They didn't defer to Father Glimar. They deferred to you." This would sway Sathred. More power.

"It doesn't matter. They have ways of keeping me in here." She climbed the spiral staircase.

Mellia kept at her heels. "Wrenching you? Braving your bees?"

"Did Father Glimar ever wrench you to keep you in line?"

No, he hadn't, obviously, since they had never been bound. And yet, Mellia had braved breaking a prisoner out of the castle for Glimar, for what he could offer her. He'd used Doloman's will to make it more palatable, yes, but Mellia was not pious enough for that to sway her, not really. She'd done it because Glimar had dangled the promise of being a handmaid, the promise of her freedom. And now he had control of everything about Sathred's life. He could give her a sumptuous feast, gifts of baubles and lovely clothes, or lock her in the keep in rags and starve her half to death—or anything in between. She could wrench him, but to what end? A few hours of satisfaction, followed by a lengthy punishment? Sathred knew. She knew how powerless she was. Her threat to wrench Glimar was empty.

"I think I can help you. Just hear me out." Mellia hung back as Sathred stepped into the handmaids' chamber. What if there were handmaids inside, chosen by Glimar for their loyalty to him? Anything they heard would go straight to the Grist father's ears, her plan wrenched even before she could set it in motion.

Sathred sighed. "There are no new handmaids yet. The keep is empty. Just me." She shivered in the draft from the open door. Come to think of it, her clothes did look thin. Had Glimar taken away her serviceable clothes to prevent Sathred from leaving the keep? More than likely, he had.

Mellia followed her into the chamber. The fire crackled, and Sathred pulled a chair up to the fireplace and put her feet on the hearth. Her shoes were soaked through—shoes, not the sturdy boots she'd left Bridge wearing. Boots, when the rest of the handmaids had been in dainty slippers. Sathred had known. If not the specifics of the plan to murder the handmaids, then at least that *something* was set to happen on that waterfall. And she'd looked out just for herself. Of course.

A pot hung on the fireplace crane, swung to the side, and an empty plate sat on a table by Sathred's chair. She lived here alone, not in the Grist queen's chamber.

"You haven't moved upstairs?" Mellia took off her wet mantle and mittens and settled in the chair opposite Sathred—the one Runas had favoured. Did Sathred not find the memories of her lost friends haunting?

Sathred shrugged. "Why? There are no handmaids to care for me, and everything I need is down here. No sense in going up and down the stairs all day."

Perhaps it also had something to do with the lingering memory of Arista's husk laid out on the bed upstairs. They'd sent her spirit downstream with the Necrophoresis Ritual, but who could forget the days she'd spent laid out up there?

Mellia leaned forward and let the crackling flames thaw her stiff fingers. "I can make them listen to you."

"And why would you do that?" Sathred was already bored with this conversation. She probably didn't believe that Mellia could do it.

"Once they do, you can help me." One reason, among a handful, but the one that Sathred would believe.

Sathred laughed coldly. "Of course. Nothing comes for free."

Rage boiled in Mellia's middle and bubbled through her words. "You are the one who betrayed me! We could all be in Falvair by now, safe and mulling our options together if you had flagged down the ship going downstream instead of letting it pass and running back to the Grist!"

"And I'll never hear the end of that, will I?" She'd hear the end of it once Mellia was gone. Her new handmaids wouldn't know anything about it. She'd just be the Grist queen to them.

"Sathred, you betrayed us for this power. You knew what it would cost you. You knew it would bind you here. You saw Arista sitting up there day after day."

Sathred had weighed her options and made the choice to come back here and be a prisoner instead of risking anything for her freedom, as the other handmaids were at this very moment.

"Arista was old and weak and had given up on life."

"And you believe that could never happen to you?"

"It won't happen to me," she snarled.

"Not if you work with me on this." Mellia drew the textured stone from her pocket.

Sathred watched her turn it between her hands, but she didn't ask what it was. It didn't matter; she would hear about it.

"I found this in the old temple near Bridge Keep. They had destroyed the statues of the deities. There was a goddess with bulging muscles, one with willow whips for hair... and this one. They'd smashed in her face. Every last chunk of rock they reduced her to, they ground to powder, all but a few bits of hair like this one. She came to me, later, in a dream."

Sathred's gaze was fixed on the stone Mellia fiddled with.

"I think you're supposed to be like her, Sathred. She stood up to Doloman. She was never afraid of him."

"And look where that got her. Smashed to pieces. Broken. Forgotten." She didn't deny that she was afraid of Doloman—or Father Glimar.

Mellia shook her head. "Not forgotten. Arista knew about her."

"Arista," Sathred spat.

"You don't have to believe it, but she was like you once, before her Grist father took everything from her."

"How would you know? Another dream?"

"No, I spoke with one of her handmaids."

Finally, Sathred had no scathing retort.

"I'm giving you the chance to do what Arista never could. Take the power that the Grist queen should have in the hive."

"And how would you do that?" Her voice still dripped with scorn, but at least she was open to hearing Mellia's plan now.

"Come with me. To the burning. In front of everyone. Tell them that Doloman wills your attendance, tell them that Doloman has spoken to you, told you that you are to take a firmer hand in the hard times ahead. Tell them whatever you think will be convincing."

The hive bells pealed, calling the comb to a special service. A service to remind everyone why Alroth was burning tonight.

"Say I get out of this guarded keep, find a way to the lists. Say I succeed in taking some power back from Glimar. What do you want in return?" She was considering it, and that was something.

"Tell them that it's Doloman's will that Alroth take control of the Marquessate of Falvair. That both Alroth and I live. That He sanctions our bond." The easy part first. Mellia steeled herself. "And tell them the truth about the handmaids. Father Glimar is trying to start a war with Carille over them. We have to stomp out the rumours. Make sure everyone knows that the handmaids went to Nordval of their own will. Destroy his excuse before it gains traction."

"No one will believe the handmaids just up and decided to go to Nordval, and I can't tell everyone the Grist tried to kill them. What reason could the handmaids possibly have had to leave New Bridge and go to the middle of nowhere?"

"Make something up. You speak with Doloman's voice. Whatever you say, they will believe. If Father Glimar tries to contradict you, he risks the people turning on him. Lord New Bridge, for one, is devotedly pious. Glimar going against you would risk his place as Grist father."

Sathred nodded. She was coming around. "And we get out of here how? If you hadn't noticed, we're both now trapped here in the keep. The guards aren't just going to let me out because I tell them it's *Doloman's will.*"

"During the service. For an occasion like this, Father Glimar can't resist having a special mass."

"Yes, a mass I will attend." The Grist queen always sat on the balcony overlooking the hive during services.

"Which is why the guard won't suspect that you're trying to leave the keep while it's in progress." The guard would still notice the Grist queen marching through the cloister during mass, but they wouldn't look twice at a plain sister slipping out. The hive balcony was high enough that anyone dressed in the proper finery would pass for the queen, and luckily, now that Mellia was here, they had a Grist queen stand-in at the ready.

34

Alroth

Alroth awoke to a boot in the ribs. His breath wheezed out, and he rolled, curled up to protect his middle, and wrapped his arms over his head. His body knew this dance, even in his sleep.

No further blows came, and Alroth rolled to his knees, clenched his fists in his lap. The cloudy grey sky outside the high window meant that he'd been out for a few hours at most, dumped here in this frigid cell. With a guard looking down on him as though he were a rat.

A boot scraped on the high threshold.

Ainsley.

No shock that the lordling didn't do his own dirty work. He hopped down, gracefully, and sauntered to loom over Alroth.

"I've been thinking about our little arrangement." Ainsley pulled a handkerchief from his pocket and wiped his hands methodically, eyeing the grimy cell as though just standing in it soiled him.

Alroth hadn't been asked a question, so why waste his breath?

"We need to make it believable that I won our duel fairly."

Alroth still held his tongue, guarded his expression. Ainsley would do what he was going to do. Opening his mouth would only make it worse.

"Don't you want to know how?" He gestured to the guard, who drew his booted foot back.

Should Alroth dodge the blow or take it? Dodging would piss the lordling off. The kick hit him in the same spot on the ribs as before. He'd have worse than a bruise there by morning.

"Come, Alroth, ask me how." Ainsley tucked the handkerchief away in his pocket.

Best to just go along with him, keep him talking. Even though the answer was likely to be *break your fingers*. "How?"

"Your mage begged me on her knees to take her from you. I can't say I'm surprised that she's so eager to be rid of you. A lady like her deserves better than a guttersnipe."

True. That much was true. And this arrangement would fix everything.

"We all know she does."

Ainsley's mouth curled into a smile. "Yes, we do, don't we? Maybe you more than anyone." He crouched so their faces were level. "Why did you keep her here? I know she wanted to run away with you."

None of your damn business, warmonger. He swallowed the snarl. It would probably get him a knee to the still-tender nose. He'd wanted to keep her safe, to run away somewhere the war couldn't reach them. Where they could have peace. "A dream."

Ainsley laughed as he rose, looked down on Alroth. "That's all a Locuplean mercenary like you has, isn't it? You certainly don't have two silvers to rub together." His face went hard. "Consider your dream shattered."

The booted guard's knee came for Alroth's face anyway. One of his arms came up of its own accord and took the worst of the blow, and the guard growled. The rivets on Alroth's cestus must have jabbed his kneecap.

"Unfortunately, I can't kill you like this, in a grimy cell. A duel is the only way for the marquessate to pass to me. We must abide by the laws of succession, you see." The handkerchief was back, despite Ainsley not so much as touching anything in this cell.

He gestured to the guard, who grabbed Alroth's hair and tipped his head back. Why did they keep doing that? Because he'd grown complacent and left his hair to grow long, into a weakness they could exploit. He should have cut his hair when he'd shaved.

The guard grabbed his arm and twisted it behind his back, the burn of his shoulder competing with that of his scalp. *Damn.* The guard stomped on his ankle, just below Miran's bite, and Alroth strangled a scream as it popped.

"Do you think that's sufficient to secure my win?"

Far off, the hive bells pealed, and Ainsley turned. He managed to make being hoisted out of the cell by a guard look dignified, and left Alroth alone.

Alroth gathered a ragged breath. His ribs twinged. His ankle throbbed. Lifting a weapon would be torture. Good thing his cesti were intact. Not that he could throw a punch with his right hand—at least not without his ribs cracking more than they already were. Ending up breathing pink foam and coughing blood like Mellia had wouldn't help anyone.

Ainsley might be a barely trained stripling lad when it came to the lists, but in Alroth's state, he might not have to throw the duel at all. Alroth untied one of his hose and wrapped his ankle. It would be stiff and hard to lace into his boot, but at least the bones didn't grind together every time he took a step.

He tucked his arm into his injured side and shadow-boxed with his other. Good thing he hadn't eaten since... last night? Otherwise, his stomach would be rebelling at that self-inflicted pain. If he was allowed a shield, any blow to it would be crushing, no matter how much of a weakling the lordling was. He could take one and live. Any more, and it would be touch and go.

He gently poked his tender shoulder. He dragged himself to the wall, held his breath, and popped it back into place—a trick he'd learned on the battlefield where healers were scarce. He bit back a howl. Dislocate it one time, and now it wanted to pop out at the slightest twist. Thankfully, that Ultio-spawn Ainsley had left him one good side. If they gave him a light sword, he could wield it, but he would tire quickly, and his wounds would only get worse. If they gave him a longsword, he'd barely be able to lift it.

Alroth took a step, trying to pace the cell and work off his nervous energy, but his ankle twinged, and he took his weight off it. He'd need it for the fight, and putting weight on it would not do him any favours.

A distant bark had Alroth pivoting to search the walls for any sign of Miran coming through. They were the one who had caused all this trouble. When it had just been Mira, Alroth had won his duel against Ainsley, proven to the Grist's satisfaction that their bond was Doloman blessed. But Miran had changed everything. Then again, without Miran, Alroth would be dead, dashed on the rocks below the crumbling bridge. Without Mellia's ability to wrench him, no amount of magic would have kept him alive. Where was the blasted creature?

Alroth stepped back onto his injured ankle and swore. He lumbered to a seat, pain shooting up his ankle and down his side as he awkwardly tried to sit without hurting himself.

Pounding on the door made Alroth scramble to his feet. The door swung open to reveal guards, and they hauled him out of the pit by the arms. Alroth clenched his teeth to keep from crying out when it strained his injured side and shoulder.

They weren't leading him to the pyre. That was a comfort. Alroth would have the chance to die for something, at least. They didn't even bother to bind him again. Did they know that he was too injured to fight? Or were they hoping that he would so that the... *score* of guards waiting outside the great hall would have an excuse to beat him bloody before the duel?

He didn't bother to dodge the kicks and gobs of spit hurled his way. Most of them landed on Alroth's boots. He'd had worse flung at him. Alroth held his head high as he was marched into the castle's outer ward, through the barbican, and down the drawbridge. Every step sent a twinge up his ankle, but he had to stay focused. The evening was nearly silent. Perhaps the town hadn't been told about the duel? Last time, the crowd had been a lake of roaring exuberance, cheering him on; through him, experiencing the glory of a nobody binding a mage.

But no, the square before the palisades was crammed with spectators, just as before, but they watched him silently, parted for him and his guards as they led him through the gap in the palisades, past the outbuildings, toward the lists. They were here to watch the monster slaughtered. Like a bear baiting.

Father Glimar and Lord New Bridge sat on the dais, as before. Alroth's pulse picked up. Where was Mellia? Perhaps she was in the crowd, not on the dais? Or maybe it was better that she not witness this.

Glimar stood, raised his hands, as though beseeching silence, even though only a quiet cough echoed about the still yard. "This duel shall reveal to us Doloman's will. When last these two opponents met, it was a bond at stake. A bond that was sanctioned by the Golden God Himself. But since then, the bond has been twisted, sullied."

Glimar gestured to Alroth. "This man has, in an act of heresy, manifested an ephemer."

A chorus of low hisses and boos rippled through the crowd. Because a man with an ephemer, doing magic, was an abomination, as he'd tried to tell Mellia, time and again. Some of the tension bled out of Alroth's shoulders. They were right. And they were right to cheer for his death.

Ainsley hefted his longsword, and the guard captain, as before, tossed Alroth a rusty old blade. But his hand knew this hilt, even ruined as it was. Ictus. Alroth whirled on Glimar, who surveyed him coldly. Was this meant to cow him? Remind him of his past failures? It didn't. Ictus had been his first weapon, bought with his own coin, earned in honest labour. She was rusted, flaking, splitting, but her core still stood. He swung her with his good arm, the whistling through the air centering him in a way nothing else could. He was armed. He was ready.

No shield was offered this time. Of course. He'd have to rely on his cesti to deflect Ainsley's blows. Surely they would give him a helm? But no, the guard captain waved at them to begin. Alroth tightened his grip on Ictus's peeling hilt, the half-decayed leather letting the iron within dig into his palms. A hundred thanks for his cesti yet again.

Alroth stilled as Ainsley approached, sword held point first as if to skewer Alroth with a single thrust. Alroth stepped aside at the last moment, the strain on his ankle now grinding bone against bone. If he did that again, no amount of wrapping would save him from ruining it. He braced for a blow that he deflected with the cestus on his good arm.

Ainsley circled him, sword at the ready, and Alroth took the weight off his ankle. It would throw him off balance, but the throbbing was distracting. Ainsley slashed at Alroth's back, the blow glancing off his jack but sending a dagger of pain lancing up his injured ribs. He swallowed a scream and turned it into a grunt. Ainsley came around and slashed at his belly. Alroth caught the blow on his sword, the impact jarring his shoulder and engulfing his side with a fiery burning that made him pull his arm in close. Ictus's tip dipped, but he couldn't bring it back up, not without the claws of pain raking his injured side. He dropped the sword and raised his fist.

When was the last time he'd fought an armoured opponent with his fists? When Alroth was just a kid, Drake had stumbled on him, barely out of childhood himself, and seen Alroth as more than just a penniless street urchin. They'd fought off a few drunk guards-for-hire in an alley. Whether they were after Alroth for his thieving or Etienne for his nobility didn't matter. The two of them had fought them off side by side. Etienne was the first to ever stand by Alroth. If he hadn't, Alroth would have been killed for sport, just another scrawny street child, a toy for the bored fighters of Munificast's underbelly. And now even Drake thought him irredeemable. Left him to die.

Using a cestus against plate would be a recipe for breaking his hand. Alroth got in close to the lordling, grappled his head, ripped at the ridiculous silver-painted bear that topped his helm, and Ainsley squealed, the chin strap on his helm no doubt cutting into his throat. A sword hilt cracked Alroth's skull, and stars danced across Ainsley's glittering armour. Alroth staggered back, and Ainsley's blade crashed into his knees, knocking his legs out from under him, and he twisted to fall hard on his good side. His hip took the brunt of it. He'd have a bruise tomorrow. No, he wouldn't. He would be a corpse by then.

The feeling echoed his feet slipping out from under him, sliding over the edge of the crumbling bridge as he shoved Mellia to safety, tumbling through the falling snowflakes, unable to stop himself... Alroth took a deep breath to calm his pounding heart. He wasn't falling now. He braced his hands on the solid, frozen dirt. She could have let him fall, could have been rid of him easily. But she hadn't. She'd seen something in him worth saving.

Alroth sluggishly got his knees under him, head throbbing now along with his shoulder, ankle, and side. Now he had to save her.

But you threw it back in her face. When he'd wrenched her. She'd been so close to safely escaping the Grist, and he'd snatched her back, wrestled her ephemer to the ground to keep her here in Sudra. Hadn't trusted her in return. Which was why he deserved his predicament.

Ainsley's sabatons padded closer and stopped before him. Alroth's hair curtained his face. He didn't need to see the look of triumph Ainsley no doubt shot his way. Once he was dead, Ainsley would bind Mellia and take uncontested control of Falvair. Feed the Grist's war, stoke the animosity with Carille, profit from the death and destruction wreaked across the lake and here in Sudra as attacking ships harried every exposed Sudran port… including New Bridge. At least he no longer had to worry about Mill Hamlet and the people he'd callously abandoned to this lordling's ire.

Ainsley's sword came to rest against the back of Alroth's neck, cold, honed to cut through flesh and bone. Alroth had sworn to protect her, and this was the last act that he could gift to her.

The blade left his nape. Ainsley's breath huffed out as he raised it. A glint of silver drew Alroth's eye. *Miran?*

Ainsley's sword whistled in the silence as it plummeted toward his exposed neck.

35

Mellia

This was not going according to Mellia's plan. She'd dressed herself in the Grist queen's finery, the smallest she could find, and strode through the corridor linking the queen's keep with the hive. She stepped out onto the balcony. Through the screen, the ripple of the restless crowd was muted. Father Glimar, standing at the altar to give his service, didn't so much as look at her—probably for the best.

His voice was barely audible from up here, and Mellia strained to hear what he was saying about her and Alroth. Something about heresy, obviously, something about his mercy. A load of mammoth shit, essentially. The stained-glass windows were far more interesting than anything Father Glimar said. Of course, they depicted Doloman's commandments: visions of the horrors in store for those who tried to defy Doloman's will and bond in ways not sanctioned by Him. A river divided in two, running over two pitifully trickling waterfalls. A foolish man, digging away at a riverbank with a shovel, trying to divert the water's flow.

Doloman's word maintained that bonds worked like those waterfalls: The magic flowed down from the source to the mage, from strong to weak, from man to woman. One source, one mage, flowing one direction, carved by Doloman's hand, by the Grist's hand. But it wasn't true. None of it was true. Mellia and Alroth had formed a powerful bond without the Grist. Their power flowed not only from Alroth to Mellia, but in both directions. Had Alroth not used magic to heal her when she was near death? Had she not been able to wrench him, like a source would their mage? Had not Del and Kai formed a bond between them the same way? The Grist denied that such a bond was possible, between two men. Though, Mellia had known that for a lie since she was a child and her brother had bound himself to his lover.

Wait, had Glimar just said Alroth was to duel for his life? For her title? If that was the case, Sathred's word wouldn't be enough. It wasn't simply a case of heresy anymore. Lord Ainsley was plotting to take Falvair, and he would not be so easily deterred.

The service ended, and the huge hive doors swung wide, spilling the parishioners into the square under Doloman's solemn gaze. Glimar tipped his head up and looked at her. Mellia didn't move. She was behind the screen. She was far away. He couldn't tell that she wasn't Sathred. He turned away and disappeared through the small door into the sacristy. Mellia let out her breath, and stood, stately, like a Grist queen. Some brothers and supplicants lingered, and she couldn't draw their attention. She retreated into the corridor back to the queen's keep.

Alroth was right. Sudra needed somewhere for folks to go, where the Grist's impossible rules held no sway. Because their rules *were* impossible. They were built on lies, on the premise that nature only had one arrangement. In their world, people like her brother—men who were mages—didn't exist. And what of Falkirk? Where did they fit into the Grist's world? What of Del and Kai, their bond ebbing and flowing between them? What of herself? She was a mage, no question, but she was also a source. Alroth's source.

Alroth, who was about to battle Ainsley in a no doubt rigged duel. She had to get there, to stop this.

At the other end of the dark corridor, she pulled off the gossamer veil. She needed to find some more practical clothes and slip out of the keep. She had to get to the duel. Alroth was in danger for as long as he was in the lists.

Mellia changed back into her clothes and hurried down the keep stairs to the inner cloister. Hopefully, Father Glimar was already out and on his way to the lists. If she bumped into him... what would he do? Never mind. She kept her head up and strode toward the gate out to the main cloister. Just a sister, going about her business. She nodded to the Grist guards on either side of the gate. They made no move to stop her, so she didn't slow down. She picked her way across the gaps where the teeth of the portcullis would bite into the ground. She would go straight to the lists once she was out and thread her way through the crowd that would have gathered for the duel. She would make her way to Alroth's side as quickly as possible, give him the best chance to—

Hard fingers gripped her arm. "Sister Mellia." Brother Padril looked down at her, jaw set. *Doloman's eye.* He knew her. Had even supported her. Until he and the guard had captured her at Bridge's temple. Until he'd seen Miran.

"Good morning." How to play this? Hope that he wasn't aware that she was a drone? Hope that he didn't know about the duel? "I'm just passing through on business for the queen—"

The fingers tightened on her arm, and she gasped.

Padril shook his head. "No, you aren't." He jerked his chin at the keep.

She didn't have to do as he said... but a barracks full of guards sat directly behind her. She sighed and let him turn her back toward the keep. "Can't have you interfering again," he muttered. "Sorry to lay hands on you, Sister."

I'm not a sister! But that wouldn't help her now.

Padril marched her up the stairs, back to the handmaids' chamber, and shoved her through the door. "I'll be standing right out here until the heretic..." He wouldn't look at her. He jerked a nod and slammed the door in her face.

Until the duel is over. Until Alroth is dead. That's why he'd looked so guilty. Father Glimar was throwing the duel for certain. If she couldn't get to him, Alroth would die.

So she had to get to him. Mellia paced to the window. Too high off the ground. She could get back into the garden, but it was a dead end. Could she climb back up the tree Sathred had modified for her? Maybe that way she could get back onto the roof. She dashed down the other stairway, fast enough to get dizzy, and shoved through the garden door. The first branch on the tree that she'd climbed down last night was high off the ground, but maybe she could—

The branch. On the other side of the frozen fountain, next to the corridor, where she had climbed across from the roof, a huge branch lay in the snow. The branch that Sathred had grown for her. Sathred had used it to get out and broken it off after her, either by accident, or on purpose. No, not on purpose. She wouldn't do that. The sap that Sathred had coaxed into it had simply frozen and split the branch so thoroughly that it had sheared off. The gap from the tree to the roof was longer now than Mellia was tall. Even if she could climb to the lowest branch and make her way up the tree, she'd never bridge that gap. She wasn't getting out that way.

There was only one way in or out of the Grist Queen's Keep, by design. Mages were coveted, not just among the Grist, but throughout The Lakes, throughout the world. It was imminently defensible, in case an enemy tried to steal the queen or the handmaids. And it also kept them all contained and under the Grist's control. She climbed back up to the handmaids' chamber slowly. She could get into the hive, to the balcony that overlooked the altar, but the drop onto the granite floor would be no better than if she jumped out the window from here—and there would be Grist brothers there to apprehend her.

But maybe there was a way down that she had overlooked. Maybe they wouldn't stop a sister trying to leave the hive. Maybe they wouldn't recognize her as Padril had at the gate. She strode through the hallway, the snow covering the window and darkening the corridor, up a narrow staircase, and emerged onto the balcony. Even higher than the chamber windows, with no snow to break her fall. No decorative pillars to slide down, no hangings to grab onto. As though they had planned to offer the Grist queen no escape—and perhaps they had modified it to prevent Arista from doing exactly what Mellia was planning to do in this moment.

Every heartbeat she spent here mulling over her options was another heartbeat Alroth had a sword swinging at his face. There must be something she'd overlooked. She descended the steps back into the corridor.

Mellia paused there. This was where she had sealed her fate. She'd snowed over this window, so determined to enter this mousetrap of her own free will. Her snowshoes made darker shadows at the top of the pane, where she'd left them. If only she'd thought to kick in the window, she wouldn't have had to climb onto the roof at all, wouldn't have needed Sathred's help to get down. She could have crawled back out the way she'd come in, no one the wiser...

Crawled out? This window was only slightly closer to the ground than those in the handmaids' chamber, but with the drifted snow, it would be easy to climb out right into the snowbank, if only the window were open.

But she could open it. By force. Mellia took the steps into the handmaids' chamber two at a time. What could she use to smash open the window? A fire iron would do nicely. She could use a chair to climb onto the snowbank. Something to cushion her from the broken glass would also be necessary. Wool? Silk? Cloth of gold. She hurried up the steps to the Grist queen's chamber. Only the Grist queens and the Grist fathers were permitted cloth of gold garments, not just among the Grist, but in all of Sudra. Perhaps the far-away emperor as well—Mellia wouldn't know about that. But there must be a ceremonial robe in here somewhere that was too fine for the wardrobe.

An ornate chest sat in the corner, and Mellia flung open the lid with a bang and dug through, tossing aside silks and jewelled beadwork. Aha! Cool gold met her fingers, and Doloman's precious metal glinted as she drew it from the depths of the chest. *Locuples's jewelled fingernails.* It was heavy! She flung it over her shoulder and staggered down the stairs. She snatched up the fire iron and went for the window; she'd come back for the chair.

She dropped the golden garment to puddle on the floor and raised the iron. Hopefully, the glass shards wouldn't hit her, though her body was protected by her dress and boots. She raised the fire iron, drew it back, and swung.

Crash! It shattered the window, breaking through glass and leading alike. Perfect. Now all she had to do was grab that chair and climb—

Crack! More cracks spidered along the leading, up and down the cracked window. *Stultitia's gnarled fingers!*

The window gave in, glass flying for Mellia's face. She hurled the fire iron aside and flung up her arms, the freezing bite of snow showering over her, chilling her head and going down her neck. At least she wasn't full of glass...

Mellia lowered her arms to spots of red speckling the snow. Or else she was. The shards were so sharp that she didn't feel them, but three shards had sliced through her dress and lodged themselves in her forearms. Mellia staggered back a step, spots clouding her vision. No. She couldn't pass out now. She gripped the first slippery red shard and yanked, tossing it into the snow, then the next.

A shout from the handmaids' chamber spurred her on. Brother Padril must have heard her smash the window. She pulled out the last shard, and scrambled up the snowbank, no chair necessary after all, though the shards of glass mixed into the snow bit at her bare hands. The cloth of gold was buried underneath it, and there was neither time to dig it out nor was it safe with all the glass scattered about. The snow was slippery and gave way as she tried to scramble up. She clawed at it, shards of pain shooting up her fingers, either from the cold or sliced by glass. It didn't matter. If Padril got to her, she would be well and truly trapped.

Her hand caught on something hard. The end of one snowshoe stuck out of the snowdrift. She'd never get it loose, but she didn't need to. She grabbed it for purchase and hauled herself up, through the ruined window, and out into the grey twilight. She scrambled to get her boot onto the meagre hold and pried herself up the snowbank. She barely took a moment to feel the wind on her face before scrambling to her feet. The snowbank was steep before her. How would she get down without slipping?

Something smacked her boot. "What in Doloman's name are you doing, Sister?" Padril reached for her foot again, but Mellia sidled away. He cursed—he'd discovered the glass shards. He wouldn't follow her. She just had to get down without breaking anything.

She crouched and leaned forward, tipping herself into a slide down the steep, snowy slope, away from hollering Padril, into the deep snow below. She landed in a heap and staggered to her feet. The snow was still up to her knees. But she knew what to do. She closed her eyes and syphoned from Alroth—he was still alive and conscious, thank Reverentia—eddies of wind whipped the powder away. A hollowed path made way for her into the yard of the Grist father's manor.

Padril had disappeared from the window. He'd be coming around to catch her. With guards. Mellia ran. Her boots splashed and slipped on the snow, but she didn't slow down. Castle Street was deserted, thankfully, but the crowd come to watch the duel spilled into the square in front of the looming castle outside the palisade.

It would take forever to push through that crowd into the palisades, past the outbuildings, to the lists. The wooden stakes towered above Mellia, not leaving even a gap to peer through. She couldn't slip through, couldn't go around... She craned her neck. The spiked tops prevented anyone from climbing over. But the lists were down this end. If she could get over, she'd have no trouble getting to Alroth.

The clash of weapons reached her even here, but no crowd noise followed. Stands full of people and no one calling out? Last time, the noise had been deafening, easily audible from the castle barbican.

If she couldn't get over the palisade, Alroth would be killed. Ainsley's piety and cruelty would leave her people in a terrible position once the war began—and he would be in favour of a war that afforded him the opportunity to not only be a hero but also profit immensely from the shipyards and supply lines that would run through Falvair.

She couldn't give up her chance to make such a difference—she couldn't give up Alroth.

Where had that come from? The man who'd let her bind his wrists when she'd seemed nervous, insisted on hearing her affirmations to keep from hurting her, and used magic to bring her back from the brink of death, despite his discomfort with the idea of being a mage. He had wrenched her. But he'd formed Mill Hamlet. Gathered drones—like her—to give them a chance at life.

Mellia called on the magic, opening the bond between her and Alroth, focused, and syphoned. The wind gusted as her legs launched her into the air, the palisade directing the air upward and lifting her. The toes of her boots caught on the rough wood as she half climbed, the wind pushing her higher, until her fingers reached the top, and she gripped the gaps in the palisade's spikes.

Alroth was revealed. A sword pressed to the back of his neck where he knelt on the lists' dirt. His head hung, and his breathing was ragged, his shoulders shuddering with each inhale. Lord Ainsley stood over him, sword hilt clutched in both hands as he brought it up—

The wind died, and Mellia's weight settled on her slipping fingers. There was nothing to grip but smooth tapered wood. No, she was too close. A scream rent the air, from Mellia's own throat, as the sword came down. She groped for the bond and syphoned sharply, using the final syphoned power to give her arms enough strength to toss herself over the palisade, her foot coming up to get her the rest of the way over.

As she fell, Alroth twisted, the sword striking his armour and shearing apart, the iron rusting through and cracking like charcoal. Now both of them were unarmed, at least.

Mellia toppled onto a thatched roof that scratched at her face and hands as she rolled down the incline and landed in a heap in the frozen mud. Guards' gauntleted hands hauled her up and dragged her to the dais where Glimar and New Bridge watched.

Glimar didn't turn from where the two men now grappled in the lists. "I see naming you a drone didn't have quite the effect I was after."

Ainsley pulled a long thin dagger from his belt and stabbed, but Alroth twisted his wrist and directed it away from his neck. Alroth tugged on Ainsley's ridiculous helmet, but a leather chin strap held it on. That wouldn't be hard to dry and crack, and having his helmet off would let Alroth end this fight. She syphoned, and it was done, the leather drying, cracking, and Alroth wrenched the helm off and tossed it, the bear figure popping off and rolling in the dirt.

"You're helping him." Glimar seemed surprised, but it wasn't a question. "He has to die, my child."

Mellia turned to him. He was calm, condescending. "No, he doesn't. And I'm not your child."

He shook his head, slowly.

"You know our bond isn't unnatural. You have your war. Go ahead and take Falvair, if that's what you want. But why kill Alroth?"

"I thought you wanted to be a handmaid. Once the heretic is dead, you will be unbound and free to join the hive again."

Join the hive as a handmaid? Wasn't that exactly what she'd wanted just this afternoon? Alroth's fist came for the side of Ainsley's head. But he blocked the blow with an armoured forearm. Alroth took another swing, right at Ainsley's armoured side. He would break his hand, even with his cestus. She syphoned, weakened the armour plate, and when Alroth's riveted fist connected, the plate cracked instead of his bones.

If she became a handmaid, she'd be trapped in the queen's keep. And what could she do from there besides know that Ainsley was mistreating her people? She would have no friends, unless Sathred counted, but she'd already betrayed Mellia once—twice since she wasn't here saving Alroth as she'd promised. The other handmaids would be chosen by Glimar, pious believers. And she would be forbidden from so much as saying Reverentia's name, of acknowledging that there was a goddess equal to Doloman.

"You know the handmaids weren't kidnapped."

Glimar shrugged. "It doesn't really matter what I know. It's what *they* believe."

"I could tell them you sent the handmaids away. Brought them a ship."

He smiled. "You could. But would they believe you over me?"

A drone. Even a handmaid. No. Righteous anger swirled hot in Mellia's belly. Alroth didn't deserve to die. She didn't deserve to be a pawn in these games. Reverentia and the other goddesses didn't deserve to be forgotten.

The wind picked up. Ainsley raised his dagger again, and Mellia syphoned. Wind whipped around Ainsley, his breath turning to a cloud, frost coating his eyelashes and his skin turning pale, lips blue, the dagger falling from his numbed fingers.

Alroth dragged himself off the ground. He winced as he staggered to his feet. He was hurt. Mellia called another gust as Glimar clawed at her arm. The wind lifted her off the dais, and she landed in the lists, staggered, and then Alroth was there.

"Don't collapse, sweetling." He wasn't just talking about her weak knees. If she used too much magic, she would go ephemeral as surely as if Alroth had wrenched her.

"I can't—" She gasped. Some of the weight was lifting.

Alroth's eyes closed as he knit his brow in concentration. The wind picked up again, keeping Ainsley frozen in place. "Like that?"

"Just like that."

He'd used his magic. Their magic. Mellia wobbled, and Alroth wrapped an arm around her waist.

Glimar nodded to someone just off the dais. A guard, who lifted… a loaded crossbow, aimed right at Alroth's belly. It would punch right through his armour—metal plates or no. Glimar wasn't taking any chances.

The guard fired.

36

Alroth

Alroth's bones burned. Mellia stumbled *through* him, to her knees. He crouched his ghostly body next to her in the mud. Something was wrong. Blood pooled beneath her hand pressed to the dirt. It ran down her arm from her shoulder... where a crossbow bolt was lodged.

Their whirlwind was dying. Ainsley flexed his hands, shook out his arms. Swiped his dirk from the mud and came for Alroth. Except he couldn't be coming for Alroth, since Alroth was as insubstantial as a breeze. He was coming for Mellia.

When would Alroth come back to himself? *Come on!* Ainsley was taking his time, but Mellia didn't move as he raised the dirk over her.

Alroth lashed out, his ephemeral cestus passing right through the lordling's smug face. Ainsley's sneer turned into terror, and he took a step back. Why would he recoil from an ephemer?

A snarl made Alroth whip around. Miran was corporeal, of course. They were in the lists, hackles raised to a mane, teeth bared, gaze fixed on Ainsley. And they were big. Shoulders at Alroth's hip, paws large as Alroth's hand. The lordling took another step back, brandished his tiny dirk. He panted, his face sheened with sweat as Miran skirted Mellia's hunched form and stalked closer to him.

The creak of the crossbow being rewound made Alroth whip toward the guard. If Alroth, injured as he was, had bested Ainsley, he would have been shot through, just as Miran was about to be. He closed the distance in an instant.

The bowstring sang, the bolt was loosed, and Alroth whirled as it passed through him—and embedded itself in the mud where Miran had been an instant before. The lordling's scream turned to a gurgle as Miran tackled him to the ground and tore his throat out, Ainsley's black lifeblood pulsing onto the hard-packed frozen dirt. Good riddance. And yet, the crossbowman was cranking his crossbow for another shot. He looked to Glimar, who nodded.

Mellia. Alroth drew back his fist. He couldn't hurt the crossbowman like this, but at least he would have done *something.* His whole body tingled, and his very corporeal fist slammed into the crossbowman's jaw with a satisfying crunch. He wouldn't be shooting anyone else.

But he wasn't the one who gave the order. Alroth vaulted onto the dais and loomed over Glimar, who foolishly waved away his guards.

"You're wasting time, Wolf."

What in Doloman's name was he spouting? He gestured at the field. Mellia had collapsed into the dirt, her own blood soaking her. *Fuck!*

Alroth scrambled down from the dais, staggered—landing on his cracked ankle would wreck him—and hobbled to her side. He'd healed her once before, and he would do it again. He rested a hand on her back and found the wound in her shoulder. He let a little magic flow into it. Her blood pulsed out.

"Careful." A soft voice. The Grist queen. "You'll make her die faster if you're not."

Not what? Careful. Right. But he wasn't *careful*. How could he wield magic he'd never practised? And what was the Grist queen doing in muddy lists? Didn't Mellia say she never left her keep?

"Magic won't get that bolt out anyway."

Of course it wouldn't. Alroth pulled his belt knife. The bolt poked out the back of Mellia's shoulder, and he could get it out. But she needed healing right away if he was going to do this.

Sathred watched him, her face blank.

"You'll heal her once I get this out?"

She looked over his head. Asking permission from Glimar? The Grist father shook his head. He wanted Mellia to die.

Sathred smiled. "Yes, of course."

The guards clattered into the lists, but their Grist queen waved them away, and Alroth set to prying the bolt loose. Either Sathred was lying or she wasn't. Either way, leaving the bolt in wouldn't save Mellia. It came free with a sucking sound that turned his stomach, but true to her word, as soon as the bolt was clutched in his hand, Mellia's bleeding slowed and stopped. She didn't move. Like Drake. Mellia had healed him, though, and the Grist queen had even more power. What had Mellia done? What had Runas told her to do? Alroth cradled her limp body into his lap.

Etienne had made some joke about his cock after... what had it been? Something about his big bones?

"Her bones."

"What?"

"Her bones. You need to magic her bones."

"Why? Are they broken?"

"You use her bones to make her wake up. Runas said something about blood. Are you a mage or not? Hurry!"

Sathred's mouth was set. She closed her eyes and muttered under her breath. "Bones, bones. Runas knows her healing, but what in all..." She nodded. Had she found whatever had healed Drake?

Sure enough, Mellia stirred, opened her eyes. Took in Alroth. Took in Sathred. "Did you do it?" Her voice was hoarse.

Sathred looked between Mellia and her mate. "Not yet."

"We had a deal."

Sathred smiled that same cunning smile she'd given Glimar right before she'd defied him and healed Mellia. "Doloman's will be done."

The grinding of Glimar's teeth was practically audible. His eyes sparked as he watched Sathred carefully peel back her veil to reveal a netting of gold over her hair. A murmur rippled through the crowd. The Grist queen. They wouldn't recognize her, but gold was an unmistakable mark—and Glimar wasn't condemning her for wearing it.

Lord New Bridge went to his knees. That's all it took for the rest of the crowd to follow suit, those behind quickly understanding the gravity of the situation as the tableau in the lists was revealed by the obeisance of those in front.

Glimar and Sathred were the only ones inside the palisade left standing.

"The Golden God has spoken to me, my children." Sathred's voice rang across the humbled crowd. "He has warned me that troubled times are upon us. He has commanded me to aid Father Glimar, to take some of the burden from him to better care for you, our children. I am here today in that spirit, to witness this act of his favour." She paced around the lists, speaking to everyone in turn. "Doloman wished to witness this duel through my eyes, and I am thankful that I am not the one who must decide who is the victor today. So thankful for Doloman's guidance on this matter. In His wisdom, He wished to teach us all a lesson in humility."

Who was the victor? Was the steaming half-eaten corpse on the ground in the running?

Sathred climbed to the dais, every eye on her as she sedately marched up the stairs to stand next to Father Glimar. She took his hand. It twitched tight and loosened spasmodically.

Would he pull away? No, he allowed her to keep it, though it seemed his fingers couldn't decide whether to go limp or crush her bones.

She didn't so much as flinch. "We believed that we could determine who had the divine right to hold Falvair through a human duel, but infallible Doloman has shown us our hubris." *We. Our.* Not Glimar, but them together. "For who among us can call this victory? Surely Lord Ainsley was on the precipice of claiming the title—but he is dead, killed not by his opponent but by his opponent's ephemer, an unprecedented outcome. So how can we name a victor?" Sathred gazed across the bent heads before her, let them all ponder her question. She was a captivating speaker. Perhaps Glimar deserved pity, but after all his manipulations, Alroth wasn't able to pluck any up for him.

Glimar opened his mouth, but Sathred cut him off.

"We cannot."

Another murmur filtered through the crowd. They had had their blood, but they wanted to know the end of the story. If Sathred didn't give it to them, someone else would.

"But the Golden God can." She pointed to Miran, parked proudly beside their kill. Was she saying that Miran would be the marquess? That was absurd. "Does Doloman Himself not say that magic syphoned from a source is as the source's own hand? Does He not say that an ephemer is merely an extension of the source?"

Alroth was the source. Except that Miran was his ephemer. Which meant that he wasn't the source this time, he was the mage. He rubbed his spinning head.

Sathred pointed at them, and Mellia lurched to her feet, pale-faced. "I present to you, the heir to the Falvair marquessate: Matron Mellia of Falvair!"

The Grist father's teeth might be cracking in his skull with the way his jaw spasmed, and was that a wince from Sathred as his fingers tightened on hers? Not what Glimar wanted, then. Good. If Sathred was his enemy, then perhaps she was the path to stopping the war before it started, the one that Mellia had so painstakingly planned.

Alroth scrambled up and took Mellia's elbow. The Marchioness of Falvair shouldn't fall in the bloody dirt.

Sathred wrenched her hand away from Glimar and flexed her fingers. "Falvair will be most important to Sudra in the coming months. I spoke earlier of a time of unrest, of struggle and hardship. Doloman has seen fit to show me a glimpse of the future, and I wish to share it with you now. Not to frighten you but to prepare you for what's to come. We will all need to work together.

"You all might remember the Necrophoresis Ritual, during which the handmaids disappeared, swept downstream. You may be wondering what has become of them, why they left you. I tell you now that Doloman has shown me the reason, and it pains me to share it with you, but such is Doloman's will. We must bear in mind that a little suffering now will serve us—serve the Golden God—in the years to come."

Mellia cursed under her breath.

"We all know that after the Grist came to bless Sudra, the heretical King Lorthran fought against their liberation and was forced to flee across the strait to Carille. I tell you that, to this day, his progeny thrive in Nordval. It was the pagan king's heir that stole the handmaids, took our most powerful mages for their own use."

Mellia cursed aloud, her un-marchioness-like objections covered by the gasps and cries from the throng.

Sathred's voice carried above them easily, through either magic or charisma. "When Doloman told me His will, I begged him for another solution, a peaceable way that would save us all from bloodshed, from the scourge of war." She choked back a sob—real or feigned made no difference to the spellbound crowd. "But His will is clear. We must retrieve the handmaids from brutish Nordval at any cost. We must show them that they cannot take from Sudra without consequence. We shall demonstrate that those of us who follow Doloman's will are undefeatable."

The crowd erupted. They leaped to their feet, hollering and cheering, shouting Doloman's name, blessing the Grist queen and Grist father. Miran growled and snapped, adding to the cacophony.

So Mellia was the Marchioness of Falvair. Sathred had secured that for them, at least. Perhaps as a marchioness she could divert Sathred's war. Except that Sathred had played her hand well. It wasn't her war. She had framed it as Doloman's war. Which meant that if Mellia—or anyone—opposed it, then they were going against the Golden God. And defying Doloman was defying the Grist. No lord wanted to be on the wrong side of the Grist.

Lord New Bridge himself shuffled forward on his knees, clutched Sathred's hand in both of his, and kissed her gold ring. A man who had never bowed to a woman in his life. No, there would be no stopping this war.

The crowd made way for the newly minted Marchioness of Falvair. It didn't much matter where they went, as long as they got out of the lists. Alroth and Mellia leaned on one another through the deserted streets outside, moving steadily... somewhere. Where was Mellia taking them? The comb? No, she passed it by. Upper Gate?

"Whoa, She-Wolf. We're not marching all the way to your marquessate like this."

She shook her head. "I have to show you something."

"Can't it wait until we're less... bloody?"

"No."

Whatever it was must be important. Alroth followed. Mellia took them off the road, onto a familiar path. He and Falkirk had found this cliffside riddled with caves when they'd first scouted New Bridge as an option to settle in permanently. But how did Mellia know about them? She headed unerringly for the entrance.

Alroth swallowed the sudden hope that sprang to his chest. They'd been burned. Drake must have told her about these caves. She couldn't have been led here by...

"Captain!" Tarrin bounded out of the cave mouth like a puppy. Whole. Safe.

Alroth gripped his shoulder, and sobs racked his aching frame. Alive. At least one. Alive. Tarrin laughed and pulled him into the surprisingly cozy cave. Selena and Vernis by the fire, the parents, their children, even a sheep or two. And supplies. His fighters must have helped move some before the waterfall. He was soon surrounded. Selena grumbled and set to healing what wounds she could. Tarrin fetched both of them food as they sat by the cheerful firepit.

Alroth's heart was fit to burst. "I have somewhere for us. Somewhere safe. Where the local nobility is very accepting. She'll make sure we're all comfortable." And safe.

"I hear the marchioness and the marquess have two ephemers, and he's also beyond reproach." Mellia wrapped her arms around him and eased him over to a bundle of pine boughs.

Beyond reproach? "Except when he's taking coin for violent jobs, foolishly refusing to do magic, stabbing his captain between the shoulder blades, or"—he swallowed—"wrenching his mate without her permission."

"He's not defined by his mistakes, Alroth. He's a good marquess and a good man."

Now that was overboard. "I wouldn't go that far." Alroth chuckled nervously.

"I would." Mellia was serious. After all he'd done, she thought him a good man. Somehow.

And all the folks in this cave agreed with her. He'd keep working to prove them right, even if he was a rich, foppish, useless noble now.

He smiled and kissed his mate.

37

Mellia

Mellia squeezed Alroth's warm hand. Her parents were receiving them in the great hall. The new year was upon them, and thus this was her father's sixty-sixth winter and final year as Lord Falvair. Tradition dictated that he stay on in an advisory role, with the title passing to his heir... well, about ten days past.

They'd planned it so that the binding to Ainsley would have fallen on the night before the solstice, the night before the title was to pass on. But since she'd been bound to Alroth then, the title had passed to him. And her, with Sathred's endorsement.

Falvair's minor lords and vassals greeted Mellia as she entered. She nodded politely, but her parents' cold faces kept her from hearing a word they said in congratulations. Alroth thanked them all and responded with appropriate humility. Mira flanked Mellia, and Miran flanked her mate on the other side. She stroked Mira's ear, no hunching required anymore. There was no question now that both their ephemers were dire wolves. They could rip someone's throat out without leaving the ground. Surely the story of Lord Ainsley had even reached folk here by now.

Lord and Lady Falvair greeted their successors from their carved thrones, a big fireplace at their backs. Falvair's Grist father and the guard captain flanked them, standing ready for... whatever happened here.

Mellia's father leaned toward her mother and murmured something. Her lips thinned, but she didn't respond. Today should be a joyful reunion. But her bond mate was all wrong. Mellia was all wrong. How did it feel that both of their children were blasphemous heretics?

Unlike her brother, Mellia had the backing of a Grist queen. She drew herself up. "I've come before you to receive the mantle of Marchioness of Falvair, by right of blood, as your sole surviving heir." The ceremonial words almost stuck in her throat as she added just a little venom to them. Whose fault was it really that they were stuck with her as the heir?

They were supposed to accept her as their successor and pass on the mantle. Then there would be a feast... Why were they just sitting there? Alroth's hand tightened on hers, and Miran growled.

"Daughter, you come to us seeking your birthright with our carefully chosen suitor murdered by an unnatural ephemer and expect to be welcomed?" Her mother's voice held the same coldness she'd shown all those years ago when Delphus came to her with the glad news of his binding. Did she know that Mellia had been watching from the peephole upstairs, balanced on a chest because she was too small to reach it? Even then, she'd noticed the glacial look on her mother's face, wondered at it.

Delphus had been so excited when he'd told little Mellia first, so determined to present the happy news to their parents. She hadn't understood where his strange sadness had come from when he'd spoken of presenting himself to them.

"You don't intend to welcome me?" She dropped Alroth's hand and planted her fists on her hips. "What do you intend?" *Give me to the Grist like Delphus? Too bad, they're the ones who sent us.*

"If I may, your ladyship." The Grist father bent his greyed head. Father Limosa, who had burned her brother. There was no monastery here, no Grist queen, no handmaids, just an old man with the ear of the marquessate. "I don't believe your daughter means any harm."

Mellia clamped her teeth together. *Let him talk.*

"The events in New Bridge were unfortunate, I grant you, but I'm certain that with solemn reflection, Miss Mellia will condemn her heretical bond and—"

Solemn reflection was Ainsley's excuse for dumping her in an oubliette. "Father Limosa. Do you know who blessed our bond?" Mellia's voice was shockingly smooth, what with her heart beating almost out of her chest.

All four on the dais—everyone in the hall—stared at her.

Father Limosa gaped but gathered himself quickly. "If you're referring to the Grist queen, I—"

"I'm not." Mellia interrupted for the second time.

Father Limosa flapped his mouth like a fish. "Grist Father Glimar has no power here."

Ah, he was resentful that the younger man had gotten the prestigious monastery post.

"Not Father Glimar, either." The fire crackled. "Doloman."

"What do you know of Doloman, silly girl!"

Father Limosa wasn't used to being interrupted or contradicted in this hall. He'd better get used to it.

Alroth rested a hand on his sword hilt. "My bond mate was a sister for two years and almost became a handmaid. Now she's a marchioness. Have a care how you refer to her."

Mira growled and lunged at the Grist father. He screeched and shrank against the wall.

"Or better yet, don't refer to her at all." Alroth almost matched Mira in tone.

"That's enough." Mellia's father hardly ever raised his voice, even now with his successor threatening his trusted Grist father, he barely added a hint of bite to his words. "It seems we have no choice."

Father Limosa spluttered, but Mira's warning growl shut him up.

"We cannot contest Doloman's will. However... distasteful it might be. I bestow upon you the Marquessate of Falvair to govern with care and courage. May your rule be peaceful and prosperous. Now get out of my sight."

Mellia's stomach dropped. He didn't accept them. He didn't accept Alroth. Mellia curtsied automatically. But he'd said the words. He'd given the title over to them, as much as it obviously pained him. That was all that mattered. The new Lady and Lord Falvair left the silent hall. There would be no celebratory feast. Not here.

Mellia took a deep breath of the crisp air. The stars twinkled brightly in the bottomless sky. They strolled to the harbour in silence.

When they were standing on the frigid ferry platform, Alroth broke it. "That Grist father is an Ignis-cursed fool."

The ferry across the harbour arrived. No one looked twice at the two of them in their plain mantles. They weren't known here yet. They boarded along with a woman carrying a chicken under one arm, and another spinning wool as she walked.

He was a fool. A powerful fool who might still manage to get them killed. "I doubt Father Glimar will grant us a replacement."

"But Sathred might. She owes you after her betrayal." He shook his head. "She could have ended the war before it even started, but instead..."

"Father Glimar would have punished her for it." But she was talking to a man who had committed treason to end a war, had been willing to give his life just to make hers a little easier. "Not everyone is as steadfast as you."

Alroth grumbled, but he couldn't keep his lips from curling up. Mellia kissed them without thinking, and Alroth's strong arms wrapped around her. Even if they struggled here in Falvair, at least they were here, somewhere they could make a difference in this Stultitian war.

The ferry bumped on the platform, and they broke apart. Mellia took Alroth's hand, and they headed for the lighted windows of a cruck nestled inside the wall. On this side of the shipyard, there were no guards hanging around, nothing to hem them in.

Alroth opened the door and bowed her into the big hall. The music stopped and the babble tapered off.

"The most honourable Marchioness of Falvair, everyone!" Alroth called.

A roar of congratulations went up from every side, and food was paraded in front of her. Mellia smiled more than she had in years, and even Alroth took a turn or two around the floor with her.

She had one last surprise, and Tarrin grinned as he handed her the long bundle.

"Picked it up while you were away at the castle."

Mellia's heart pounded. What if Alroth didn't like it? What if he thought it was a violation—

"Go on, Lady Falvair." Vernis prodded her with his bony elbow.

Alroth had his back to her. Everyone was watching, though they were pretending not to. Mellia tapped him on the shoulder, and he turned. He took in the bundle, and his eyebrows drew down. She'd overstepped. She should just—

"What have you got there, sweetling?" He still called her that sometimes.

"It's a gift for you." She shoved it at him. "With any luck, you'll never need it."

He unwrapped the cloth, took the hilt, and drew the blade. He looked at her, awestruck. "How? Magic?"

"No, I had it reforged. Got Etienne to tell Livine how it used to be, and there's a good armourer here. I sent the ruined one ahead so that—"

He laid the blade on the table and kissed her, held her close, until they were both breathless, the younger and more rowdy onlookers oohing and aahing.

"You like it?"

"It's perfect." He ran his hand over Ictus reforged, caressed it the same way he would Miran. His cheeks reddened. "I have something for you, too." He grabbed his clay cup and strode to the hearth, laid it in front of the fire. "Watch."

What was she watching? She stood in silence, along with the rest of the room, openly watching now.

Selena caught her eye and jerked her chin at the cup. A thin tendril of steam curled into the air. Alroth had heated it. He'd learned to use their magic.

He grinned, took her hands in his. "I'm not too good for it. Never was. The men who look down on mages are fools." His eyes were so bright. "I was a fool, Mellia."

"You can say that again!" Selena was grinning, though. She winked at Mellia.

Her fool. It had taken him long enough to come around, but he was learning now. Just like they would learn to govern a marquessate. Together.

Epilogue

Livine's letter had informed them that the handmaids and the mercs had reached Nordval safely, despite a winter storm blowing them off course. Thankfully, they had arrived intact, and the storm had kept anyone else from following them across the strait. They were safe in Lacune, Nordval. They'd been aiming for the more heavily fortified Olenast, but Lacune was a fortress in its own right, and they would be safe.

Mellia and Alroth were doing everything in their power to keep the war from escalating. Though, going flatly against the Grist would be more likely to get them ousted from Falvair than to stop the war from building.

A messenger hurried into her study and bowed over a letter. From Livine. Mellia thanked him and urged him to read it to her.

Dearest Lady Falvair,

As strange as it is to address you as such, it's no stranger than the predicament we find ourselves in over here in Carille. We've been told that we will only be safe if we are bound to Carillan sources and given the protection of becoming citizens of Carille. In order to determine who is to have the honour of binding a handmaid, the Duke of Nordval has arranged a tournament. Runas is furious. She's already demanded that we be released from the requirement, but even she can see that there is no other recourse. If we don't want to be returned to Sudra forthwith, this is our only option.

Our newest friends—you know who, the ones who fell over the waterfall with us—have insisted on participating in the tournament, along with the nobles of Nordval. There won't be time for nobles to come from further afield. I've tried to explain to them that this will only reinforce the notion that Nordval kidnapped us to gain our power, but no one is thinking logically at the moment.

The Grist here are different—they act in an advisory capacity, but I think they have more... subtle connections. I don't doubt that they will try to influence the tournament. They are not as fixated on suppressing stories of the other deities besides Doloman, and I'll send you any that I hear, since you asked about them in your last letter. You're right that Reverentia is said to be Doloman's equal, in all things. Lots of households here have altars to their family deity, and Reverentia is a popular choice. It's fascinating how their perspective on Doloman is completely different from ours: They see Him as an angry, violent god, trampling all who oppose him under His golden feet. Not many altars to that, understandably!

Their perspective on King Lorthran is totally different too—did you know that King Lorthran and Queen Olena had two ephemers like you and Alroth? Can you imagine? Two firebirds! No wonder the Empire gave up on conquering Nordval with the two of them defending it. Anyway, I've heard unsubstantiated rumours that the exiled prince, their heir, will be competing in the tournament. I bet Dayma would swoon at the chance to bind herself to a prince, even an exiled one. They're probably just rumours, though. I doubt a prince would have trouble finding a mage to bind to him.

I'll keep you updated on all developments here.

Love,

Livine

P.S. Alinace misses you terribly, but it turns out she brought a *rat* with her from New Bridge! In her pocket!! —L

P.P.S. D and K are getting absolutely amazing at syphoning. I sometimes watch their technique. It's truly mesmerizing. —L

And a note scribbled at the bottom.

> Don't worry about us, Mellia! We have everything under control here. We'll stop the war from our end. —Morath

Oh, Morath. No doubt she would do her Metoian best to stop the war single-handedly. But this war had been generations in the making, back to King Lorthran and Queen Olena themselves—with two ephemers as well, it seemed: firebirds.

Alroth's heavy tread made Mellia look up from the letter. He tapped on the doorframe as he came in.

"Time to hear petitions. Don't want Father Limosa to beat us there."

"Too true." She had to get ready.

Alroth caught her arm gently as she made to slip by through the doorway. "One moment, Lady Falvair." He grinned down at her. "Thank you, sweetling."

"For what?" Her breath shallowed, being this close to her bound mate, their bodies close together in the doorframe.

He sobered. "For making a place for my folks. A safe place. I couldn't have done this without you."

"It was an accident of birth that—"

Alroth shook his head. "Now, don't go doing that, She-Wolf. A hundred times you could have given up the title, given me up for dead. But you didn't. And here we are."

"Here we are," she echoed. His lips were fascinating from this close up. She tipped her head up, and he brought his down to meet her.

Mira and Miran let out a chorus of hearty barks and dashed through the wall next to them. They were practically the size of small bears these days.

"And thank you for that." He jerked his chin at the ephemers.

"For making our ephemers? We did that together, as I recall…"

He shook his head. "I've been thinking about that second crossbow bolt. How did the crossbowman miss? Miran was two ells away."

And she'd given Miran just enough power to spring out of the way in time. Her stomach knotted. It had been far too close, that crossbow bolt. If she'd been even a moment later, if she hadn't seen the crossbowman in the crowd… but she had. And Sathred had come to her aid. Mostly. Why in the name of a score of different gods had Sathred almost single-handedly started a war between Sudra and Carille? She had seemed to hate Glimar so much, so why go along with his plan? Maybe one day Mellia would be in a position to ask her. But until then, she would do the best she could for her little corner of the world.

"Let's go get your folk settled, Wolf."

He growled theatrically. "They can wait a few minutes." He kissed her neck. "Or a few hours."

Mellia laughed, the feeling so sudden, she didn't have a chance to consider it. With war on the way, it seemed wrong to be so happy. But she was. She threaded her fingers through Alroth's hair. Her source. Her mage. Her bound mate.

Thanks so much for reading *A Bond of Storms and Stitches*! If you liked it, please leave a review on your platform of choice. Even a line or two is very helpful for other readers!

If you want to be the first to hear about new releases, consider joining my newsletter at join.elizabethshearly.ca and get a free novella featuring Brother Padril and Etienne's sister.

If you want to know more about King Lorthran and Queen Olena of legend, consider joining my Patreon at patreon.com/ElizabethFShearly at any paid tier for the story of their binding ritual.

The handmaids' story continues in *A Bond of Armour and Artfulness*, a *Guys and Dolls* retelling. Join Dayma and Blaise as they spawn a magic stork bird, learn to wield their magic, and brutalize their enemies, both on the tourney field and in the banquet hall.

Acknowledgements

Thanks so much to my editor, Maggie Morris, for your careful and thorough feedback. So many moments in the book hit harder because of your suggestions, and I appreciate all the time you take to check and double check everything.

Thanks so much to Gayle Morrow for checking my horrendous Google translate Latin phrases and sprucing them right up. (All errors are, of course, my own.)

Thank you to the wonderful Laura Robson my top-tier Patreon supporter for your support all year. Having direct support from readers like you means so much to artists and artisans like me!

And thank you, Lovely Reader, for reading! You're a glittering star twinkling back at me from the void. <3

Dear Lovely Reader

Dear Lovely Reader,

A Bond of Storms and Stitches is just the first part of a brilliant idea I had in my kitchen one day. Historical fantasy romance novels based on the movie musicals I used to watch with my grandma. I knew I had to start it off with *Seven Brides for Seven Brothers*, since it provided so many characters to follow through the rest of the series. I had no idea that the characters were going to pop off the page and come alive so thoroughly.

At the end of 2024, I was finishing up Project Pardus, which I wrote without an outline and taught me a very important lesson: writing without an outline doubles my drafting time. So I jumped into outlining *Storms and Stitches* at the start of 2025, using a new outlining method that works with my brain.

I won't talk too much about my state of mind this year, since I know so many of us are hanging on by a thread, but know that the Grist and the nobles in Sudra were inspired by my frustration with patriarchy and capitalism. In my book, I can rip the throat out of my fictional representation of patriarchy—and I hope you found it as satisfying as I did.

Mellia has so much faith in those patriarchal structures, and she is so fixated on working within them, even when they don't serve her, and in fact bring her down. It took a lot to break the Grist's hold on her. But she came around and realized that those structures never served her. Even the so-called freedom they were offering with just a form of servitude.

Alroth never asks for help, even when he needs it. He's too proud to learn a new skill, too set in his ways to admit that he might be wrong and he might need to change. He thought that the worst thing he could be was weak, feminine. But femininity isn't weakness, and Alroth finally realized that using magic doesn't mean you're weak, it's just another form of strength.

Community building is only going to get more important in the coming years, as fascism continues to rise, and my handmaids are struggling with it like so many of us. They try, they fail. They keep at it. And they will prevail.

Hang in there, my friends.

I hope *A Bond of Storms and Stitches* meant something to you, as it means so much to me. <3

Looking forward to our next adventure,

Elizabeth F. Shearly

E. F. Shearly

A Tourney Bond

A Syphon Bound Novella

She needs a bond mate.
He's sworn to celibacy.
They absolutely should not fall in love...

Katya needs a suitor. Any suitor. And this tourney will gather all the eligible lords in one place for the first time since the war. If she doesn't find someone soon she'll lose her family's lands...

Brother Padril has his orders, and carrying them out is the only way to restore the war-ravaged province. His feelings for Katya are immaterial: the Grist never relinquish their bound brothers.

But Brother Padril needs information only Katya can provide to carry out those orders, and none of the eligible lords will speak to Katya regardless. How could spending the tourney together possibly make their plights worse?

If Katya can't attract a suitor, her lands will be forfeit, and besides, any dalliances will see Padril ousted from the only family he's ever known...

A Tourney Bond is a very loose State Fair retelling as a historical fantasy romance novella, set in the Syphon Bound world.

Get it **free** when you join my newsletter.

A Bond of Armour and Artfulness

Syphon Bound Book 2

War is inevitable. The Five Mages have fled the Grist zealots and fallen into the hands of the heretical nobility across the lake. Noblemen have come from across the province to win their hands---and their magic---for themselves. But only four can prevail.

Dayma will never be brought low again. She will marry well, and build a strong bond with a wealthy protector. But it's not up to her. Who will win her hand in the tournament? To make matters worse, the Grist have followed them across the lake, and are tying to fix the tournament so their chosen pious nobles capture the handmaids.

Blaise doesn't do "work". If he never tries, he can never fail, right? Good thing his father assigned a surrogate to fight in the tournament for him. He can sit on his ass and still win a handmaid's magic for his father. Except one of the handmaids deserves more than that. She deserves a good man, a good mate.

Join Dayma and Blaise as they spawn a magic stork bird, learn to wield their magic, and brutalize their enemies, both on the tourney field and in the banquet hall.

Coming soon!

About The Author

Elizabeth spent 21 years tinkering with a dozen different manuscripts. She finally gave in to the urge to write romance in 2022, and published her first sci fi romance novel, *Endless Sea of Stars*, in 2023. The denial continued when she thought her second book might not be a romance (it was), but she embraced her romance-writer nature and joined Ottawa Romance Writers in 2024. Now she writes sci fi and fantasy romance with a good bit of spice and super-cool world-building. She's all caught up with some of the most popular romantasy series (team Rhysand in ACOTAR book 1, thank-you), and devours alien, shifter, and orc steamy books with abandon.

When she's not watching characters play-act in her head or delving down research rabbit-holes, you can find her relaxing on the couch with her black and orange cats, playing an anime RPG or knitting a sweater for her kid.

Join the monthly newsletter for news about the *Syphon Bound* series at http://join.elizabethshearly.ca to get a free Syphon Bound novella, *A Tourney Bond*, featuring Brother Padril and Etienne's sister.

- Join Elizabeth's Patreon to get access to bonus scenes and short stories every month for as little as a dollar, https://www.patreon.com/ElizabethFShearly

patreon.com/ElizabethFShearly

instagram.com/ElizabethFShearly

bookbub.com/authors/elizabeth-f-shearly

facebook.com/ElizabethFShearly/

goodreads.com/elizabethfshearly

pinterest.com/ElizabethFShearly

Also By Elizabeth F. Shearly

Endless Sea Of Stars

Dread Spring

Project Pardus

Syphon Bound

A Bond of Storms and Stitches

A Bond of Armour and Artfulness

Syphon Bound Novella

A Tourney Bond

Second Acts of Weary Warrior Women

The Swordswoman and the Vampire

To Break A Dragon Bond

A Pentagram Of Candles and Spectres

Her Castle, Her Howl, Her Pack

The King's Pixie Seer

www.ingramcontent.com/pod-product-compliance
Lightning Source LLC
La Vergne TN
LVHW041053080826
845145LV00007B/1561

* 9 7 8 1 0 6 8 9 3 4 6 4 3 *